THE BOY CALLED IT
... IT BEGINS

WALLACE E. EDSON

Copyright © 2022 by Wallace E. Edson

All rights reserved.

No part of this publication may be reproduced, distributed, or transmitted in any form or by any means, including photocopying, recording, or other electronic or mechanical methods, without the prior written permission of the author or publisher, except as permitted by U.S. copyright law. For permission requests, contact WallaceEdsonBooks@gmail.com.

The story, all names, characters, and incidents portrayed in this production are fictitious. No identification with actual persons (living or deceased), places, buildings, and products is intended or should be inferred. Any resemblance to real places or people is just too weird to imagine. It is recommended that you avoid people and places that are like those in this book as the people carry swords and the places have hideous creatures that may eat you.

Should symptoms of mixed realities caused by this book persist, seek medical help immediately. Psychological help may also be advised should you believe anything in this book is even remotely real.

If you purchased this book without a cover you should be aware that this book is stolen property. It was reported as "unsold and destroyed" to the Author and the Author has not received any payment for this "stripped book." If you are aware this book was stolen and you continue to read it, shame on you.

ISBN: 978-1-959358-00-8 (paperback)

ISBN: 978-1-959358-01-5 (e-book)

Cover image: Original artwork by Mike Murray (commissionmike@gmail.com)

To Sgt. James G. Ellis, United States Marine Corps:

For your friendship, your service, and your sacrifice.
I wish to one day be at least half the man you were.

To Randy Culpepper:

For making me laugh when it was hard to do so.

FOR ALL THEY DO OR DID

Some people can make it on their own, while others have those who have helped them to reach their dreams. Here are a few of my dream makers:

Wallace William Edson: Without you, son, I would have no story to tell. You are what makes me whole.

Marge and John Vasilik (Ma & Pop Vasilik): I wouldn't have my weird sense of humor and the confidence to wield it if not for you. Of course, I'm still not sure if that's giving you the credit or blame. Either way, I have no complaint with the way you raised me.

Susanne Mulcahy and Jan Raissle: Every Moose needs his Squirrel and Squirrelette. Thanks for being mine. You're the best two sisters ever!

Bob, Marie, Sammy, Sydney, and Fiona: For the many ways you were there for me and the inspiration you provided me. Thank you for taking me and Will into your family—forever corrupting our minds and souls.

Jennifer Oneal: For being that little voice in the back of my head screaming "You can do it! Just don't screw it up!"

Debbie Belmessieri (debbie.belm@gmail.com): Without your editing skills, my book would read like poop. Thanks. You're awesome!

Mike Murray (commissionmike@gmail.com): I love the cover you made for me. Of course, if this book doesn't sell, I'm heaping all the fault onto your artwork. I'm too fragile to bear the criticism. JK

CONTENTS

ONE ○ A False Start ○ 1

TWO ○ Chute Ride ○ 9

THREE ○ Squirrels, Birds, & Elephants ... Oh My! ○ 23

FOUR ○ It Deepens ○ 35

FIVE ○ Meeting Lord Stronghide ○ 49

SIX ○ Did Someone Say "Party!" ○ 55

SEVEN ○ Marching With The Elephants ○ 67

EIGHT ○ Magic Doesn't Exist ... Does It? ○ 77

NINE ○ I Said Sorry Already ○ 85

TEN ○ Watch Your Step ○ 95

ELEVEN ○ Is There A Healer In The House? ○ 105

TWELVE ○ And Then There Were Four ... Or Was That Five? ○ 111

THIRTEEN ○ As Easy As Hitting A Fallon With A Stick ○ 121

FOURTEEN ○ Dark Orders 129

FIFTEEN ○ Buttka's Public House ○ 135

SIXTEEN ○ Dinner At The Big House ○ 147

SEVENTEEN ○ Familiar Faces ○ 157

EIGHTEEN ○ The Word Is "Covert" ○ 163

NINETEEN ○ Troubles Washed Away ... Human Boy And All ○ 175

TWENTY ○ Can't Fool An Old Squirrel ○ 189

TWENTY-ONE ○ Death Of A Friend ○ 195

TWENTY-TWO ○ Dry Socks And Render Beasts ○ 207

TWENTY-THREE ○ Beasts Of A Feather ○ 217

TWENTY-FOUR ○ A Belly Full Of It ○ 225

TWENTY-FIVE ○ The Name Be Vasilik ○ 231

TWENTY-SIX ○ Just A Hint Of Prophecy ○ 241

TWENTY-SEVEN ○ O.M.G. It's A C.I.M.U. ○ 247

TWENTY-EIGHT ○ She Who Is To Be Obeyed ○ 255

TWENTY-NINE ○ Some Mirrors Are Just Not Nice ○ 261

THIRTY ○ Fun In Fishmonger's Alley ○ 279

THIRTY-ONE ○ The Messes Fallons Make ○ 289

THIRTY-TWO ○ Vasilik Is Sneaky. Who Knew? ○ 295

THIRTY-THREE ○ Not A Creature Stirred ... Ok, Maybe Just One ○ 303

THIRTY-FOUR ○ Rumors On The High Seas ○ 307

THIRTY-FIVE ○ Betrayal Revealed ... Kinda ○ 315

THIRTY-SIX ○ Which Feral Mystic? ○ 329

THIRTY-SEVEN ○ The Red Lion ○ 339

THIRTY-EIGHT ○ Getting Away ... Hat And All ○ 349

THIRTY-NINE ○ A Long, Short Boat Ride ○ 359

EPILOGUE ○ A Warm Welcome Ahead ... Unlikely! ○ 371

ALL ABOUT ME, BEING ALL ABOUT YOU, BEING SOMEWHAT ABOUT ME

SHOUT-OUT

THE AUTHOR

ONE

A FALSE START

Ellis lost control and his adrenaline spiked as the rumbling of the conveyor belt brought him further up the chute—trapped inside the barrel. Inch by dread-building inch, it drew him closer to being vaporized if he didn't somehow break out of the industrial canister that he had selected for its near-impervious attributes. Faster and harder, his heart pounded in his chest as he slammed his fists against the curved walls. The inside of the barrel was tinted an eerie blue by the glowing Jot Light that cast dim shadows over the boy's cringing face. "Help! Izak, help me!" he screamed, but his desperate shrieks, though echoing loudly inside the container, drew no one's attention from down below. Outside of the barrel he heard the mechanical sounds of gears turning, along with the scraping of metal on metal which muffled every other noise, including the boy's futile calls for help—which looked to be the last sounds Ellis would ever make…

Actually, that isn't where this tragic event truly started. There were a few ill-conceived ideas leading up to Ellis being vaporized into nothing.

In a world of committees and social compliance where everyone was expected to do as they were advised to do, Ellis stood out like an elephant at a squirrel party. To say the least, he had a notorious tendency to resist standards and regulations in a time and place when few people ever stepped out of line because … well … because it just didn't happen … or it didn't happen often when Ellis wasn't involved.

He liked to think that beneath the surface of his rebellious façade was a heart of gold. After all, he was a devoted friend who would do anything for his buddies. And from his perspective, he believed that most of the trouble he got into was because he was trying to help, or impress, a friend, whether they wanted his help or not. One of those friends was Izak—his best friend and total opposite. It was Izak that gave Ellis his shortened name. Well, he didn't give him the name so much as Izak had trouble pronouncing the name Elliston when they were toddlers and finally started calling him Ellis. At the time, Ellis didn't mind—who knew it was going to start a trend and become a thing for all the other kids and even adults to start calling him.

The two boys stood face to face on a semi-crowded walkway somewhere in sector PO72. They weren't literally face to face as Ellis was easily four inches taller than his friend. With his height advantage, he could look over his buddy's head at the drably dressed crowd of people in their monochrome slacks and shirts as they went about their day doing whatever boring thing they had to do. Ellis groaned at the tedium. But that was the problem with Ellis—if it weren't for his occasional antics, he would have surely died from boredom by now.

Izak nodded his head as he spoke while gesturing casually with his hands. "At the Education Center, or at home, rules are a boy's best friend and will serve him well when he is a man," he said, repeating the words his father was so often professing. The boy's voice was even and tempered as he peered intently at Ellis. "… and I think you wouldn't get into so many bad, avoidable situations if you followed the rules and would just not be … be … be you," Izak added as his head slumped on the last few words.

Ellis looked at him for a long moment. "Are you done?" he asked with a smile stretching across his face. "Just help me get the canister to the Bin reclamation center." He gave a kick to the large charcoal gray industrial barrel laying at their feet.

Izak's narrow shoulders dropped even lower than before. "You haven't heard a word I've been saying."

Ellis looked back to his brilliant, but less adventurous buddy, "Not particularly, but don't you feel better getting it out of your system?"

Izak's head shook slowly, "Not particularly."

Under a perpetually gloomy sky ruined by centuries of negligence and pollution, the two boys made their way down the monotonous gray sidewalk where they received odd looks by the equally monotonous people passing by.

"We are so going to get caught." Izak whined, while nervously glancing around.

"Not if we look like we are supposed to be doing this ... act natural," Ellis responded with his typical forced confidence.

"I am acting natural. It is natural for me to be scared out of my mind when you include me in your insane schemes."

"Then try looking at the ground, like me."

Both boys stared at the ground as they went. The view was rather bland since all the streets and walkways of Consolidated Earth were made of the same translucent and extremely hard material called Kraytite; something Izak swore was made from a composite material containing a substantial amount of Thistine, the 120th element on the periodic table. Of course, Ellis had learned to shake his head yes and say, "uh huh," whenever Izak talked that way. To Ellis, chemistry was a foreign language that never flowed well off his tongue. History and engineering were more his style. He found them to be both useful and straightforward, though, he did admit that history had many more gray areas and flexibility of fact. He always knew that the truth pertaining to anything depended on who was recording the history at the time.

The two boys rolled the barrel for a couple of blocks. Though Ellis was taller and much wider than his very thin friend, they had the same light brown hair and similar features with hazel eyes. It wasn't unusual for strangers to assume they were brothers, and Ellis always insisted on being the assumed older brother even though he was a month younger than Izak.

They weaved in and out of the towering housing structures which were made of stacked cubicles with basic electric conduits and plumbing pipes attached to their exteriors. They had tiny viewing portals providing a minimum of natural light inside—a feat of architectural dullness.

Ellis had been taught, at the Education Center, that many years after the feuding countries and corporations ended the wars that nearly destroyed the planet and greatly reduced the population, they focused their combined efforts toward a mutual ideology dedicated to planetary preservation. From this came the renaming of the planet to Consolidated Earth, or C-Earth for short. It was also the beginning of a spartan, uninspiring existence—which was still better than unending conflict.

Before long, the boys rolled the barrel up to the point where the community sector ended, and industrial sector began. They stood staring out at the countless nondescript buildings spread out over the vast expanse of industrial machinations made real.

Izak grabbed his nose. "Ugh! I hate coming out here. How can you stand the stench?"

Ellis looked back behind them at the oppressing stacks of community cubes stretching high and wide over PO72. If it weren't for the uneven staining of the cube walls by time and weather, there would be no way to tell one cube domicile from the other. "This whole place has a stench to me," Ellis said with a heavy breath.

"Are you going to start that 'I don't belong here' speech like you do every other day?" Izak groaned.

"Well, I don't." He spread his arms out and gestured all around him to all the gray in every direction. "There is nothing here for me ... there is nothing here at all ... not even color."

"But there is also no hunger, no illiteracy, and no killing," Izak reminded him with a knowing shake of his head.

"... or fun ... or excitement," Ellis answered back.

"You are about to climb onto a garbage chute where at any minute a discarded chunk of wall or a piece of an old transport vehicle could fall on you and squish you into a goo. How is that not exciting?"

"It is exciting, but it is also illegal; not to mention we only get to do it every other week or so. I want something like that every day," Ellis said, with his eyes glazing over, lost in a fantasy that will never be.

The boys turned back in the direction they were going. Ellis forced a smile back to his lips. Before him was their destination, a sector dedicated to trash disposal—Sector TR09. Each one of the many buildings had at least four conveyor chutes stretching up to the sky, delivering an endless amount of garbage. Garbage that was the result of many centuries worth of neglect and waste.

"Have you ever opened one of the panels to the communications console in the Education Center?" Ellis asked without looking away from the chutes.

"No. I don't do things I'm expressly restricted from doing," Izak said with a shake of his head.

"Well, if you did, it would look like that," Ellis said as he pointed out toward the tangle of trash chutes nearly blocking out the horizon. "Just a wad of wires clumped together and stretching off in different directions."

"Yeah ... but I highly doubt there is one of those inside the communications console," Izak replied, gazing up at the sky where the clouds should be. Instead, there loomed an immense rectangular mass with a viscous, shiny, fluid-like surface alive with electric sparks flowing across the top of it in waves.

Ellis shook his head. "Nope. There is definitely not one of those inside the console."

They stared upward at what was commonly referred to as the Bin. It floated hundreds of feet in the sky above. It was suspended in the air by numerous hovering bulbous electrodes scattered around its perimeter and sending out waves of sparks across its surface. It was positioned nearly perpendicular to the ground and covered at least a thousand acres of the sky.

Izak swallowed hard. "I never cared much for this place. Besides the smell, it looks like a lake of lightning hanging in the sky that could fall at any minute ... and it is only a prototype."

Ellis' smile dropped away. "When I stare up at it ... I ... I feel it mocking me ... it took everything from me, and it now dares me to face it," Ellis said with more sadness in his voice than determination.

Izak's voice softened but retained a slight edge to it. "Is that why we are here today? Instead of just proving you're braver than any other kid, you want to taunt the thing responsible for your parents' death."

"They called it an industrial accident, but it was that thing they were working on when they died ... it's alive ... it killed them," Ellis said calmly, with a nod toward the Bin above.

"Try not to think about that while you are in the chute. Those kinds of thoughts will make you lose focus," Izak said.

"Not today. I won't be losing focus this time. I'm going to beat Mohamed's record," Ellis announced with renewed excitement. "Tomorrow they will be talking about the kid from Sector PO72 who made the longest Bin ride ever." His eyes beamed with anticipation.

Izak frowned. "Or they will be talking about the kid who died stupidly in a completely avoidable Bin accident ... or maybe they will be talking about the kid who got arrested for the umpteenth time for being a community nuisance ... or maybe they will not be talking at all if you come to your senses and forget riding on a freaking garbage chute."

Ellis looked at Izak as though his friend had lost his mind. "And what are the chances that any of those bad things will happen?"

"High ... very, very high chances," Izak quickly responded, with a pitch of irritation in his voice.

Arguing was not only common for the two of them, but it was how their friendship worked best. Without knowing it, they enjoyed it. As the contradicting pair argued the finer points of the law and the physics of dying in a moronic manner, a local security bot on patrol stopped in front of them and leaned in close.

To put the community at ease, the automaton officer was shaped roughly like a human as it had a plastic shell with a curved bottom and top, not unlike a dress maker's pattern dummy. It had a view screen where the head should be with a poorly designed CGI officer's face. Ellis had never met anyone at ease around these things, himself included.

The security bot stood there focused on the boys. An awkward moment or two passed between them as Ellis and Izak stopped talking and nervously looked to the side. They were now very much aware of the security bot's presence as they turned to gaze uncomfortably back at the bot.

"What should we do," whispered Izak after what felt like an eternity.

"Running comes to mind," Ellis whispered back.

"That's your answer for everything."

"Because it's a good answer," Ellis whispered more loudly. "And it applies to most situations for me."

"But I'm slower than you," Izak hissed.

"So?"

Izak, now frustrated, turned to Ellis. "That means your answer has a reduced probability of success for me."

"How is that my fault?" Ellis replied.

Izak's eyes narrowed. His lips tightened. "Really? REEEALLY? You actually don't see how us always having to run from trouble is your fault? Mister 'Let's throw gear gunk at the girls during fitness session so they chase down Izak and force gunk down his shirt!'"

Ellis' face cringed as he remembered that it required some creative explaining to talk the girls out of multiple humiliations that they were planning regarding Izak and some ugly payback. "Ok, I can see how that one may have looked like my fault."

"May have looked like your fault?" The smaller boy took in a deep breath to begin a long list of things that most definitely looked like they were Ellis' fault, but the motionless security bot began humming as the internal processor kicked in. The dormant face on the screen sprung to life as it exited sleep mode. The boys stopped their arguing as it now appeared that they may be in trouble—whether or not it was Ellis' fault.

A faint crackling static sound came from a hidden speaker. "Greetings, citizen. What is your name and committee number?" The robotic guard's voice sounded like an antiquated recording with the words not quite matching up with the animated face. These older model bots lacked the finesse, appearance, and functionality of the newer community service bots in the central sectors, but they were perfect for someone who was skilled at manipulating their software bugs.

There was another long pause as Ellis pondered how to answer. He had experience dealing with the security bots and he knew they would be nice to you and wish you a warm greeting just before they arrested you for things that were only slightly illegal.

After a moment, the bot repeated his question, "What is your name and committee number, please?"

Ellis' face stretched, and his eyes looked suspiciously to one side. "It depends," he said with a sneaky assurance in his voice. "Are you looking for us?"

The bot straightened up. Quiet whirling and some unusual clicking could be heard from within the machine. "Negative," it responded.

"Then what makes you think we are the ones you're looking for?" Ellis said.

Whirl ... click, click, click ... whirl. "You are not the subjects of a fugitive acquisition," the bot responded.

Ellis smiled as the clicking sound was a giveaway that the bot was either an older model than he thought it was, or it was in need of some hardware updates. So, he said, "Then how is it that you located us?"

"You were not located ..." the bot paused. "You have been detained for suspicious behavior."

"If you didn't locate us, then how were you able to find us so quickly?" Ellis leaned in and up toward the bot as Izak's wide-eyed expression begged him to leave the bot alone.

The metal cop made a few more clicks and then answered, "Location was not quick as it was not necessary. You have not been located as you are not the subject of an investigation." The face on the screen had a perpetual eerie smile, causing Izak to avert his eyes; it creeped him out.

"So ..." Ellis scratched his chin. " 'We are free to go' is what you're saying?"

After several clicks and whirls the bot stated, "Please stand by for a Community Officer to help you in this matter." The bot leaned forward and went silent for what appeared to be an intentional deactivation. After a soft reboot, the automated security bot stood upright. On the display screen was the face of an actual human officer, but the defective speaker still made the voice sound distorted. "This is Officer Martinez, please state your name and committee number for the record." There was a long silence. "Hello ... citizen ... hello!"

The bot stood alone on the sidewalk with the officer calling out to no one. Ellis, Izak, and the canister were nowhere in sight.

TWO

CHUTE RIDE

A sizable gathering of kids formed near a Bin chute access point outside of one of the many garbage process centers. Izak and Ellis stood at the front of the group with their canister sitting next to them.

Ellis raised his arms as a cheer from his friends brought a huge grin to his face. Izak, on the other hand, didn't look nearly as confident, or content. He glanced back at the massive chute that stretched nearly twenty feet wide and was filled with every kind of hazardous trash, big and small. The metal plates of the conveyor screeched and groaned under the heavy weight of its load. *Crack!* —A broken rusty propeller blade toppled over, smashing a discarded clay pot into hundreds of pieces. Izak cringed.

With his voice barely sounding over the crowd, Izak tried to reason with Ellis. "It's not too late to turn back now!" The boy looked around at the eager faces of their neighborhood friends. "Ok, it's a little too late to turn back now without incurring some serious social consequences … not to mention the relentless jokes made at your expense, but that will go away with time. Death will take a lot longer to get over than that." Izak's eyes trembled as he looked to the conveyors filled with trash coming from other locations via large, automated ground transports.

He watched as both ancient and current constructs and technology headed up the long haul to the vaporization point at the top. He turned back to Ellis. "You do realize that death is one of the possible outcomes here? No one has ever tried to go as far as you're planning to go."

Ellis took a break from the cheers and adoration to glance to his best buddy in the world. "You and I both know that there are way too many check points and scanners that will stop me long before I get to the top. I'm just afraid I won't make it as far as Mohamed did last time. He was smart to wrap himself in that reflective insulation padding." He gave a nod to his rival in mischief, Mohamed, who stood looking overly assured that Ellis was no competition.

"I have to beat his record, and I can do it with this plan." Ellis said as he held up a C.I.M.U., a small flat piece of glass with a rounded border made of blackened Kraytite. It was a communication device referred to by its users as a Cimu, pronounced *seemoo*. Nobody called it a Comprehensive Interfacing Media Unit when Cimu was much easier to say.

"Let's test out the Cimu connectivity," Ellis added.

"Whatever," Izak said as he held up a similar object. He reluctantly spoke into the device. "Cimu, activate." The glass screen flashed on. "Cimu, engage with Ellis Culpepper."

The device in Ellis' hand lit up, and a series of pings rang out. He lifted it to his lips. "Cimu, accept engagement request." The screen flashed again and Izak's face appeared on the display. "Cimu, hologram mode." Another flash and a three-dimensional image of Izak's head was projected an inch above the screen. "Hey buddy," Ellis said, as he waved to the miniature version of Izak's face. "Test, test, test. Am I coming through?"

Izak shook his head, and the hologram mimicked him. "Considering that you are standing right next to me, yeah, I would say you are coming through very clear."

"Aww, why so glum and grumpy? Hey, what's that in your nose? Let me check," Ellis said as he stuck his finger out and inserted it into the hologram's nostril. He twisted his finger around. "Yuk, it is gross up in here. Don't you ever clean it?"

The crowd of kids around them erupted into hysterical laughter which only encouraged Ellis more. The hologram head winced and shook with disappointment.

Izak glared into his screen at the close-up view of Ellis' finger. "Why don't I hate you? I really should hate you much more than I do."

"Because I'm the only friend you have who will help clean your face holes," Ellis said as he pulled his finger back and shoved it into the hologram's ear. "Why's it so icky and sticky in here, too?" Ellis' face wrinkled with an overly dramatic cringe of disgust as he pretended to dig deeper into the 3D Izak's ear.

Izak sneered at Ellis. "I'm going to terminate the connection."

"No, wait!" Ellis yelled. "We have to try it in the barrel."

Ellis lifted the lid on the gray canister. The hinge was worn, but very secure. He swung one leg over and into the can. With little effort, he nimbly pulled the other leg over the edge and stood upright inside. A mischievous grin crossed his lips and he dropped down, closing the lid behind him.

Izak stood there for a moment staring at his screen which couldn't focus well on the dark image of Ellis. Soon, his face became clear as the light from Ellis' device brightened on its own.

"Test, test, and a retest to you. Can you see me?" Ellis called out.

Izak sighed loudly. "Sadly, yes I can."

"You know, a real friend would be a tad more supportive."

Izak lifted the lid and stuck his face down in the barrel only inches from Ellis' head. "A real friend wouldn't make his friend help him to vaporize himself in front of an entire sector of kids."

Ellis looked a little uncomfortable at having the real head of Izak too close to his face, but he could tell that his friend was waiting for a response. "There is no way an entire sector of kids is out there … I mean, come on, maybe a quarter of a small sector."

On Izak's C.I.M.U. device, his glowering face could be seen next to Ellis'. He wasn't the slightest bit happy. Izak pulled back out of the barrel, slammed the lid closed, and pressed the C.I.M.U. hard against his head. "Ugh! You are so frustrating!"

The lid flipped open, and Ellis popped up. Glancing around, he calculated the crowd numbers. "No, really, at best we have only half of a sector of kids here." He looked down to see a close-up of Izak's forehead in 3D on his C.I.M.U. "Whoa, is that a pimple?"

Izak glared at his friend for a moment as he collected his nerves. "Please, just shut up and get back in the can. I want to get this over with."

"I need to get it in the access port before I can do that."

Izak stepped back and gestured wide with his arm to invite his friend out of the barrel. Pretending to be afraid of Izak, Ellis sheepishly pulled one leg out at a time until he was standing alongside of the big container.

"Maybe I should ask Mohamed to help me get it up onto …" He stopped talking when he noticed how hard Izak was trying to remain calm.

Realizing he may be asking too much of his friend, Ellis caught Mohamed's attention with a wave of a hand and then motioned to the canister. "Can you help me get this barrel set up?"

Mohamed nodded and pushed through some of the kids. He was taller than Ellis, and nearly as strong, but his complexion was much darker. And even though Ellis was constantly making disparaging remarks about his rival, they actually liked each other more than either would admit. So, he helped Ellis lift the can up and place it bottom first into the access port. The lid was now positioned to the side like a door. He whispered to Ellis. "I think you got the little guy wound up into a bunch this time … even I'm a little scared for him."

Ellis leaned in close to Mohamed. "With friends like him, who needs babysitters?"

"Come on, man. I wish I had a friend who cared that much. I suggest you make it up to him when you get back."

Realizing Mohamed was right, but resisting to give into the guilt too soon, Ellis nodded his head and then grabbed the top of the access portal to pull himself up and into the canister. A smile crept across his face. "Don't be silly, you don't have any friends," Ellis laughed. "Just kidding, I'll apologize to him when I get back."

Izak walked back over. He placed his hand on the lid and took in a long steady breath as he looked sincerely at his friend. "Will you at least jump out if I tell you to?"

Ellis smiled widely at him. "Will you promise to not overreact and tell me to jump out before I get to the second landing?"

"Ok. I think I can do that."

"Cool." Ellis crouched down in the canister. "Now, don't get all sappy on me. Help me shut this lid."

Izak closed the lid. "See you in a few," he said as he pushed the canister the rest of the way into the access portal—of course, how could he have known that he wouldn't be seeing Ellis in a few?

The kids swarmed in around Izak as the barrel began its long ride up the chute. Many of them, including Izak, pulled out various telescopes and binoculars, ranging from homemade tube and lens gadgets to Izak's high end digital binoculars that he borrowed from his father's closet—in this case, borrowed meant *taken without permission.*

Normally, such a commotion would draw a lot of attention from security, but where the kids were positioned near the base of the chute, they were out of the programmed sensor range for the waste processing center. With everything being automated and observed by robotic sentries inside of the center, there was no need to monitor outside the fences; so, the unusual crowd of kids watching the trash ride up the chute went unnoticed.

As the canister reached the halfway point to the first sentry landing, Izak lifted the C.I.M.U. to his lips without dropping the binoculars from his eyes. He saw the canister wedged in between a large red bench-like object and a dirt-encrusted chunk of marble slab.

"Alright, Ellis, you are halfway up the first zone," Izak said and waited for a reply, but nothing happened. "Did you get that?"

Inside the canister, it would have been pitch black if not for the slim beam of light coming through a small hole in the wall. The sound of the conveyor was loud and occasionally screechy. Izak's voice was faintly heard in the darkness. "Hey, you're scaring me. Answer already!"

A bright flash filled the small container, then dimmed to a blue hue. Ellis was upside down and on a slight angle. With much grunting and groaning, he struggled to twist around as a small hourglass-shaped flashlight in his hand went on and off while he accidently covered and uncovered it through his efforts. "Enough, already! Talk to me!" Izak's voice sounded more nervous than mad.

After fighting with his own body and the awkward position he was in, Ellis got as vertical as he could. He felt around for the C.I.M.U. which was lying face down in the barrel and now blaring with unpleasant statements regarding Ellis and something about an acrid smelling trash coaster. Ellis flipped the device over to where the scared hologram image of Izak continued shouting.

"Okay. Okay. Okay. You can stop freaking out. I'm here," Ellis said to the irate hologram Izak that went silent and then disappeared from the screen—which was not a good sign. "Hello? Izak? Hello?" Ellis called out.

There was nothing for a long agonizing moment and then Mohamed's 3D face appeared above the screen in Ellis' hand. "Uh, Ellis? This is Mohamed. Izak is not talking to you right now, but if you could see his face,

Dude, you're gonna have some serious apologizing to do when you get back."

"I figured as much," Ellis said honestly. "Could you tell me where I am until he's done pouting?"

"Sure. Actuallyyy ... you're now passing the second landing. You can jump out now before you get too far. You beat my record!" he said, with more than a hint of fibbing in his voice.

"That's a lie, you buggle-head!" Izak yelled from the background. "Give me that." The hologram kept disappearing and reappearing with different views. Ellis saw a hand, then a shoulder, another hand and someone's knee, and then finally it was Izak's face again. "I'm here," his tiny head said. "And you are only just now reaching the first landing. Mohamed was trying to trick you into quitting early." Izak had regained his composure. "How's the ride so far? Is the air fine; you can breathe? Did you remember your Jot Light?

Ellis braced himself after the canister shifted unexpectedly. Apart from a bump on the head, he did well with the tussle. "All fine here. A little rougher than normal. I got an air hole for breathing, and I got the light on, too."

Down below, Izak rocked with anxious energy. His voice was more than a little tense. "Uh ... you're coming up to the second landing." Through the binoculars, he saw multiple rays of light begin scanning the trash. He jumped up and down. "They started! The scan has started!"

On Izak's C.I.M.U. display, Ellis could be seen smiling as he listened to his friend overreact to the scanning process. In the background, and among other excited voices, Mohamed said, "This is where they busted me. It's all over, now."

The crowd of kids watched as the canister neared the second landing. The excitement quickly quelled as every breath was being held, and a silence washed through the whole area. They cringed as the many rays of light crisscrossed over the canister above. Izak sucked in more air on top of the air he was already holding in, but no alarms sounded, and the conveyor kept on conveying until Ellis' barrel was on the second landing and heading up to the third. He was now the all-time champion of the chute ride—and the crowd went wild!

"No way! You did it!" Izak moved the C.I.M.U. away from his face and he turned to Mohamed. "He did it. He really, really did it!" A satisfied grin washed over his face as he watched Mohamed drop his head in disgrace.

After a moment, the cheers began to dissipate as the kids watched Ellis' barrel making its way up to the final platform high in the sky. Izak's grin gradually dropped away, and the concerned wrinkled brow reappeared.

Mohamed leaned in next to Izak. His voice had a slight tremble in it. "Why didn't the heat scanners pick him up? ... Izak, what is that container made out of?" Mohamed was now staring full on at Ellis' co-conspirator.

"I don't know ... I didn't think to ask." Izak's words barely made it out of his mouth.

***

Inside the container, Ellis was having a little celebration of his own with no idea where he was. Rocking in the dim blue light, he had hardly enough room to swing his arms, yet he managed to party. His frivolity was cut short when he got distracted by the stern voice coming from a not-to-happy hologram Izak. "Ellis?" an uncomfortable quiet moment passed as the hologram head held back its anger. "Ellis?"

"Ellis here, Mr. Navigator ... what's the news?" Ellis reveled in the idea of returning to the sector Education Center as the new local hero.

"Where did you get that can?" Izak said, his voice shaking.

"Do what?"

"The barrel. Where did you get it?"

"What difference does it make?"

"You passed right through every scanner and sensor for the second level! There is only one material that can do that."

"Yeah, I know." Ellis said nonchalantly. "I got this from the bio disposal plant on the edge of the old TN12 sector. This thing can make it past any scanner."

The hologram's mouth dropped open wide and there was no sound from anyone on the other end of the communication feed. Ellis grimaced as he gazed at the gaping mouth of the hologram. "Hey, man. That's a little unnerving with your mouth and everything like that. You want to knock it off? You're beginning to scare me."

"Scaring you? You think I am scaring you!" The tiny hologram face twisted with anger. "What were you thinking? Never mind, like always you weren't thinking! How incredibly stupid do you have to be to ... just get out! Open that freaking lid and get out of there ... for crying out loud, you are halfway to the third landing!

"Cool!" Ellis said with a nod and a grin.

Izak's hologram turned away as if to talk to someone sitting next to Ellis. "I'm going to kill him ... if he lives through this, I'm going to kill him."

Mohamed's voice called out in the background. "You may not get the chance."

The hologram head looked back at Ellis. "Please ... please, remind me to kill you when you get down here!" Ellis looked oddly at Izak's projected image as it added several more 'pleases' to the request—not to mention a few unpleasant accusations.

"Now, why would I do a stupid thing like that?" Ellis responded, still smiling.

"Stupid?" The hologram became a close-up view of Izak's eye. He had obviously brought the C.I.M.U. to his face. "You think that would be a stupid thing for you to do?" The eye darted around as Izak's voice trembled. "How about climbing into the one and only thing that keeps you from not getting vaporized and then riding it towards the only one thing in the world that can vaporize you? Doesn't that register with you as being more than a bit stupid? Those canisters aren't supposed to be on this chute! It's even illegal for a citizen to have one!"

Ellis held the screen with the freaky eye away from his body as it was seriously creeping him out. He shrugged his shoulders and bobbed his head back and forth. "Ok, in retrospect ... you know ... with all things considered ... I could have given a touch more thought to this idea."

"A touch more thought!" The eyeball screamed.

"Alright, I'm sorry. I'm just playing with you," Ellis chuckled. "I thought of everything. That's one of the reasons why I drilled a hole in the side, besides the purpose of not suffocating ... I'm going to stick my fingers out for the bio scanner to see and have the bots catch me before I hit the third landing. So, lighten up. And get your face away from the Cimu."

※

Among the kids below, Mohamed, who had been listening to the conversation while looking through binoculars, interrupted them. "He better start poking those fingers out. He is more than halfway there, and the sensors are scanning like crazy."

Izak lifted up his binoculars to do some scanning of his own. "Pop open the lid and stick your big stupid head out," Izak instructed. "It will work just as good."

"No. I can't do that."

"Yes, you can ... put your stupid hands on the stupid lid and push. Then stick your stupid head out!"

"I'm detecting a little sarcasm and a lot of hostility in your voice," Ellis said sarcastically.

"You haven't begun to see hostility, and I'm not being sarcastic about that."

"Relax. I can't stick my head out because that would be me quitting ... if I stick my fingers out, the alarms will go off and they will catch me without me being the one to quit."

Izak stood staring at Ellis' face on the display screen. Mohamed, who was still gazing through the binoculars, shrugged his shoulders and said, "Dude ... that is why he is your friend ... I may be stupid, too, but at least I make sense."

"You did what you needed to do. Open the lid already. You promised," Izak said more calmly into the C.I.M.U. screen.

In the dim blue hue on the screen, Ellis gave a reluctant grunt. "Fine, I'll stick my fingers out a little earlier than planned. Will that make you happy?" He was now the one with disappointment in his voice.

"We are well past happy. Happy is not a place I will be until you open that darned lid!" With the binoculars in hand Izak zoomed in on the dark gray canister and saw a finger poke out the hole, and then another appeared as the scanner beam got closer. Izak breathed out heavily. He realized that Ellis' logic wasn't completely wrong since it doesn't matter how much of the body is sticking out of the can. The scanners were programmed to pick up even the smallest trace of bio matter, and that made him feel better, just not a lot better.

For the first time in chute ride history, all the kids were rooting for the security scanner. They watched on as multiple streams of light passed back and forth across the trash in the chute. Every time the lights came close to Ellis' fingers, the mob gave out a loud singular gasp of hopeful optimism. The fingers wiggled back and forth. Now they were in a direct path for one of the beams. As the glow of the ray neared a fingernail, Izak smiled wide. It was almost there ... but Ellis curled his finger up at the last second.

"Ow, they're cramping!" Ellis whined.

"I'm going to hurt him so bad," Izak grumbled under his breath.

"Don't worry, he is about to reach The Wall," Mohamed assured him. "With that solid wall of sensors, there's no way he'll get through."

Izak grumbled to himself, "He wouldn't have to rely on The Wall if the idiot would come to his senses and open the lid, and that's not likely to happen. It requires maturity and sanity to do something like that; not that a mature and sane person would even be in this position to begin with."

"Are you talking about me?" Mohamed asked.

"No. I'm just making an observation."

"He's talking about me," came Ellis' voice from the C.I.M.U. "He forgot to mute his Cimu first."

"I didn't forget anything," Izak continued to grumble. "Ok, you're about to hit The Wall, keep those fingers out and wiggling." As he watched through his binoculars, the fingers disappeared into the can. "Ellis! What are you doing?" Panic flowed through the boy's body.

Giddy laughter was heard over the C.I.M.U. "Sorry, man. I'm just messing with you," Ellis said, as he stuck his fingers back though the holes and outside the can. "I couldn't resist."

"Yes, you could have resisted. You just don't have the brains to do it." Izak's expression made it clear that he was tired of the emotional roller-coaster ride.

Ellis was now at The Wall and the bright red light of the scanner beam started to envelope the gray barrel. The beam crept closer towards Ellis' fingers as the crowd of onlookers began to tense up with eager anticipation of the alarms. If the mischievous boy curled his fingers, he would have touched the red glow and start the automated panic of the security bots

Screech! A loud metal on metal noise shattered the silence and threw the tension into overdrive as the trash on the chute shifted unexpectedly causing Ellis' canister to rotate forward with the air hole pointing down. Izak's eyes sprung open wide, filling the binocular's eye pieces.

From inside, Ellis lost his grip on the C.I.M.U. which fell to rest on the air hole, covering it completely. To make matters worse, Ellis tumbled onto the device with his shoulder securely holding it in place.

"Get out of there, Ellis! You have to get out now. You're passing The Wall and almost on the landing. Get out!" Izak's muffled shrieks could be heard coming from somewhere under Ellis' shoulder.

"I'm with you there," Ellis grunted as he worked to get into a less painful position. "I'm out of here."

<hr />

Looking through his binoculars, Izak saw the lid open after the barrel passed The Wall and Ellis' head stuck partially out as the canister was still laying on its side. With no shock to anyone, alarms pierced the air with high pitched shrills that had the kids covering their ears. In an instant, the chute conveyor came to a screeching halt and Izak let out a 'yahoo' that no one could hear over the blaring alarms.

Izak wrapped his left arm in such a way that it covered both ears while he watched through the binoculars with his right hand. He saw a security bot move toward Ellis' location on the chute. It was finally all over and Izak could relax, but strangely, the bot stopped a little short of Ellis' position and reached into the garbage. After a moment, the mechanical arm pulled out something small and furry with four legs. The alarms shut off.

Mohamed, who was also looking through his binoculars, yelled, "Is that a mouse?"

Izak zoomed in to see that it was actually a mouse that somehow found its way into the trash chute and made it past the sensors. With another loud screech, the chute lunged back into motion. Izak whipped his binoculars back toward Ellis where he caught a glimpse of a large, dirt encrusted, marble slab as it fell against the canister, slamming the boy back inside.

Interestingly enough, there were two types of reactions to this occurrence from the crowd of children below. The first was an uncontrollable urge to flee as a portion of the rabble fell over each other while running as fast as possible away from the process center. The other reaction was that of terror-filled screams and the flailing of arms as the kids tried desperately to get the attention of the security bots, who happened to be programmed to not notice this kind of behavior outside of the process center. Of course, Mohamed was among the first group.

<hr />

"Uhhhh," Ellis moaned from inside the dull, blue-lit canister. After he shook his head a few times to clear his senses, he pushed on the lid expecting it to flip open. Nothing happened. He pushed even harder, but still nothing. In an awkward panic, he twisted quickly around to kick at the lid, but there was no way he was going to move the huge slab leaning against his only escape hatch. For the first time, it was Ellis who had fear in his eyes.

The frightened boy turned back around and scrambled to find the C.I.M.U. He desperately needed to call Izak. After a moment of pure frenzy and no communication device, Ellis froze. He knew where it was. Peeking through the hole that had rotated up a few inches when the slab fell on the canister, he saw the hologram head of Izak just outside of the barrel and partially blocked by a broken toilet seat still clinging to its porcelain base. Somehow, the device slid out past the opened lid when the barrel shifted—this was when all the yelling began.

Ellis lost control. His adrenaline was spiking as the rumbling of the conveyor belt brought him further up the chute—trapped inside the barrel. Inch by dread-building inch, it drew him closer to being vaporized if he didn't somehow break out of the industrial canister that he had selected for its near impervious attributes. Faster and harder, his heart pounded in his chest as he slammed his fists against the curved walls. The inside of the barrel was tinted an eerie blue by the glowing Jot Light that cast dim shadows over the boy's cringing face. "Help! Izak, help me!" he screamed, but his desperate shrieks, though echoing loudly inside the container, drew no one's attention from down below. Outside of the barrel he heard the mechanical sounds of gears turning, along with the scraping of metal on metal which muffled every other noise, including the boy's futile calls for help—which looked to be the last sounds Ellis would ever make.

Izak stood at the bottom with his hands now dropped to his sides. The look on his face showed that his mind was whirling. He knew his friend would do something to get out of trouble. "He always gets out. That's what he does. Everyone knows that," he mumbled to no one particular.

The fog of disbelief had now flowed over all the kids from the sector, or at least the ones who didn't run away. No one said a word. There was nothing to say. The dull gray canister from the bio matter disposal plant reached the end of the chute. It rolled over the edge and onto a large, curved flipper plate that dropped down and then quickly up again. The barrel wobbled slightly as it was tossed into the air with the marble slab and broken toilet seat. A single finger could be seen sticking out of the air hole. The container made one last half turn in the air before disappearing into the lightning covered surface of the Bin—in a flash, Ellis was gone.

Streams of tears rolled down Izak's face.

THREE

SQUIRRELS, BIRDS, & ELEPHANTS ... OH MY!

There was darkness. But inside that darkness was an even darker, blacker whirlpool with a brightly glowing purple mist intertwining with the darkness itself, as though the combination of the two were eerily alive. It was calmly twisting, a living maelstrom with the cloudy purple light revealing a dingy white toilet floating alongside of a gray barrel canister. A C.I.M.U. device passed by with the three-dimensional image of a crying Izak fading away and then blinking out altogether.

The seat of the porcelain toilet swung gradually open with no gravity to direct its motion in either direction, or at least until it brushed listlessly against the canister which forced it closed and sent the commode on a collision course with a rusted fire hydrant. Off in the distance, and further down the swirling dark funnel, was a heavily corroded yellow school bus and what appeared to be the top half of the Statue of Liberty. Beyond that was an endless collage of trash and debris drifting away into nothingness—and the only sound was that of the faint screams emanating from inside the barrel. In time, they too grew quiet.

For the moment, everything was still, and the inside of the container was bathed in the soft blue glow of the Jot Light. Nothing moved and only the quietest of sobs reverberated off the container walls. The air hole that had been drilled to ensure safety from suffocation was far from a perfect circle and the jagged edges gave evidence to the hasty effort made to cut it. Some of the haphazard cuts appeared deeper and darker than the others—until they started moving. They weren't cuts at all. They lifted into the air, vaporous tendrils of pure black that billowed in through the hole. They twisted, swirled, and creeped across the open distance.

With a long draw of his arm across his face, Ellis wiped tears from his eyes and the dripping snot from his nose as he lifted his head. Before him were the writhing tentacles of blackness. The boy froze. Of everything and anything he could ever expect to see, this wasn't it. Sitting there, he couldn't force himself to scream, or breathe, or … or do anything. He only caught his breath and relaxed the painful grip he had on his leg when he saw the glow from his Jot Light form into droplets around the tendrils. Ellis watched on with squinting eyes and a questioning brow as the droplets of light drifted toward the black mass of tendrils. One by one they pressed up against the living darkness and disappeared, absorbed into the twisting nothingness. The tendrils floated in Ellis' direction. The light was all but gone when the darkness wriggled in closer to his face. "Ok, now what?" Ellis whispered to himself in a controlled panic, as he pressed his back hard against the container's wall in a useless attempt to stay out of reach from … from whatever it was that was coming ever so slowly at him. The very tip of one ghostly tendril paused in front of Ellis' face. The boy breathed out a stuttered breath as he relaxed, gazing at the thing that hovered frighteningly close to his face. The lines on his forehead arched with curiosity. It was as though the slivers of darkness were saying something to him that was just beyond his ability to hear.

The edge of the boy's lips loosened and turned up slightly as though he might smile. The black tendril of vapor split into two strands and the two tips mimicked the boy's lips as though they might smile back. Ellis' shoulders dropped as he released tension in his neck muscles, but the relief was brief as the two haunting vapors shot out, piercing into both of Ellis' eyes. There was the hint of a shriek when the light in the canister went out completely. All was dark—again.

Zap!—Ellis jerked wildly as he was overcome by an intense electric shock that coursed throughout his body. There was no doubt that he was being disintegrated. Of course, it felt much less instantaneous than he thought it would. After a few more brief seconds, the shock became a tingle and then stopped all together. For what seemed a lifetime, there was nothing but the sounds of Ellis' heavy breathing. He could see nothing except what looked to be a pinpoint of light glowing almost within his reach. He held out his hand. In that instant, he was blinded, as a mini sunburst of purple light poured through the little hole and into the barrel.

The bright purplish glow washed over him in a shower of liquid color, which literally soaked into the pores of his skin. He pulled back his hand to see beads of the living light cascade over his palm and between his fingers where they, too, sank deep into his skin. When the wispy light was completely absorbed into the boy, the barrel was dark once more.

Flash.—the blue Jot Light flickered on, and the tumbling resumed—and so did the screaming.

Ellis fell hard against the container wall as he was tossed around inside. Seeing the air hole next to his face, he stopped screaming and pressed his eye against the opening, but he could only catch quick glimpses of the outside as the barrel rotated in the air. During one of these glimpses, he saw the brilliant blue sky outside the container. He couldn't believe what he saw—*this isn't right. Where is all the gray?*

Another sight flashed in front of his eye of a mountain-sized pile of junk coming straight at him. Then he saw what looked to be a large squirrel walking upright on two legs. His heart raced so fast that it was more of a continuous hum than individual beats. He strained to see the creature better when he felt the jolt of an electric shock zap through his body again, causing him to yelp. Shaking it off, he pressed his eye harder to the hole and the view became clearer, almost as if he was looking through a telescope.

He *did* see a squirrel-person on the ground below; then there was the bright blue sky with fluffy white clouds and a brilliantly yellow sun; then the junk pile; then another squirrel-person; and then back to the serene sky with large breaks in the clouds for the bright rays of light to come down. "Wait a second!" he said as he pushed away from the hole. "A two-legged squirrel?" Ellis put his eye back to the hole only to see that the previously mentioned huge junk pile was going to crash into him, or he into it.

The canister plummeted toward a large pile of junk located on the edge of what looked to be a swamp. Near the top of the pile was a humongous orange and green striped canvas tarp flapping in the breeze like a circus tent being blown in a windstorm.

The barrel and its panicky cargo dropped from the sky, missing the top of the junk mountain, but hitting near the center of the canvas. It briefly got caught up in its billowing folds, causing a rapid deceleration of the barrel's descent. A dense thudding sound emanated from inside followed by a partially, yet painful yelp. The pause must have given Ellis some hope that he had miraculously landed safely and without harm as he could be heard calling out, "Yes! Finally!"

Like his luck, his hope lasted only a second. The tarp rustled loudly and blew open with a snap, releasing its hold on the barrel as it rolled out of the canvas and bounced down the surface of the junk pile. With every bump and bang, Ellis could be heard yelping in pain from inside.

Just one last thud and the canister rolled to a stop with the lid popping open wide. Ellis crawled out dazed and dizzy from the ride with a roaring sound ringing in his ears. It sounded like clanging metal or wood, or maybe both, doing battle in his ears.

He stood on trembling legs and shook his head as he felt his balance and clarity coming back to him, but that irritating clamoring noise was still ringing in his ears. Behind him was the mountain of junk that caused him much grief, yet also saved his life, as he would have surely crashed to the ground had it not been there. In front of him was a large open field with the greenest grass the boy had ever seen, not to mention it was the only grass he had ever seen as C-Earth had little to no grass in its populated areas. Ellis rubbed hard at his eyes. The daylight was overwhelmingly bright.

When his vision adjusted to the light, he could see that at the opposite side of the lush green field was what looked to be two armies preparing for battle. Each side was threatening the other by smacking their swords against their shields, or clanging war staffs together. The now-bewildered boy could make out two distinct human-like groups of creatures facing off with one another. One looked almost human with the exception of a squat, trunk-like nose on their faces, mustard yellow skin, and enormous elephant-like features such as ears and tusks. Besides those differences, and the fact that they were at least nine feet tall, they looked humanish. The other army was the upright walking squirrel-people that Ellis saw from the air hole of his barrel. They had tails, fur, and every other squirrel-like attribute except they were the same height as Ellis if not smaller.

As his mind struggled with what his eyes were seeing, a few trunk-faced combatants stopped bashing their swords against their shields and looked strangely at the boy. Soon the cacophony faded away as more soldiers stopped to gaze at the oddity that was Ellis. A wave of silence flowed over the battlefield. The warriors from both sides halted in place to see what everyone else was looking at. All eyes were on the strange-looking boy who fell from the sky and now stood staring back at them. Nothing was said and no noise was made—it couldn't get any more uncomfortable.

"Awkward ..." Ellis whispered to himself as he shifted nervously. Finally, he flipped his hand while his arm stayed low by his side to offer a very weak and uncommitted wave. "Hi guys, how's it going?" His voice cracked—it just became more uncomfortable.

The soldiers from each side were unsure what to do. They scratched at their heads and shrugged their shoulders at one another. Some of the elephant-looking creatures even tugged with curiosity at their trunks; the same way humans might rub at their chins while pondering something peculiar. Many of the creatures even exchanged glances with their enemy as if to ask, "*Now what do we do?*"

An enormously large trunk-faced soldier stepped forward in front of his army. He wore a black leather jerkin with an intricate weave design and bright shiny clasps running in a row down his mighty chest. His biceps were bigger around than Ellis' shoulders. Wrapped tightly around the massive arms were white and blue strips of cloth. He stood out as the only one dressed that way, and his stance made it clear that he was in charge.

Across the field, a squirrel warrior walked out and stood in front of the smaller furrier army. He was almost half as tall and only an eighth of the weight of his opponent. His much lighter looking leather armor was dyed a bright red. Ellis noticed that only a few of the squirrel soldiers wore the red armor. The others had on green leather jerkins.

With one paw, the warrior removed his leather helmet to reveal the gray fur on his head. In his other paw was a long staff with metal plating at the ends.

On C-Earth, where Ellis was from, war was not much more than a distant memory and only students of history knew any details surrounding it. Since Ellis loved history, he was able to conclude that the two creatures appeared to be the leaders of the opposing armies. "Ok. I guess I'll be talking to one of those two ... now which one looks the friendliest?" Ellis whispered to himself with fake courage.

The squirrel-warrior shrugged his shoulders. The elephant-like creature turned to glare at the human boy with a measured stare. Ellis felt him gazing into his very soul. The boy stood there helpless and exposed, not to mention stiff as a board. After a moment, the creature's mouth curved up into an unnerving smirk under its mammoth tusks as he gestured to a few soldiers and roared, "Bring it to me!"

"Yeah, you're not the friendly one," Ellis groaned loudly to himself.

It appeared the battle was postponed as multiple trunk-faced warriors split off from their unit and were charging full on towards Ellis. The others maneuvered into a position to cut off the squirrel army that was also moving to converge on the now very confused boy.

As might be expected, Ellis was the only one left feeling befuddled as he watched this bizarre scene unfold. He desperately tried to grasp this new reality, which he was beginning to question as not being real at all. By the time it occurred to him that he should be running, it was too late. A muscular trunk-faced warrior stepped in front of him with his sword held up in an extremely unfriendly manner.

For the first time in his life, Ellis was frozen and unsure what to do. It wasn't necessarily fear that kept him from reacting, but instead, his normally quick thinking and creative resilience was clouded by an overwhelming lack of belief in what he was seeing. The grotesque yellowish humanoid with the trunk for a nose was now standing in front of him with his sword held high over the fifteen-year-old boy, who was now most likely not going to see sixteen.

Clang!—the sword rang out as it glanced off a shiny slim pole that appeared from out of nowhere. The giant warrior was thrown off balance. The pole whipped around and down, slapping the ugly warrior's knee, which buckled and sent him crashing hard to the ground. A whirl of metal pole and reddish-brown fur flashed in front of Ellis as a small squirrel-like person stood in front of him, poised to strike anyone who dared to come near the human boy.

Ellis was stunned. Before him, and with their back to him, was one of the squirrel-fighters standing guard. The tiny thing couldn't have been much more than four and a half feet tall with a bushy tail protruding from a hole in the green leather armor. Ellis couldn't think of what to say except for the only thing you should say in a moment like this. "Thanks."

Turning to face him, the squirrel warrior smiled a bucktoothed grin and in a high pitch squeaky voice, she said, "You're welcome," as she pushed back the teal cat-eye glasses on her face with a thin claw of her little paw.

At Ellis' feet was an old white fedora hat that had fallen out of the pile of trash. The squirrel-girl snatched it up. "You dropped your hat." She leaped up and flopped it on his head. "Quick now, we have to go before another Fallon catches us," she squeaked urgently, while grabbing his hand and tugging at him.

"But it's not my hat," Ellis said as he was jerked away.

She didn't hear him as she was busy running for her life with the weird looking boy in tow.

Ellis ran with her around the edge of the junk pile and away from the battlefield. As they neared a path leading into the swamps, a shield appeared from behind a giant tree and knocked both of them off their feet—it was a huge shield. Ellis hit the ground hard, and his new old hat flew off.

The squirrel-girl rolled away and quickly jumped to her feet with beyond-lightning speed. Ellis was fast, but he had never seen anyone move like that before. Without any hesitation, she was caught up in a staff-to-sword fight with two of the ugly Fallon things from what Ellis had now determined, at least for the moment, was the enemy side of the battle. One of the warriors was a bit taller than the other, but even the smaller one was almost double Ellis' height; and Ellis was five foot two. Except for their height difference, they looked almost identical, right down to the tribal-looking tattoo on their right cheeks just above the tusk.

The furry little girl moved with grace as she deflected the forceful blows with her staff. It was useless to try headshots, as the Fallons were using their tusks as well as their shields to block her strikes. Being low to the ground, she could take better advantage of her position, which she did—*crack!*—She smacked the bigger guy on the ankle and dropped him hard with a yelp.

The other Fallon launched several frenzied strikes at the little squirrel-girl that she deflected, but when she went to hit his ankle with her staff—*thump*—her staff stopped short as he lifted his boot to receive the blow with the sole of his foot. Stomping down hard, he snapped the staff a third of the way up and trapped it under his boot. The squirrel-girl's eyes shot open wide, filling the lenses of her glasses. She was completely stunned that her move ended with such catastrophic results. Seeing she was distracted, the Fallon swung his shield, catching her in the chest and slamming her flat on her back. He towered above her grinning.

Having never been in a fight, and not knowing what else to do, Ellis used the only weapon he had to try and save his new little friend.

"Hey … you! Elephant-face … guy … thing … whatever you are!" Ellis stammered as he had also never had an enemy before and was uncertain how he should insult him. Back on his world, all fighting was abolished, and confrontation took the form of disapproving glares at a committee meeting.

He thought to remark on the creature's yellowish skin and how it reminded him of vomit, but the Social Acceptance classes engrained in him kept him from judging someone based on their appearance—it was part of the Consolidated-Earth education doctrine.

The creature turned toward him. Ellis stood his ground though his legs trembled, wanting badly to run away. "Stop … and I'll … do something!"

The huge Fallon wrinkled his brow. "Don't you mean 'or'?" His voice was deep and gravelly.

Now, Ellis had a wrinkled brow. "Or what?"

"You said 'stop and you'll do something,' instead of 'or'."

"No, I didn't," Ellis lied. Why not lie? It was helping him to stall for more time as he tried to keep the furry girl from being mushed.

"Yes, you did. You said 'and'. I heard you say 'and'." The Fallon turned to look at the squirrel-girl on the ground. "Didn't he say 'and'?" He looked back to Ellis. "You said 'and' … I heard you."

The girl sat up and nodded to Ellis as she straightened the glasses on her tiny furry nose. "He's right, you did say 'and'," she squeaked very matter-of-factly to Ellis.

With wide eyes, Ellis threw his arms in the air and glared at the girl. "Whose side are you on?"

She looked confused by the question. "Mine."

There was a weird pause as all three of them looked at each other, seemingly uncertain as to where they go from here.

After taking in a deep breath, Ellis said, "Alright … alright." He gazed up at the hulking beast and said, "Stop ... and ..." He shook his hands out in front of him as he nervously tried to figure out what to do. *What should come after someone says and?* A small electric shock shot through his body and was gone. He paid it little attention as his current situation was much more pressing. He glanced to the ground hoping to find a plan or scheme down there. It took a second, but he bent over and picked up an apple sized rock. "... and I'll hit you in the face with this." He held up the rock.

Laughter blared out from the mouth and trunk of the Fallon while its mustard yellow face turned to a bright shade of orange. This alone wouldn't have been so embarrassing if it wasn't for the fact that the squirrel girl was also chittering away in what must have been rib-tickling hysterics.

The Fallon warrior looked at the little girl as they exchanged knowing glances. What Ellis was saying was so incredibly ridiculous. To imagine a puny boy hurting a Fallon with a puny rock was beyond the realms of any reality.

When the big fellow turned back to laugh more at Ellis—*smack!*—His lights went out as the hefty rock bounced off the ridge of his trunk between his eyes. The blow sent him tumbling backwards over a tuft of grass.

Though violence was not condoned on C-Earth, every citizen was required to choose multiple forms of physical discipline training to maintain a healthy body. Target throwing was one of Ellis' disciplines, and he was particularly good at it, but something seemed off. The boy looked at his hand and arm as he realized he threw the rock much harder than he would have thought possible. The Fallon's laughter left the boy feeling a little mad, but more so than that, he also felt an uncomfortable tingling sensation as if charged with a low volt of electricity. He didn't know what to make of it and assumed it was some natural reaction that occurs in the body when you participate in physical conflict.

Ellis walked over to the squirrel-girl whose eyes were still glistening from giggling. Her reddish fur was also standing up like it had been brushed the wrong way. He knelt beside her, pretending to be mad more than actually being mad. "... and I'm not helping you up." He paused. "Ok, I'll help you up, but I'm considering not liking you." As his hand was inches from hers, he got launched on top of her from an excruciating slap to his back.

Standing over Ellis and the girl, with a shield in his hand, was the other warrior who had been smacked on the ankle. He had waited for the right moment to get back into the fight and gain the upper hand.

"Not so funny now ... is it?" the mastodon of a brute sneered. This Fallon was much nastier and more vicious looking than his fallen comrade; not to mention he was furious at seeing Ellis take out the other guy so easily. "Let's see how you like a hit in the head," he growled, raising his shield high over his right shoulder—*Thunk!*—The trunk on his face twitched forward as his eyes rolled up in his head.

After a second or two, he dropped to his knees and slumped over to the side. Standing over him was a squirrel warrior in full green leather armor and a large staff. Her fur was longer and less red than that of the younger squirrel-girl on the ground, but Ellis saw a resemblance between the two of them.

The warrior-squirrel scowled at the two kids as they got to their feet. But when Ellis was standing up, he realized the larger squirrel was his same height—she looked bigger from the ground.

"Sydney, what is that?" the larger squirrel girl squeaked angrily, while gesturing to Ellis. Of course, even the angry voice of a squirrel-person had a chipmunky sound that made Ellis smile. The taller squirrel was not pleased about this at all, but then, maybe not all squirrels have a happy temperament.

Sydney stiffened up and pushed out her chest in defiance. "I don't know what it is, but he's with me ... if he is a he, or she ... whatever it is, it's with me." She looked to Ellis and half-heartedly motioned to the other squirrel gal. "This is my sister, Sam. We are Seeuradi."

Sam took a step toward Ellis and sniffed the air around him a few times. "It smells awful!"

Ellis' face tightened with disbelief. He waved his hands toward the trunk-faced creatures on the ground who were now both out cold and snoring away. "We are standing next to these two nasty, reeking ... things ... and on the edge of a garbage dump ... and you think I smell?"

Sydney bobbed her head reluctantly and leaned towards Ellis. She whispered frankly, "You do smell a bit."

Sam took a step back quickly. She had an ah-ha moment. Her head twisted slightly as she examined the unusual creature. "U-man ... I think he's a U-man! But it can't be. They haven't been around here for decades."

Sydney's pointy little ears perked up. "Wow!" She looked closely at Ellis; uncomfortably close, with her nose practically on his. "We have never seen an ooman," she said, not sure of the vowel sound.

Ellis put his finger on Sydney's forehead and his fingernail disappeared into her fur as he pushed her back away from his face. "You're both wrong … it's pronounced human. You gotta add an 'H' sound in there." He turned back to look at Sam. "Can you say hhhhhuman?" He ended with his classic condescending grin.

In a flash, Sam leapt into the air and spun around. Her foot shot out and caught Ellis on the chin. His world went dark as he flopped down and across the chest of the snoring elephant soldier hit by the rock. Sam glared down at the boy who was now snuggled up to the Fallon. "hhh-U-man." She gave a wide bucktoothed smile as she kicked the white fedora hat, causing it to flip over and onto Ellis' shoulder.

As Sam walked away, Sydney squeaked out in her factual tone. "I think you're still saying it wrong!"

FOUR

IT DEEPENS

A hazy glow came slowly into focus as Ellis tried to open his eyes. Reaching up to touch his jaw, "Ow," he called out, wincing with an intense pain shooting through his entire face. Even in the low light, the black and blue hue of his chin was more than a little visible; it was obvious.

The boy sat up with a labored effort to see what looked to be the inside of a large sparse hut made from branches and mud.

Under him was a pale green tattered blanket which must have been stretched over some excessively dry and brittle leaves as he made loud crackling sounds with every movement. A rock slab to his right had a single candle flickering in a losing battle against the darkness. Actually, he could see that it looked to be brighter outside than inside, as slivers of the setting sun worked their way through the dead foliage, creating sheer curtains of light in the floating particles of dust.

It took a little rubbing of his neck and stretching of his head from side to side, but the boy's noggin eventually cleared. From outside the leafy thin walls, he heard many voices and shuffling of feet coming in and out of the area. Nothing sounded familiar, but at least he didn't hear any swords clanging against shields or giant yellow elephant people threatening to kill him.

Crawling on all fours, Ellis crept toward a shabby leather flap that he assumed was the door. Ever so quietly, he pulled it open to peek out.

A horrendous odor assaulted his nostrils and made his eyes water. The stench was emanating from a large boot-shaped object wrapped at the bottom in leather, or some form of animal hide. The shape of the boot was odd in that the foot portion was short as it only extended out six inches from where the calf and ankle would be. It would be accurate to say that at the base it looked like a circle with a bulge sticking out in one direction.

He followed up the object with his eyes to see that it really was a boot, and a leg, and an entire body of one of the Fallon warriors. This one, Ellis noticed, had a bulbous bruise on his forehead and two painful looking black eyes on either side of its trunk. The boy could see the bruised eyes as they were now glaring down at him from above two menacing tusks. Ellis shook his head and whispered to himself as he recognized the Fallon warrior he had hit with the rock, "There is no way my luck is this bad."

The creature slung open the flap and snatched Ellis up with one hand, holding him inches from the yellowish trunk on his face, which was easily eight feet off the ground.

"Go'n somewhere, rock-boy?" the guard sneered. Evidently, he carried a grudge.

"Not if you don't want me to," Ellis peeped.

Standing on the opposite side of the doorway was another Fallon guard; of course, luck again would have it that it was the other Fallon from the swamp that tried to kill Ellis.

The larger one grumbled, "Put him down, Evan." As Evan put Ellis down, the big one snorted, "We gotta bring him to the surrender meeting."

"So, who surrendered, Mr. …?" Ellis waited for what felt like an eternity before the large guard filled in the blank.

"Brandor."

"Ok, Mr. Brandor."

"Just Brandor!" he trumpeted.

"Of course, you're not the formal type, that's ok, I guess. So, who won the war, just Brandor?"

Evan shook his head and sarcastically replied, "That's what the surrender meeting is for … nitwit," he huffed, with a breath that made Ellis nearly gag.

Evan hovered close over Ellis, checking him out as he bent over. "For the time being, the Seeuradi agreed to have you remain under our protection if we ceased all hostilities and promised to not harm you."

"Seems fair ... I especially like the not-harming-me part," Ellis said with his voice cracking, as he looked to each side at Evan's tusks that were now projecting out past the boy's shoulders. With the tusks on either side of his face, he got a better view of them. Instead of being smooth throughout, the majority of the boney surface was pitted with grains running the length. There were, however, some chips and cracks that did not seem natural, unless being formed by blocking sword and axe blows was considered natural for a Fallon's tusk growth.

Having Evan's face that close to him, Ellis also got a good view of the handy work he did with the rock. It was much worse than Ellis had realized. Not only did he put a lump on the warrior's forehead and give him two black eyes, but the area around his eyes had begun to swell up as well. The dark hue of the bruising was a drastic contrast to the vomit-colored skin. It looked seriously painful.

As they began to walk away with Ellis in tow, Brandor stopped. "Wait a minute." He stepped over to a log by the hut to retrieve the white fedora hat Sydney had put on Ellis' head when they were next to the trash heap that morning. With his huge four fingered hand, the creature pressed the hat onto the boy's head. "Don't forget your hat."

"But it's not my ..." Ellis was stopped by the hostile look on Evan's bruised face.

"It's not your what?" Evan growled.

Peeking out from under the rim of the crushed hat, Ellis' voice cracked again as he said, "Nothing. It's ... not nothing. Thank you ... for the hat."

"Be happy we didn't just leave it there," Brandor huffed.

With the hat issue resolved, one of Brandor's eyes squinted tightly and he leaned in, poking the boy in the shoulder with his trunk. He said, "hey ... what's your name?"

This was never Ellis' favorite question to be asked because it was usually coming from someone he had offended, someone he may still offend, or someone he was currently in trouble with; most often it was a security bot. He took a moment to decide if his usual answer was best for this situation.

Brandor's trunk pulled back and lifted high on his face as he barked louder. "What is your name?"

Whether it was self-preservation or stress, the boy did not know why he decided that he was going to go with his usual response, which he had come to regret on multiple occasions thereafter. "It ... depends," he stammered.

Content with the answer, the big guard stood up and repeated it to make sure he got it right. "*It* Deepons."

Evan corrected him. "Deepens," he said as if he were an authority on the subject.

"Deepens," Brandor repeated. Both guards nodded their heads in agreement.

"Actually, that's not right," Ellis sheepishly protested.

"What's not right?" the guards snarled in unison, with a double dose of noxious breath blowing over the boy.

Ellis gulped as the stench caught him off guard and caused his voice to shrill with his answer. "Nothing ... actually ... I'm good ... how are you?"

Brandor and Evan each took one of Ellis' arms, lifted him in the air between them, and walked off—and every thunderous step was the echoing sound of an encroaching doom in the human boy's head.

Brandor and Evan walked up to the main entrance of a particularly large stone building and stopped under an archway with Ellis dangling between them. From inside, many voices of various unusual sounds filled the air. Deep booming tones of Fallons, like Brandor and Evan; high pitched chittering that must have been from more of those squirrel people; and ear-piercing squawks and shrieks from something Ellis could not identify echoed around a massive stone pavilion at the center of an expansive, yet primitive village.

The entire valley was a centralized meeting place; a neutral ground where the many races could meet to resolve issues or collaborate for a common good. The village and its rarely used buildings and huts were the hub where all trails led into the valley. Each race of the Giverkind had set up camp on the outskirts of the village, but here in the middle is where they all met to resolve their issues.

It was an ancient site developed to bring the races together as one during their darkest hour. Because of its success at uniting the races, it had become unnecessary. Long ago during those dark times, the many different creatures of this world gathered in an alliance that lasted for centuries—only in recent years had the village resumed its purpose as the once invulnerable bond of their racial unification became fragmented; and the alliance wavered under the weight of suspicion and greed.

Ellis saw two types of humanoid creatures here like the ones he saw before; the Seeuradi squirrel-people, and the nasty-smelling trunk-faced Fallons; but now there was a third—bird people.

Unlike the squirrel and elephant beings who all looked alike within their own race, Ellis noticed that these new bird creatures were not alike. They each had bird heads and legs on humanoid torsos with feathered wings starting from below their claws at the forearm to the shoulder, but not all members of their race was derived from the same species of bird. Some had the head and feather colors of hawks, while others looked similar to owls. There were also flamingos, finches, cranes, and even pelicans—too many types for Ellis to count. And far too many for Ellis' comfort. His head swung around frantically as he tried to take in the sight of an ever-increasing and disturbing barrage of images flashed before him.

Normally, one might expect a surrender meeting to have less yelling than there was here, but then again, like Ellis, most people from C-Earth wouldn't have a clue as to what a surrender meeting was. His world had not had a war in nearly three hundred and fifty years. And that ended in the establishment of the Committee-Based society that is now Consolidated Earth.

At the front of the room, two members for each of the three groups sat at a long, high table. Two bird men sat in the center, a hawk and a heron. Two Fallons were to the right of them, and two Seeuradi sat to the left.

Around the room was a mixture of the races in various groupings. The air was vibrant and alive with talk regarding a strange and mysterious visitor.

"I heard someone say he was here with a message from the Oomans," one brilliantly pink flamingo lady gasped to a squatty hen.

"Maybe they have had a change of heart. I do so hope so," the chicken-woman replied.

"Yes, of course, I hope so as well. If the Oomans don't return to the council, this war could escalate across all of Fentiga."

The deafeningly loud conversations were at a fevered pitch when an uneasy hush spread across the room. Brandor and Evan stepped in through the grand archway with Ellis still hanging by his armpits a few feet off the ground.

"No, this isn't at all embarrassing," Ellis moaned.

"Shut it," Evan barked from the side of his mouth.

At the table, a Fallon in a leather jerkin with a patch over his eye and his tusk on that side broken two thirds of the way motioned for the guards to come forward. As they made their way through the crowd, Ellis noticed everyone staring at him. Their gaze felt like little fingers poking at him to verify that he was real.

As he was midway down the center aisle, Ellis saw a familiar furry-faced squirrel-girl up ahead standing in the front of the crowd and at the beginning of the row. Sydney had leaned out into the aisle, waving frantically to make sure he saw her. Ellis flapped his left arm in a pathetic acknowledgement, and with much less enthusiasm than his furry friend. He would have already succumb to despair if the situation wasn't so ridiculously insane that his mind still hadn't caught up with the reality of it.

When the guards got within ten feet of the table, they stopped. Brandor snapped to attention, which jerked Ellis violently to one side. "We have brought the U-man boy."

The Fallon with the eye patch cringed at Ellis' ugliness as his good eye pivoted around to inspect the hideous boy with mushy pale skin, hair all over his head, and a puny frame; not to mention some dumb-looking white hat was pressed hard onto his head. He huffed with a whip of his trunk, "Set him down. He's not a criminal." The guards set the boy down as the one-eyed Fallon continued. "What's his name?"

Brandor tried to stand even more at attention than before. "*It*, sir! The boy is called *It*."

"Deepens ... sir," Evan piped up out of turn, but with equal respect and rigid body.

"What?" The Fallon at the table said while scratching his fingers against the rough dirty-yellow skin of his bald head.

"Deepens, Sir?" Evan responded.

"What deepens?" His voice was stressed and gruff.

"The boy, sir."

"The boy deepens?"

"Yes, sir," Evan said nervously and let his posture relax as he thought through his words. "I mean ... no sir, the boy does not deepen. He is Deepens." Evan snapped back to attention as if he had successfully explained his comment—sadly, he had not.

The Fallon with the eye patch groaned as his hand slid down his face and grabbed at his trunk in frustration. "So, how does the boy deepen?"

Evan's face lit up as he now realized the misunderstanding. "No, no, sir. The boy doesn't deepen ...obviously ... he doesn't do that." He looked at Ellis and whispered, "You don't deepen, do you?"

The insanity of the situation was getting to the human boy, and he gave a weak grin. "Not today, I haven't."

Evan turned back to the table stuttering as he talked. "No ... of course not ... I meant to say ... actually, he says ... his name is Deepens...*It* Deepens." At this point, Evan needed to stop talking but didn't. "... The boy ... his name is *It*."

A low grumble flowed from the Fallon at the table. His weathered and scarred face tightened as he let go of his trunk. "You are dismissed," he said to the guards, with a broad wave of his four fingered hand. Evan and Brandor ceremoniously turned around and walked to the back of the room to take up post at the archway.

After the guards moved off, Ellis saw Sydney was standing to the left of him at the front of the audience. She waved again and gave him a thumbs-up.

The Fallon at the table turned to the Seeuradi squirrel-people and the bird-people next to him. "Ladies and gentlemen of the panel ..." He turned to the crowd. "Ladies and gentlemen of the Seeuradi and Ave community ..." He held both hands out towards Ellis. "The Fallon folk present to you, the boy called *It*."

A murmur flowed over the room like a gusting breeze gaining strength and volume as it rolled. Everyone was discussing the odd-looking human creature and his equally odd name. Even the people at the table murmured amongst each other. The name *It* was repeated over and over.

At one point, Ellis considered sneaking off while everyone was distracted. That tactic worked well on the security bot back home, so he thought it might work here. The only reason he didn't ease out of the crowd and into the darkness was that he wouldn't know where to go if he did get away. Alone in the dark with strange creatures everywhere was not a good idea; besides, it could be worse, at least he didn't get vaporized. Where he stood now would have to do for the time being.

"So, that's Jagger Large-Bottom. He's like the second-in-command of the Fallon army ... and a real twogg," Sydney squeaked into Ellis' ear. She had crept up to stand beside him. Leaning into him, she pointed to the large creature at the table with the eye patch. "He got the patch on his eye from fighting the Kroncal."

Ellis turned to see Sydney was only inches from his face and standing on her tiptoes. He whispered back, "He doesn't look much too friendly."

"Oh, he's not," she said, as she reached up to snatch the white hat from his head.

"Who is the other one in the orange robe? He almost looks like a nice guy." Ellis nodded toward the other Fallon who sat with a calm and steady demeanor. It even appeared that he may be smiling.

Sydney straightened her glasses, then punched her little paw into the hat and knocked out the dents while she talked. "I'm sure he is. He's a mystic, and a very powerful one I'm told. I think his name is Kandula." When she had the fedora back in shape, she gave it a quick wipe across the top and deftly set it back on the boy's head.

"A mystic?" Ellis gave her a look that questioned her sanity.

She grinned and nodded her head.

The Seeuradi squirrel-lady at the table stood up on her chair, as the table was built to accommodate a Fallon-sized person. Like the other Seeuradi on the panel, she wore a dark purple robe with ornate yet dingy white trimming. The trim of her hood wrapped around her head, creating a crown-like effect with smaller red and blue trim interwoven into the dingy white.

She raised her arm with the baggy sleeve of her robe spreading out in the shape of a big purple wing. As with any courtly setting, the raising of the hand by one of the leaders in authority was to result in the quieting of the audience and a respect for the presiding officials—but that's not what happened. If anything, the murmuring had become an all-out free-for-all of conversation and laughter.

"She's our Prominence and also a powerful mystic!" Sydney squeaked loudly as she pointed her paw toward the table. "She is mentoring me with my healing mysticism!"

Ellis could barely hear Sydney over the commotion. He leaned in closer, but that didn't help. A deep bellowing trumpeting echoed off the pavilion ceiling and caused Ellis to lean in tightly against the girl. Jagger was standing there with his trunk pointed straight up. The crowd quieted down in an instant, except for Sydney.

"... and if I focus my heart into my mystic studies, I may one day be Prominence myself. That would be so awesome," she squeaked.

Sydney was oblivious to the room going silent. Trying not to move the rest of his body, Ellis nudged her hard enough to bring her attention to the table where Jagger was glaring at her with his one good eye.

"See, I told you he was a twogg," she whispered.

The huge Fallon breathed out deeply and took his seat. The Prominence nodded her thanks to him and gestured to the bird-people at the table. "I would first like to thank the Ave flock for once again taking on the role of arbiter to help facilitate this amicable, albeit temporary, arrangement in regard to the mutual ceasing of hostilities. They have been there from the start and helped the Seeuradi and Fallon folk weather the storm of this growing dispute." She glanced at the Aves sincerely. "You have our gratitude."

She now turned her attention to Ellis as she cleared her throat with multiple little squeaks and addressed him with her paws stretched out. "*It*, I am Prominence Susanne Janli of the Seeuradi people. On a day that began in contestation for the offering rites of the Great Giver in this region, you have arrived, and in doing so, you have given us pause."

Ellis couldn't help but snicker at her squeaks as she presented herself with all seriousness, yet sounded so gut-wrenchingly funny. And the fact that she said "pause" with her paws stretched out only made it worse. Ellis visibly fought to not lose control.

Susanne noticed the few giggles that slipped out of the boy, but as she had no experience with human customs, she did not address it. "As it appears that you are a sign from the Great Giver ..."

"To some it appears that way," Jagger grumbled, cutting her off.

Again, she nodded to Jagger. "Yes, to some." She looked back to Ellis. "We have called this surrender meeting in order to determine how to interpret the significance of your arrival and how we should move forward with the joint surrender based on our findings." She touched her chin and tilted her head as a thought struck her. "But, before we are to continue, we must first verify that you are indeed a U-Man child."

"Ha!" yelled Sam from the audience's second row. She leaned forward over Sydney's shoulder and pointed a crooked clawed finger at Ellis. "I told you it was pronounced U-Man!" She shoved Sydney hard enough that the young Seeuradi girl nearly lost her glasses. It's a good thing she had a strap that wrapped around her head, holding them on. The little squirrel-girl still had to adjust them on her nose.

"Enough," squeaked Susanne, as she chastised Sam with glaring eyes and a squinched up nose.

Sam tucked her head back into her shoulders as she shrunk away, but whispered loudly to her sister, "I wasn't wrong … he was!" She trailed off muttering the word U-Man a few more times under her breath.

The majestic squirrel-woman turned her attention back to Ellis. "As I was saying, could you please verify for the panel that you are indeed U-Man? We have seen none of your kind in so many years that we are not certain if you are one."

For a boy who normally always had something to say, Ellis was at a loss for words, or even an idea as to how he would prove he was a human. He had never had to prove his humanity before. A silence gripped the entire room. All eyes were fixed on the human boy. As a rare choice of options, he decided to tell the truth—what could it hurt? "I don't know what a U-Man is, but I am a human," he said with an exaggerated H sound.

Again, there was a wave of murmurs flowing through the room. The members of the panel looked to each other. The hawk-headed Ave on the panel leaned on the table and inspected the boy from a distance. A crooked line of missing feathers and scarred skin stretched across his face and ended next to the beak where an ugly scratch continued partially over the bridge of the beak. The eye on that side of his face had a milky white film over the black pupil.

With jerky movements, he twisted his head back and forth, taking turns looking through each eye. "In my travels of the lands to the west, I have heard this pronunciation of their peoples' name." He looked back to the group at the table. "Hooman is correct." He looked back to the Ellis. "You are correct, boy," he added with what sounded to be resentment, if not contempt for Ellis' presence.

Ellis shook his head slightly as the absurdity of his situation continued to befuddle him. With the rest of the room, he watched the panel as they discussed in low voices amongst themselves.

Sydney stood on her tiptoes again and whispered in Ellis' ear. "I think that Ave is called Edroy. I don't know much about him, but that he is very important, and he dresses really fancy."

Ellis looked at Edroy in his shiny forest green jacket with glittering buttons and matching vest. Underneath the vest, the birdman wore a billowy white collared shirt. A silky golden scarf tied around his neck flowed over his shoulder and down the front of his jacket.

Ellis grinned, "Yeah, I'd say fancy is an understatement."

Occasionally, one of the Fallon raised their deep gruff voices in protest of something being said, or maybe they were in agreement with the others and angry tones were just part of their typical speech; it was hard to tell with them. After a few moments, the panel faced Ellis.

Susanne addressed the room. "It is the panel's decision that the surrender shall stand as is with no one conceding loss or claiming victory." She dropped her eyes to Ellis. "Though we all agree that you are U-Man ..." She was stopped instantly by a loud squeak from the crowd.

"Hooman!" Sydney asserted from the first row. "You need to stress the 'H' and the oo sounds." She leaned in toward Ellis' direction with her hand near her mouth to direct a very loud whisper at him. "That's right, isn't it? Hooman?"

Ellis groaned back to her, "Close enough."

Pleased with herself, Sydney smiled with her buckteeth gleaming and turned to stick her tongue out at her big sister. Sam gave her a look of *"you're gonna get it when we get home."*

Susanne nodded. "Yes, of course," she began again. "As we agree that you are ... hooman, it stands to reason that you may not have been a direct gift from the Great Giver, but your timely arrival has brought about a temporary end to our disagreements." She bowed her head in reverence. "And that is certainly a great gift to our people on all sides."

All at the table nodded in agreement with the exception of Edroy. Something with the way he turned the scarred side of his face with the milky white, lifeless, eye toward Ellis gave the boy a chill.

Ellis looked to the others and bounced his head and shoulders in confused acknowledgement and said, "Glad to help." Of course, it almost sounded like a question the way he said it.

Susanne took in a reluctant breath. "Sadly, we are unable to agree as to what we are to do with you. It is for this reason that the status quo shall be maintained, and you are to remain as a temporary guest of the Fallon folk and under their continued supervision and hospitality."

Sydney looked at the scowl on Jagger's face. "He doesn't look hospitable to me."

Ellis' eyebrows pulled in tight together and very slowly he responded, "So ... I'm a prisoner?"

"Of course not!" Susanne squeaked out, offended by the accusation. "You're a guest ..." she thought for a moment, "... who can't leave."

"Yeah, we call those prisoners where I come from," Ellis said, with an excessively snarky tone.

Susanne gestured to the Fallon at the table. "Through his emissaries here, Lord Granger Stronghide of the Fallon folk has assured the panel that you will be afforded all the courtesy of a welcomed guest, and that you will be free to come and go as you please under their supervision." She nodded to Jagger and Kandula at the table. They nodded back in affirmation. Of course, the robed mystic had a genuine smile for her, while Jagger's look was nothing short of irritated tolerance.

"Where would I go?" Ellis said in a high pitched, stressed voice. His question was more rhetorical than anything.

"I'm sure I do not know. That is for you to decide, but until the council has agreed to a more permanent solution, you will travel with the Fallon to the city of Utuska where you will remain until we have a consensus on the most expeditious way to return you to the hoomans."

Sydney took a step forward in protest. "He should stay with us! After all, I found him; and the Giver Common Law states that first retrieved, or in hand, has first rights."

Ellis nodded his head vigorously up and down even though he had no idea what she was talking about. Staying with the squirrel people who saved him was much more preferable than being a guest of the creatures who tried to kill him. To Ellis, this was a "*no brainer.*"

Susanne waved Sydney off. "He isn't a piece of metal or a contraption of some sort. He is a living being and not covered by that particular Giver Common Law ... it has been decided." She looked up to the audience. "As per the stipulation of our joint surrender agreement, the boy called *It* is to remain with the Fallon folk."

The room erupted with heated arguments of who should host the "hooman" boy.

Susanne placed her hands on the table to lean out as far as she could towards Ellis. "By the way, dear, it is not proper to wear your hat during official assemblies."

Ellis' shoulders drooped as he moaned, "But it's not my hat."

While the room around him roared with debate, Ellis thought back to when Izak was pleading with him to not get into the container and ride the Bin chute. How he now wished he had listened to his little friend as he watched the trunk-faced guards walking in his direction. So lost in his head at the moment, Ellis didn't see that Sydney moved even closer to be against his side while she whispered a divination incantation to herself and made strange gestures with her paws. She, too, was watching the hulking guards approach as she ended her incantation with a frown.

"Sorry to hear you might die." She said with sincere regret in her voice. "What a bummer."

Ellis looked at her with wrinkles of disbelief across his forehead. "Yeah, bummer."

"So, your name is *It*?" Sydney squeaked in a perky tone, as if she had forgotten what had happened only moments earlier.

The guards were now within ear shot of the two kids. Ellis nodded his head yes with the resolve of a boy who had nothing left to lose. "Yes, *It* … I am so *It*."

"I'm glad to have met you, *It*." She reached out to shake his hand excitedly. "And don't worry, I don't think they really will kill you. There's probably a rule or something about that being inappropriate." She paused to calculate the probability. "Yeah, they probably won't kill you … that sounds right." She smiled.

As Brandor and Evan walked up, Jagger joined them and said, "Lord Stronghide will want to see him. Take him there straightaway."

The guards nodded and said, "Yes, sir," in unison.

"Excuse me. May I ask a question, Mr. Large-Bottom, sir?" Ellis asked respectfully to Jagger.

The tension multiplied a hundred-fold as Brandor's and Evan's jaws dropped open under their large tusks. But it was Jagger's face that glowed bright orange with rage.

"What did you call me?" The Fallon's fists were clenched and shaking as he towered four feet over the boy.

"I'm sorry, I thought your name was Large-Bottom."

"Who told you that?" the mammoth barked with near seething rage.

Sydney slipped in behind Ellis, disappearing completely.

"Well ..." Ellis started to speak when he heard a fearful squeak from behind him.

"Well, what!" The enormous beast growled.

"I thought I heard someone refer to you that way."

"Which someone?"

"I don't know. Maybe a Seeura ..." He felt a tiny claw stab at his back. "Maybe not a Seeuradi ... No ... Not at all." He glanced out into the audience and his eye landed on a turkey-looking Ave. "A bird. The turkey. I overheard him say it to someone as we walked in."

Jagger looked at the turkey bird-man with death in his one good eye. The turkey-man happened to see Jagger glaring at him and his head started nervously bobbing around as he glanced about to see if the evil eye was meant for someone else—it wasn't.

Jagger growled again. "I should have known. Those backstabbing beakheads speak one thing to your face and another when your back is turned. I don't trust their entire race any further than I can throw them." He bent down close to Ellis with his tusks on either side of the boy. Ellis could see that the broken tusk had an ornate white metal cap at the end. Jagger's breath washed over the boy as he said with an ominous growl, "... but then again, I can throw a body pretty far."

"I so believe you could," Ellis coughed from the Fallon's stench-filled breath.

Jagger stood back up to talk with Brandor and Evan.

Ellis tilted backward and whispered harshly to Sydney who was still hiding against the small of his back. "His name isn't Large-Bottom!"

"Apparently not," she whispered back.

"Then why did you tell me it was?"

"Because I don't like him ... and who would believe his name is Large-Bottom, anyway? That's just silly ... but he does have a large bottom."

Jagger walked back to the table while Brandor and Evan grabbed Ellis under each arm as they had before and lifted him high in the air. The glare in their eyes and sneer on their lips was more than enough to easily clear a path to the exit. As they walked, Brandor pulled *It* to mouth level and grumbled, "Lord Stronghide wants to see you."

FIVE

MEETING LORD STRONGHIDE

Wistful clouds drifted across the starry sky, making the darkness of the night thicker than normal when they passed by the moon. A moth sizzled as it flittered accidently into the flames of a single torch poised outside of a large mud hut.

Little creatures of the night scurried across the ground on the hunt for food. Not quite rats or lizards, the hairless scavengers looked to be a combination of the two. They skittered away, knocking around twigs and leaves, as two large shadowy figures lumbered slowly into the torch light. Between them floated a much smaller shadowy form with a white hat.

As the dark trio moved into the dim glow of the torch, it was clear that the two large creatures were Brandor and Evan. Between them, still dangling by his arms, was Ellis; or actually, as he was now known, *It*. He made the choice to accept the change of his name to *It* as it was easier than admitting he lied in the first place. Sometimes you just have to stick with the lie when you are already in too deep to be saved by the truth.

"What were those?" *It* said as he squirmed around trying to see the little critters on the ground as they disappeared into the bushes.

"What? The verms?" Evan said looking down.

"I'm not sure. They look like rat things."

"All I saw were verms," Evan said.

"They're scavengers," Brandor added.

"I don't think I like them," the boy whined.

"I'm sure they'll be heartbroken to hear that." Evan groaned.

They made their way past the firelight and around the corner of the aging structure. Another very large Fallon guard stood in front of a flimsy door. In his hands was a sword with a blade the size of the human boy, and its hilt was wrapped in some sort of black animal skin. The huge sentry turned quickly as he heard the others approach.

"What comes?" he bellowed.

Brandor called back, "Brothers. Fallon kin." Brandor and Evan thrusted *It* out in front of them. The boy hung in the air like a toy doll, and his expression made it clear that he was so over being carried around like this.

"We are bringing the hooman to Lord Stronghide as ordered," Evan announced.

The sentry gave *It* a look over and then waved them on as he opened the door to the hut. As they passed him, the guard winced and said, "That thing smells."

Without thinking, *It* retaliated with, "You're one to talk. Is the word bath even part of your vocabulary?" Immediately after the words flew out of his mouth, the boy knew he had made a mistake, but what were they going to do, imprison him?

Luckily for him, the sentry did nothing more than give him a surly glare.

"You just can't stop that mouth of yours, can you?" Evan snarled.

"Restraint has never been one of my finer qualities," the boy responded.

Brandor snickered. "You don't say. I hadn't noticed."

It was shocked to see that Brandor almost smiled. "So, you guys do have a sense of humor."

"Nope," Evan said, while pushing the boy to the door.

As Evan was passing through the doorway, the sentry got a closer look at his face and noticed the black eyes and the knot on his forehead. "What happened to you?" he said to Evan with a knowing smirk.

Evan growled his reply.

The thatching hung over the roof edge and the straw drug across the heads of the two Fallon goons as they turned sideways to get through the door with their prisoner/not prisoner.

Inside, the spacious room was warmed by numerous candles set throughout. The fireplace was stacked with logs, but it lacked an actual fire. Along one wall were large tables occupied by more Fallon folk scratching at paper with feathers longer than the boy's arms. *It*'s face crinkled with curiosity as he whispered to himself, "Quills ... and paper?"

He took note of how amazingly similar every Fallon looked and wondered how they could tell each other apart. In his own world, all children are test tube babies. Through gene manipulation, the Genetics Committee had made certain that mankind's need for individual identity was satisfied by making every citizen unique.

More of the Fallon folks were scattered around the building, involved in various chores of repairing clothing, organizing scrolls, and packing up supplies. A small Fallon of no more than seven feet tall pressed a finger into her trunk and wriggled it around. *It* was not sure if she was scratching or picking, but either way, it looked so gross.

At the far end of the room was a sturdy wooden table with broad legs made from mismatched and rusty round metal posts. One post had a faded symbol of a car inside a circle with a slash across it. Behind the table was a mammoth-sized Fallon wearing a leather vest and bands of red and green cloth wrapped around his tree trunk arms. *It* recognized him from the battlefield.

The guards stopped in front of the table and presented the human.

"We brought *It*, as requested," Brandor said.

"Then put him down. He is a guest and will be treated as such," the large Fallon said in a voice that was deep, but not nearly as gruff.

The tiny human was caught off guard by the social grace and good diction of the creature.

"What's its name?" asked the Lord.

"*It*," said Evan.

"What?"

"*It*."

Lord Stronghide slowly rose from his seat. One of his tusks was broken at the tip. Deep gashes and scars covered much of the exposed parts of his body. On his shoulder, one of the scars was a series of puncture marks forming a half circle. *It* thought to himself, *What on C-Earth could be so big as to leave a bite that size?*

The trunk on Stronghide's face stiffened and his brow was tight with restraint as he made his way to where Evan was standing. He leaned in, pressing his trunk against the now trembling guard's trunk. Their tusks meshed together. "The next word out of your mouth had better be ..." He grabbed the top of *It*'s head, turning him to face Evan, "... this boy's name ... and even the Great Giver cannot help you if you say the word 'it' one more time."

Evan shrunk and trembled even more. The Lord breathed heavy into his face. His gaze was a searing flame reaching through to the soul of the poor guy.

"*It! It! It!*" Loud and clear, the words rang out through the room, but not in the gruff voice of one of the Fallon folk. It was a softer voice; a human voice.

Lord Stronghide whipped his head to look at *It* while his face was still pressed hard against Evan's face. His tusk clacked against Evan's as he actually dragged the young warrior's face with his as they both now looked from an angle at the frustrated boy.

Realizing that things were on the verge of getting ugly, *It* gathered the courage to speak again. "We are not going there again ... My name is *It*," he said a little louder and more annoyed than he may have intended. "That is my name."

Without moving his head, the gargantuan pulled the boy closer to him. Now all three of them were practically nose to trunk to trunk with the white fedora getting pushed to the back of the boy's head by the overlapping tusks. *It* was standing on his tip toes on the cuff of the Lord's booted foot to keep from dangling by his head. This Fallon was even bigger than Jagger.

The tension in the air was broken. "Your parents named you *It*?" the Lord huffed.

It didn't want to lie, but he was now in way too deep to turn back. He stammered his answer. "Sure."

The Lord thought for a moment. "They are wise." He stood back to his full height which had to be close to ten feet tall by the boy's estimation. "I think I like them." He let go of *It*'s head and walked back to his desk. "Having a strange name would lead to defending that name often. It will build you up physically and strengthen your spirit ... your resolve."

Both *It* and Evan relaxed, releasing a long-held sigh. Even Brandor's body shifted to a more comfortable position as the three of them exchanged grateful nods.

After returning to the desk, Lord Stronghide sat back down and gestured to *It*. "I'm sure you have been made aware of the situation as it stands."

It nodded his head with only the slightest confirmation as he was still completely bewildered by this new world.

The Lord continued to gesture while looking over a document on his desk. "As per the joint surrender terms ... all participants and their Lordships ... blah blah blah ... yada, yada, yada ... the U-Man as stated above." He pointed at *It*. "That being you." He continued to read. "... is to be hosted by the petitioning party ... that being us ... and will remain as such until a permanent resolution is in place." He stopped gesturing and leaned forward. "You got that?"

The boy swallowed deeply with a full understanding of his situation and said, "I'm not going anywhere."

Lord Stronghide winked at him. "I see we understand each other." The giant warrior leaned back in his chair. "But we can't have you wandering about without protection, so we need to get you a Host Custodian." He looked to Evan and focused on the bump bulging out from his forehead where *It* had hit him with the rock. He pointed one of his thick fingers at the Fallon's head. "That's a sizable lump."

"Yes, my Lord," Evan responded while looking down in shame.

Stronghide tilted his head towards *It* as he talked to Evan. "This one did that to you?"

"Yes, my Lord."

"And the black eyes?"

"Yes, my Lord."

"With a rock, I'm told."

"Yes, my Lord."

"You had a sword ... and a shield ... he had a rock."

"Yes, my Lord."

Still looking at Evan, he took on a softer, more mentor-like tone. "As much as we can learn from our elders and our instructors, we can also learn from our enemies, and not underestimating them. Don't you agree?"

"Yes, my Lord."

Stronghide glanced down at *It*. "And you. Do you agree?"

It was barely listening, as he was worried about the rock-throwing incident being brought up again. "Huh, sure."

"Good." He turned back to Evan and said, "Because you are now his

Host Custodian. You can learn from each other."

Evan looked up with wide pleading eyes, but he said nothing.

Lord Stronghide nodded to Brandor. "This is your son?" He pointed to Evan.

Brandor nodded his head and spoke proudly. "Yes, my Lord ... this is my son Evan; the eldest of my brood."

It lost all composure. "No way! I thought you were the same age! That explains why you got so mad at me for clobbering him this morning."

The three gargantuans gazed down at him as if he might have more to say but shouldn't. The boy looked to the floor and didn't utter a word more.

Lord Stronghide turned back to Evan and grumbled, "Has he been fed?"

Evan snapped to attention. "No, sir. Not since he has been with us."

"Then take him to the Seeuradi camp. They are celebrating with a feast. He needs sustenance for the morning departure and the festivities will be good for him. He looks a little stressed." He glanced over to Brandor. "Send for Jagger and Kandula. I want to speak with them before they turn in for the night."

"Yes, my lord," said Brandor, as he headed for the door with *It* and Evan.

"Oh, and boy!" Stronghide called to *It* before he was out the door.

"Yes." *It* called back from under his crumpled fedora.

"I don't mind it here, but you will do well to remember to remove your hat during official sessions with the other Giverkind leadership. They can be a bit touchy about those things ... decorum and the such."

It's shoulders dropped. "But it's not my hat."

The Lord snorted. "That's a shame, it looks good on you."

It gave a reluctant shrug as Evan led him to the door.

"He's right you know. You look less ugly with it on," Evan added as he pushed the boy out into the darkness.

SIX

DID SOMEONE SAY "PARTY!"

The darkness of the road opened up to bright firelight and the sounds of laughter and strange-sounding squirrel and bird voices. The mirth grew louder as the human boy walked into a large open pasture with his guards, Brandor and Evan, alongside of him. Several campfires blazed up into the sky, competing with the stars to light the night.

Just beyond the fire, many carts and tables were decked out with platters of varied meats, fruits, vegetables, and some odd looking pasty green stuff that just didn't resemble anything familiar. On one table, a pig-sized creature lay stretched out in a long and shallow wooden platter. It had two extra hind legs and antler stubs above its ears. Sliced fruits garnished its sides with several chunks cut from its rump.

It's nose uncontrollably sniffed the air as he was overwhelmed by a delicious wall of aroma; decadent smells that had never been smelled before. His eyes glassed over as he became entranced by the aromatic majesty of the moment—*Swock!*—in an instant, he was knocked out of his trance. Sydney had climbed up on the boy with her feet resting on his hips and her paws still against his face where she slapped him.

She was in the middle of a one-sided conversation with him, but he hadn't heard anything until now. "Did they beat you or something?" She practically stuck her nose on his face as she sniffed and examined his head for signs of abuse. "Because they can leave a bruise easily with those big dumb fingers of theirs ... They don't even have to try to crack your skull open. They can't always control their strength. It's a fact."

"What?" *It* pushed Sydney away. "What are you talking about? They haven't hurt me."

"Well, you had a dizzy look in your eye, so I thought they knocked your head around and gave you brain damage or something."

"And so, you slapped me? How was that going to help if I was brain-damaged?"

Sydney wasn't sure how to answer as he had a very valid point.

"Well, you don't have to worry. They didn't hurt me. I'm fine."

Brandor looked down on the tiny human and squirrel-girl and leaned in toward his son, Evan. "They do realize that we are still standing here, don't they?"

Evan shrugged. "No, I wouldn't assume that. I've been around them for a very short while, and yet I'm quite sure they don't see the obvious."

"Lucky for me, I don't have to stick around, Mr. Host Custodian." Brandor slapped Evan on the back and walked off. He left his son the honor of guarding the very peculiar-acting boy.

It went back to inhaling the air with both nostrils flexed open wide. He made his way toward the banquet table with Sydney at his side and Evan in tow. They maneuvered between many Seeuradi and Ave people dressed in colorful celebration garb. One Ave with the head of a peacock wore an elaborate cloak of brilliant blue, green, and purple hues that was such a compliment to his own plumage that it was nearly impossible to tell where the Ave feathers ended and the cloak began.

As *It* and Sydney darted in and around the others, the mammoth Evan parted the crowd with no effort or intention at all. No one wanted to be under him as he went by.

"What is all this?" *It* gazed over a table bulging with glazed treats, breads of all kinds, and fruits like none he had ever seen in any digital library. Sydney looked strangely at the boy, as he pushed between a tall crane-headed Ave man and a short gray Seeuradi lady.

"You act like you have never seen food before," Sydney said as she studied the table in case there was something odd there that she hadn't seen at first.

"Of course I have. I've read about it and seen vids on our media boards, but never in person."

"What's a meatia board?"

It never looked away from the table. "A link on a Cimu device that connects me to a media data stream and my virtual lessons and stuff. It also depends on the platform or app."

Sydney cocked her head to one side. "What's a seemoo?" She paused. "What's a data?"

Evan, who had been listening the whole time, leaned down and pressed his large head between the two. "If you have never seen food before, then what do you eat?"

"Not this for sure!" *It* held his hand up with his fingers coming together to make a circle like he was holding an invisible cup. "We eat simfood discs about this big. They come in different colors with slight changes in flavor. They have all the vitamins and minerals we need to survive and are tasty ... if you like eating cardboard." He looked at Evan and Sydney whose faces reflected that they were completely lost. "Fake food. Our world is running out of food, so we have smart people who make fake food out of things you wouldn't normally eat." He looked back to the table. "We have nothing like this." Drool was building up in the corners of his mouth as he smacked his lips together.

A concerned brow lifted on Evan's forehead as he leaned down to say, "I'd keep that talk of another world to myself if I were you. We don't need people thinking that the gift from the Great Giver is nutters."

It had many questions in the look on his face, but Evan tilted his head with a gesture to the table and said, "Eat up. After all, you are the reason they are celebrating." The big man stood tall and turned away as he said to himself, "Giver's gift ... my bulbous butt."

"Really?" *It* said as a response to Evan's comment about not talking about his world.

Sydney nodded her head excitedly. "Yep. This all about you ... sort of."

She picked up a grape and popped it in his mouth. The boy instantly forgot his question to Evan. His eyes rolled back in his head as he bit down on pure heaven.

An eternity passed by as he savored every drop of juice. Groans of joy and bliss emanated from every pore of his body. When he opened his eyes again, he saw that everyone within twenty feet of him had stopped to look oddly at the oddly-acting human boy.

It shrugged his shoulders at them and said, "What? These are the best things ever."

Sydney's face crinkled up. "They're just grapes. Wait until you try the Pecan Wallies ... yum!"

After a lengthy feeding frenzy of overly sweetened pecan flavored candies, *It* was forced to tell Sydney everything about everything related to his adventures with the Fallons. The human and his two companions rested next to a crowded fire. Their bellies were full.

The young boy couldn't help but be ever aware that Evan was only with them out of a sense of duty, and he watched *It* constantly. No matter how the small human tried to include the hulking warrior in the discussions, Evan stayed aloof—ever vigilant, but aloof. *It* felt that his needing to be guarded was an overly exaggerated burden, but he was not about to let his fun evening get rained on by Evan's astringent nature.

Soon a group of Seeuradi and Ave people showed up carrying various objects as they spread out around the fire. They were followed by several Fallon, some of which held enormous drums. The crowd, including Sydney, clapped and yelled in excitement. Even *It* let out a few hoots and hollers though he didn't know what was going on.

"So, what's this?" He looked up to Evan.

The trunk on Evan's face lifted up slightly with a hint of a smile underneath. "Music."

Drums began beating. The trill of a flute filled the air, and the melodies of harps and horns joined in. The atmosphere was charged with lively melodic energy which was exhilarating ear candy to someone from C-Earth who had never known or heard music before.

One by one, people sprung to their feet, twirling and leaping around the fire. Sydney grabbed *It*'s hands and pulled him into the merriment. He stumbled along with Sydney who obviously knew how to dance and was very good at it. *It*, on the other hand, bumped into several other Giverkind and had to apologize several times before the clumsy boy figured out that he could use some of his gymnastic exercise training to look nimble and fleet of foot.

After several spins around the fire, Sydney was pulled away from *It* and lifted high into the air by another, much taller, Seeuradi man. This was no problem for *It*. He continued dancing alone as he spun, jumped, and even tumbled—the smile on his face could never be chiseled away.

He wasn't alone for long before a white feathery flash blocked his view of the party around him. As he blinked to clear his eyes, he realized he had a bright white Ave girl embracing him with her winged arms and cupping his head gently with her talon-like hands.

She had tiny fluffy feathers spreading across her stunning dove face. *It* was instantly enamored by her beauty as they twirled together, oblivious to the world around them. When she brought her hands down to his shoulders, he saw other dancers lifting feathery girls up above their heads.

The boy had little faith that he was strong enough to do that, but he didn't have a choice as his partner slid his hands down to her waist and smiled an enchanting smile. His hands began to shake as his nervousness was manifesting something inside him. He felt a tingle throughout his body similar to the electric shock he got earlier that day. After one more spin, the girl leaped into the air as *It* lifted hard to get her overhead. His hands hurt from some unseen electric charge just under the skin.

Unfortunately, the girl weighed little to nothing, and with a strength the boy had never known before, *It* threw her soaring into the air high above him. His face cringed in horror as he realized he no longer had his hands on her waist. She rocketed above the crowd and her human partner. The boy could only hope that he didn't toss her in the direction of the fire.

He watched on helplessly as she reached the apex of her upward motion to begin her catastrophic crash to the ground, but in that moment of pause as her upward momentum ceased, she spread out her wings and performed two fascinating flips, gliding back down to *It*, who instinctively caught her in his arms.

A roar of cheers and applause exploded from every Fallon, Seeuradi and Ave in the area. The girl hugged him tightly as others patted him on the back and commended him on such an extraordinary performance.

However, not everyone was impressed. Sydney, who had been watching them dance, scrambled up the body of one Fallon and bounded to another Fallon's shoulder where she leaped as high as she could, twirling in the air with a final twist to land in front of *It* and the angelic dove-girl.

Sydney squeezed between them, forcing the Ave girl to the side. "Get your own hooman. This one is with me." She grabbed *It*'s hands and started twirling with him. She gave him a look of stern accusation. "You never tossed me in the air like that."

"I just met you this morning," he said jokingly.

"Yes, but you still never did that."

"Besides, you're not my girlfriend. I'm not with you."

Sydney looked at the beautiful dove-girl who continued to glare back at her. "Yeah, but she doesn't know that," Sydney chittered out with a giggle. "Besides, I am your best friend."

It looked at her as though she were nutters. "You're my only friend."

"Which makes me your best friend."

"Which also means it makes you my worst friend." He smirked.

She chittered out loud again. "Good point."

They continued to dance around the fire, and *It* noticed that Evan never took his eyes off of him. Even with two young squirrel-girls shaking their tails at him and trying to dance with the stoic behemoth, Evan stood alert and watching *It*'s every move. However, *It* did notice that Evan's unflinching dedication to duty was betrayed by the slight tapping of his huge, booted foot to the beat of the drums. The boy smiled. "So, there is a chink in his armor."

"What was that?" Sydney asked.

"Nothing."

After a few more twirls, *It* and Sydney stopped to have a drink. Like with the food, he drank down his glass of what they called "freat" with long enjoyable gulps. The fruity liquid had him fascinated with the flavor and texture. He only set his cup down when he noticed his watch dog was not at his side.

"That's odd," he said looking around.

"What's odd?" Sydney glanced back and forth but saw nothing unusual.

"Where's Evan?"

Sydney scampered halfway up one of the poles used for a wagon canvas cover. "Wait, there he is." She pointed to some big forms just outside of the party circle at the edge of the field. They were partially obscured under an outcropping of trees.

With his squirrel friend trailing behind, *It* moved closer to where he could see the Fallon people in the shadows under the limbs of a strikingly beautiful tree covered with a purplish bark and massive teal leaves. They spied on Evan standing with some other Fallon who looked almost identical to him with mustard yellow skin, bald head, and broad shoulders. If it weren't for her wearing a leather skirt and flowing blouse, along with a slight difference in height, *It* would have had trouble telling them apart.

"So, is that his sister, or something?" Sydney whispered.

"Could be. I have no clue," *It* responded.

Evan reached out and grabbed the Fallon girl's hands in his. She leaned in closer with their tusks angled so that their lips pressed together. Their trunks intertwined as he pulled her close.

It and Sydney both ducked down and pressed their backs against a fallen log.

"Nope, that is most definitely not his sister," *It* gasped.

"At least we sure hope it isn't, or I would have to find you a new Fallon bodyguard," Sydney replied.

"Ew! Don't be gross. That's not his sister!"

As if two thieves in the night, they stealthily crept up to peek over the log.

Evan was back to holding the girl's hands. He looked to be saying something to her, when she broke down crying.

"No way! I think he just asked her to marry him ... way to go master of the smooth," *It* quietly cheered.

The girl's crying turned into sobs as she looked at Evan pleading, "Don't! Please don't do it!"

Sydney shook her head. "You know, I'm pretty sure that wasn't a marriage proposal. I'm a girl, and I know about these things."

"Then why do you think she's crying?"

Sydney was also taken aback. "I have no clue. Until now, I didn't know Fallons could cry. That is seriously strange."

"Yeah, well, strange has become an undefinable term for me since I got here."

While *It* and Sydney were busy snooping, a small group of Fallon folk walked into the center of the dance circle near the fire. Without warning, the tallest one, who stood feet above the Seeuradi and Ave crowd, lifted his large trunk toward the sky and let out an ear-splitting trumpeting noise that stopped the merriment in its place and got the attention from people at several other campfires as well.

It whipped around so fast he slipped and fell to his butt. As he regained his composure, he recognized the eye patch and scarred face from the surrender meeting. The party crasher was Jagger.

"I'm sorry to interrupt the festivities, but I wish to request that all my herd brothers and sisters return to our encampment as we will be making our return journey home in the morning."

A few grumbles of protest came out from the crowd ... but only a few. Jagger was not someone you would challenge.

He continued to address the crowd. "We wish to thank both the Seeuradi and the Aves for their hospitality." He paused as the crowd erupted in cheers and applause as they showed their racial pride. "And, I would also like to express our acknowledgement of the serious nature and responsibility for hosting the hooman boy by announcing the appointment of Evan Bulltusk, Eldest son of Brandor and Ginora Bulltusk, as the Host Custodian for the boy." Silence—the air was thick with some unseen pressure which weighed heavily on the crowd, except for *It* who couldn't have been anymore clueless.

After a moment, a whisper of sorrowful murmurs cascaded through the crowd, and the girl with Evan resumed her sobbing. *It* was completely lost as to why everyone was so sad for him having to be hosted and appointed a custodian from the Fallon folk.

For a moment he felt touched that these animal people, who he had just met today, were so moved by his unfortunate situation. Of course, it didn't take him long to see that everyone had turned to look at Evan as he stepped back into the circle and up to shake hands with Jagger. The Fallon girl ran off.

It turned to Sydney. Even she had water-filled eyes. The boy shrugged. "Why is everyone sad for him ... I'm the one who has to tolerate him constantly watching me."

Sydney wiped the back of her paw across her eyes. "The Host Custodian is responsible for the visiting guest."

"Yeah, so?"

"So, he is responsible for you. He must protect you with his life. He will pay for any mistake you make." She took a sad breath. "For many Host Custodians, it could be a death sentence." She looked to *It* and saw by his wide eyes and slack jaw that he was now affected by the seriousness of the situation.

To chipper him up she squeaked, "They only assign someone a Host Custodian if they are very, very, important. Important enough that someone might try to kill them." She paused for a moment with a genuine grin. "You must be excited knowing how special you are!" Her left eye closed as she pressed her glasses against her head, thinking very hard. And in her typical matter of fact manner she said, "... but I sure hope you don't get killed soon. I've hardly gotten to know you." She beamed another smile at *It* who had gone ghostly white. "Hey, look at it this way, now we know why the Fallon girl with Evan was crying."

<hr />

A low candle flame barely lit the hut where *It* first awoke this day. From one side of the room, a low and deep grumbly breath sucked air in and blared it out again. Huddled close to the glow of the candle, *It* laid quiet on his bed of leaves at the opposite side of the hut listening to the thundering snores coming from the giant mound in the other makeshift bed across from him.

After some long moments, the little human opened his mouth. "Are you awake?" He got no response. There was just a short trumpeting snore. "Hey, Evan ... rotund rump!" Evan twisted under his cloak. The snoring stopped. The room was dead quiet. After the long uncomfortable silence, *It* started in again. "Evan, dude, are you up!" The mountain on the floor raised slightly.

"What on the Great Giver's great green turf do you want ... you pebble stuck in the fat-fold of my backside?"

It cleared his throat. "Uh. Well, first off, good job on such a descriptive insult ... very creative there." *It* paused as it occurred to him that he didn't plan out what he was going to say, let alone how he was going to say it. "Also, I was just checking to see if you were awake."

A menacing growl filled the darkness.

It's voice cracked. "And, I was also checking to see if we should talk about this whole Host Custodian thing."

Another eerie silence amplified the effect of the darkness on Evan's side of the hut which made it seem more distressing. The boy peered into the shadows hoping to see something reassuring. He tapped at his chin nervously as he wondered if he should say anything. Yep, he couldn't take the silence anymore. He opened his mouth and squeaked out "Helloooo."

With great effort and annoyance, Evan grumbled some more as he sat up. His head was only a few feet from the roof. "What about it?"

It popped up, thankful that Evan didn't smash him like a bug. "I was thinking I don't need a Host Custodian, with no offense to you. I will still stay with the Fallon folk as decreed, but, you know, without all this Host

Custodian ... you-have-to die-for-me stuff."

"It is the will of our herd Lord," Evan huffed. "I'm none too happy with it either, but we do what we have to for our herd and our honor."

"I hear you saying that, but doesn't the dying for me seem a bit much?"

"I'd rather not have to, but ..."

It cut him off and said, "I know ... we do what we have to for our herd and our honor." His voice reeked of sarcasm.

Evan sat up straight and, surprisingly, his voice came across friendlier than before. "Do you have a herd?"

It's eyes squinched together. "A herd? No. I'm human. We don't have herds. We have chat groups and community display settings. Does that count?"

"I doubt it." It was a for-sure thing that Evan had no idea what a chat group was, but by the sound of it, he was quite certain that it was nothing like a herd. With another belabored huff and some effort, Evan laid back down. "Then you couldn't understand. Besides, hoomans know nothing of honor."

"What do you mean by that?"

"I mean, the hoomans brought our many races together for over a thousand years of relative peace, and then after all that time they mysteriously pulled away from the union with no regard to the degradation that followed—that's what I mean about your people having no honor."

"Well, I don't know anything about that."

Evan sprang up to a seated position again with unexpected agility and speed.

"Exactly how is it that you know nothing about that? Why don't you know more about your kind? And don't try that 'I'm a gift from The Great Giver' bunk, because no Fallon worth his sword would fall for that. Only a Seeuradi or Ave would swallow that shovel-full of tonk droppings."

"I never said I was any kind of gift from your God! And I have no idea what a tonk is!"

"Then why didn't you say something at the meeting?"

It's internal sarcasm switch flipped on again. "Well, let me think about that. Maybe because I fell through a waste disposal disintegrator that turned out to be a portal to a world full of strange animal people ... who, by the way, introduced themselves to me by trying to kill me on sight! So, when a creature who outweighs you by at least six hundred pounds says you are a gift from their God, you go along with it; even if you know there isn't a God and that the gifts are just our useless garbage, you still go along with the charade."

As before, the room went deathly quiet, with the exception of some very loud popping sounds.

"Was that your knuckles?" *It* asked with less sarcasm.

Evan raised up and knelt down next to *It*'s bed. He leaned in close enough for the candle to light up his now bright orange face. The yellow complexion was infused with the deep red of rage as his tusks flanked the boy on both sides. "Don't you ever speak about The Great Giver like that, or my soul be damned, and my honor lost, I'll squash you myself."

Something snapped in *It*. The boy glared back into the giant eyes only a foot from his face. There was no way of knowing whether it was exhaustion or irritation giving him courage, but his voice was clear of intent. "I'm done being scared of you! Of all of you … but I am also sorry for offending you. At least now you know how I feel after having Fallon after Fallon treat me like … like I'm nothing more than a hideously ugly burden. I got enough of that from the community home back on my world."

Evan paused after now seeing the first sense of honesty in the boy's eyes. The yellow came back to his cheeks. His trunk lifted slightly from a weak snort. "Well, there is that."

"So, truce?" *It* said extending his hand.

Evan took the boy's hand and half of his forearm into his grasp and shook it. "For now." He retreated to his bed and dropped down hard. The echo of leaves crackling under the heavy load gave way to quiet once again.

"They're beasts of burden," Evan's deep voice breathed out, breaking the stillness.

"Excuse me?" the boy replied.

"You said you didn't know what a tonk was. It's a beast of burden. They pull wagons and plows and such."

"Oh."

It laid there for a moment, not making a noise, with the contentment of knowing they may have just broken the ice between them. The hut was blissfully silent once more, but not for long. Now that they were on better speaking terms, the human kid risked another interaction.

"Hey, Evan?"

"What?" the warrior grumbled back.

"Where are the toilets around here?"

"What's a toilet?"

"A place to relieve yourself. You know. I gotta pee. I've been holding it all day and I'm about to explode."

Evan gave a deep chuckle. "You call that place a toilet?"

"Yeah. What do you call it?"

"We call them trees."

The room grew quiet again. After a few moments, *It* got up with his knees pressed tightly together. "Where can I find some toilet paper?"

Evan grunted. "We call them leaves."

It said nothing more. Cringing, he shuffled out the flap door.

SEVEN

MARCHING WITH THE ELEPHANTS

Even with a slightly overcast sky, *It* was ecstatically happy as he craned his head upward to peer into the vast blue sky dotted with blotches of gray. Never had he seen so much color. His white fedora hat with the black hat band was pushed tight on his head to keep it from coming off.

As he thought about it, in the flash of one day, he found himself ripped from his world and his people to a land full of odd creatures where he was considered the freak—yet he didn't care. The blue sky and those little blotches of puffy clouds, combined with a crisp clean smell in his nostrils, pushed any conflicting emotions to the outer edges of his thoughts.

"And we are looking at what?" Sydney's squeaky voice broke the serenity.

It didn't stop looking up and replied, "The sky." He breathed in deeply.

"I see," she said with eyes searching the clouds. "And you don't have one of those where you're from?"

"Not like this. Mine is a never ending murky gray haze. And the air tastes thick and acrid."

"It must be a miserably peculiar place."

"Yep. It is," He answered softly.

They stood there for a few minutes longer when Sam and a few other Seeuradi warriors in green armor walked up to see the two kids staring at the sky. Sam shook her head and squeaked, "What are you two nut-heads doing?"

Sydney shrugged her shoulders. "I have no idea." She kept her eyes skyward.

"You look ridiculous," Sam chided. "You should have better things to be doing …" She nodded her head towards *It*. "Especially you."

The boy looked to Sam with a squinched brow. "Why me?"

Sam's face crinkled in disgust. "That giant beast stands alone in the Fallon Host Custodian ceremony, where he's swearing to die for you, and you would rather be looking at clouds … are all U-mans as thoughtless as you?" She stressed the incorrect pronunciation of humans.

Instead of questioning why Evan wasn't around, *It* had been enjoying the big oaf's absence. Shame washed over the boy's face. "Evan? I had no idea … when did they start?"

Sam bounded away with her friends and called out as she went. "Like you care."

It turned to Sydney. "How bad will it look if I'm not there?"

Sydney concentrated for a moment. "I guess, it would be like getting an award from a high priestess."

"But, that's not bad," he said with comfort in his voice.

"… and then knocking the award to the ground and kicking it around in the mud." Sydney kicked at the dirt.

"Ok, that is bad." The shame returned to his face.

She continued to elaborate with enthusiasm. "… and then stomping on it until it breaks into a hundred pieces."

"I get the idea!" he said louder than necessary.

Sydney got carried away in the excitement. "… and then spitting on all the little pieces."

"Alright already! I got it! It's a very rude thing to do."

"… and maybe then lifting your leg to pee a little on it." Sydney lifted her leg slightly and mimicked a dog peeing.

Full of frustration, *It* glared as the squirrel girl concluded her description with that ever-present smirk on her face.

With their hearts pounding away, *It* and Sydney ran through the many camps heading back to the Fallon encampment where they would find Evan and the Host Custodian ceremony. Sydney bounded back and forth just as a squirrel should. Had she been running in a straight line; she would have left *It* in her dust.

He watched his little furry friend's erratic behavior and realized that she was enjoying herself as she let out gleeful squeaks each time she bounded across his path. The boy couldn't believe that he was being beaten so easily on foot. Back home he was the fastest kid in his sector and probably the fastest in all the nearby sectors as well. But now, compared to Sydney, he was a snail.

His lungs burned from the exertion as he pushed harder. Off in the distance he saw Evan and another Fallon folk standing on a wagon surrounded by the Fallon herd. A multitude of emotions started to swell in the boy as he pressed his limits beyond what he thought he could do.

A painful tingling sensation filled his body like the one he felt the other day when he was in the canister as it fell through the Bin and onto the junk pile. The tingling turned into a vibration, and he started to pick up speed.

"Yaha!" Sydney squealed as she saw *It* catching up. She stopped holding back and started to leave the boy behind again.

Something gradually took over *It* as his face strained with intensity. Little black veins stretched across the whites of his eyes. He felt that something was wrong in such a wonderfully right way. Whatever it was, it had taken over his body.

As the two kids reached the edge of the Fallon crowd, Sydney changed direction to avoid a flatbed cart parked in front of her. *It* saw the cart too, but he was unable to stop himself. The black lines in his eyes and the fierce expression on his face had him looking like someone else, or something else.

Sydney glanced back and stopped in horror as she watched her friend careening straight for the cart at a pace that could kill him if he hit it. Just before he smashed head-on into the cart, *It* leaped with one stride onto the cart and launched his body up into the air. "Raah"—he let out a roar as he flew well above the ground. After what felt like forever, the boy became aware that he was now plummeting to the earth.

The intensity quickly faded, and the black veins in his eyes retreated as he flailed his arms in a panic. He now had control of his body again, but it did him no good as he tumbled fifteen feet above the ground. Sydney watched the boy's awkward flight as he flipped through the air. He came crashing down into the crowd that had now spread out to let him smack hard into the dirt, where he rolled to a stop. He looked up to see he had landed in front of the wagon where Evan was standing with a disapproving scowl.

Sydney remained outside of the crowd, watching where *It* disappeared. She said to herself, "Now, that's different."

"Ow," *It* whimpered on the ground. The large Fallon folk who stood over him with blank expressions on their trunk-nosed faces stared at the disheveled human. "Hi?" He said as he got to his feet and moved to climb up onto the wagon with Evan.

Above him, he saw that the other Fallon on the wagon next to Evan was Lord Stronghide. The boy clumsily scrambled atop the wagon and brushed the dirt off his pants and shirt with his hat. "Am I late?"

Lord Stronghide resisted saying what was really on his mind and just grumbled, "Exceedingly." He straightened up to his full height and took in a deep breath before addressing Evan. "As I was saying, Evan, do you, before your tribe, and your herd; before the Seeuradi and Ave Giverkind; and before our hooman guest; take on the responsibilities of the Host Custodian?"

Standing at attention, Evan barked out his response. "I do!"

"Without complaint or pause, will you accept death, injury, punishment, and incrimination in his stead?" He stressed the word incrimination and stared at *It* as he said it.

It could not believe what he was hearing and from deep in his soul he wanted Evan to scream "*no, this is ridiculous ... are you people insane?*" But that is not what Evan said.

"I will!" Evan replied quickly and with dire devotion to the words.

"Then let it be done!" The mammoth leader turned back to the crowd. "Here is your herd brother who is put to task and whose life is no longer his own." The leader saw Evan's mother in the crowd standing tall next to her husband, Brandor. Tears streamed down the deep crevices of her leathery face.

Lord Stronghide offered a smile of comfort. "Mourn not for our brother. As we all must pass a final challenge to earn our commission in the leading ranks of the herd; let this be his." He turned back to Evan. "Should you survive this honor, you will have set your place and title, and be worthy of the right to your own brood as your eighteenth year comes to a close." The crowd remained respectfully quiet as it should for such a somber and austere occasion.

Taking advantage of the pause in action, *It* stepped forward. "Why don't I get a say here?" He started to turn to the Fallon leader, but then stopped to look back at Evan as something important had just dawned on him. "You're eighteen? You're only eighteen years old? You look fifty … or at least a hard forty-five."

Evan squinted one eye, as he was unsure what to say.

It turned back to Lord Stronghide. "Look here, I appreciate all this attention, and banquets, and ceremonies, but I can take care of myself. And, definitely, nobody has to die for me."

Stronghide had an unnerving smirk cross his lips. "Really? You can protect yourself?" He said as he looked hard at the boy. *It* said nothing out of fear of the odd look on the giant's face. Lord Stronghide peered out into the crowd. "You there!" He pointed at a Fallon guard toward the back of the gathering. "Skewer this boy!" The guard nodded with his tusks dropping low as he lifted his spear out of the dirt.

Within the crowd, there was a slight commotion as a reddish-brown furry streak among the large bodies flashed in and out of view.

Without a word of question, or pause for clarification, the Fallon guard pulled the spear back behind his head.

On the wagon, *It* stood tense as he wasn't sure how this joke was going to play out. After all, it had to be a joke. Lord Stronghide winked at the boy as the guard in the back grunted and launched his weapon at the chest of the human.

It was as if time slowed to a crawl; the metal point glistened at the end of the spear that flew over the heads of the crowd, making its way toward the trembling target on the wagon. *It* saw the sharpened tip spinning through the air only feet from his chest. He had no time to react—and this was no joke.

In the span of a microsecond the young human had accepted his end, but to his side, and coming up from the crowd, the reddish-brown flash appeared. Sydney leaped with one bounding stride high into the air. As she glided upward, her right hand spun her staff like a propeller. As if in slow motion herself, she reached *It*. He could clearly see the cheesy grin on her little squirrel face, buckteeth and all.

In that moment, the grin turned to a look of horror as she realized that the spear would hit its mark before her staff could reach it—*Kathunk!*

Crack!—*It* was shoved back as the weapon sunk deep into a huge meaty arm stretched across his chest while the spinning staff snapped off the back portion of the spear's shaft.

Time sped up again for *It*. Sydney landed at the far end of the wagon and flipped backwards to land in a protective stance next to the boy, who was still alive.

It stared at the broken spear now protruding from Evan's arm. The giant Fallon stood tall again without removing the weapon. Stronghide's smirk turned into a genuine smile as he said to the human boy, "It appears you have two Host Custodians."

⁂

A long caravan of immense Fallon-sized wagons and some smaller rust covered metal vehicles from the Great Giver were pointed west. They made for an eclectic and strangely anachronistic convoy. Some of the scavenged vehicles had faded names on them like Chevy, Ford, and US Army.

Giant beasts called tonks, which loosely resembled dinosaur-sized hippos with strong horse-like legs, were harnessed to them. Most of the Fallon folk were on foot, as it was their custom to use the wagons for gear, materials, and supplies. *It* stood near a wagon with a group of Fallon warriors and artisans who had stopped by to give him gifts.

Everything from a hooded cloak to leather for shoes and belts had been bestowed upon him. And they were all way too large. He held up a shirt for inspection and quickly figured it would be better put to use as a blanket or sleeping bag. Regardless of their questionable usefulness, he received the gifts with sincere respect and appreciation. For the first time since he arrived, he had really looked into the faces of these large beings to see their humanity and how they truly wished him a warm welcome. He could have said no to the presents as the Seeuradi people had given him clothing and a backpack the night before, but he felt it best to just accept what he was given with a smile.

The young human looked out over the large field to see that all the camps had been packed away. The Seeuradi were loaded up and ready to head northeast while the Aves had already marched off to the south hours ago. *It* looked around to see the empty pavilion and various huts on the road.

"Kinda different when it's empty," a deep voice said from behind him.

It turned to find Evan standing guard with his arm bandaged up. The wagons began rolling, and the two talked as they walked.

"Why isn't someone staying?" the boy asked.

"This is only a place of meeting and used for the many people of the land for disputes and ceremony." Evan pointed to a hill. "Over that ridge and down in the valley is where one of the Great Giver sites is located."

"There is more than one?"

"A good many actually ... throughout the world ... I believe." Evan gestured to the wagons. "Much of what we have or make was either given by the Great Giver or made with the help of something from the Great Giver."

"And the war was because you and the Seeuradi wanted equal share of what the Great Giver gives."

"Yes. All claim to have more rights or need of the offerings."

"So, technically, the Great Giver gives you war?"

The warrior grunted sadly. "It hasn't always been this way. For many generations we were at peace and worked together. We even stopped seeing ourselves as separate species and became one species. The Giverkind ... made up of many races." Evan's eyes dropped to the ground, as he knew he had played his part in what has become a shameful display of infighting.

With an awkward pause in the conversation hanging over their heads, they both looked uncomfortable as they walked along. *It* kicked at the dirt nervously and decided to break the silence, but when he noticed a tuft of reddish-brown fur flop out from under the bottom of the wagon and then dart back under it, he held back his comment. This happened two more times when the boy bent over to rub his leg as if something was wrong with it.

He peeked under the wagon. With no surprise to him, he saw Sydney gripping tightly to some metal braces near the wheel. A pack was strapped snuggly to her back and her staff was securely tied to the pack. She winked at *It* and put one finger over her lips. "Shhhh."

The boy straightened up and kept walking.

"If you were at peace, why did you start fighting?" He pretended that there was nothing sneaky going on under the wagon and tried to reengage Evan in conversation.

"Some time back, about thirty years, you hoomans pulled back from trading and communicating with the other races."

With his face scrunched in confusion, he looked honestly at the big man. "Why would that start a war between you and the Seeuradi? What did humans have to do with that?"

"I'm not sure, but from an early age, I was taught that your people were the bond holding all the races together ... looking at you, I can't imagine how it's true, but it is what it is."

"I'm sure I should be offended, but as you say, it is what it is." A wry smile crossed the boy's face.

Evan cleared his throat and trunk then stretched as he lumbered along. "Maybe now you might understand why you may need protection from those who are not as hooman-friendly as the rest of us."

"And you trying to kill me is your idea of human-friendly?" *It* looked up to see a snarl forming at the edge of the giant's mouth and decide to change his tune. "Yeah ... sure ... protection and all that."

"... and we really need to start your training soon."

"What training?"

"Combat for one. Your rock throwing skill won't get you very far," Evan said as he rubbed at the still-bruised area between his eyes.

"No, it won't," he said with a chuckle.

The big Fallon swung his tusks as he shook his head, then added a slight snort of sarcasm from his trunk. "And, if you are just now noticing the rodent under the wagon, then we have a lot of work to do on your observation skills."

It gasped. "You knew she was there?"

"Long before we started rolling."

"Why didn't you say anything?"

"I figured the longer we held off acknowledging she was there, the longer we could go without having her come out and start chittering at us."

It broke out with honest laughter.

The two continued chatting. Evan told his human guest more about the world of Fentiga and *It* did his best to describe the drab reality of C-Earth. The enlightening discussion made the long walk much less tedious, and it signaled the beginning of a strange and awkward friendship, or more accurately put, non-enemyship.

During a break on the road, *It* noticed two vehicles toward the front of the wagon train being pulled by young tonks. They looked familiar to him. He recognized them as antiquated forms of transportation from his world. When he walked up to them, his assumption turned out to be true. One vehicle was long and yellow with rusty patches and many windows. The words Smyser Elementary were written along the side with embossed letters. Sections of the metal had been cut or rusted out and were draped in multi-colored tarps of leather.

The other metal vehicle was much smaller and had the word Toyota on the back. The boy remembered that it was called a van because he had once researched cargo transports called haulers on his world, and their designs had evolved from ancient things called vans. Of course, all the vehicles back on Consolidated Earth were automated and ran on electricity—no tonks needed.

As he got closer, the flaps moved on both vehicles and then they flipped outward in the air with poles coming out from under them to hold up the leather like tent roofs. Little furry people, yet not people, came rushing out in a whirl of activity. Large tables were set up and pots slammed on top of them. Big spoons rang out as they were tossed into the pots to announce that lunch was soon to be ready.

The human boy sheepishly walked up to a few of the small furry people in an attempt to get a better view of them. "Cripes!" They were not the prettiest of critters. Actually, if the ugliest chimpanzee and the ugliest opossum got married and had a baby, these would be their offspring.

"Some place else, please," a sharp shrilly voice hissed.

It looked down to see where the voice was coming from. One of the small creatures stood looking at him. *It* pushed his lips out and cocked his head to one side. "I'm sorry, were you talking to me?"

"Ohhh, but no. I was talking to some other long-legged git standing in the way." The creature was not short on sarcasm. "Matter of fact, why not start swinging them long legs around and make it even harder for us to work." He shoved past *It* and grumbled the word, "Lumber."

With a crinkled forehead *It* took a step or two to one side as he questioned himself, "Lumber?" He thought out loud. "Why lumber?"

"Many reasons," another shrilly voice said.

It turned to see one of the busy creatures setting various vegetables out on a nearby table. This one looked to be younger than the previous one. The white of his opossum face was brighter.

"Lumber doesn't move. Lumber doesn't think. Lumber grows tall but has no sense about it ... lumber is best used to light on fire and watch it burn." The creature paused and pointed a wooden spoon at the boy. "Hopefully, you got the idea by now."

"Yeah, I'm in the way," *It* said.

"You got it. But then they call me that a lot too, so I would be one to know," he said with a wink of his tiny black eye.

"Can I at least ask why you're here, doing this?"

"Where should I be?"

"Well, you're not a Fallon, so I didn't know why you were here making food for the wagon train."

"That's what Didelphi do." He smiled with his sharp pointy teeth in a sketchy way that had *It* feeling slightly disturbed.

"Fair enough." The boy grimaced. "Well, I'm Ellis, I mean *It*. My name is *It*."

"Okay," the creature said, with a questioning look on his face.

"And you are?"

"Confused."

"No, your name. What's your name?"

"Toyota."

It looked at the embossing on the back of the rusted van with the word Toyota on it. "I see how you got your name."

"How?" Toyota said, with an authentically serious raised brow.

It was bewildered by the sincerity in the Didelphi's voice. "You know ... the vehicle." He gestured to the van, but the small creature still could not make the connection. *It* gave up. "I think I should go."

"Alright."

The creature went on about his work and *It* went on getting in everyone's way.

EIGHT

MAGIC DOESN'T EXIST ... DOES IT?

The fire crackled, spitting tiny sparks across the ground. Many enormous, booted feet encircled the burning logs with one pair of small paws standing out amongst the tread-worn leather. Even more of a contrast was the gray and white sneakers next to the paws—the paws belonged to Sydney and the shoes were *It*'s.

The human boy and Seeuradi girl had joined their Fallon hosts around the fire before turning in for the night. It had been a long day of traversing what *It* deemed the most "phenomenal" landscape he had ever seen. Then again, C-Earth was the only other landscape he had ever seen until now, so his perspective was remarkably narrow.

The air boomed with laughter from everyone but Evan, who sat with the ever-present stoic look to his brow.

Brandor stood with his hand clutching his gut while retelling a side-splitter of a story. "So, the boy says, 'Excuse me Mr. Large-Bottom' ... and oh my Great Giver, I thought Jagger was going to pop a tusk. His face was drawn in so tight. It was anger beyond the limits of anger."

Evan's mom, Ginora, looked at *It*. "Oh, dear, you didn't call him that. Did you?"

It gave Sydney the evil eye. "I wouldn't have if someone hadn't told me that that was his name."

"I can't help that you believe everything you're told," Sydney responded with a chittering giggle.

"Oh, it gets so much better. When Jagger pressed the boy to tell him who told him to say that, the boy blamed a Turkey Ave," Brandor said, with his own laughter making it hard for him to talk.

"That's not right," Ginora chided the human again.

Brandor slapped his hand to his thigh. "And when the Ave saw Jagger looking at him with death in his eyes, the bird was shaking so much from fear that it looked as though he would lay an egg on the spot."

"Just count yourself lucky that Jagger is a Fallon of principle and didn't tear your head off," Evan piped in with a glare at *It*.

Brandor snorted. "Principles or not, that was funny."

Out of respect for his father, Evan held his tongue, which was hard for him to do knowing how insolent it was for them to laugh at the expense of a herd champion and general.

After a few more chortles, the crowd quieted down. Unspoken words loudly declared the group's exhaustion. They sat still and introspective.

Once again, *It* stared into the sky with no desire to ever look away.

"You're doing it again," Sydney said like she had said so many times that day.

It tore his eyes away from the sky. "How can you not want to watch them? It's like a giant black blanket with a billion white marbles spilled over it." He grinned.

Evan's mom smiled. "You act as though you have never seen stars before."

Out of reflex, *It* started to say that not only had he never seen stars before, but the night sky in his world had an never-ending glow of the man-made lights, which added to the despair of the gray clouds. However, he only got the words "I haven't" out of his yap before Sydney's elbow caught him in the ribs, and Evan's foot hit him so hard in the shin that they could hear the *thunk* noise over the cackle of the fire—both of which caused a substantial amount of pain.

"Ow! ... I meant I haven't taken the time to actually look at the sky lately ... been busy ... you know, with all the being nearly killed and stuff."

Ginora nodded. "Yes, dear, it always seems to be that there isn't enough time, or something is trying to kill you."

The look on *It's* face screamed, "*I can't believe you think being nearly killed each day is a normal thing.*"

Before Ginora could ask any more questions, *It* noticed that Evan was no longer wearing a bandage on his arm and that the wound from earlier today had healed completely. There was barely even a scar. "What in the heck happened to your arm?" he said louder than intended.

Evan's eyes squinted in confusion as he hoisted his arm up. "Nothing. Why?"

"You had a spear sticking in it this morning and now it is almost healed! How can that be nothing?"

"I had the shaman treat it."

"You had the what do what?"

"Our shaman healed it."

"With what? No medicine works that fast."

Ginora spoke up again. "He used a mystic poultice, I believe."

Sydney squealed in excitement. "Oh, what kind? Was it a Calendula recipe?"

It sat, unable to speak.

"I have no idea what he used. I've never understood the mystic arts and how it works," Ginora replied.

"I'll bet it was Calendula." Sydney squeaked again. "Or maybe Gotu Kola. Yes, it might be Gotu, but I bet it was Calendula used with a chant ... shamans are more chanters than incanters," Sydney said, while looking at *It* as if she was describing what she had for lunch.

Her typical factual nature made it even harder for *It* to grasp that his new friends were discussing magic as if it actually existed.

"Yes, he did chant," Evan added to the conversation, while rubbing at the rough hide of his arm.

"See, I knew it. That's what my Prominence taught me about shamans. I'm studying to be a healer, even though my sister thinks I should join the Seeuradi guard. We prefer incantation with our potions and wraps ... and stones. We are all about healing stones." Sometimes it was an endless stream of squeaking once she got excited.

It held up his hands. "Wait a minute." He paused as he got Sydney's attention. "How can you possibly believe in magic? That's ridiculous!"

The air grew silent and heavy. The way everyone squinted their eyes at him made the boy feel as if he were the crazy person there.

"No, it's not!" Sydney squeaked her resentment. The fur standing up on her neck and head also sent a loud and clear message to *It* that he was somehow out of line with his comment, so he tried to smooth things over.

"Okay ... I realize I'm new here, but ... really ... Magic?"

Sydney reached into a pouch on her belt. She pulled out a small, red polished stone with a strange intertwining symbol etched into its smooth surface. She held it out in front of her and whispered, "Rizon." The stone rose from her hand and floated a foot above it. The Fallon around the fire applauded excitedly. Even Evan was impressed.

It couldn't believe what he was seeing. The stone was glowing with a light purple hue surrounded in a blackish mist that wasn't steam or smoke. The dark mist stretched down from the stone to Sydney's hand. It appeared as if the little wispy pillar was holding up the stone. Now *It* was impressed. "I don't know how you're doing this, but it is ... wow ... incredible."

"Part of my healing studies included a few other mystic concentrations, but this is the best of what I can do outside of healing at the moment." The stone wobbled a little as she talked.

"What's a mystic concentration?" *It* asked innocently, but the looks he got from the group made him feel as if he had just asked if the sky is up, or is water wet?

"It's basically the talent focus of your mysticism, or as some species call it, magic," Sydney replied.

"So, how do you do that?" *It* leaned in closer.

"You have to use the right incantation and lots of focus." The stone wobbled again. "See, when I talk, I lose focus and the stone isn't stable."

It was more intrigued with the black mist as he reached a finger out toward it. "But what's up with the black smoky stuff and the glowing?"

The stone dropped as the ever-friendly squirrel lost her temper. "Enough! If you can't respect me, at least respect my beliefs!" She jumped to her feet. "You don't have to make fun of me! It took me a year to be able to do that." She bounded off without retrieving her stone.

It's eyes opened wide. "What did I do?"

Evan swung his tusks as he shook his head. "That wasn't cool."

"What? I just wanted to know how the black stuff worked."

Evan's mom stood up. "I don't know if this is some kind of hooman humor, but it isn't funny. She is your friend. She deserves better." She walked off as the others stood up to leave.

"I wasn't making a joke." *It* said with his hands out to his side, but no one wanted to hear it.

Brandor got to his feet with great effort and a deep groan. "To many people, mysticism is a sacred thing ... a life of devotion." The nearly nine-foot-tall mammoth stretched a little after having sat for so long. "That poor girl was sharing with us ... with you ... a special part of her, and you tease her about black smoke and glowing stuff." He started to turn away. "Let's see you make a stone float." He walked off with the loud thuds of his footsteps trailing off into the darkness.

The rest of the Fallon thundered off without a word or even a look toward the inconsiderate boy. As the last to express his disappointment, Evan got to his feet and collected his sword. "You know, I may not show much concern for the rodent, but what you did was wrong." The big Fallon turned to leave. "Lucky for you, all the crazy in that squirrely brain of hers will have erased this by tomorrow." He walked just outside of the firelight. "Her kind are like that." He stopped. "... and don't hang out here pouting over your screw up for too long. The morning will come quick."

Only the sound of the campfire flames hung in the air. *It* stood motionless with his self-pity and embarrassment fighting for bragging rights over the stupid move he just made. After a moment, he shook his head in disbelief. He was sure he saw a glow and black mist, *so why didn't anyone else see it?* The boy pushed around the dirt with his foot as he started working out in his head how to explain what he saw to Sydney while at the same time avoiding any chance of upsetting her again.

A weak smile made its way to his lips as his foot kicked Sydney's red stone out from under a leaf. She was so upset that she ran off and left it behind. More guilt washed over the boy's face—with everything she had done for him, he repaid her by acting like a complete and total twogg.

He picked up the stone and looked it over for traces of the something that wasn't there. *Maybe it was never there*, he thought. Holding the stone in front of him, he glanced around to make sure he was alone. He wondered to himself if all this magic nonsense could actually be real. After all, he did see the rock float in mid-air. How can that be harder to believe than animal people and a trash portal in the sky?

As he peered down at the stone, he felt drawn to it. "Could it be real?" He said to himself as he shifted his weight into a position where he could dart away if necessary. With one more look to make sure no one was watching, he whispered "Rizon"—as he expected, nothing happened.

So, now he was standing there looking foolish with his hand out and no stone floating above it. More embarrassment flowed over him. He got mad at himself for even trying.

Talking to himself, he said, "Good going, Ellis, did you actually think all you had to do was say Rizon …?"

Wooosh!—Black lines flashed across the whites of his eyes, and the stone shot straight up into the air with a trail of dark glowing mist behind it.

"No way!" the now-astounded boy shouted, as he stood gazing up into the night sky. "That did not just happen." A few more moments passed with him still blown away by what did just happen.

His look of amazement turned to one of curiosity when a faint whistling sound could be heard above him in the distance. He turned his ear up to hear more clearly. The whistling grew louder. It was then that he remembered that what goes up must come down. He took a sudden step back just as the stone whizzed past his face and slammed into the ground.

Relieved that his head wasn't just cracked open, *It* squatted down to dig the stone out of the small hole it made in the dirt floor. Bringing it up to his face for closer inspection, he caught the last glimpse of the black mist and purplish glow as it disappeared.

His head shook in disbelief. It was hard enough for him to take in the existence of all the weird creatures and this crazy new world in just two days, but now he had magic to wrap his mind around. Life was surely not cutting him any breaks this week.

With a deep exhale of breath, he stuck the stone in his pocket and walked off to use a tree before heading to bed. He had no idea what he was going to say to Evan and Sydney in the morning about the rocketing stone, so he concluded it would be best to keep his mouth shut and remove any risk of inadvertently offending anyone.

After a few moments, the boy's shadowy outline disappeared as he walked off toward his bedroll. The fire was all but out with just a few tiny flames dancing around the brightly glowing embers. The bushes off to one side began to rustle. Twigs broke and leaves crackled as a small form pushed through the shrubs.

Little feet, looking similar to hands, waddled slowly to where the boy had been standing. The hole made by the stone was barely visible by the campfire. The little feet stopped next to it. A cool breeze blew a leaf past when a crooked black finger jammed into the hole and twisted around inside it.

The flickering fire reflected off the deep black beady eyes of one of the opossum-faced creatures as he pulled his finger from the hole and tasted the dirt. A sinister smile wormed across his snout as Toyota gazed out into the direction where *It* walked off.

NINE

I SAID SORRY ALREADY

The morning came, and *It* was still infatuated with the brilliant blue sky and every tree and shrub he saw. He couldn't imagine ever getting tired of it. Back on C-Earth, he always dreaded waking to the drab-gray view of the smog-filled sky and the equally drab-gray domicile-cube buildings, not to mention the only slightly shorter industry buildings which were ... take a guess ... yep; they were gray. Gray, gray, gray to infinity gray.

With Evan following close behind as always, the boy made his way to where the Didelphi had breakfast served for the wagon train. Unlike the banquet he received two nights ago, *It* had discovered that meals on the road were a lot less extravagant, but because it was real food and not a food-like substance, the boy had no complaints about the cuisine. He quickly scarfed down some juicy orange fruit shaped somewhat like a fat banana. Then, with equal fervor, he devoured a thick brown piece of bread slathered with a green gooey paste—it tasted way better than it looked.

Before he could begin munching on a second piece of bread, he saw the squat Didelphi he met the other day. *It* dropped his bread and ran over to where Toyota was shoving plates into a crate.

"Hey, Toyota!" *It* called out as he ran up. "How's it going?"

"How's what going?" the creature said, with a sincere smile, yet weaselly look. The problem with Didelphi is that all their expressions were weaselly looking. When happy, they look weaselly. When sad, weaselly. Scared, same. Infuriated, no difference. Asleep and dreaming of wonders beyond imagination ... yep, still weaselly.

"Nothing. I'm just saying hi."

Toyota's snout crinkled. "Then why not just say hi?"

"Okay," *It* said as their greeting turned a little awkward rather quickly. "Then, hi." The two stood looking at each other until *It* moved the conversation forward. "So, by any chance, have you seen Sydney?"

Toyota continued to place the plates in the crate while he talked, as the Didelphi are an efficient and industrious lot. "And a Sydney is what exactly?"

"No. I meant ... she is a ... she ... my friend Sydney?"

"I haven't seen any other hoomans here."

"She's not human."

"A Fallon? You have a friend outside of your race?"

"No. I mean, not no, that I don't have a friend outside my race, but no, that she is not a Fallon. I obviously have friends that are Fallons, or at least since two days ago. What I'm trying to say is that she is a Seeuradi person and not a Fallon person." He took a deep breath. "There are only two of us traveling with the wagon train that are not Fallons and are not one of your people." He paused to look Toyota in his beady little black eyes and sighed. "So have you seen her?"

"Yep." Toyota just looked at him.

"Aaaaaaand," *It* said, shaking his hands out in front of him.

"She's come and gone." He motioned up the road. "Up front of the train is my guess."

The boy let out a disappointed breath, as he was hoping Sydney was not so mad as to go off without him.

Toyota leaned in toward *It*. "So, how is it that a hooman is friends with a Giverkind?"

"I like making friends. It's always a better deal to make someone a friend than an enemy," he said, with a little hokier sound to it than he intended.

A slightly unnerving smile crossed the opossum's face, but *It* didn't notice. "A deal? Your friendship is a deal?"

The boy thought for a moment and nodded his head. "Yeah, you can call it that."

Toyota lowered his head a little too dramatically. "I never had a friend outside of the Didelphi." He added a little shrug to sell the performance. "I can't imagine what that would be like."

It gave the small creature a wide grin. "You and I are somewhat friends now."

"Really?"

"Sure. Why not?"

"We're friends?"

Without a second thought *It* said, "Yep ... friends ... it sounds like a good deal to me." He held out his hand.

Toyota's eyes opened wide, and his pointy teeth showed through his wiry smile. His small monkey hand shot out to *It* and he shook eagerly. "A deal ... a very good deal."

Evan was lifting a cup to his mouth with what appeared to be milk, but in this world you can't bet on anything being what it looked like. From across the way he watched *It* talking to the opossum-monkey creature and didn't think anything about it until he saw the boy reaching his hand out to Toyota.

The cup and its milky white liquid barely hit the dirt before the large Fallon was charging over the ground and crashing through everything in his way. Though it seemed unlikely, he leapt over a pile of firewood with more agility than a being his size should have.

He reached *It* as the boy was letting go of Toyota's hand. Without stopping or even slowing down, Evan's gigantic hand wrapped around the boy's shoulder and snatched him up as the big Fallon ran past. After several strides he stopped and shoved *It* high up against the scratchy bark of a purple Elum tree. His trunk was curled upward with his eyes narrowed and intently focused on the now startled boy pressed hard against the bark.

Evan's voice didn't have its usual even cantankerous tone. Actually, he was outright peeved. "What did you just do?"

It struggled to speak, but the pressure against his chest was not making that possible.

Evan continued to yell. "Why were you shaking his hand?"

It was still unable to speak, but even if he could, he was not sure what he should or shouldn't have said as he didn't want to make Evan more furious than he was now.

Realizing that the boy couldn't make a sound beyond gasping for breath, the big yellow beast loosened his grip and set *It* down. Only now did he notice how everyone within fifty yards was gawking at them with bizarre expressions. But, then again, anywhere the human goes, he draws attention and strange expressions. What an odd-looking creature he was.

With his feet now firmly on the ground, and Evan looking very uncomfortable by his own behavior in public, *It* cleared his throat and attempted to communicate. "Are you completely nutters?"

Evan took in a few deep breaths to remain calm. "I need to know what you were doing with that Didelphi."

"Nothing," *It* said, completely confused.

The big Fallon talked in a softer, yet still gruff, accusatory voice. "You were shaking his hand, so don't say you did nothing."

"What the ..." He threw his hands up. "Are you serious? You can't be! So, I shook his hand. What kind of crime could that be?"

Evan leaned down close to make sure he was heard as he used a specifically hostile whisper to get his point across. "They don't shake hands!"

It looked around the breakfast space at the makeshift Didelphi camp. The little critters rushed around with little interaction outside of work-related communication.

Evan waved his arm to encompass the whole area and said, "Have you ever seen them shake hands?"

The boy scanned back and forth and shrugged his shoulders. "No, but I haven't not seen them shake hands, but then I didn't even know these people existed until yesterday. So, my database on them is very minimal." Evan's trunk started to curl upward, and his yellow complexion threatened to turn orange again. *It* shrunk away. "Now what did I do?"

In an ire-filled hiss Evan said, "I don't know what a database is."

After a few unsuccessful attempts at explaining to Evan the definition and purpose of a database, *It* asked if they could just drop the subject and head for the front of the wagon train where Sydney had gone.

As they walked, Evan continued his warning. "Since you don't understand our world, you don't understand the Didelphi. They are exceptionally disciplined in living life through contractual obligations. For them, it is a matter of comfort and survival. This particular band of

Didelphi have had a contract with us for a couple hundred years. Other bands are more nomadic and take contracts where they can find them."

"A couple hundred years? And so, they just cook for you?" the boy replied in awe.

In a low chuckle, Evan said, "No, they also provide other domestic services such as cleaning, sewing, and even some farm work. As part of the contract, they also co-exist in the same valley where the Fallon provide protection from the more violent races of Fentiga. And there are some very violent races out there."

"Yeah, I got the feeling I'm the guest of one of them," *It* joked, but Evan didn't smile. "Lighten up, will ya? So, all is good with these contracting guys?"

"Well, the downside of working with the Didelphi is that they insist on having at least a verbal agreement for every aspect of their lives. This is why they don't shake hands. A handshake is just as good as a signed parchment." Evan looked to *It* with sincerity. "So, you can see why I was concerned when I saw you shaking hands."

"I do see—now." *It* was a little hesitant with his response.

"And you need to always be careful when using words like contract or agreement around them."

"Or deal?"

Evan snickered. "Definitely. Never say the word deal with them, unless … if you are actually making a deal with them, then it's okay."

"So, what if you used the word deal and you shook their hand?"

"Oh yeah, that would be a pretty solid agreement there," Evan said without skipping a beat. After a brief moment of silence, he looked down at the now quiet human boy. "Do you need to tell me something that is going to peeve me off?"

"Well … it's my experience that most things peeve you off," *It* said, as Evan came to a halt and stared a hole through him. "So, I may have told him that I would be his friend … and he said something like 'really' and I said something about yes, we are friends … and it's a deal … and … and well that is about it … what we said that is."

"You contracted with a Didelphi to be his friend?" Evan fought to be calm.

It bobbled his head around in a reluctant yes to the question.

Evan wrung his hands together to keep from strangling the boy. "Do you hate me?" Evan asked seriously. "I mean, do you really hate me that much?" He didn't let the boy answer. "You have been here for less than three full days, and you have embarrassed me on the field of battle, you have caused me to be your Host Custodian, I had to break off my engagement to keep the woman I love from being a widow …" Evan, for the first time since *It* has known him, sounded almost sarcastic. "And now you have entered into a contract with an oversized field rat ... to be his friend!"

The boy bobbled his head up and down again. "Yep, that about sums it up." He became worried about the scowl now solidifing on Evan's brow. "But I don't hate you at all … not one bit. That part of your rant is incorrect."

Through a growl, the hulking Fallon grumbled, "Well, I guess that makes it all better, don't it?"

It was not sure if he was supposed to respond, but he did anyway. "I'm thinking … no?"

"No!" Instead of snapping the boy in two, he just turned and continued toward the head of the wagon train.

"Did you really break off your engagement?" *It* asked, genuinely concerned.

"When you love someone enough, you would do anything to keep from hurting them, but I got the feeling you know nothing about that," Evan said with a voice full of regret and anger.

They walked the rest of the way in silence.

———

At the front of the line of wagons, four Fallon warriors stood gathered at the edge of the road on a small ridge. They were staring down at the open brush field leading up to a thick forest line a quarter mile off. Evan and *It* walked up to the group and look out as well.

"What is it?" Evan whispered to the others.

The largest Fallon turned to look at Evan with his one good eye. It was Jagger. He replied, "A glint, or light flash of some sort just inside the woods."

The group stood in silence studying the terrain. *It* began shifting back and forth. Patience was not one of his many skills. "Where I come from things are constantly flashing."

"Yeah, we don't get a lot of flashing here, which is why when we see it, we give it our fullest attention," Evan followed up.

"So, now we just stand here?" *It* added.

Jagger glared down at the boy. "No." He looked back out toward the woods. "We sent a volunteer scout to investigate. We can't leave a possible threat unchecked and at our backs. If all is well, we will move on."

"Like there is even anything big and bad enough to attack an army of Fallons?" *It* snickered, as his question was as rhetorical as it was absurd.

Evan and Jagger gave each other a knowing look that sent chills down the human boy's back.

Evan looked back to the woods. "Well, if the scout doesn't return, then we'll at least know something is wrong."

The boy's brow lifted as he tilted his head to one side. "No offense to you guys, but how is someone as large as a Fallon going to sneak around out there without being seen? Besides, if there is something bad out there, it will know he's coming."

Jagger didn't take his eye off the woods. "That's why we didn't send a Fallon. We sent the squirrel."

A multitude of emotions rushed through *It's* body as he knew immediately who they were talking about. Unable to control himself, he stepped in front of Jagger, and though he was yelling into the Fallon's belly, he had no fear. "Sydney! You sent a little girl out there?"

"Nope. She volunteered." He leaned in close. "She made the same point you did about us being ..." He searched for the word. "What did she call us?"

One of the other guards leaned in. "Rotund lard butts, sir," he blurted.

The very round and plump Floks added, "She called me a billowing mass of fat, and said something about us thundering around like blind tonks."

Jagger turned back to *It*. "So, you can see why we were quick to take her offer to scout for us. Besides, she was driving me insane, and it was a convenient way to get her to leave. That girl is about as bizarre in the head as a sack full of cats with a gore snake tossed in the middle."

"I don't even know what that means ... and it doesn't matter what she said to hurt your so sensitive Fallon feelings. She shouldn't be out there!" *It* turned to search the area. His breath came in short, determined huffs as he forced his mind through the fear that could no longer hold him back. He grabbed his hat from his head and leaped off the ridge. At a full-out run, he was off toward the trees.

Evan must have known what the boy would do because he too was off the ridge and charging through the brush right on *It*'s heels.

Being a small human, the boy had to dart around and over the shrubs while Evan tore noisily through the vegetation as if it wasn't even there.

"I guess we do sound a little thunderous," Jagger remarked, as the group of Fallon guards watched Evan and *It* run across the field of brush.

"I don't think I like what he said about our feelings," Floks added.

Jagger growled.

Just as they were reaching the edge of the woods, *It* passed a familiar lump of fur crouching in a bush. Sydney popped up and watched her friend run by. She stepped to one side to avoid Evan who, now at full momentum, continued past her with a very confused look on his face as he saw her waving hi to him as he charged by.

It stumbled after a few more strides, then stopped and turned back. His eyes sprung open wide when he realized his large mammoth friend was not as agile as he wished he were. Instead of making the boy roadkill, Evan scooped up *It* in his meaty arms and did a controlled drop and roll that sent the two bowling over stones and branches. Sydney heard her human friend yelp from inside a cloud of dust.

Evan and the boy laid in the dirt coughing up the dust from their lungs. Sydney walked up to the two with that ever-present happy grin on her face. "So, I see we changed our minds about being quiet and sneaky and went with the loud and clumsy approach."

She knelt beside *It* and smiled down at him. Picking his hat out of the dirt, she slapped at the dust until the fedora was almost white again, then plopped it on his head. He looked up through the dust and broken branches of the bush he landed in and quickly shoved his hand into his pocket to retrieve the stone which he held out to her. She looked at it with squinched eyes as she couldn't make out what it was through the dirt covering it.

The boy smiled a dirty-toothed smile and stammered. "It's your stone. You left it behind when you stormed off last night ... I mean walked off ... left ... gone to bed." Sydney took the stone as her human buddy sat up. He looked at her with soft eyes. "I'm so sorry for hurting your feelings and disrespecting your beliefs. I promise, I'll never do anything like that again."

"Cool. My healing stone. I'm glad you found it. I was looking all over for it this morning. Thanks." She stood up. "You guys ready to go? Stealth is obviously not an option anymore." She grinned and started walking toward the woods.

"But I'm trying to say sorry," *It* called out as she kept walking away. He let out a last frustrated mumble. "I said sorry, already."

Sydney glanced back over her shoulder. "Are you okay?" she said with a chitter. "Let's go." She took off walking with a spring in her step.

Evan got to his feet and flailed at the dust on his leather tunic. He reached down and lifted *It* up in the air to give him a quick look-over for injuries and then set him down. "I told you she wouldn't even remember that you offended her. They're a little quirky that way."

"How could you have gone to war with them if they are so non-confrontational?"

"Trust me, it wasn't easy ... It was also weird that they would do the things they did to cause a war." Evan glanced around at his surroundings before they headed into the woods. "Our three races, when you count the Aves, are the largest, but also most peaceful of the Giverkind." He paused. "Or at least until the start of the conflict."

"When was that?"

Evan stopped. With a deep gaze he looked into the boy's eyes. His voice revealed a sense of regret. "Many years ago, before I was born." He smiled. "But it ended when a hooman boy fell from the sky—a gift from the Great Giver." He laughed aloud. "And some gift you turned out to be. You're more of a blight if you ask me."

He pressed *It*'s hat down around his ears and started walking after Sydney.

TEN

WATCH YOUR STEP

The boy and his Fallon bodyguard caught up with Sydney and made their way to the treeline. Sydney sniffed at the air, as did Evan, his trunk twisting with a cringe. Pressing her glasses back and twitching her nose, she pointed off to their right and deeper into the woods. Evan nodded his agreement and took the lead as he said in a low voice, "I smell it too." He drew his sword and pumped it twice in the air before entering the woods; a signal to his Fallon brothers on the road watching. Jagger held his arm out to the side and then bent it back, bring his fist to his chest; a sign that he received the message.

Feeling rather incompetent since he couldn't smell anything but trees, *It* whispered, "What do you guys smell?"

Sydney whispered back with a huge grin, "Bad things."

The boy stopped in his tracks and shook his head. "So, the two of you smell bad things and your first reaction is to go find it?"

Evan glanced back with a smirk. "Basically, yes." He turned forward again. "Besides, it's better to know than not know what enemy or peril you face."

"But aren't you supposed to keep me out of danger?"

Evan stopped and looked to Sydney. "Are you going to keep going into the forest if we turn back?"

"Duh ...," she said without hesitation.

Evan looked at *It*. "Are you going to go back without her?"

"I see your point," the boy groaned.

"Then we check this out and head back. We only observe." The big yellow warrior turned back to Sydney. "You understand? ... observe only. Now, why don't you get a higher view and tell us what you see."

"Sure thing," she squeaked as she scampered up to Evan. In a heartbeat she had scrambled up the big Fallon's leg, across his back to his shoulder, and perched with one foot on his head and one on the side of his neck. "I still don't see much," she squeaked.

Pulling from his vast reserve of calm, Evan grumbled, "From a tree."

Giggling and chittering out loud, she leapt to a nearby tree and bounded from branch to branch until she was quickly at the top.

It grinned. "She knew what you meant the first time."

"I know. She enjoys being a pain in my ..."

"Neck?" *It* snickered.

The Fallon snarled, "I was thinking much lower."

The two didn't have long to wait before Sydney was back on the ground. "So, what did you see?" Evan asked.

"Trees and birds—and more trees," she replied and then pointed off to her left. "We need to go that way."

It wrinkled his forehead. "Why that way? I thought you didn't see anything but trees and birds."

"No, I said I saw trees and birds."

The boy's brow wrinkle again. "There are trees and birds all around us."

"Yes, there are, but over that way is a small area where there are no birds," she squeaked, with more wisdom than her years would suggest.

Evan gazed off in the direction where Sydney was pointing. "Which means they're afraid of something over there."

She smiled. "Yep."

The three made their way slowly and quietly through the woods, or at least as quietly as they could with one of them being an eight-foot-tall elephant-person with seven hundred pounds of crunching power in every step.

It was once again finding himself overwhelmed by the sights and sounds of this beautiful new world as they moved deeper into the woods. The last two days had been a shocking contrast to his former reality of buildings and industry with grayish streets and sidewalks.

There were no metallic security bots or driverless transports here. He was now surrounded by an explosion of color in every tree and shrub. Even the ground was covered with an intricate system of roots that weaved in and out, forming endless rainbow patterns across the soil. Bright, multicolored hues soaked into the moss on the sides of the trees and rocks with their soft cushy fibers that formed around his hand as he pressed up against it. Beauty was just so beautiful—yet he cringed whenever Evan and Sydney walked past without taking note of the singular wonderment surrounding them, as they might ignore a pile of tonk droppings on the side of the road.

"Twoggs." *It* whispered under his breath.

Evan came to a stop with the rainbow roots snapping under his mammoth boot. "Did you say something?"

"Yes. Yes, I did," he grumbled as he walked off.

Sydney, who had paused when Evan stopped, watched the boy stalk away. "Well, what was it?" *It* didn't respond. "What did you say?"

Sydney turned back to Evan as if he had the answer, but the befuddled Fallon just shrugged his shoulders and lumbered off after the strange human boy.

Before long they came across a small opening in the trees with an outcropping of large boulders scattered about. Having checked them out from a nearby tree, Sydney gave the "okay" for them to look closer. They cautiously approached the open clearing between some of the boulders where the ground was scorched with the remnants of a campfire. The acrid odor that *It* could not smell before now permeated the air.

"What is that awful stench?" *It* groaned while grabbing at his nose.

"You think that's bad, try sniffing with my nose. It's ten times worse," Sydney griped.

Evan looked hard at the ground. *It* noticed the Fallon's distraction with the dirt and asked, "What do you see?"

"It's what I don't see ... no footprints. There should be footprints." His voice was tense. A small piece of cloth partially covered in the dirt near a large rock caught his eye. After seeing the piece of cloth, he then noticed four more similar scraps of cloth or leather covered by dirt. If he had hair on his neck, it would be standing up high and twitching wildly.

The warrior looked to his two companions and could see that they were contentedly unaware of what he now knew was a big mistake. He shook his head, knowing that Jagger never would have made such an amateur screw-up. Evan took in a deep breath and casually walked towards one of the cloth swatches without looking at it. As he got closer to it, his fingers made the leather hilt of his sword squeak as they tightened. He stopped a foot or two from the boulder.

"Sydney?" His tone was dead serious.

"Yes?" she carelessly answered.

"Could you take out your staff, please?" he insisted calmly, while lifting his left foot high off the ground. Sydney reached for her staff, and *It* watched on, confounded as Evan stomped down hard near the piece of cloth. His mammoth foot sank down several inches into the dirt with the sound of cracking bones coming from just under the loose soil.

An ear-piercing scream shot out from under Evan's foot, and wrapped around his boot was some sort of humanoid creature writhing in pain.

In unison, several areas of ground erupted with dirt and ashy-skinned creatures. They had been lying in wait under blankets and cloaks covered by dirt. Bone and branches tied together to make armor covered their chests and backs. With the exception of the demonic teeth and two holes where a nose should be, they were the closest things to a human *It* has seen since he arrived in this world. They even stood at roughly the same size as an average human.

By the time the boy could grasp the severity of their situation, Evan had dispatched two more creatures while Sydney beat down a third with her staff. More of them flooded out of the woods and skittered across the boulders. Evan's trunk raised towards the sky and a trumpeting call filled the air. Off in the distance, several trumpeting responses could be heard, but by the sounds of them, they were too far off to be of help.

It's vision was momentarily blocked as one of the creatures leapt at him from a rock ledge with a stone dagger clutched in his hand. A large yellow hand wrapped around the creature's head and snatched it away in midair before it landed on the boy. Evan stood holding the creature by its head and using him as a mushy club, slamming him left and right into the oncoming rush.

Between Sydney and Evan, the two kept the creatures at bay with *It* standing between his guardians. Unfortunately, more ashy men leapt down from the rocks behind *It*. The boy grabbed a stone club dropped by one of the now dead creatures and started to swing it. Having taken historic self-defense exercise classes, he was able to avoid being hit. To his misfortune, education programs on C-Earth never offered any offensive exercise classes—there was no violence where he was from.

Two creatures moved in on him. He could have called out to Evan or Sydney, but they had their hands full. He knew that if they saw him in trouble, they would sacrifice themselves for his safety, and that just wouldn't do.

It's time to stand on your own, he thought to himself. So, with an uncertain and feeble attempt at a war cry, he struck out at one of his gruesome attackers to test their resolve—with pointed rotting fangs dripping saliva and a heart-stopping shriek, the creature showed himself to be amply resolved. He blocked *It*'s strike with ease.

From off in the distance, a high-pitched screech echoed through the air and caused a pause in the action as both sides tried to determine if it were good or bad for them. A small furry form launched out from a tree and made several bounds and rolls from rock to rock. As the critter hit the ground near *It*, the boy recognized his new Didelphi friend, Toyota.

Toyota loped across the ground on his feet and knuckles just as you might expect a monkey to do. He came right up to one of the creatures in front of *It*. With his left hand he grabbed the ash-covered thing by one foot and yanked hard, flipping it into the air. With his other hand, he grabbed a piece of straight iron with a bend at one end that had been strapped to his back and swung the bent tip of it into the head of the creature before it finished its flip. The creature flopped unconscious to the ground.

Without slowing down, Toyota grabbed the other creature's foot and flipped it into the air the same as before, but this time, as the opossum-monkey boy swung his iron rod at the creature's head, the stone edge of *It*'s club struck the creature first. The human boy from C-Earth was now in the fight.

The four were holding their own with *It* being the least effective combatant, or at least that was the case until the adrenaline and fear kicked in. And boy, did it kick in. Small black lines streaked out across the whites of his eyes. His friends didn't notice the change, but the ashy thing fighting him had taken note of the boy's freaky eyes.

The creature was not at all happy about it as the boy's hands began moving faster than the creature could track. *It* felt his every sense heighten. His club easily struck down the creature in front of him, but then he stopped and stood motionless. Among the many sounds he could now hear, he heard a faint whistling that grew louder. Instinctively, he twisted his body to the right just as a tiny dart flew past him and into the neck of a creature directly behind him.

It squinted his eyes. He saw past the rocks and beyond the trees deep into the woods; further than any human could see. There was something there, but what was it? A form unlike the others was hiding in the shadows. He could barely make it out.

The dark shape held out a small pipe—*fwwt*—another dart flew out towards *It*. The boy didn't move this time. Just as the dart was about to hit its mark between his eyes, another creature leapt in front of him with the intent to strike the boy down. Just like the last dart, it sunk deep into the neck of the creature who slumped to the ground.

Evan and Sydney worked together as the slower Fallon held his ground by striking and blocking while the agile squirrel girl would swing and dodge. Several times she leapt from, or bounded off, Evan to strike attackers he was blocking. Having her yipping loudly and darting in and around him during battle frustrated the warrior Fallon to no end. A few times his sword swung close enough to Sydney's head that she wasn't certain as to whom was the intended target.

At one point the tiny Seeuradi paused. She was perched on Evan's shoulders after whacking two creatures in the head. She saw three of them charging Toyota across the way. "Watch out!" she screamed.

Though he was trained to fight, the young Didelphi was only good with one opponent at a time, and the look of fear on his face showed it. As the three fiends drew near, Toyota launched himself backward into the air as if hit hard and rolled to a stop in the dirt. His arms and legs aimed skyward while his tongue dangled from his opossum mouth. The emptiness in his still-opened eyes was more than convincing that he had somehow died.

"No!" Sydney screamed again. The creatures stopped their rush toward the motionless Toyota and refocused their attention toward *It*. As they made their way to the boy, Sydney saw Toyota lift his head up and look around. Seeing that the creatures had their backs to him, Toyota got to his feet and went in for a surprise attack. He was able to leap in the air and hit two of them in the head before the third could fully turn and fight.

Sydney let out a loud "Ha" before leaping off Evan to take on another creature herself. However, her excitement was short-lived as she looked around to see even more Ashmen crawling over the rocks.

Chaos ensued all around. It looked as though the sheer numbers of their enemy made it obvious that *It* and his friends were fighting a hopeless battle—or at least it appeared hopeless, until, without warning, the bushes at the edge of the small clearing seemed to explode inward as they were ripped up by their roots by some of the fiercest Fallons the Stronghide herd had to offer.

Jagger and Floks crashed through the underbrush with several other Fallon warriors from the wagon train following close behind. Jagger carried a giant battle axe, while Floks swung a massive flail. Foliage and dirt blew into the air along with hurled javelins launched by the Fallons in the back. Each javelin found its mark, piercing six Ashmen and pinning them to the ground as they fell. One javelin was thrown with such force that it continued traveling through its target and into the dirt in front of Evan.

With one swift motion, Evan snatched up the javelin, struck one Ashman in the face with it, and turned to throw it at one of the creatures attacking Toyota. Toyota was both surprised and relieved when the Ashman in front of him sprouted a javelin from his side.

Evan groaned as he was struck by rusty swords, one across his back, and one across his ribs, as he had three of the noseless humanoids taking advantage of his turned back. As he whipped around to face his attackers and the third creature's sword that was now stabbing up at him, he too found himself surprised and relieved as a giant battle axe, thrown sideways, swiped all three of the attackers away so quickly that it looked as though they just vanished.

Jagger, who no longer had his axe in hand, slowed to a jog as he came up to Evan. He reached over to grab the hand and the club it carried of an Ashman attempting to attack Sydney. He lifted the creature into the air and threw him and his club over his shoulder with little to no look of concern on his face. Before the creature hit the ground, Floks ran by and hit it with his flail like it was a humanoid shaped cricket ball. The creature flew off to the side, slamming hard onto a boulder.

Floks cried out, "Send out the fast bowler!"

Jagger called out to Floks as he was running by with his rotund belly shaking as he went. "Floks! Secure the area!"

Floks paused, and though he was breathing heavy, he said, "Stuff that. I'm not going to let the young ones have all the fun." He turned to run off. As he took his first step, Sydney slammed her staff into the ground, launching herself up toward Evan's shoulder and then leaped onto his tusk which she used as a springboard to fling herself onto Floks' back where she clung onto the top of his leather tunic.

"Yee ha!" she squeaked out loud, as she rode into battle with Floks as her steed.

Having just been a springboard for a war-raging squirrel-girl, Evan stood before Jagger and breathed out a heavy sigh. He did his best to stand at attention, though he was bleeding and utterly exhausted.

Jagger took in a deep breath. "What happened to just reconnoitering the area?"

Evan shook his head. "The Ashmen were not fond of that plan."

Jagger surveyed the scene. The numbers were now against the ashy creatures who had begun retreating into the woods in all directions. Jagger saw *It* just standing amongst the mayhem, staring into the forest. "What is the hooman doing?" he asked with his head cocked to one side and his brow arched high.

Evan grabbed the base of his trunk and sighed. "I don't know."

Off in the distance Floks was taking on the few Ashmen that didn't have the chance to flee. For the first time, Sydney got to see the portly warrior in action, and she had a front row seat as she clung to his back watching over his shoulder. He took on every opponent that came at him with more grace than someone of his bulk should have.

After the dust had settled and Sydney disembarked from her Fallon ride, she scurried over to *It*, breathing heavily. "You alright?" Sydney said, leaning up against her friend and taking his hand into her paw. The boy said nothing and continued staring off into the forest.

Evan lumbered over, holding his bleeding side. He had multiple cuts and purple bruises all over his body. "So, what's up with him?" he gestured with his trunk toward *It*.

"I don't know." She looked out where *It* was gazing. "I think he's doing that staring at nature thing he does. You know, like when he stares up at the sky with that whole, 'the beauty of it all' infatuated attitude."

"So, we're in the middle of a battle for our lives and he stops to admire the view?" Evan growled.

"Yep." She squeezed the boy's hand and leaned her head against his shoulder. "It's so romantic to be in love with nature."

Evan leaned down with his trunk next to the boy's ear. "For Giver's sake, it's a tree. Get over it." He tapped the back of *It*'s head, but even a small tap from Evan was a jarring experience. *It*'s head bobbed forward painfully. The boy snapped a *don't ever do that again* look to Evan. The black streaks were still fading away until the white of his eyes were all that was left, but in that moment, Evan saw something.

"Ow!" *It* winced as he woke up from his daydreaming. "Did you just hit me?"

Evan's expression was blank, and his trunk drooped low—*did he, or didn't he just see something in the boy's eyes?*

Evan's voice cracked as he cleared his throat. "Yeah, it's time to wake up."

The sun was high in the sky as the four made their way across the open brush area back to the wagon train where the healer would be waiting. Sydney had used up the limits of her healing when the fight ended. Now she was still full of nervous energy.

"… And did you see me and Floks? He was just swiping through those guys like they weren't even there. He even used his big belly to crush one of them against a tree—who would have known he was actually a great warrior? Did you know, Evan? Did you know Floks was even better than you?" Sydney chittered on as her adrenalin was still in full force.

Evan grunted a response that didn't really answer the over-excited squirrel-girl's questions.

Even though Evan and *It* walked at a slowed pace while Sydney bounced in and around them, Toyota had to lope on his feet and knuckles to keep up with the group. A cut above his eye was covered in dirt and sweat.

Sydney stopped chittering when she noticed Toyota following them. She looked oddly at the opossum-monkey boy. "Why were you there? Just now, I mean … in the fight."

"Because of you and the Fallon," he said with a gesture of his snout toward Evan.

"Us?" Evan added. "What did we have to do with you being there?" he said dismissingly.

"You were both fighting with *It* ... for *It*." He was a bit out of breath as he tried to maintain the pace.

"Of course!" Sydney poked *It* in the arm and grinned at him. "He's our friend."

Toyota laughed. "Exactly. You are his friend, and you fight with him. I am now his friend, so I fight with him. I have to ... I'm sure it's an unspoken part of the agreement."

Sydney leaped up onto Evan's back and held herself upside down as she looked at Toyota. "Yeah, friends are like that."

Evan grumbled quietly and clutched his sword hilt. "I never said *It* was my friend."

"But he is," Sydney squeaked as she bounded off Evan's back, then darted back and forth in front of Evan. "He is. He is. He is. *It* is your friend!"

"I never said that ..." The Fallon huffed with a few added grumbles and a feigned kick at the tiny Seeuradi girl who quickly dodged away.

The four walked along with loud debates going back and forth about who is and isn't a friend to the human boy. *It* said nothing. He just grinned and enjoyed the moment — but, in the back of his mind, he thought of the mysterious form hiding in the woods. Then more thoughts came to mind. *How did Toyota know where we were? How did he get there just in time to save me? Is that a tire iron he had strapped to his pack? ... I wonder what's for lunch.*

ELEVEN

IS THERE A HEALER IN THE HOUSE?

*I*t and his battle-worn companions sat beside a large, covered wagon, rubbing their various aches and injuries. Evan appeared to have taken the brunt of the damage, as he had a deep gash to his leg with additional minor bloody wounds to his torso and head. As the surge of adrenaline was now long gone, the emotional and physical crash that followed was heavily weighing on them all.

"Is it always like this?" *It* moaned.

"Is what always like this?" Sydney squeaked weakly.

"Fighting. I've never fought before."

Evan smiled down at the boy. "Well, that was obvious—I'm not even sure if you could call what you were doing as fighting ... but what a rush!"

"Rush? What rush?" The boy held out a trembling hand. "What's this? Why can't I stop shaking?"

"It's called the battle shakes," a soft, deep voice said from inside the wagon. After a few moments of bottles clinking and loud rustling of paper, a robed Fallon stepped out through the rear tarp carrying a large satchel embroidered with brightly colored rainbow hued beads. At a little over seven feet tall, he was short for his race. *It* recognized him as the other Fallon at the table with Jagger during the surrender meeting.

"Every warrior gets it after a skirmish. Even old-timers like Jagger get the shakes after battle. It's natural. As a matter of fact, it's when you don't get the shakes afterwards that you should be worried," said the Fallon, looking down at *It*.

"Why?" said the boy, still holding out his arm.

"Because it's the ones who don't shake afterwards that are either too accustomed to it, or worse, they enjoy the bloodshed and chaos." He walked over to *It*, pushed his arm down, knocked his hat off his head, and looked him over.

"Yeah, I'm only five and I can't stop my tail from shaking," Sydney squeaked as she stood up to show that her tail was twitching uncontrollably.

"Five what?!" *It* asked.

"Five years old," Sydney responded with a grin.

"What?" *It* jumped to his feet. "How can you only be five? You can't be five!" the boy yelled out and then turned to Evan. "Is she only five?!"

"That was my guess," Evan said with a raised brow.

"You mean you people knew she was only five and you let her go out to be killed by those ... creatures ... thingies?" *It* gestured widely with his hands as the healer struggled to continue looking him over.

"Well, actually, I'm more like fifteen in hooman or Fallon years," Sydney said in defense of her maturity.

"How is that?" *It* snapped.

"They don't live as long as us," Evan grumbled.

"Huh?" The look on his face made it clear the boy was caught off guard.

"Yeah, Fallons live to be about two hundred years, while Seeuradi have only forty-five or so—that's why we don't make friends with them. We would go through too many of them in one lifetime." Evan said with a snort at the end.

With his face frozen in shock, *It* stared at the still-grinning Sydney.

"Yep, so I will be all grown up and old when you are still a young hooman," Sydney squeaked as if it were something to be proud of.

It sat back down with his hand still shaking.

Seeing nothing wrong with the boy other than post-battle stress, the healer reached into his bag and started to pull out a bottle.

Glancing into the top of the bag, *It* saw more black, glowing mist within the bag.

The healer handed him the bottle. "Here, drink some of this." He began to turn away but stopped. "And I'm called Kandula; the herd mystic and all-around dispenser of dubious wisdom."

It took a gulp from the bottle and spit it out violently. "Yuk! What is this?"

"Hey! Don't waste that! It takes a long time to ferment." The aged Fallon reached into his bag and pulled out a feather the size of *It*'s arm and waved it around Evan's head as he chanted. Again, *It* saw a black, glowing mist, and this time it was not only enveloping the feather, but he saw wisps of it coming from Kandula's mouth which intertwined with the feather's smokiness. The combined mystical vapor wafted over Evan's face. His entire head glowed with it.

It looked back to the bottle he was holding. "This is nasty." The boy wiped at his tongue to get the taste out of his mouth.

"It will help with your nerves and stop you from trembling." Kandula looked back to Evan and poured some purplish liquid over a deep cut on the warrior's leg while again chanting. The wound began to heal as the skin pulled together. The liquid had a purple glow with a black mist around it.

It watched the bloody cut on his friend's leg magically close up. "No way!" He lifted the bottle to his lips. "This place is nutters." He drank in deeply, though the taste almost made him vomit.

After a few more applications of the liquid, the healer finished with Evan and moved on to the little squirrel-girl. "So, you must be Sydney?"

"How did you know my name?" she squeaked. "Did you divine it?"

The old Fallon's cheeks cracked with laugh lines as he chuckled. "No, I most definitely did not divine it, little one. I would be one sad case of a mentor if I didn't know my own novitiate." He smiled broadly. His mustard yellow skin being blotchy around the mouth made his grin come across as being wider than it was.

"Oh, my Great Giver!" Sydney squirmed with excitement which made it hard for him to heal her as she kept bumping his feather aside. "No way! This is too cool! I'm really your novitiate?"

"Yes. Now hold still."

"What's a nofishatate?" *It* tried to say with a hiccup at the end.

"Novitiate," Sydney squealed. "He's going to teach me. I'm going to get to learn shaman mysticism."

"Well, you won't have time to learn all the shaman mystic arts, but while you are with us, your Prominence has asked that you continue your training," Kandula said, leaning over to wipe the wound on Toyota's head, followed by a dose of the purple elixir and more waving of the feather. "There, that should do you all just fine. The Giver is the spirit, and the spirit is in you." He packed up his bag and headed for the wagon. Sydney followed close at his heals bounding back and forth, nearly being stepped on. The others remained outside in the shade of the tree.

"So, when do we start? Are we starting today? What will you teach me first? I'm a fast learner." Sydney stayed behind Kandula up to and then into the wagon with non-stop chattering. From inside the wagon, she could still be heard. "Wow, look at this place ... Hey what is this? Oh, my Great Giver, what is that thing?" A good deal of clanging was heard from inside the wagon as Sydney chattered on.

"Put that down before you blind yourself," Kandula griped from inside the wagon.

Evan leaned back against a tree, causing the lower branches to rustle. "It's nice to hear her annoying someone else for a change."

"Annanoy wif who?" *It* slurred.

"With the tree verm ... Sydney."

"Who isth Snidney?"

"Your friend. Sydney."

"Neber hert of her."

Evan reached for the bottle in the boy's hand. "How much of that did you drink?" He took the bottle and sniffed it. "Good Giver! There's fermented tarin root in this. A lot of it. You're snockered."

It held out his hand and gave Evan a huge cheeky grin. "Lowok no shakies." The boy fell over into Evan's lap. He was out like a light.

Toyota waddled over and inspected the boy briefly, picking up his hand and letting it drop. He looked up to Evan and said, "Can I have a snort of some of that stuff? I have the shakes too."

Evan glared at him.

Toyota's head drooped. "Yeah, I expected as much."

◦―⌒―◦

Inside Kandula's wagon, a jungle of herbs and plants hung from a network of twine near the tarped ceiling. On the left side, high up, a long thin counter was covered in bowls, bottles and several crude instruments for cutting and grinding. Sydney stood at a round table under the counter. She was hard at work crushing something in a bowl with a stone pestle.

The wagon lurched to one side as Kandula stepped in through the back tarp flap with a goatskin water bladder in his hand.

"What are you doing on my stool?" he said, as he looked accusingly at his student.

"I thought it was a table ... I'm preparing a tonic for *It*. Someone gave him a lot of fermented tarin root and this should help him with the headache he will have later."

"Did you use Drot seeds?"

"Of course. I'm almost ready to channel the healing stone into the mix."

"No, you're not," Kandula snorted.

"Sure I am." She examined the bowl. "I got the mixture right."

"No. I meant that you aren't using your stone."

"Then it won't be as potent."

"You're here to learn the shaman ways." He hung up the water bladder and gathered Sydney's bowl and pestle. After bumping her away with his leg, he sat down on the stool to work at the counter. "Come up here, little one." He set the bowl on the porous wood surface.

Sydney scampered up his leg and arm to squat on the table. Kandula pulled out his feather and a wad of twigs tied together with one end charred from being burned. He held the wad of twigs with the burned end inches from his face.

"That stone of yours is the yoked beast in the field. You pull the mystic essence from the world and tether it there for use later. The shaman gathers the essence and channels its flow." He held the wad of twigs closer to his lips. "This is our smudging stick. With it, we call on the life-giving breath of the Dragon." He chanted in a light and low voice; just barely more than a whisper and then said, "Kesta Fir." The smudge stick ignited in a small flame which he put out with the palm of his hand. Smoke trickled out and up in front of him. "The Dragon brings life," he said, as the wisps of smoke began to twist around, tumbling and rolling in the air. Gradually two swirling amorphous clumps of smoke merged to form the shape of leathery wings. The remaining wisps of smoke floated under the wings with one end taking the shape of a tail, and the other the resemblance of a dragon's head. A misty dragon was formed, flapping around in circles and loops just above Sydney's head.

"Wow," she squeaked.

Kandula gestured with the smudging stick. "... but the Dragon can also breathe death." The smoky beast opened its maw and drifted down toward the squirrel girl as if to devour her.

Sydney fell back with a yelp as she was about to be eaten. Kandula flicked the feather in the air through the dragon, dispersing the smoke. "The Shaman's feather is the world's strength and fragility. With its breeze, the spirit of the world takes flight." He twirled the feather, gathering the smoke and blowing it toward the bowl containing Sydney's mixture. "So, the smudging stick and the feather bring the essence of the Dragon's breath and spirit willingly to a union of healing and wellness of the being as a whole." The smoke disappeared into the mixture. Kandula picked up the bowl and handed it to his young novitiate. "Now it is potent."

Sydney stared into the bowl, transfixed on the powder. "Wow."

TWELVE

AND THEN THERE WERE FOUR ...
OR WAS THAT FIVE?

After three weeks, the wagon train entered the Fallon territories and *It* got to see more of their lifestyle with every village they passed. They weren't just thick-skinned, stuffy giant warriors with superiority issues. They were professional craftsmen, artists, seekers of self-enlightenment, and even entertainers.

Evidently, Evan was stuffy by his own choosing and not the product of his culture. But he did have a few indulging habits that made him less of a twogg—he loved to dance. On multiple occasions, *It* caught Evan jumping up and down around the evening campfires with some of the locals. While his fellow tribesman beat on drums and chanted in rhythm, Evan and others painted their faces and danced in some sublime ritual around a blazing fire.

The scene was reminiscent of the ancient tribal dances *It* had studied in his knowledge enhancement programs back on C-Earth. Seeing these behemoth beings leaping and twirling then slapping their chest and yelling would normally bring the average teenager to tears with laughter, but not for *It*. There was some sort of eccentric majesty that earned his respect ... a spiritual conjuring of community unity ... and it was just so awesome.

The caravan dwindled as they went along. Each day a few more tonk-drawn vehicles and a number of the troops would split off from the main column and return to their villages. For *It* this meant there were less Fallons for him to train against for his daily combat lessons. Of course,

Sydney loved the training, as she was given an opportunity every day to heal *It*'s cuts and bruises. She had become his personal medic along with solidifying herself as the boy's best and most loyal friend.

By the end of the fourth week, they reached the main herd city where many of the troops were stationed. Unlike the other hut-filled villages speckling the landscape, the city of Utuska was surrounded by a high wall made from vertical standing tree trunks, reminiscent of the Earth forts of old. Along the main road stood buildings constructed from timber and others made from stone and mortar. Of them all, only a few were two story buildings—Fallons didn't typically trust high structures to hold their weight, so they preferred to be low to the ground.

The large gate at the main entrance was wide open and manned by only two warriors. Fallon folk traveled around as they pleased without interference. Even the resident Didelphi enjoyed the freedom to come and go without concern.

For a society thought to be at war, they had an earned sense of comfort that no one would be attacking the Fallon at home. Even the children here were large enough and strong enough to crunch the average humanoid into people-butter; and it doesn't hurt that they all have been trained to fight regardless of their profession.

Because of *It*'s "offensive deficiency," any free time while on the road had been spent on his learning how to fight. When they got to Utuska, the self-defense training increased tenfold. Unfortunately for the tiny human boy, the majority of this training ended up with him being held upside down by one of his legs. The other times, he was either knocked flat on his back, or sat on—the learning curve was painful.

"Is there ever a time when you aren't training to fight?" *It* asked, as he wiped the dirt and sweat from his eyes. The blazing sun was beating down on him as he stood in the practice arena.

Evan towered over the boy. "Sure. When you are asleep, and when you are dead. Now, stop lollygagging around and kill your opponent." He pointed back to a plump familiar looking Fallon—Floks.

It reluctantly picked up a wooden practice shield and sword made special for his diminutive stature. Though exhausted, he moved in on the jovial Floks who laughed as he swiped at the boy and just barely missed taking off the top of his head with a practice flail.

It took a step back. "You almost cracked my skull open!"

Floks laughed even harder. "Then defend yourself better, fluff-bug."

From the side Evan yelled, "Charge in there! Like a proud Fallon, charge your opponent!"

"I'm not a Fallon and I'm feeling less proud with each beating I get!"

Floks grinned. "I tell you what …" he dropped his practice shield and flail. "I'll make it easier for you, fluff-bug."

"Great! Adding insult to the injury!" *It* started forward when he got distracted by loud screams from the other side of the arena.

"For my friend and for victory!" Toyota leaped out from behind a barrel and charged at Floks.

From the opposite side, another shriek filled the air as Sydney bounded across the ground with Floks as her target. "Death to the tyrant! Victory for *It*!" she squealed.

Toyota and Sydney threw themselves on Floks and scurried over and around his bulbous body while pummeling him with their tiny fists.

Though he couldn't even feel their blows, Floks waved his hands around trying to swat them off, but they were just so fast. "Hey! Stop that!"

Seizing on the opportunity, *It* threw his shield to the side and flipped the wooden sword in the air to catch the blade end. Flailing the sword around like a club, he charged at the plump Fallon. "Oh yeah!" he cried out.

Evan shook his head and sighed as Floks tried to defend himself from his munchkin attackers. Even *It* was getting in a few good shots with the hilt end of his wooden sword.

Floks stumbled as he swiped the air. "Stop it … Evan! They're cheating!" He knocked Sydney to the ground, but as he reached for Toyota, Sydney leaped back into the fray.

Evan pulled at the top of his trunk as the chaos went on for way too long.

⁂

The glaring afternoon sun shone brightly through an unusually large window. Actually, everything in this room was oversized. From the chairs and table to the water tankard and plates. It was obviously a room designed for a Fallon.

Standing in a row and silent as mice, Floks, *It*, Sydney, and Toyota waited for the consequences of their actions. Each one of them had bruises and black eyes as evidence of their mischief. Off to the side was Evan.

With an orange face and creased forehead, he did not look happy. It could have had something to do with this being Lord Stronghide's office, and Stronghide was at his desk, staring holes through Floks and the kids.

Leaning against the desk beside the Fallon Lord was the one-eyed warrior, Jagger. A long uncomfortable silence had the row of rioters shifting nervously. Even Floks, a full-grown adult, wrung his hands with the worst of anticipations.

Finally, the agonizing quiet was broken as Stronghide grumbled, "An entire morning of training has been wasted on this …" He was at a loss for words, but his angry eyes filled the emptiness until he had the fitting term, "… fracas of yours." He targeted his gaze on Floks.

Floks pointed a large chubby finger at the children. "They cheated."

"I'm not interested in the minutia of that display." He turned his gaze on Evan. "My concern is the responsibility we have as hosts to the hooman. He should be getting prepared for the journey home. I'm beginning to question my trust in his supervision."

Evan stood tall, but the sullen squinting of his eyes betrayed his shame.

Now that Stronghide had made his disappointment clear, he looked to his General. "Jagger!"

"Yes, my Lord?"

"Bring them in."

"Yes, my Lord." Jagger headed for the door and shoved passed Evan as he exited.

Once again, the room was filled with a deafening silence that was too uncomfortable to bear for some of them. A low whistling tune drifted through the room. It didn't take long for all eyes to be on *It*.

Holding his hat in his hand and tapping it against his leg, he whistled for a moment longer, but the gaze from Evan stopped him dead. "What? You guys are way too intense," *It* said, then looked to Sydney and Toyota for support. "Right? Aren't they?"

Both the Seeuradi girl and the Didelphi boy nodded their heads in agreement until they, too, were caught in Evan's gaze, at which time they both shook their heads *"no"* with much emphasis.

The door opened and in walked Jagger. He was not alone. Behind him was Sydney's sister, Sam, and a teenage Ave boy they had never seen before with dark blue feathers. Smaller black feathers circled his eyes with a tapered streak reaching back along the side of his face. The rest of his humanoid shaped body was covered in the same blue feathers as his face.

Sydney's cheeks stretched with excitement as she tilted her head toward *It*. "Wow, a Blue Jay Ave. I've only seen a few of them."

Sam immediately walked over to Sydney and tussled the fur on the girl's head. "Hey kid, we've missed you!" she continued, as Sydney pulled her head back with a huff. "So, how's your little quest going?"

"It's not a quest!" Sydney squeaked.

"That's not what you were saying before you left." She grinned. "Your quest with the hooman boy."

It leaned sideways toward Sydney. "What quest?"

"It's not a quest," she squeaked again with a tensed jaw.

Then Toyota leaned in. "Can I go with you on your quest?"

Her cheeks puffed out. "I'm not going on a quest!"

"Well, if you do go on a quest, can I go with you?" Toyota replied.

She dropped her head.

It looked over to Toyota and said, "I think we're already on the quest."

Toyota's face lit up. "How splendid! I've never been on a quest before." He was then struck by a brief moment of befuddlement. "So, what should I be doing for this quest?"

Before *It* could reply, or Sydney could protest some more, Lord Stronghide cleared his throat through his trunk and nodded toward Sam. "You may know Defender Sam Laap of the Seeuradi." He then gestured to the Ave. "And this is Lucas Alan Bazillion ... something of something ..." He looked at the Ave boy. "You're going to have to tell them yourself."

The young Blue Jay stepped further into the room and stopped. He placed one clawed foot out in front of the other and posed. "I am Lucas Alan Bourdillion Traherne, Second Assistant to the Established Regent Elect of the First Talon, Edroy Nalyd Kayne Grondol." He ended with a flourish of his feathered arm and a bow. Not a word was uttered as everyone watched the bird-boy who stayed in his bowed position.

After a few seconds Jagger placed his hand near the side of his mouth and leaned close to Lord Stronghide. "I can see why you didn't try saying the whole thing."

"So, is anyone else feeling a bit weird and awkward?" Sydney squeaked softly.

Toyota shook his head with his typical clueless grin. "Not me. Why?"

"Weird and awkward is normal around here," *It* snickered.

Realizing that the Ave boy couldn't stand back up until his introduction was received or rejected, Stronghide elbowed Jagger in the ribs and gave him the evil eye. It took a moment for Jagger to get the message.

The one-eyed Fallon stepped forward and stretched out his hand, palm up. "We welcome you to Utuska and to this assembly."

The boy stood upright and took a step back.

Lord Stronghide got to his feet and moved around to the front of his desk where he leaned back with his right haunch resting on the desktop. "Before Sam and Lucas arrived, I had a few communiques with some of the other races. It seems we weren't the only ones to have an incident with the Ashmen. Others have reported being attacked or followed by them. Apparently, they're hunting for something …" He looked at *It* and said, "Or someone."

He waved his hand toward Sam and Lucas. "Which brings us to why they're here. We have decided to work together, as we once did, for the moment at least, to bring *It* back to his people in hopes that his presence is the catalyst for reuniting the hoomans and the Giverkind."

Sydney whispered to *It*. "Wow, the fate of our world is in your hands. No pressure on you." She grinned.

The boy raised his hand. Stronghide rubbed at the bridge of his trunk as if trying to keep a headache at bay. "What?"

"Can I not be a catalyst? I'm quite happy the way things are now and the whole catalyst thing sounds … complicated."

"Not to mention unhealthy for you." Sydney whispered to *It*.

"And continue with you being a pain in the …" Jagger began to say.

"Knock it off," the Lord barked and then turned to *It* with an uncharacteristically sympathetic look. "There is too much at risk here. The plan is that you are the catalyst, and we are sticking to that plan."

"My Lord Stronghide," Lucas interjected with an arm flourish and bowed head. "Pardon my regretful, but necessary interruption. May I request the nature and specifics of the plan so as to report the course of action to the Ave Regents Council?"

Sam studied Lucas' regal posture and attempted to copy him. Her arm flailed out as she bent over way too far. "Yeah, me too. I need to know that stuff to tell my people."

"Well, you can both report to your leaders that the plan at this point is for the hooman to continue his training. The rainy season will be upon us soon. We will want to hold off for better traveling conditions on the roads after they have passed. At that time, I will give you the specifics to report, but for now it is best if few knew the details of the plan. The way I see it, the Ashmen had information that they should not have had. I don't want that happening again."

Lord Stronghide stood up and walked over to Evan. "I have asked Sam and Lucas to assist you in the boy's training. He will also need a position in the community to earn coin and learn an appreciation for hard work. See to it that you match one to his skills."

"What if he has no skills, my Lord?" Evan said, foreseeing the challenge ahead of him.

"There is always a need for muckers in the tonk stables," the Lord replied.

It turned with a raised brow to Toyota. "What is a mucker?"

"Beats me. I'm still stuck on the word catalyst. Does it have something to do with cats?"

Jagger stretched out his arms to hustle everyone toward the door. "Alright, you heard our Lord. Back to training. Get out there and get to it."

Evan was the last to head out, but Stronghide stopped him. "Evan?"

"Yes, my Lord"

"As for the antics during training ..."

"Never again, my Lord. I'll make sure of it."

"Let me finish."

"Yes, my Lord."

"You have been pushing hard and meeting my expectations, but sometimes a leader needs to know when to give his unit time to let off steam and unwind. You just can't have them know that it's okay to do it. Besides, seeing Floks out there getting bested by a band of miscreants was hysterical." He smiled at Evan. "You need to see the pleasures in life as well as the duty. A great leader strives for balance."

"Yes, my Lord." Evan forced an uncomfortable smile and headed out, closing the door behind him.

The Lord and Jagger stood alone, looking out the window at Evan attempting to wrangle the kids into the practice arena. Across the room and behind the two giant Fallons, a door opened. Kandula walked in from a side room.

"So, you still think it's best to keep the boy in the dark?" He said as he walked over to Stronghide and watched out the window as Toyota and Sydney teamed up with Floks to attack *It*. They were all laughing hysterically as they played.

Stronghide took in a deep breath and exhaled with a burdened sigh. "It's the best chance we have at getting him to the hoomans alive. Even if it doesn't work, we should be able to get his body to them."

"It must be a difficult decision for you."

Stronghide shot a curious glance to Kandula.

Kandula huffed. "Don't try that look of ignorance with me. I see you're starting to admire the boy."

"He is a disrespectful and undisciplined mess, but in the short time of his being here, the boy has the Seeuradi and Fallon talking about peace. He is also building hope in our people that the hoomans may once again open up communications."

Kandula patted Stronghide on the back. "And he grows on you."

"Yes, that he does ... like a fungus." He lumbered back to his desk. "And how are things with your new student? Will she also help to secure our relationship with her people?"

"That isn't why I agreed to take her on," Kandula said offended by the statement.

"Are you telling me that you didn't give any thought to the strategic advantage of having her train under you?"

"Yes, that is exactly what I'm saying."

Jagger, who had been watching out the window the whole time, grunted. "She is a non-stop nuisance with a few straws missing from her bundle."

Kandula laughed so hard he snorted. "That she is, my friend. That she is. And it is both refreshing and exhilarating trying to keep up with her. She will either be the death of me, or the revival of my spirit. Either way, it won't be boring."

"That may be." Jagger placed his hands on the window frame and leaned heavily against it as his voice took on a more solemn tone. "But will all that be of any use to her or the boy when the darker times come?" He turned to face Stronghide. "Without our walls to protect them, they will face those things that we have faced and maybe more." He looked back out the window. "And by the looks of it, they won't be ready."

He watched out the window as Lucas stood to the side watching on.

Floks was now on the ground with the kids, including Sam, on top of him. This time he was laughing too hard to fight back.

THIRTEEN

AS EASY AS HITTING A FALLON WITH A STICK

Sam's Seeuradi unit and a few Ave warriors stood with Evan, Floks and the kids at one end of the practice arena. In the center, Lucas strutted back and forth with a gracefully measured pace.

"Welcome gentle Giverkind and honored hooman guest," Lucas called out to the crowd with an overly elaborate bow. "We shall begin with a combat exercise designed to aid you when faced with a much larger opponent. Of course, I do realize that this exercise would be pointless for a Fallon as few beings are larger than them, but they will make for great instructional devices. So, I will need one Fallon and Seeuradi volunteer, please," Lucas added with several more flourishes.

Sam bounded into the center of the arena before the Ave could finished his sentence.

"Wonderful." Lucas looked to Evan. "And a Fallon, if you wouldn't mind, gentle sir?"

Evan sneered and took a step backwards and nudged Floks out of the crowd. The portly Fallon stumbled forward, whipping his trunk around in defiance. "Hey! Hold on there!"

"Thank you, sir ... Floks, I believe it is?" As is his practice to be elaborately eloquent with an inclination toward the dramatic, Lucas held his arm out, making a wide flamboyant gesture for Floks to join Sam. So, the big Fallon made his way to the center, dragging his feet as he went.

Lucas looked to *It*. "Up until now, your gracious hosts have instructed you on how to fight a Fallon as a Fallon. What we propose is that you utilize your smaller stature and speed to your advantage; something the Seeuradi are renowned for having." Lucas turned to Sam and Floks. "Please, if you would, Mr. Floks, attack your opponent—and don't hold back."

Floks' eyes widened. "If I do that, she'll be annihilated."

"Please, sir. Don't worry yourself about her wellbeing. Just attack," Lucas said with a wink.

Floks looked to Evan, and Evan just shrugged his shoulders. Floks shrugged back at him and turned on Sam. He charged her with little enthusiasm and weakly swung his wooden flail. Sam easily deflected it with her practice staff.

"Please, Mr. Floks. Don't be so gentle. It's important for the lesson that you try hard!" Lucas called out.

"That's okay, Lucas. He is probably a little intimidated by me," Sam yelled back. Her comment set the crowd off into hysterical laughter, considering that Floks was at least three feet taller and eight hundred pounds heavier than her. "Besides, with all that jelly around his stomach, he might have heart failure if he moves any faster," Sam added with a taunting snicker.

"Why you tree verm!" Floks lunged forward swinging down hard at Sam.

Sam deflected the blow and scampered to the side as Floks went past her. To make it worse for the rotund Fallon, she smacked him on the butt with her staff as he went by. "Wow, I bet that would have hurt if you didn't have so much padding back there," she squeaked.

"I'll give you padding," Floks grunted as he turned on her again.

Lucas faced *It*. "Note how she uses her wit to antagonize her opponent into attacking carelessly and then dodges him easily—but it is imperative that you follow up your move with a calculated strike."

Sydney turned to *It* and said, "This is where her being a twogg pays off. Do you have twoggs where you come from?"

"Yep."

"What do you call them?"

"Jerks." *It* smiled.

"Ooo, I like the sound of that word."

Sam was now taunting Floks relentlessly. He chased her around the arena, rampaging from one end to another. Though the Fallon had much longer strides than the Seeuradi warrior, Sam was still easily able to stay just ahead of him. He was swinging his flail wildly and missing by a far margin. His face glowed orange with anger.

Sam veered straight towards a large wooden crate full of training equipment.

Evan whispered to himself as he watched on, "Don't fall for it."

Just as she reached the crate, she leaped on top of it and sprang off the other side. Floks, who was now at full berserker speed, couldn't stop or even change direction. He careened into the crate with all of his weight, shattering it into a hundred pieces. His momentum carried him through the wreckage, but he tripped on a piece of practice chest armor and went sprawling into the dirt. His tusks made deep trenches into the ground, and he was temporarily blinded by the dirt they kicked up.

Sam raced back over to him and, once again, smacked him on the butt with her staff.

Panting heavily, he got to his feet and charged once more without wiping the dirt from his face. Sam did another deflect and dodge move. This time, as the Fallon went past, she swung her staff to strike the inside of his right knee. When the hard wood made contact, the giant warrior collapsed instantly with a yelp.

Lucas spun back around to *It*. "And that is how you employ agility and cunning to triumph over a larger opponent."

Evan put a hand on *It*'s shoulder. "But it doesn't work every time. So, you need to have many combat strategies in your battle bag."

Sam walked up and offered an arrogant grin. "It works most of the time."

"It's my experience that nothing works most of the time," Evan said with more than a little self-confidence of his own.

"You care to try?" Sam replied with a snarky squeak.

"What's the wager?"

Lucas stepped up. "I implore you both to employ equanimity here, please. This was just an exercise."

"No, bird-boy, let him try." She glared at Evan. "Loser buys the winner drinks tonight and rubs her sore feet for all to see at the pub," she chittered, with the Seeuradi soldiers chittering with her.

"Works for me," Evan said with no concern for his pride.

The large Fallon faced off with the tiny Seeuradi. He took off his leather jerkin which he held it in his right hand and fought with his wooden training sword in his left.

"If you are both ready, commence," Lucas said reluctantly.

"You're bigger and dumber than your friend," Sam taunted as she darted back and forth trying to make Evan charge her.

"That may very well be," Evan said calmly.

"I'm sure you get your fat-headedness from your mother," Sam said, getting a little annoyed herself that he wasn't taking the bait.

"Oh, yeah! You rodent-brained mongoose!" Evan took two sudden strides forward. Sam anticipated his move and started to dart to the right when Evan threw his sword at her. She quickly changed directions and leapt into the air to the left. Unfortunately for her, Evan was a step ahead. He threw his large leather jerkin to his right where she was flying in the air with no way to change direction. As Sam's feet hit the ground, she was knocked down and covered by the heavy leather garment.

With unexpected velocity, Evan leaped over to her and swept her up in the leather vest. He wrapped her up tight in a roll and walked back over to the group. It was as if Sam were a novice, and the embarrassment showed in her face.

The muscular Fallon held her above his head. He looked over to *It*. "And this is how you eat a squirrel burrito." He opened his mouth and turned Sam upside down as if to eat her headfirst, but he stopped just before she reached his teeth.

She had closed her eyes but opened them again as she realized he wasn't eating her. Embarrassing her further, he gave her a huge cheesy grin and said, "I can drink a lot, and I have a few growths on my feet that could use a good rubdown."

Evan snapped the vest in the air like a whip and it unrolled, launching Sam several feet off the ground with a not-so-graceful landing in the dirt where she tumbled several times before coming to a dizzying stop—she was covered with dirt and partially blinded by the dust.

Sydney cocked her head to the right and squinched her eyes. "I guess it doesn't work most of the time, unless this is one of the times not covered by the most."

Evan shot *It* a wink as he walked over to console Floks and his bruised ego.

It put his arm around his little Seeuradi buddy and said, "I got the feeling the outcome would have been the same no matter what."

After a moment or two of snickering, *It* and Sydney walked over to Sam, who was still brushing off the dirt from her lesson.

"So that was an interesting exercise. I would never have thought that being wrapped up and turned into an entree was a successful strategy for beating a larger opponent," Sydney squeaked with a giggle.

Sam reached out to grab her sister by the ear, but Sydney ducked and ran off. She hollered back over her shoulder, "I'll catch you later, *It*. Kandula needs me."

"She'd better run," Sam sneered.

It wasn't sure if he was expected to make conversation with Sam, so he said the first thing that came to mind. "If you ignore the part where you were almost eaten alive, your technique was solid."

Sam glared at him for a quick moment but was distracted by something behind him. *It* turned around to see a group of Seeuradi warriors laughing and goofing around. One particular warrior stood out, as he was the tallest at five foot four inches, and the only one wearing red leather armor. The others wore green armor like Sam's.

It looked back to see that Sam was staring at the tall one. "So, you like this guy, I take it?"

She snapped out of her lovelorn trance. "What? Who? No way!" She grabbed him around the shoulder and clasped her paw over his mouth. "Shhh … you tell anyone I like him, and I'll feed you to a Kroncal!"

"Whaf isb a Crofkul?" the boy mumbled through her paw.

"What?" she barked at him. "Speak clearly."

"I kanf spec clarlea wiff yo hanf own mife mouf."

She took her paw off his mouth. "You're weird."

"I asked what a Kroncal was," he said while spitting dirt and squirrel hairs out of his mouth.

"How can you not know what a Kroncal is?" she said with a squinched forehead.

"I guess not hearing about them is a good cause of my not knowing about them."

"They are the only race of people, if you can call them people, who are a near match for the Fallon." Her eyes narrowed as she took on a solemn tone. "They're hideous beasts. The only ones who eat other races."

"That's messed up ... wait a minute. You said they are the only people to be a near match for the Fallon."

"Yeah."

"But you were at war, or are at war, with the Fallon."

"So?"

"How is it you're at war with them if no one but the Kroncal are a match for them?"

"Oh, that. They would have destroyed us if they wanted to."

"What! Then why were you about to do battle with them?"

"We were just showing them that we would stand up to them to defend our Great Giver rights," she hissed and let out a gasp of annoyance. "For many years they have been playing dirty tricks and being deceitful about their gift retrieval process; also, last year our high mystic died suspiciously." Her eyes softened. "He was a wonderful person. The Aves did an investigation and found some proof that the Fallons may have been involved."

"That doesn't sound like Fallons." He waved his hand around to encompass the whole of the city. "I've been around them for some time now and I can say they are occasionally ill mannered and often arrogant, not to mention their severe lack of hygiene and the stench that accompanies it ... oh, and boy can they be a bit touchy about rules." His voice softened and a genuine smile crept across his face. "But they are honest and an honorable people."

Sam sighed. "I was told they were that way too, once, but that was long before I was born."

"Maybe the whole thing has been a huge misunderstanding."

"It doesn't matter, now. It looks like we are on the path to fixing things between us. This is the first time we've worked together on anything in almost twenty years."

From across the way, the group of Seeuradi warriors let out several cheers which distracted Sam.

It noticed her leering at the boy again. "Why don't you talk to that guy if you like him?" *It* said with a big smile on his face and while twitching his eyebrows up and down.

"Because he is a Seeuradi Adept, an elite guard. Besides, I have issues with boys—I can't seem to talk to them right." Her eyes popped open wide. "Wait a spot, you're a boy, right? Or at least boyish."

"Yeah, I'm a boy."

"Then you can tell me how to talk to him. What do boys talk about?"

"Whoa, I know nothing about relationships. I'm the last guy you want advice from."

She grabbed his arm and squeezed tight with a pathetic helpless look in her eyes. "Please. You got to know something."

He swung his head in hopeless resignation. "Alright, it seems to me that the best way to get to know someone is to find something you have in common and go from there."

"Like what?"

"I don't know. What does he do that you also do?"

"We're fighters."

"There you go." He pointed her in the direction of the Seeuradi warriors. "What's his name?"

"Khal."

"Go to Khal and show him that you are interested in what he is interested in." He pushed her on her way. "Show him that you are a good match for him."

As Sam reluctantly walked toward the other Seeuradi, Lucas came up behind *It* and said, "Well, sir, shall we embark on some Ave combat training?"

"Huh, what?" *It* glanced back. "Yes sure, but give me a sec. I want to watch this."

Lucas looked to where Sam was walking up to Khal. "Are we eavesdropping? It is not at all proper."

"Sam just asked for some advice on talking to boys. She likes Khal."

"What advice did you offer?"

"Um ... I just said to find a common interest and show him you are a match for him through that interest," the boy replied.

"Sagacious advice for one so young. What was the common interest?"

"Fighting. She said they both have that in common."

"Intriguing. By any chance did you consider that you just told an emotionally questionable Seeuradi female to prove that she is a match at fighting with this Seeuradi gentleman?"

It turned to Lucas. The boy's expression went from one of giddy expectation to one of "*oh cripes!*"

They both turned back to see Sam talking to Khal.

"Okay. So far so good. Nothing to worry about," *It* breathed.

"Have patience. I'm confident misfortune is ensured," Lucas said in a knowing voice.

They watched as Sam raised up her staff and pointed it at Khal. He looked to be confused but raised his staff and dodged as Sam swung at him. He defended two more strikes, but the third one caught him in the gut. When he bent over from the blow, she smacked him on his back and dropped him. Two of Khal's buddies jumped in, but she made short work of them as well.

There were now three squirrel boys rolling in pain on the ground. Sam turned toward *It* with a huge bucktoothed grin and gave the human boy a big thumbs up while her tail darted back and forth with excitement.

Lucas exhaled heavily and said, "And there it is."

It gave Sam a thumbs up as he spoke out of the side of his mouth to Lucas. "And when she figures out that she shouldn't have beaten him up?"

Lucas nodded. "Yes, well, it would be shrewd of you to provide her a wide berth for the next few days."

FOURTEEN

DARK ORDERS

Torchlight flickered off the damp cave wall while the sound of water droplets dripping into puddles echoed softly in the shadows. At the center of the near empty subterranean chamber was an immense white stalagmite with streaks of green stains left by years of calcite formation. Contrasting the natural surroundings, an enormous red framed mirror was built into the limestone spike jutting from the cavern floor. The frame was an ancient, rust-coated metal with curious symbols covering its surface. Odder still was the lack of reflection in the glass. Where there should be an image of the opposite cavern wall in the mirror, there was only an eerie unending milky whiteness.

The stillness of the cavern was interrupted when the mirror began to pulse and the white emptiness within swirled violently in a maelstrom of black and dark purple mist overtaking the white. Wisps of smoke stretched out from the nexus and into the cave as it began to form fingers; then a hand; then an arm. As the mist dripped away, the arm appeared covered by a golden yellow silk sleeve. Finally, an entire cloaked form stepped through the mirror.

With the hood drawn, no face was visible, but the decorative trimming and fine material was evidence that this was no commoner. The mysterious individual spun around searching for something, or maybe hoping to find nothing. Seeing that he was alone, the stranger scurried with unsure, almost clumsy, steps from the large cavern into a small tunnel to disappear into the dark. The sound of his shoes scuffing the hard stone trailed off, leaving only the cadence of the steadily dripping water.

⁂

A hidden stone door scraped loudly as it creeped open into a dilapidated courtyard. A tangle of dead vines covered the rock floor surface. What once looked to be a lovely mountain garden with a scenic view of the surrounding valley was now the victim of time and the elements overlooking an expanse of rock and sand. If ever there was a sign of life in the valley below, it had long since been wiped away.

As the door opened wider, the cloaked stranger in the gold robe stepped out and moved cautiously across the vines. Fearfully avoiding the edge of the cliff, he hastily moved up a set of winding stairs leading up the mountain. The sounds of labored breathing made it clear that he was not accustomed to this much exertion. Occasionally, rocks slipped out from under the fancy leather shoes worn by the stranger. At one point he slipped and fell forward, striking one knee hard against the granite stair.

"Chances be damned!" A high-pitched male voice rang out in pain. "I'm late enough as it is."

Hobbling with great effort, the stranger made it to the top of the stairway rubbing at his knee. Before him was what was left of a grand double door. Large iron bands held together the remains of the wood that looked to have been torn apart, as much of it was smashed inward. One door was slightly ajar with a gap of a few feet, which the stranger walked through.

His head emerged on the other side just as a long blade swung out and stopped inches from the front of his hood. He put his hands up, and with his fingers, he pulled the hood back and down behind onto his shoulders. Thin stringy brown hair was matted against his wrinkled forehead as sweat dripped down and over his round cheeks. With the sleeve of his robe, he wiped more perspiration off of his very pronounced nose—he was most definitely human.

With the same hand that he used to wipe his face, he now pressed the back of his sleeve against the blade and pushed it slowly away. "Do not delay me. I do not wish to be later than I am," he said looking straight ahead, not taking the time or effort to turn his head.

To one side, a scratchy hissing sound was followed by an equally scratchy hissy voice.

"What does it matter, Neevit? You're still late. I'm sure that won't cost you much more of your soul."

The hissing came from the shadows, but Neevit didn't turn to look as he confidently responded, "And what have your services cost you, Slagg? The likes of you don't even have a soul."

The sword retreated back into the shadows. "Which is why you should be more careful in how you speak to me. Opening you up would only bring me pleasure, regardless of the retribution."

"I'll be sure to bear that in mind," Neevit said with no fear or sincerity in his voice.

⁂

The sweaty, robed man shuffled along even quicker than before through a dank corridor until entering a huge anteroom; it was like one found in a palace, but time and neglect has taken its toll on it. He paused for a moment, glancing around, and then continued shuffling his feet across the stone and dragging his robe behind. There were no verms; no insects; no signs of life anywhere. After going through a series of smaller hallways, he walked through an open door.

His face blanched, instantly drained of life and any last ounce of happiness as the air around him reeked of death. He stood at the top of a stairwell looking over the railing. Down below stood several tables with beakers and Bunsen burners on them. Unfamiliar metal contraptions were also scattered about the room on other nearby tables.

"I'm sorry, have I inconvenienced you?" A very pleasant-sounding feminine voice drifted out from somewhere below. It was sweet and melodic. "Surely if you cannot be here when called for, then obviously I have become an inconvenience for you," the voice called out gently again.

Neevit's voice cracked, and his body trembled. "No, your highness. Never."

In an instant, a misty form of darkness appeared before him, hovering in the air. Behind a smoky veil was the outline of a hideous visage. Its partially visible mouth opened. "Empress! How many times do I have to tell you … Empress?" the specter shrieked with the pleasant feminine voice replaced by a terror-causing screech. Through the veil, piercing glowing eyes stared out at the sweaty, shaking man as they looked him up and down hungrily. After a tense moment, the soft sweet-sounding voice returned. "I like Empress. It feels good rolling off the tongue. Don't you think?" she asked, as her snake-like tongue slithered out of the mist and twisted in his direction, before pulling back into the smoky blackness.

"Yes, my Empress!" Neevit practically squealed.

"Good. I'm glad that is settled. Now, why didn't you come when I first called ... and who is this interloper that I am hearing about?"

Neevit cleared his throat, as the specter had now moved within inches of his face. "That is actually why I am late. I was gathering information for my report. The Fallons and the Seeuradi have called for a temporary truce. It appears a human boy arrived and put a stop to the conflict. It is believed that he is a gift from the Great Giver and may be some sort of a divine redeemer."

"A redeemer? From their ridiculous made-up deity?" she quipped.

With the large fog of evil inches from his face, Neevit could only peep out what sounded like a confirmation.

The Empress pulled back. "Where is this ... redeemer?"

"He is a guest of the Fallon and with Lord Stronghide himself."

"So, he is smart enough to seek out a powerful and competent ally. What else do we know of this boy?"

"Not much more than that which I said, but I have my sources working to get me more information. I have one of our faithful embedded in the boy's company. Also, I hear the boy is to be escorted to the city of Yolanrym after the rains have passed."

"That gives us time."

"The Ashmen set a trap for the boy, but he escaped."

The room grew colder as Neevit could now see his breath. The misty form flashed with a demonic image just under the black surface. The horrific screechy voice returned. "Under whose authorization did they make such an imbecilic move?"

"It was a misunderstanding. They were instructed to only track, but an opportunity presented itself and they attempted to kill the boy," Neevit whined with fear.

"Exactly! ... They attempted to kill the boy, which they failed to do. Now we may have been exposed." The empress descended slowly to the floor below. Her softer voice returned, echoing as she drifted downward. "I don't want him dead yet. Find out all you can first. I need the data on this boy."

Neevit cleared his throat with a great deal of effort. "And what happens when he reaches Yolanrym?"

"He won't reach the human kingdom. I want him dead before then, regardless of whether or not we get any useful information from him first." The empress had drifted completely out of sight, but her lovely voice could be heard trailing off. "Oh, and I want you to make an example of those moronic Ashmen. We can't have our associates making haphazard decisions."

"I'll select a few from the raiding party to be punished," he said with fake confidence.

"No," her voice whispered back seductively. "All of them."

"My Empress?"

"Kill the entire raiding party ... I don't wish to appear ... indulgent."

The room was once again deathly quiet. The light of a nearby torch gleamed in the depths of Neevit's trembling eye. "Yes, my Empress."

FIFTEEN

BUTTKA'S PUBLIC HOUSE

The Warrior's End Pub, also called Buttka's Place, was louder than normal as she not only had her usual Fallon patrons, but the addition of some Seeuradi and Ave warriors had the place hopping. Many Seeuradi sat or stood on the tables in order to see as all of the furniture was Fallon-sized. The taller Ave folk had it a little easier as they stood or knelt on the chairs. With that being said, the most burdensome issues caused by oversized furniture were the many injuries due to those Seeuradi and Ave old enough to drink fermented fruit and roots; they had much further to fall when they had too much to drink.

Most of the tables had their own self-imposed segregation as the different races tended to only sit with their own kind. One table stood out, as there was a variety of Giverkind hanging together. *It's* entire crew was there, with the exception of *It* himself. Sitting at the head of the table, Evan held out a tankard that was twice the size of Sam's head.

"To the Seeuradi! Though they may not be wise when it comes to making a bet, they are honorable in the payment of that debt," Evan said, gesturing to his freshly pedicured feet and then lowering his tankard down to Sam, who took her cup and clinked it against his. Of course, it made no louder sound than that of a thimble against a wash pot. Across the room, several Seeuradi heard the loud Fallon's toast and cheered out above the crowd. One of the squirrel-looking warriors had had too much to drink and fell off the table with a painful thud as he hit the floor.

"Had I known you were analyzing my moves in the arena today, I wouldn't have made that stupid bet," Sam squeaked with a loud chittering laugh.

"Now that is the wisest thing that I have ever heard you say," Evan replied with a swing of his trunk.

Toyota and Sydney were sitting on the table with Sam who was, oddly enough, snuggling up to Khal. All four giggled hysterically after Sam's comment to Evan. Lucas, however, stood on a chair next to the table, but his laughter was precisely measured and most appropriate.

After a few more moments of laughing, Sydney turned to Toyota. "I've been meaning to ask you … so, how do you do that playing dead trick that you do?" she squeaked.

"It is so easy. All you have to do is practice laying still."

Her nose squinched up. "Really?"

"Yeah, I practice every night, but I never know how good I'm doing because I always fall asleep—I'll teach you sometime. It's all about the tongue." Toyota stuck his tongue out and let it hang to one side. "See," he said, as he swung his head back and forth with his limp tongue slinging around.

To the others it looked gross, but not to Sydney. "You'll teach me? That would be wonderful!" She squeaked and chittered on, as they continued discussing the details of looking dead and sticking their tongues out for practice.

At the other end of the pub, the front door opened and in walked *It* and Floks. They attempted to make their way through the crowd, but even one Fallon was hard to get around for someone *It*'s size. He snatched the white fedora hat off his head and waved it as he struggled to get past a particularly unaware Fallon when a loud trumpeting sound echoed through the room, causing the boy to nearly jump out of his skin. The trunk on Flok's face stood up straight as he took in another deep breath and yelled, "Clear a way! Make a hole!"

The mass of Fallon bodies parted to give room for *It* and Floks to walk unimpeded. *It* settled his fedora back on his head like a boy of some importance and looked up to his Fallon friend. "Thanks, big guy. You are handy to have around."

"Any time, fluff-bug," Floks snorted with a broad smile.

"What is a fluff-bug anyway?" the boy asked.

"It's a tiny fragile little insect with a poofy body and delicate wings."

"Yeah, I kind of imagined that's what it was. I don't suppose you'll ever stop calling me that?"

"I wouldn't get my hopes up if I were you," he laughingly snorted.

The two reached the table. *It* climbed onto a chair next to Lucas, while Floks plopped down into a chair and threw his feet high in the air, bringing them slamming down onto the table. Toyota, Sydney, Sam, and Khal went rolling from the tremendous jarring of the table. Their drinks flew out of their hands and covered them in Freat Tea. All four of them wiped at the green liquid on their clothing and gave the portly Fallon a piece of their minds in the process.

After order was regained, *It* noticed Sam and Khal being rather friendly and sitting close to each other. He nudged Lucas and gestured toward Sam and Khal. "What's going on here? Didn't she beat him up?"

"Yes, indeed she did," Lucas replied with the same tone of confusion as *It*.

"And yet he is with her?"

"Might you now have a better understanding as to where the term 'squirrely' comes from?" Lucas asked with a judgmental smirk and shake of his head.

"Uh huh, I guess so," the boy replied, still staring at the two infatuated Seeuradi.

A rather slender Fallon in an apron, or at least slender for a Fallon, lumbered up to the table. She slapped a towel against Floks' feet. "Get those mud stompers off my table before I stomp a hole in you," she bellowed.

Floks whipped his feet to the floor as quickly as his robust body would let him. He pointed at the kids standing on the table. "What about them? They have their feet and whole bodies on the flipp'n thing." He gestured around the room to show that most all of the Seeuradi were standing on tables, and those not on tables were standing on the bar. "You got at least thirty pairs of paws running around on your tables."

"They are too small to matter," she replied and then looked to *It*. "Hello there, wee one. What can I get for you?"

It smiled widely. "Hi Buttka. I'll have a Jugosh Freat, please."

"You betcha," she said with a wink.

"Wait a minute!" Floks sat up straight and scowled down at *It*. "Why does she get to call you 'wee one' and you complain if I call you 'fluff-bug'?"

Buttka's jaw dropped open. "Because fluff-bug is an insulting thing to call him!" she said with another swat of her towel, but this time to his head.

"Yeah, well, you haven't seen him fight." He looked to Evan for support. "Am I right?"

Evan shrugged his shoulders. "That is true. A fluff-bug even hits harder than him."

It rolled with the punches, as teasing each other was status quo for this group. It's kind of how they say they like each other without actually having to say the words. He yelled out over the noise as he pointed a condemning finger at Floks and said, "She can call me anything she wants, because she is by far a mile or two prettier than you."

Of course, with every Fallon looking so much alike and none of them being beauties, *It* wasn't being completely honest with his assertion, but he had become more fond of the Fallons than he ever would have thought possible.

Buttka waved off Evan and Floks with her towel. "Don't you listen to those two bullies. I'm sure you can more than hold your own against the likes of them," she said with a gentle motherly nuzzle of her trunk against *It*'s cheek and turned to walk away. "I'll be right back with your drinks."

"Hey, you didn't even ask me what I wanted," Floks bellowed out as Buttka walked off.

Sydney bounded across the table and sat on the edge facing *It* with Toyota following suit.

"Where did the two of you go?" she squeaked as she gestured toward Floks with a nod of her head.

Floks laughed. "You're going to like this ... Go on, tell them where you just came from, fluff-bug."

"I had dinner with Lord Stronghide," *It* replied.

Though everyone at the table was amazed, Evan was astonished. Lord Stronghide isn't the type to have dinner with the lower-level troops, let alone a common human.

"Wow, what was that like?" Sydney chittered while scrunching her face.

"Well, you know that feeling when you have to trump off a gasser but you're in a place where you can't do it because there are people around you?" the boy asked.

Toyota's eyes narrowed together as he was thinking very hard. "No. That has never happened to me." He noticed *It* looking at him oddly. "I just do it when I need to."

"We know what you're talking about," Sam interrupted to keep the topic of conversation away from Toyota's bodily functions.

"Well, imagine feeling like that the whole time you're around Stronghide," *It* groaned.

"Lord Stronghide!" Evan insisted.

"Lord Stronghide," the boy replied to avoid another argument with Evan about hierarchy, respect, and a hundred other things he never seemed to do right. "And the sad thing is, I didn't have to trump, but I felt like I did the whole time—I always feel like he thinks I'm a mess."

Floks nodded his head. "Yeah, that's about accurate."

Evan too sat there nodding his head.

"So, what did you talk about?" Sydney asked

"Well, he kind of just kept going over the plan for escorting me to Yolanrym after the rains come and go, and that we would be disguised as a caravan of merchants."

Evan smacked the table with his hand to get everyone's attention. He had a slight tint of orange in his complexion. "If Lord Stronghide called you in for a secret meeting about a secret mission, then he wouldn't want you blabbing it around at the pub!"

"But that wasn't all we talked about. He asked me about my training and gave me advice. He even said he wants to do this weekly so as to be sure I'm ready when the time comes."

"You're going to meet every week?" Toyota hissed, as if he just bit into something nasty.

"How nutters is that!" Sydney squeaked as she jumped to her feet. "I guess now we will have to say, 'yes sir' and 'no sir' with a salute when talking to you." She snapped to attention and whipped her paw to her forehead, accidently knocking her glasses to one side.

"Being asked to sit at the table of a Lord is quite the honor and could mean an elevation in status ... congratulations," Lucas offered with a bow of his head. With *It*'s new position, Lucas may have realized that he, too, would need to be cautious around him now that the boy was a much more important human than he was when he first arrived.

Sam, Khal, and Toyota joined Sydney in a mocking salute to *It*. Even Floks scooted his chair back so he could sit up straight and slap his hand to his face for the tiny boy. Of course, the evil eye he got from Evan had him slipping his hand back down to his side and acting as if he was just wiping something from his cheek.

The grimace on Evan's face also made it clear that he wasn't happy with what the boy was saying. "So, what have you been telling him about my leadership of this rabble?" he grunted with a scowl on his brow and a curl in his trunk.

It has been around the proud Fallon long enough to know when something was wrong, but when isn't something wrong or disappointing to Evan? The boy just answered as though all was well in the world. "Actually, I told him I was surprised that, in light of the misfits you had to train, you have exceeded any expectation I had … I mean, look at us. Who would ever have thought a bunch of duffer-heads like us could not only fight, but as a unit we're not that bad."

The expression on Evan's face relaxed as the authenticity of the boy's words made him take note that these kids were possibly starting to appreciate his efforts; even if they never do show it and are constantly disregarding rules and discipline. "So, what did Lord Stronghide say when you told him that?" he said, acting as though only a little interested in the answer.

It was distracted as Buttka arrived with his drink and was handing it to him. "Ah, I don't know, he said something about him not doubting he made the right choice, and then he said something that made absolutely no sense at all." *It* took the cup from Buttka and started slurping the foamy green syrup dripping over the edge.

"What! What did he say?" The big Fallon leaned forward, forgetting that he wasn't interested. In all the years he'd been serving as a soldier this was the first time that he'd had the opportunity to work closely with Lord Stronghide, and he was anxious to hear what the mighty leader thought of him. "Put down that scrabbing cup and tell me!"

Evan had yelled a little louder than he intended, and it got the attention of the entire pub. His trunk dropped in embarrassment as all eyes were on their table, and him in particular.

"Alright already! Keep your shorts on." *It* set his cup down, but kept his voice raised. "Lord Stronghide said something about you being the one he would choose to be … or to do something or the other in a time of Kathawn … or Kathow. I'm not sure how it's pronounced."

The already quiet room became even more silent as every Fallon in the place gazed somberly at Evan. The Seeuradi, Toyota and *It* looked lost as to what just happened, but not Lucas. As a politician in training, he understood the impact of the human boy's words.

Floks patted *It* on the hand and spoke with a genuine affection for him. "You got it right the first time, boy. It is Kathawn."

After a strange and uncomfortable pause, *It* said, "What's a Kathawn?"

No one leaped to answer the question, so Buttka smiled weakly to *It* and said, "It's the name of a battle that began the first horrible war between the Fallon and Kroncal nearly eight hundred years ago." She placed a mammoth finger on the boy's shoulder and breathed, "It was a sad time for the Fallon."

Floks pushed his shoulders back and his chest out. "During a time of war, you become close to those at your side. But for most, there is that one Fallon you are closest to."

"It's called your war wife," Buttka added with a serious chuckle.

Floks smirked. "Yes, some have called it that … or your battle buddy. However, you say it, this is the person you would most willingly die beside. At the battle of Kathawn, there were no Fallon survivors. For a Fallon to tell another Fallon that he would 'Weather the Kathawn' with him … well … it was a sign of trust and respect beyond any other. It is rarely spoken." He looked on Evan with pride.

Evan's head dropped as he stared blankly at the worn cracked floorboards. "And for a Fallon Lord to say it of a herd member is an honor with no equal," he breathed just barely loud enough to hear.

Floks gazed up toward the roof beams as he appeared to be calculating something in his head. "It's been at least one hundred and fifty years since a Fallon Lord declared the Weathering of the Kathawn oath."

The room was still, and the reverence washed over the Seeuradi warriors who bowed their heads in respect. A Fallon dressed in a dirty smock from a day of hard labor at the mill raised his trunk and emitted the strangest yet most harmonic note *It* had ever heard. Not quite a hum, or a murmur, the tone drifted through the room, picking up volume as more Fallons joined in. Soon the room vibrated with an unbelievably beautiful noise.

Though he would deny the truth of it, Evan's eye glistened with the threat of a tear. *It* noticed the look on his large friend's face and, in that moment, he realized how lucky he was that this Fallon was his Host Custodian. That was also the moment when *It* stopped referring to himself as a guest who couldn't leave. He was even tempted to say that he wasn't a guest anymore. For the first time in ever, some place, somewhere, felt like home to him.

Pllllthhhhh—an offensive sound with an even more offensive odor came from behind Toyota, ruining the moment and the quality of the air. "Pardon me, but I told Buttka that deep fried Caleon meat gives me gas."

"Aw, gross!" Sam squealed, as she shoved Toyota off the table.

"That boy ain't right," Sydney squeaked with her fingers clasping her nose below her glasses.

Toyota hit the floor and tumbled. When he came to a stop, he let out a mischievous snicker and made his way toward the door.

"Where you going? You don't have to go." *It* called out to him.

Looking like she was surrendering, Buttka waved her towel in the air with frantic swipes. "Honey, you can stay. If I kicked out everyone who trumped off a gasser in this pub, it would be as empty as a hog pen on Great Giver's Day." She continued flapping the towel around as she walked back to the bar.

It wasn't sure what she meant by that, but he agreed that Toyota shouldn't have to go. "Get back here!"

"I actually do have to go. I have contract obligations to do."

"Alright, just come back when you're done," the boy said through his hand that now covered his nose and mouth.

Sydney let out a muffled yell, still holding her nose. "No, for Giver's sake don't come back if you're going to be trumping off like that."

Toyota waddled out the door, still grinning as the others went back to chatting away.

⁕

The weathered and worn sign above the door of the Warrior's End public house was an image of a mighty Fallon warrior wielding a great sword and wearing full metal armor with a missing butt plate. He was slightly bent over with his enormous rump shining in the bright sunlight.

Below the sign, the door opened up and Toyota waddled out. He headed around the corner and stopped below a window. With a sigh, he slowly climbed up an awning post. The light beaming through the glass glinted off the tiny black globe of his eye, and the laughter from within brought that sketchy grin to his lips.

He saw *It* across the room putting Sydney in a headlock and laughing, while the others were completely enthralled in some story or instruction that Evan was giving. Again, Toyota sighed and reluctantly slid down the post. As he glumly walked away, the beak and blue-feathered head of Lucas appeared and pressed against the window from inside the pub. He watched the little Didelphi walk off. The feathers above Lucas's eye raised slightly as a sliver of suspicion invaded his thoughts.

After a moment, Toyota shook off the sadness of leaving his friends and glanced back to see the now empty window. He then glanced around, making sure he was alone. Seeing the coast was clear, he scooted off behind the building and made his way down various streets and through small alleyways with a sense of urgency pushing him along.

The monkey-opossum boy paused; a flash of moonlight raced across the black of his beady eye as he looked over his shoulder. He was sure he hadn't been followed. When he reached the city wall, it looked as though he could go no further. With another quick scan of the area, he bounded onto the wall and dug his claws in between the logs. He climbed effortlessly to the top and swung over the edge, all of which was excessively unnecessary as the nearest gate was only a few meters away.

Once on the other side, he let his hands glide against the log wall for a controlled fall. He hit the ground with a roll. In the shadow of the wall, he reached into a pouch on his belt and pulled out a piece of glass. Holding it to his eye, he looked through it as he slowly turned it in different directions until the glass started to glow. After more reassuring looks of his surroundings, he took off towards an outcropping of trees.

The Didelphi boy made his way through the trees and was not nearly as quiet as he had been before, but then who was there to see him sneaking around outside the city parameter. The glass that had been glowing in his hand grew brighter as he walked and then began to blink. As he approached a massive tree with crackled looking purple bark and leaves the size of a Fallon's hand, a hooded figure stepped out into the moonlight. Toyota froze.

A harsh masculine voice called out to him. "I do not like waiting."

"Sorry. I couldn't get away until now. I had to trump to make an excuse to leave."

"That's a detail I don't need to hear ... what do you have to report?"

"*It* is now meeting with the Lord of the Fallons once a week. And he said that the Fallons will be taking him back to the hoomans after the rainy season."

"I already knew that."

"Yes, but he says they are going to dress up like a caravan of merchants."

"What else?"

"That's all."

"What about his behavior? Has he been acting strange?"

"He's a hooman—he's always acting strange."

"Besides that. Does he show any mystic inclinations?"

"Nope. But then, I don't know what an inclination is. Not that it matters, because he seems to really not know much about mysticism at all. That's odd, isn't it? He said they don't have it in his world."

"What? What do you mean his world?" the stranger barked as he bent down, his hood was only inches from the Didelphi boy's snout.

"Yeah, every now and then he starts talking about some world that he comes from where they don't have wars, or mysticism, or even freat tea. It's kinda weird. Evan and Sydney usually shut him up before he can say very much more about it. That's kinda weird, too."

"The next time you get the opportunity ... which means you are to make the opportunity ... to start up a conversation with him about this other world, make sure the Fallon and the squirrel are nowhere around when you do it—You got that?"

"Yeah, sure. Talk to him about the other world. No problem. I like talking to him. He's a great guy and the first friend I have ever had outside of my kind."

"Well, don't you forget that we have a contract, you and me. Even though it is an inherited contract, I expect you to fulfill the obligation no matter how good of friends you are with the boy."

The shrouded figure reached into his cloak and pulled out a tiny marble horn and handed it to him. "Take this. It's a hearing horn. I will contact you through it. You hold the open end to hear from and speak into the smaller end. When you feel it vibrating, you will know it's me trying to reach you. If it is ever discovered by anyone else, destroy it immediately—These meetings have become too risky."

"Okay," Toyota whispered respectfully, while he examined the hearing horn. "What if I need to reach you?" he said looking up, but the cloaked stranger was gone. He shrugged his shoulders, stuck the horn in a small pouch at his waist, and waddled off.

After several meters, Toyota heard a twig snap. He nearly jumped out of his skin. Spinning around, he saw nothing and eventually convinced himself that he was alone. Again, he waddled off until he was out of sight.

Above where he had been standing, the branches quivered, and leaves fell to the ground in the shadows of the forest. A dark form glided down landing softly, even daintily, on the forest floor. As he stood there, a dim sliver of moonlight caught the side of his feathered face. It was Lucas. He paused, staring out into the darkness after Toyota. Though his beak couldn't smile or grimace to give away a sign of what he was thinking, his right talon was clenched and the feathers on the back of his head and neck were high and ruffled. He hissed out a whisper, "And what is your treachery, I wonder."

SIXTEEN

DINNER AT THE BIG HOUSE

The morning had just begun, and *It* was busy mucking out a tonk stall when Lord Stronghide walked in. The boy was covered in dirt and tonk droppings, with the exception of his white hat, which kept its clean appearance due to the efforts of a doting Toyota who was around more often than ever before.

The mighty Fallon looked around while sniffing the air. He shook his head and grinned. "I wasn't being literal when I said you could muck out the stables if no better job suited you."

"Actually, I do have another job, but it doesn't start for another hour or so. I help Buttka and some of the other merchants with their books, and I'm teaching classes at the schoolhouse in math and reading. It turns out that I know more in some subjects than the teachers here."

"Then why are you in here covered in tonk manure?"

"I love it."

"You love tonk manure?"

"No, of course not. I love being around the animals and I do this on my free time so I can see them."

"You mean you do not receive any reimbursement for this?"

"Nope," the boy said through a gaping smile.

"You hoomans are definitely strange. I had forgotten that about your kind," Stronghide said and then huffed. "I'm going to need you to conclude these other jobs. I want your martial training stepped up. We can discuss the new schedule at dinner tonight."

"Actually, I was hoping to talk to you about that. As much as I appreciate the special attention I'm receiving, I feel uncomfortable attending these dinners while my friends are thinking that … I'm … you see, the problem is …"

Lord Stronghide cut him off. "Because you are receiving special attention, they think you're special, and that bothers you."

"Sort of. I'm sorry. I know that makes me look ungrateful."

"No. It makes you honorable …" he paused for a moment. "And they are all your friends?"

"Of course."

"Even Evan?" Lord Stronghide said with his tusks twisted to the side and one eyebrow dipping low.

"Especially Evan—he's the man! Or the Fallon!"

"And he likes you?"

"Like is somewhat of a strong word for it. I would say he dislikes me a lot less than he claims, and he tolerates me much more than his Fallon temperament would normally allow."

"That sounds about right," Lord Stronghide said as he straightened up. "A Fallon and a hooman … friends. I like that." he said and folded his arms. "Well then, I guess we can't have you feeling special. So, no special treatment. It is done. Anything else?"

"No. I'm good. Thanks."

Stronghide grinned. He found the boy's cluelessness as to how he should act around a Fallon Lord rather refreshing.

―――

The day was hot, and there wasn't a cloud in the sky. *It* had quit his other work obligations and was at the practice arena sweating like a four-ton tonk pulling a wagon full of Fallons. In other words, just another day. The only thing different is that for the past couple of training sessions, since the night at the pub, Evan had been working the team harder than ever before. It had become his mission to make them the best they could be—in turn, he was becoming a better leader.

Sydney followed *It* around trying to heal wounds he didn't even have. He was becoming more than annoyed with every chant he heard, and every feather stuck in his face.

"Will you stop already? I haven't even been hit yet," *It* griped.

"Yes, I know, and that is beginning to bother me. Your improved fighting skills are getting in the way of me practicing my shaman healing skills," Sydney chittered back in an aggressive tone that still sounded cute.

She continued to shadow *It* around and looked depressed after each dodged blow or parried sword that left the boy unscathed from Flok's attacks. Evan saw how irritated Sydney was getting and felt obligated to help her practice her craft.

Evan called out to Lucas. "Hey, bird-boy! You want to give Sydney a hand? She needs someone to heal."

Lucas, who had been uncharacteristically watching Toyota practice his playing dead trick, flourished his arms out as he bowed deeply. "It would be an honor and a privilege to help the Lady Sydney." As he was standing up, Lucas reached into the feathers under one of his arms and pulled out several throwing knives. He began throwing the razor-sharp blades at *It* while twirling across the ground in exaggerated, yet graceful motions as if he were dancing. The first knife whizzed past *It*'s head, as the boy blocked one of Floks' strikes.

"Hey!" the boy yelled out, and then had to start doing a dance of his own with his practice shield to catch the knives coming at him while avoiding more strikes from Floks. "Come on already! That's not fair!" he screamed, as the small sharp pieces of metal kept flying at him much faster than they normally do in practice. He was also not used to having two opponents. Then it happened. One of the blades missed the shield and sliced across the upper arm of the human boy.

"Ow! Gosh scrabbit! That scrabbin hurt! You scrabbin idiot!" The boy dropped his shield to grab his shoulder.

"Yay!" Sydney squealed. "Thank you, Lucas! Thank you, Evan!" she squeaked with joy as she ran to *It* and began her first-aid routine with that ever-present grin on her face.

It scowled at her. "This is your fault!"

"Oh, belt up, you big fluff-bug." Floks called out as he boomed with laughter.

"And don't swear like that. They were just trying to be helpful." Sydney squeaked.

"You call this helpful?" *It* said as he gestured to his bleeding arm.

The laughter came to a stop when a deep and gravelly voice came from behind them. "Don't ever let me see you drop a shield like that again!"

They all whipped around to find Jagger standing there.

"I don't care if you just got your arm cut off, you don't drop your shield!" he said with more anger than was necessary for the situation. He shot a look to Evan. "What are you teaching this boy?"

"Sorry, sir. It won't happen again," Evan hastily responded.

"Good then. Now go ahead and start wrapping this up. It is almost time for the dinner with Lord Stronghide."

"But I talked to Lord Stronghide this morning. I thought there weren't going to be any more dinners," *It* complained as Sydney dabbed at his arm.

"That's not my understanding. And I would move quickly to get ready if it were me," Jagger hissed.

It began to shuffle off to retrieve his hat with Sydney still trying to tend to his wound. The others stood there staring at the ground.

"I thought I just said, you should be moving quickly! Why are the rest of you faffing around there like slugs in the mud?"

"Excuse me, sir?" Evan asked, perplexed by the order.

"Are you daft? Lord Stronghide wants all of you at the dinner table tonight—and be prepared to give your reports." Jagger stalked off towards Stronghide's office.

"Holy Giver! We're going to the big house," Sydney squeaked.

"Well, this is entirely unexpected," Lucas commented as he retrieved his throwing knives from *It*'s shield.

"Tell me about it," Evan grumbled as he was not taking the news as well as one might think he would.

"What's wrong with you?" *It* asked.

"I am not prepared to deliver a report this evening. And with you dropping your shield every time you get sliced open ... I don't have much progress to report on."

"Yeah, I know how you feel. I hate giving reports when you have nothing to say," Toyota whined.

They all looked at Toyota as if he was speaking another language. They had no clue what he was talking about—but not Lucas. He stared at the Didelphi boy. He knew Toyota was referring to his dark meetings with the dark stranger.

"Well, we all have things to do to get ready. Let's get going," Evan said as he headed out of the practice area.

The others took off, while *It* and Toyota lagged behind. "But I'm still bleeding," *It* complained. He glanced down at Toyota.

Toyota put up his hands. "Don't look at me. I don't even want to go. We always have to be so serious when we are around the big Fallon."

"Tell me about it," *It* replied.

"I could always trump a few times and get us both thrown out."

It shook his head. "You know, let's talk about how there are times when you don't do that … like around girls, or leaders of great armies."

"Why not around girls?"

"Well …" *It* thought for a moment. "You just don't do it. And come to think about it, it would probably just be faster to cover the times you can do it." *It* put his hand over the cut on his shoulder and winced. "Like when you are alone in a room with Evan."

"Really?"

"Oh, yeah. That's the best time. Fallons, especially Evan, are all about stink."

Toyota smiled as they both turned to leave.

Lord Stronghide sat at his desk looking over some parchments. A pair of thin, oversized reading glasses perched awkwardly atop the bridge of his trunk—or at least they were thin for a Fallon. For anyone human-sized, they were like viewing portals. A knock at his door snapped him out of his intense focus so quickly that he snatched the glasses off his face and tried to hide them under some parchments.

"Come in."

Jagger walked in and closed the door behind him. As he made his way across the room, Lord Stronghide huffed in relief and put his glasses back on.

Jagger cleared his throat before reporting. "I talked to Kandula about the upcoming Giver Festival. He agreed with you that inviting the Seeuradi and Ave to celebrate with us is a mutually beneficial idea. He is setting up the communication enchantments and will have them ready for you as early as tomorrow morning."

"Good. What about our little custodian tribe? How are they coming along?"

Jagger shook his head, swinging his enormous tusks. "I find it hard to believe, but Evan has stepped up his training intensity and he seems to have earned some respect from them. I've even noticed other members of the herd giving him much more consideration and respect as well lately."

"Good, he needs to have some wins."

"Yes, well ..."

"Out with it, Jagger."

"I believe the respect he has earned is partly due to a rumor that has been spreading like demon-fire."

"And what rumor would that be?"

"Somehow, the herd is under the misunderstanding that Evan is a Fallon you would Weather the Kathawn with." Jagger cringed slightly expecting the Lord to launch into an irate tantrum and seek Evan's head.

"Yeah, I kind of thought putting that rumor out there would have that effect."

"You started the rumor?"

"I figured if we were going to expect great leadership from Evan, then we would need for him to see that he is a great leader ... pretty good idea, huh?"

"Yes, of course. Very good."

"Anything else?"

"Uh, no. Except that they will be ready for dinner as requested."

"Fine. I should like for you to join us as well."

"Of course." Jagger turned on his heels and headed for the door. Halfway across the room he stopped. "So, it's only a rumor?"

Stronghide was distracted with something he was reading. "What's that?"

"The rumor. About Evan and your selection for Weathering the Kathawn with him. I mean, it's not true?"

"What? Great Giver, no. I only let that slip to get the most out of him. Even you said there's been a change in him."

"Oh." Jagger lingered for a moment.

"Is there something else?"

"No, it's just ... I guess ... well, I always thought that if you had to pick someone from the herd ... you know ... I always assumed."

"Yes, Jagger. It would be you."

"Yes. I thought so. And me you, too. I mean. I would choose you as well." Jagger thudded lively to the door. "I'll see to dinner," and he left.

The room was quiet and Stronghide stared at the door. "Well, I'll be scrabbed; I got two birds with the same stone." He looked down and continued reading.

<hr />

Clank, clank, clank—forks and knives tapped at the dishes as ***It***, Sydney, Sam, and Toyota ate feverishly, enjoying every bite of an extraordinary meal. Stronghide, Jagger, and Evan took even measures as they quietly sliced pieces of meat from their entrée. Stronghide looked across the table and watched the feeding frenzy for a moment. He turned to Evan and said, "And they say we are the brutish barbaric race." He paused and winced. "Are they always like this?"

Evan set his fork and knife down and sat up straight. "No Sir, I asked them to behave themselves this evening."

"You hear that, Jagger? They are behaving themselves," Stronghide huffed.

Jagger shook his head and said, "I've seen packs of verms with more manners."

Lucas, who had been eating elegantly at the end corner of the table leaned forward to say, "If I may, Sir, they are behaving remarkably well … all things considered. I, for one, am impressed." He went back to delicately shaving small slices of what appeared to be a purple spider-shaped vegetable.

"Good, I now know where to set the bar before moving forward." He addressed Evan again. "So, ***It*** tells me that you are his friend."

Evan coughed as he choked briefly on a bite of food. "Actually, Sir, I have been diligent in affording him all of the courtesies as our guest."

"See, I said he didn't dislike me so much anymore, but he still won't admit I'm his friend," ***It*** snickered while gesturing with his fork.

Evan sat there nervous and uncertain as to what to do.

"I don't think Evan has ever had a friend," Sydney added.

Evan shot her a chastising look, but she just stuck her tongue out and then chittered away. "But we all know he likes us, and we're his friends even if he doesn't want us to be."

Again, Evan gave her that look of warning.

"I'm not his friend," Sam mumbled loudly with a mouthful of food.

Evan glared at her as well.

"What? It's true. And if you keep staring at me like that, you'll be wearing your trunk as a scarf."

"Well, I don't have a friend contract with anyone else but *It* ... and I'm very content." Toyota sat smiling, unaware that Lucas was glaring at him. The young Ave knew clearly as to what degree Toyota wasn't *It*'s friend.

"A contract?" Stronghide perked up. "What's this about a contract?"

"Yeah, me and *It* have a binding contractual agreement to be friends," Toyota's beady little eyes glistened as again he gave that unnerving smirk of his.

"Yep. We sure do." *It* put up his hand for Toyota to slap.

Stronghide turned again to Evan. "So, our guest, while under our care, has signed a friendship contract with a Didelphi."

"Oh no, they didn't sign anything. I think it was just a handshake," Sydney blurted out, with a piece of food shooting across the table. She turned to *It*. "Right, it was just a handshake?"

"Yeah, but it's all the same," *It* added nonchalantly.

"Interesting," Stronghide said, while giving Evan a look that the young Fallon warrior wasn't sure how to interpret. "So, how's the training coming along?" Stronghide asked *It* in an attempt to change the subject.

"Well, I have calluses where I shouldn't have calluses and I have cuts and bruises where I know I don't want cuts and bruises," *It* said with a mouthful of a blue biscuit-like bread.

"We've been pushing them pretty hard," Sam added.

"But with Evan's guidance, I am confident *It* will be amply prepared by the completion of the rainy season," Lucas interjected with a gracious nod of his head to the Lord.

"I'm glad to hear that, because I want the training to be stepped up a notch," Stronghide announced.

Evan's face went blank, as the others at the table dropped their forks.

"Stepped up? What about the calluses and bruises I was telling you about?" *It* added with a look of shock on his face.

"Now you can look forward to giving Sydney many more opportunities to practice her healing mysticism," Evan said with a hint of humor—but just a hint.

"Yes!" Sydney chittered.

"But I don't *want* to give her any more opportunities," the boy whined.

"Luckily for you, this isn't a request," Lord Stronghide said, while watching *It*'s face drain of happiness and color. The great Fallon pushed back from the table to get to his feet. "Which weapon have you selected as your primary?"

It looked at him unsure what to say.

"Sir, we haven't established a primary for him. We are attempting to figure out which sword would be suitable for his style. He is still clubbing more than precision striking."

Stronghide glanced around the room for a moment and then his eyes fell upon Toyota's backpack. The large Fallon walked over to it and grabbed the iron rod attached to it. The shaft had some tightly wound leather wrapped around it for gipping. At the end of the bent potion, there was a little hexagon shaped socketed indent.

"Well then, try this as your primary. I've seen the Didelphi use this metal staff proficiently. It's a Didelphi Fighting Staff. I suspect that it will work even better as a club for you." He turned to Evan. "There, that was simple enough."

"Pardon me Sir, but that would be completely ineffective against a Fallon," Evan said respectfully and with much reluctance.

Stronghide's brow wrinkled as he leaned down toward ***It***. "Are you planning to declare war against the Fallon?"

"Not that I'm aware of," the boy replied sheepishly under the Fallon's tusk.

"Good. We can all rest easily tonight in that knowledge." He turned back to Evan. "Not only do I want the training stepped up, but Jagger has informed me that as of today you still have not practiced any form of Kroncal combat strategy."

"Yes ... well ... I didn't see any reason to spend precious time practicing for an enemy that is nowhere near where the boy will be traveling."

"Yet, you were spending precious time training him to fight a Fallon when he himself says he will not be going to war with us."

"Yes, sir, but ..."

"Preparation. It's all about being prepared. I want you to include Kroncal training."

"Yes, Sir."

"You still have a problem," Jagger said, and wiped his mouth with a large towel. "That toothpick he'll be training the boy to fight with is going to be useless against the ferocity of a Kroncal. The lower back of their heads is the only place that will do any good."

"True." Stronghide rubbed hard against his chin. He reached around behind his back and pulled up his blouse. "Here, this should do." He pulled out a sheath with a stiletto dagger in it and handed it to the boy.

Jagger leaned back in his chair and turned his head to the side. A look of confusion crossed his face. It was clear that this was no ordinary stiletto. "Are you sure, my Lord?" he asked.

"I am most certain," he said with an authentic smile as a distant look in his eyes hinted to thoughts of a different time and place. Lord Stronghide cleared his throat loudly and looked down at the human boy. "With this, you only need to thrust the point in just the right spot. Evan will instruct you on those spots. And Lucas," he turned to the Blue Jay Ave. "I believe you can show him how that Didelphi Fighting Staff can be used as a thrown weapon."

"Yes, indeed I can instruct him so," the Ave responded.

"Good. I suspect you will all need plenty of rest as you will begin the new training at dawn, but first, who is up for some dessert?"

Little hands shot up all around the table—Evan sighed.

SEVENTEEN

FAMILIAR FACES

Dawn came and went, and then many more dawns flew by as well. The young ones trained diligently and painfully through to the end of summer. The days became cooler, and the occasional shower heralded the arrival of the rainy season.

The city was alive with activity and excitement for the coming Great Giver celebration. Scarecrows were erected with swords and shields made from vegetable husks, and the city streets, as well as the buildings, were decorated with colorful gourds and wreaths of all kinds.

The crops having been harvested and fall seeds planted, the Fallon folk enjoyed the respite from their summer labors. On many evenings the drums could be heard beating late into the night with singing and laughter filling the air. The best of all gifts the Great Giver could provide was the rain from the sky, and the Fallons were abundantly grateful for that.

Evan and his motley crew of under-aged warriors were the only ones not enjoying a moment of repose. In the practice arena, they drilled every spare moment, and Sydney got more than enough practice healing *It*'s wounds.

"Stop it!" *It* yelped, as Sydney cleaned some mud from a cut on his forehead and then used her purple healing liquid to close the wound.

"You know, it wouldn't hurt so much if you would duck when you're supposed to," Sydney chided him.

"You don't say?"

Evan stood in the center of the arena. He had some odd-looking contraptions attached to his hands which made each finger look like it had a long razor like claw. On both forearms, he had small round shields attached with little pointed barbs across the front surface.

"You have to keep moving. Don't stand still for a moment," Evan yelled to *It*. He wiped his palm against the top of his head. "And for the Great Giver's sake, don't forget to duck. How hard can that be?"

Sydney smirked to punctuate Evan's comment.

It held a practice Didelphi Fighting Staff in one hand and an oversized blunt stiletto in his other hand. He was still not ready to tell everyone that the traditional Didelphi Fighting Staffs were really just discarded tire irons from C-Earth. He shook off his thoughts and gripped his weapons as he complained loudly. "But there are two of you and one of me."

Sam popped out from behind Evan with a nubbed practice mace. "I'm not a person, I'm a tail." She swung the mace around and flipped it in the air a few times.

"Then just be a tail and stay behind him," *It* called back.

"A Kroncal can strike a target in front of them with their tail if they have the room. So, you need practice that way. Now get to it, you big whiner," Evan cried out as he advanced on *It* and began swinging. *It* dodged and parried every strike, and in between strikes he got in a few shots of his own with his stiletto into strategic targeted areas. "Very good. Yes, very good!" Evan hollered as *It* kept him at bay and poked him with the stiletto.

After a few more strikes, while *It* was busy blocking Evan's attack, Sam jumped out from behind Evan and struck the boy hard in his ribs with the mace. *It* dropped to the ground, groaning.

"I think you broke a rib; you nut-job of a twogg," *It* gasped.

Evan looked down to Sam. "Try to be a little less of an enthusiastic tail."

"But what fun is there in that?" Sam chittered.

While Sydney attended to her human friend's injury, some Seeuradi riders rode in from the front gates on horseback and galloped up to Stronghide's office. It's rare if ever at all that Seeuradi come to the Fallon city of Utuska. With the exception of Sydney and Sam's group, it had been decades since so many squirrel-people had been there. Of course, *It* and his crew had to run over to see what was happening. The boy meandered more than ran as he collected his white hat and clutched at his side as he joined the others. They reached the riders in time to see Jagger and Lord Stronghide thud out onto the front porch of the wood slat building.

The Seeuradi riders dismounted and bowed. One of the five stepped forward after bowing. "Great Giver be with you, Lord Stronghide."

"And with you ... Greetings and welcome," the great Lord said with a nod of his head and gesture of his trunk.

"We have come to announce the arrival of Prominence Susanne Janli of the Seeuradi. She's accompanied by a unit of our Red Elite and is escorted by an Ave representative who goes by the name of Edroy Grondol ... well, actually, his name is too long to remember."

"The Established Regent Elect of the First Talon, Edroy Nalyd Kayne Grondol," Lucas called out from behind.

"Yes, that's the guy. He, too, has a unit of Ave Peacekeepers charged with mitigating any and all aggressive conduct."

Jagger leaned in close to Lord Stronghide and whispered, "One unit of birds against the Fallon home front. This should be interesting."

"It's just a reminder that they have to have their beaks in everything," Lord Stronghide hissed with a whisper back. He then addressed the riders. "How far out are they?"

"They will arrive before day's end," the lead out-rider responded.

Sydney and Sam began jumping up and down hugging, squeaking, and squealing while repeating over and over that Susanne was coming.

It stepped up to Lucas. "So, who is this Edroy guy?"

"He is one of the nine Established Regent Elects, and my direct superior," Lucas replied.

"So, you're happy he's coming?"

"Of course, I relish the opportunity to serve my master in person." Lucas' expression didn't match the words coming out of his mouth, but *It* was not about to question him.

"Did you say master?"

"It's just a title of respect used to denote a mentor or instructor. Nothing more," Lucas stammered.

It doubted it was nothing more. His Ave friend was standing much too rigid, and it was not like him to stammer, or lie.

The end of the day arrived along with the Seeuradi and Ave procession.

They were greeted with honors, as Jagger had two squads of troops in leather uniforms standing in formation and saluting with respect. As the word had spread from the city earlier, many Utuska citizens showed up as well. It was quite the spectacle.

After Susanne was practically mauled by Sam and Sydney, as well as the other Seeuradi warriors, they went inside. Lucas greeted Edroy with a flourish and a deep bow. Edroy glanced down at his minion and then looked away as he took his time acknowledging the young Ave, forcing Lucas to stay bent over for much too long. *It* grimaced as he watched his friend being humiliated in front of so many people. The boy remembered the fancy-dressed scar-faced Edroy from the surrender meeting many months ago. If he wasn't sure then what to think of the Ave, he was clear on it now.

"Twogg," *It* grumbled under his breath.

Eventually, Edroy acknowledged Lucas and dismissed him with no further acknowledgement. Susanne and the Ave representative were escorted into Lord Stronghide's office where he brought them up to speed with the training and the scheduled caravan trip to occur at the end of the rainy season.

Sitting around a long dinner table was Lord Stronghide, Susanne, Kandula, Edroy, and Jagger who all wore their typical social event eveningwear. Jagger and Stronghide looked earthy in brown casual pants and loose-fitting blouse shirts, while Susanne had on a slim fitting olive colored dress with matching cloak. Kandula had donned a pale blue robe with a paisley pattern, but as would be expected, Edroy was full-blown primped and preened as if dressing for a gala event of the highest order—and his table etiquette made the others look as though they were commoners.

"So, you are welcomed to remain as long as you wish after the Giver celebration has concluded next month," Lord Stronghide informed Susanne and Edroy with a nod to each.

Edroy gingerly set his utensils down and dabbed his beak with a lace napkin that he brought with him. "Your hospitality is without equal, and I'm without necessity for anything more. However, if I may beseech you with a request of the Flock-State. The Council has suggested that I accompany the caravan to Yolanrym in order that I may offer my aid as a regal advisor for your interactions with the hooman's royal court ... that is with your honored permission, of course."

"I see no reason why not. You would be a welcomed and appreciated addition to our company," Lord Stronghide responded and then nodded to Susanne. "How about you? Would you care to take the journey and represent the Seeuradi in the hooman royal court?"

"Sure, why not? Who doesn't enjoy an adventure?" Susanne squeaked with honest enthusiasm.

The feathers on Edroy's face tensed as he resented the frivolous way that Susanne accepted such a stately invitation. However, he quickly forced a friendly lifting of his cheek bones, which was the Ave equivalent to a smile, and gestured gracefully in her direction. "We would most definitely be the worse for the lack of your company had you not accepted such a cordial and virtuous invitation, dear Prominence."

"As usual, dear Established Regent, you are overly gracious in your considerations," she said with a forced sense of formality.

Kandula chuckled. "I think you're both full of tonk stank. You accepted the Giver celebration invitation so you could insert yourselves into the caravan. Not that you shouldn't be welcomed to go. I would've insisted so as to make our requests to the hooman king more complete with a representative from each of the major races," he said, while cutting his steak and then popping a large piece into his mouth when he was done talking.

Susanne grinned. She has always enjoyed Kandula's frank, and often abrupt, disposition.

"That is preposterous, and I take offense," Edroy declared.

The Fallon mystic reached into his pouch and pulled out what looked to be a small wooden circlet with a web of strings stretched over it and feathers attached to its edge. He placed it on the table and said nothing.

"What is this?" Edroy asked.

"It looks like an everyday dream catcher, but this one is special. It doesn't catch dreams. Instead, it catches falsehoods. Any false statements spoken into the web results in the actual truth coming out the other side," Kandula said and looked to Edroy. "Would you mind speaking through it and saying that you did not plan this whole time to travel with us to the hooman kingdom?"

Edroy huffed and sat back in his seat.

Susanne squeaked with glee, "Don't ask that of me. I'll tell you straight outright that I wanted to be invited. I think it will be a rollicking fun time."

"Put away your truth catcher, Kandula," Stronghide said, while restraining a smile.

"Yes, it is unnecessary. I merely misspoke, as I did not wish to appear assertive or imposing," Edroy confessed, as he adjusted the ruffles of his blouse which billowed out from his satiny turquoise dinner jacket.

"Then that is settled, and we can focus on more pressing matters," Lord Stronghide added with some faux seriousness in his voice.

Both Edroy and Susanne looked at him with curiosity in their eyes.

Lord Stronghide let out a boisterous laugh. "Our dinner. It's getting cold. Enjoy."

As everyone relaxed and began eating again, Lord Stronghide leaned in close to whisper to Kandula. "I didn't know you had something to detect lies."

Kandula spoke from the side of his mouth. "I don't ... but he doesn't know that." He smiled and nodded courteously to Edroy.

EIGHTEEN

THE WORD IS "COVERT"

A week before the Great Giver celebration was to commence, the hard rains came early. The air had turned unusually chilly, and the streets had become a slew of endless mud puddles, but you couldn't tell by the attitudes of the Fallon folk that the weather was not fair. The common houses were always filled with loud talk and laughter, as all within them were happy and excited to celebrate the autumn rains and the hopes for good prospects in the future harvest.

It and his friends continued their training and often would move their practice indoors. On one occasion the leaders from each of the races had asked to observe the progress being made. It was a shared belief that if the human boy were to learn many skills from the different Giverkind races, it would improve the chances of the human courts accepting the request to reunite as an authentic offer of mutual collaboration.

On one particular day, *It* was performing exceptionally well in the indoor practice area and had earned the praises of the elders who had all decided to attend the training.

Evan stood in the center of a barn with Sam behind him as they performed some intense Kroncal combat training. They lashed out feverishly, but *It* moved fluidly, dodging all of the attacks, including Sam's sneaky tail attack. As he finished delivering a death blow with his wooden tire iron to the back of the neck of the mock Kroncal, the barn door flew open with a gust of wind and rain blowing up dust and straw. A Fallon, worn and weather-beaten, lumbered through the doors and straight up to Lord Stronghide.

"Pardon this intrusion my Lord, but Chieftain Torst of the Palham village has requested some assistance with a tonk drive that was disrupted by a pack of wholven. He does not have enough Fallon to wrangle the tonk and drive off the wholven at the same time."

Jagger stepped up. "I can do it. I'll get a few warriors and head east. I can be ready in a day."

"Yes, but I could really use you here for the celebration preparation," the Lord, said eyeing *It* as the boy walked over to a barrel where his white fedora hat rested.

"Who would you send in my place? It shouldn't be that difficult of a task," Jagger continued.

The Lord kept watching *It* as the boy reached out, grabbed up his hat, and with a twist of his fingers, he flipped it up and onto his head in one deft move.

Edroy saw the way Stronghide watched the boy. He could see that there was some admiration there, but the look in the Ave Regent's eye was that of menacing calculation.

Jagger glanced at Evan who was removing his Kroncal armor, and then the one eyed general nodded towards the young Fallon. "We could send Evan and his unit. It will give him the opportunity to field test his leadership skills. If they succeed, and they should, it will prove that they will soon be ready for the caravan to Yolanrym as well as solidifying their usefulness in a joint effort to aid the Giverkind."

Lord Stronghide took in a breath and heaved out his chest. "That is a very fine suggestion." He turned to Evan and barked, "Evan, take today and tomorrow to prepare. You will leave the day after next for the Palham village." He glanced back to Susanne. "Do you object to Sydney accompanying them on this short errand? It won't take but a few days and they will be back in plenty of time for the celebration."

"Of course not. If she is lucky, one of the boys will hurt themselves and she will be able to field practice her new Shaman healing skills," Susanne squeaked proudly.

"Wonderful, that would be perfect," the Lord replied.

"And may I offer the services of my second assistant, Lucas? He has many skills beyond that of a liaison and secretary, as he has exhibited through his combat instruction," Edroy added almost insistently.

"I think that would be an outstanding idea. They have been acting as a unit and I believe they could only benefit from his company," Lord Stronghide said with an exaggerated grin.

"What about me?" Toyota excitedly piped up.

Jagger gave him a questionable look. "This isn't practice. They will bring only what is essential."

"I'm not as good of a fighter, but I'm a much better cook than all of them put together, and I'm very handy with cleanup," Toyota pleaded.

"Yeah, we could really use him," *It* added.

"Yes, please, let him go! He's a hoot to be around," squeaked Sydney with her paws clasped together as she begged.

"I guess if we are to keep the unit whole ... ready yourself as well," Jagger said to Toyota who was shaking with anticipation.

Crack!—A bright flash of light followed by another boom not only woke *It* up, but it startled him so much that he nearly fell out of his cot. His heart was beating as fast as the rain pelting against the window to his room. In the morning he was to leave for Pelham and his first mission.

Groggy and only remotely awake, he swung his legs over the side of his hay-stuffed mattress and felt for his boots. He slipped them on and shuffled over to the window. With each flash of light his room lit up, projecting distorted shadows on the walls behind him.

It was a sparsely furnished room similar to his cubicle living space on C-Earth, so he felt comfortable here. Staring into the turbulent night sky, he couldn't believe that he had only been in Fentiga for half a year. It seemed like a lifetime ago that he first fell through that portal. He wondered if his Papa and Izak stopped missing him by now. He had been so busy living this fantastical life that it was only moments like this when he had time to reflect. He even momentarily forgot that tomorrow he would be turning sixteen. Somehow, birthdays just aren't significant anymore. What could possibly make his sixteenth birthday memorable now?

Down below, the streets were practically flooded. The storm made it impossible for torches or lanterns to be used and the clouds cut off any moonlight. *It* couldn't see anything through the heavy darkness, but the lightning strikes came often enough that every few moments he saw still shots of the world outside his window.

The weary boy was ready to turn back to his bed when the sky lit up again, but this time the street wasn't empty. Two hulking shadowy figures were making their way down the road with what looked to be a long sack on their shoulders with something in it.

The lightning was gone in an instance and the darkness shrouded the streets once more. The boy pressed against the glass, straining to see the figures below. With another flash of lightning, he caught a glimpse of them disappearing behind a building.

Without stopping to think, *It* snatched up his cloak and tire iron then dashed out the door while jamming his hat on his head.

It scrambled out into the muddy streets. The water was up to the top of his boot and he slipped and stumbled every step as he hurried to the corner of the building where he last saw the shadowy figures.

Peeking around the corner, he caught a glimpse of them as they sloshed their way into a nearby barn. The hooded figure in back stopped and shot a look over its shoulder. *It* ducked back, slamming himself against the wood slats of the building. Raindrops pounded against the brim of his hat, making sounds like little explosions in his ear that he feared might give him a way. He breathed in deeply and willed himself to look around the corner.

"What are they up to?" he asked himself.

The white fedora edged its way around the corner. No one was there. After a short gulp, he took off, leaping over puddles and splashing down the road until he reached the barn. Light crept out through a slim crack in the door which was left slightly ajar. The boy tried quietly to sneak up for a closer look, but his boots made a sucking noise each time he lifted them out of the mud as he walked. It was agonizingly long and noisy as torch light from the barn fell across his face.

At the door he peered in to see cloaked figures loading a covered wagon with various sized sacks. One of the sacks already in the wagon was at least eight feet long and bulky. Just the right size for a Fallon folk.

"I got to get help," *It* whispered.

From behind him he heard the sucking sound of the mud. He spun around as lightning streaked across the sky. For a moment he was staring up at a giant hooded being. He swung his metal tire iron, and it thudded hard against the arm of the giant figure standing before him. Nothing happened. He raised his arm to strike again, but everything went dark as the lightning disappeared and a scratchy burlap sack came down over his head and engulfed his body from behind him.

He struggled and called for help, but he was lifted off the ground and, after a moment of being jostled, he felt himself flying through the air and landing hard on what felt to be hay and wooden boards. Alongside of him he could hear other muffled voices, and he felt people bumping against him as they struggled in their sacks.

"Heeya!" A voice yelled out from somewhere beyond the scratchy sack.

It was tossed around violently as the wooden boards began to bounce under him. He figured out quickly that he must be in the wagon with the other sacks and that the wagon was now moving quickly through the storm and the town. Occasionally he felt one of the other people brush up against him.

"Hello? Can you hear me?" he called out to the others. "Who are you? Can you talk?"

He heard a deep menacing growl from nearby—he knew that growl.

"Evan? Is that you?"

"Rawca! Ish Meyf!" came the angry reply.

"Ok, I'll take that as a yes. Who else is there?"

A sound emanated from one of the other sacks. "Cacoo, cacoo."

"A bird call? Wait a minute. An Ave ... Lucas? Is that you?" *It* said.

"Cacoo, Cacoo."

"Anyone else?" the boy cried out.

"Rahwsh! Mehf!" echoed the angry voice.

"Ok, Evan, we have already established that you are here." *It* heard a loud thud, followed by a painful squawk. He sighed and shook his head. "My guess is that you just tried to kick me and hit Lucas instead."

A sad "cacoo" validated his assumption.

There was a slight whimper and low crying. *It* whispered harshly, "Hold up guys; I hear something."

The bags stopped shuffling as they all tried to hear what *It* heard. The quiet whimpering turned into a muffled sobbing and squeaks.

"Sydney? Is that you?" the boy asked.

The crying got worse.

"Hey, it's ok. I'm here. You're going to be alright."

"Mawk! Herp taw!" the angry voice called.

"Evan is here too, or at least I think that's what he's trying to say." *It*'s voice softened. "Don't be afraid. I'm going to get you out of this. We are all going to get out of this."

It heard the weeping slowly come to a stop. A meek little squeak let him know that she was alright.

A weak smile crossed his face. "Fine. Good. We will figure out a way to get out of here."

As the boy pondered an escape plan, he heard what sounded like chewing.

"Rut rat!" Evan grumbled.

"I don't know what it is," the boy replied.

After a few frightening moments, *It*'s sack pressed against him hard and he felt teeth gnashing at the bag trying to tear their way to the boy.

"Evan!" *It* shouted with terror in his voice. "Help me! They're eating me!"

All the sacks began kicking and screaming as they heard their human friend being devoured, but there was nothing they could do. Finally, the sack tore open and tiny razor-sharp teeth stopped inches from the boy's face.

"Hi, *It*. What's up with all the screaming?" Toyota said, with his snout still in the boy's sack.

It looked up at his Didelphi buddy. "Toyota! I'd kiss you if you weren't so ugly."

"Hey! That's not nice. You're not so pretty to look at either, you know."

They both sat there for an awkward moment or two, with Toyota's absent-looking face still inches away from *It*'s nose. *It* nodded to his left as he said, "You can get off me now."

"Oh, right. Of course," Toyota replied and quickly pulled his head out of the torn burlap.

After Toyota chewed through his friend's restraints, he and *It* began setting the others free. Toyota explained how ridiculous it was for anyone to use a cloth gag on a Didelphi when they are so easily chewed through. Their loud and frantic attempt to escape ended when the wagon came to an abrupt stop. Everyone froze. The only sound they could hear was the rain beating heavily on the canvas top. Evan had a hint of fear in his eyes as he was still tied up and gagged. The strongest of them was still helpless.

They all stared at the front tarp flap where they knew the driver must be sitting just on the other side.

The flap flipped up and a large, hooded head popped in, tusks and all. "Will you shut it!" a gravelly-voiced Fallon said as he jerked his hood back. It was the one-eyed Jagger. "For crying out to blazes! You're making enough noise to startle the dead. Does the word 'covert' mean anything to you?"

"Isn't that the cabinet where we keep the dishes?" Toyota offered proudly.

"No, my little and intellectually deficient friend, that's the cupboard," Lucas said, while shaking his head.

"Oh, I know. It's the thing we put our mugs on so they don't leave a ring on Miss Buttka's tables at the pub?" Toyota smiled.

It put his hand to his forehead. "Coaster, that's a coaster."

Toyota gave Jagger a sincere and disappointing look and said, "Then nope. We have never heard of a 'covert' before."

Jagger's yellow face turned orange with frustration. A large four-fingered hand set lightly on the big Fallon's shoulder as a familiar voice next to him could be heard saying, "Be calm. They are just scared."

The friendly face of Kandula came though the tarp flap next to Jagger. "Hello little ones. I am sorry we had to do this to you, but we had to ensure that no one followed us. Be patient and quiet until morning and all shall be explained. Also, do not stick your heads out of the canvas. It is imperative that you are not discovered," he said, and started to pull his head back out but stopped. "Oh ... and could someone please set Evan free. He looks most distressed."

It was well into the morning when the wagon pulled to the side of the road and the rain gave no sign that it was going to ever ease up. Jagger hopped down from the driver's seat and, as could be imagined, he made a sizable splash in the mud. After slipping a few times he got to the rear of the wagon and used some poles to hold the rear tarp flap up as a canopy.

The kidnapped crew piled out of the wagon and huddled under the makeshift shelter. Having discovered bedrolls and packs full of their gear, they were all dressed for the weather and what looked to be a lengthy journey. *It* was even wearing his white fedora hat.

Kandula came around from the side of the wagon and said, "As you may have guessed, you will not be visiting the Palham village today as planned. Instead, you will make your way to the hooman city of Yolan-rym."

"I thought we were going to wait until after the rainy season for that," *It* asked, with a tilt of his head.

"That's what we wanted everyone to think," Jagger added.

Kandula pulled his cloak in tighter around his neck and leaned in closer. "It was decided that you four would leave at a time most unlikely. This way you will be harder to track, and it will be sometime before anyone knows you're gone. Since we do not know how, or by whom, the information regarding *It* and his movements had been discovered, we thought it best to keep your travel plans secret. Only Jagger and I know where you were dropped off and which route you will be taking."

"How will we not be noticed missing?" Evan asked.

Jagger gestured behind them. "Because everyone back there knows you are leaving today for Palham. They will even see your wagon head off that way. We have decoys making a trip in your stead. This way, the only two people who know where you are will be me and Kandula. So, if word gets out about your location, I'll know that Kandula is a spy and I will dispatch him myself," Jagger said candidly.

Sydney gasped, "You can't do that!"

"Don't worry little one, he is just pulling your tail," Kandula assured her, with a chastising glare to Jagger.

Jagger gave a reluctant shake of his head. "Sure, a joke. Just a joke."

"What about my people? I am expected to report into the Regents Council," Lucas asserted.

Jagger shook his head. "No, you won't be reporting into the Council. We have no idea who is after the boy, so we assume anyone could be. That includes the Aves."

"So, we won't be in contact with anyone the whole time? What if we need help?" *It* said with much apprehension.

"If we sent anymore warriors or chaperones with you, it would raise suspicions." Jagger pulled a parchment from his cloak and spread it out on the wagon bed. "You can see by the mark here where we are dropping you off. Follow this line ... and I mean only this line, to the hoomans. Do not deviate! You will notice this is not a direct route. That is intentional."

Evan looked it over and pointed to a spot on the map. "I'm not one to complain, so this is just an observation, but this area here is almost into the Kroncal's territory."

Jagger nodded and winked his one good eye. "Yes. No one would expect you to go in that direction. And once you skirted passed the Kroncal's border, you should have a clear shot the rest of the way with trade roads. No one would expect to look for you traveling those roads. We're not saying that this is the safest route, but it is the last path anyone would think you to take."

He wiped away the rain droplets that had beaded up on the wax coating covering the map and rolled the parchment up. Jagger handed the map to Evan and pulled him away from the others. "I know I don't have to remind you, but I will. You are his Host Custodian. If you should fail to protect him ... if you fail to get him to his people ... you can never return to the herd."

Evan breathed in deep with his chest puffing out. "I will die before I fail."

"I know you will, and our Lord knows it as well. You've shown courage in battle and an exceptional tactical mind, but it is your devotion to the herd that has been most noticed. As Lord Stronghide would put it, 'you have a mighty resolve' and you know how he is always going on about bolstering resolve."

Evan smiled. "He loves that resolve."

"Yeah, he does." Jagger put his hand on Evan's shoulder. "But then, so do I ... and to that end, I need you to know that I understand that you are friends with the boy ... I can't see how that is, but I understand it ... just know that your place within the herd is secure as long as the boy reaches Yolanrym ... even if he is dead."

Evan's body tensed, and his eyes gave away his rejection to the idea, but he nodded in obedience.

While Jagger and Evan went on to discuss evasion strategy, Kandula pulled out a mystic's pouch identical to his own, but much smaller. He handed it to Sydney and said, "You will need this."

Sydney quickly grabbed the pouch. "No way. This is so cool. My very own shaman mystic bag!" She opened it up and rummaged through the contents. Amazingly, her hand reach in far deeper than the outside of the bag appeared to allow. With a loud squeal, she pulled something out. "A smudging stick." She shoved it in Toyota's face. "Look, Toyota, I got my own smudging stick!"

"Wow! Awesome!" The monkey-opossum was excited for her though he wasn't sure why a bunch of partially burnt sticks were so important.

She leaped onto Kandula and hugged his neck as hard as she could. Though he could barely feel it, his eyes glistened with affection. "Yes, hugging. Not a Fallon tradition, but your appreciation is not without reciprocity."

She dropped back to the ground, put the smudging stick back in the pouch, and hugged it to her chest.

"I have also added a kit to Evan's backpack. I'm sure he won't notice the extra weight. It contains items to aid in finding your direction and other useful mysticism," Kandula told her, but then paused to look deep into her eyes. "I expect you to bring them back when you return to continue with your training."

"Return? I thought I was going back to my people."

"Your Prominence and I had a discussion. We both agree that you should return to your shaman studies. You will then bring back what you have learned to the Seeuradi. This will hopefully be the start of a prosperous alliance."

"What about me?" Toyota said with a grin.

"What do you mean?" Kandula asked.

"Do I get anything?"

"Um, well, of course." The Fallon shaman pulled a bag from the wagon and dug through it. "Here we are." He brought out a very small brush and handed it to Toyota.

"Holy Giver! This is for me?"

"Yes, it is. And I'm sure no other Didelphi has ever even seen one of those."

"It is so awesome."

Lucas leaned down toward Toyota and said, "You don't even know what that is, do you?"

"I haven't a clue, but I'm the only Didelphi to ever have one."

Kandula snickered. "It is for brushing your teeth. The mystic effect is that it will allow you to make friends more easily. Clean your teeth with it twice a day and it should start working for you in just a few short weeks."

"I always wanted to make more friends. *It* was my first non-Didelphi friend, and now I can make more."

Jagger and Evan rejoined the group as everyone finished gearing up.

Jagger looked to *It* and said, "Maybe you will return to the hoomans and encourage them to align with the Giverkind again. Either way, I wish you luck. You weren't always annoying and irritating."

It laughed. "Not always?"

Jagger chuckled and extended his hand. *It* reached out with his hand, and his arm disappearing into Jagger's giant grasp as they shook. The Fallon warrior let go and pointed away from the road and into the woods. "Don't stay on this road. Head due west for two days and then follow the river north. It's all on the map."

The five took off into the woods. Sydney turned back before they were out of sight. "Will you finish teaching me the dragon in the smoke conjuring trick when I return? Mine is still just a blob-shaped puff of smoke."

Kandula gave out a snort of laughter. "Of course, I will, little one. When you come home."

The two Fallons on the road watched the motley group of unlikely friends disappear into the rain and woods.

"Don't you mean if she comes home?" Jagger said with a burdened concern.

"Hope, Jagger. Hope is what makes all things possible." Kandula wiped away at a rain drop near his eye.

NINETEEN

TROUBLES WASHED AWAY ...
HUMAN BOY AND ALL

The drenching rain showed no sign of letting up and the leather ponchos they wore kept out most, but only most, of the dampness. After having left Jagger and Kandula, the young ones spent half of the day climbing down into the valley west of the main road and then took the better half of the afternoon crossing the great prairie.

Evan slogged along the mucky bottom of the valley with Lucas and *It* on each flank. By the looks of it, they had already suffered their first losses as Sydney and Toyota were nowhere in sight.

"How are they holding up back there?!" *It* called out to Evan over the pounding rain.

"You tell me!" He stopped and turned his back to the boy. Attached to the Fallon's huge pack were two makeshift hammocks, one on top of the other, covered by leather tarps. Sticking partially out of one hammock was Sydney's face with water droplets covering the lenses of her teal cat-eye glasses. Some of the droplets were trapped in the empty spaces once occupied by cheap rhinestones. Her eyes were closed as she slept soundly; a tiny rivulet of rain ran between two freckles and dripped from her cheek. *It* peeked under the tarp of the other hammock to catch Toyota digging way too deep into his nose with his finger.

Toyota stopped but left his finger where it was. "So, are we there yet?!"

"We have a few days to go before we hit the river and turn north! Then we have another 534 miles before we can head back east!" *It* yelled out over the rain.

"So ... no, then?!"

"Yes. No!" ***It*** dropped the flap and slapped Evan's side to indicate that he could turn back around.

"And?!" Evan grunted.

"All is well with the guests at hotel Evan!"

"Good." Evan began walking again, but he was having to go slower as Lucas and ***It*** struggled with the deep sucking mud. Lucas' talons made it easier to walk than the boy's human feet, but not by much. Evan's strength negated the fact that his weight forced him deeper in the mud.

"Can I ask you a question about something I've been wondering?" ***It*** shouted out over the down pour.

"Would you not ask me if I said no?" Evan grumbled loudly.

"Probably not."

"Then ask away."

"That day when we first met?"

"You mean the one where you embarrassed me in the field of battle and made me the tonk butt of many jokes?"

"Yeah, that one."

"What about it?"

"You could have killed us easily ... Sydney and me that is."

"Yep."

"Why didn't you?"

"I didn't kill you because I was ordered to bring you to our Lord."

"What about Sydney?"

A hint of a smile lifted the side of Evan's lip under one of his massive tusks. "Look her in the eyes and tell me that you could possibly harm her in any way."

"I know what you mean. I got sick to my stomach just at the thought of her being mad at me for making fun of her magic stone trick. I couldn't even think of her physically getting hurt."

"Me too," the big Fallon said, giving in to a full smirk.

"She got under your skin."

"Like a bore leach," Evan chuckled, as ***It*** stumbled from laughter.

Lucas turned to face the two. "I do so much hate to interrupt, and I beg your pardon, but has anyone else noticed the thunder is getting louder?" Lucas interjected with his usual flare and flourish, though the mud and rain hampered his ability to appear graceful.

"Yeah, it did seem to get louder when we passed that bend by the canyon a few moments ago," *It* added.

Evan stopped and aimed his large floppy ear to the sky. His face tightened. "That's not thunder—move!"

It and Lucas began slogging through the muck harder and faster, but they couldn't nearly match the pace of those giant Fallon steps. Evan turned back to them. "Let's go, we have to make it to higher ground!" he yelled, but then his eyes popped open wide as he saw thirty Ashmen coming up from behind them. "I said, move it!" He took a few steps back in their direction and swooped Lucas up in his left arm, and *It* in his right arm. *It* clung to Evan's right bicep and was facing back to now see, with a higher view, the reason they were running.

Sydney's paws stretched out inches from *It*'s face. She yawned and said, "Good afternoon, I think." She wiped the water from her glasses and looked behind them to see the small army of Ashmen catching up to them. "What did you boys do while I was sleeping?"

"It wasn't us!" *It* cried out.

Toyota stuck his head out of his hammock and started to say something when he saw the Ashmen. He quickly pulled the flap back over his face and retreated further into his hammock.

It hollered out to Evan, "Does this thing have a higher gear?"

"What?" Evan yelled.

"Faster, you have to go faster!" he hollered frantically, with his fingers trying to dig into Evan's poncho for a better grip.

Evan took a moment to glance behind him and saw that the Ashmen were dangerously close. He grunted, tossing *It* up, and switching him over to his left arm where the boy smashed into Lucas. They were now held pressed against each other, face to beak.

"Hi," *It* said awkwardly.

Lucas turned his head with one eye glaring at the boy. "This is most inappropriate," Lucas gasped.

It looked back over Evan's shoulder at the oncoming mob of death. "It could be worse."

Evan continued running, but with his one free hand he pulled his sword.

"Evan, they're on us!" *It* yelled, as the Ashman caught up to the slower moving Fallon. Looking to one side, Evan brought his sword up as the first Ashman pulled up alongside him, but the mighty Fallon held his swing. He glared at the creature, who glanced back at him with a face flush with fear. Evan's brows arched with an unasked question about the creature's bizarre behavior as the Ashman sped away.

To his left and his right, Ashman after Ashman passed Evan until he was literally surrounded by them. It was as if they were all one panicking herd stampeding together. Sydney crawled halfway out of her hammock and was hanging on the side of Evan's back. She looked down and saw a few of the Ashmen running alongside of Evan. They glanced up at her and she smiled—"Hi?"

They continued running with a dreaded fear on their faces. Sydney looked back behind the mob and called out, "Hey guys, I don't think they are after us."

"What do you mean?" *It* shouted.

Sydney crawled on top of Evan's shoulder and pointed behind them. "They're running from that."

It and Lucas looked back to see a wall of water thundering through the valley.

"What is that?" *It* yelled.

"That, sir, is most commonly called a flash flood" Lucas remarked with a false sense of calmness.

Sydney scrambled down to Evan's chest and held on to his tusks as she swung herself in front of his face. "I think you're going to want to see this."

Evan glanced back with Sydney still dangling from his tusks. The leather around his eyes wrinkled with wide creases in his mustard skin as his eyes sprung open. The crest of the wave was taller than him.

By now most of the Ashmen had passed Evan and turned on a slight angle, headed for some higher ground near a small cliff. Evan's face cringed, as he must have realized he had no choice but to do the same. He would have to worry about fighting the creatures after they got out of the way of the oncoming flood.

Though the ground was still slippery, it was firming up with less mud for them to sink into. Evan put his sword away and grabbed *It* in his right hand. In one swift ducking move, he set both *It* and Lucas on the ground while still at a gallop. The boys hit the ground running alongside of Evan as they reached the cliff wall.

Many of the Ashmen were struggling to climb the wall when *It* and his friends arrived. The creatures scratched and clawed in a frenzy. For a brief moment they paused. Their evil-looking faces stared pleadingly at Evan. Without any words, a silent agreement dictated that killing each other would have to wait until after they delt with their mutual dilemma.

"So now what do we do?" Sydney asked while perched on top of Evan.

Evan reached up and plucked her off his shoulder. With a grunt he said, "This," as he threw her skyward toward the top of the Cliff. She missed the ledge, but there were plenty of roots hanging out of the cliff wall near the top that she was able to grab onto. In a flash she had latched on and scrambled up over the edge.

"Okay, now that we know that works." Evan took off his pack and dropped it to the ground. Toyota came rolling out from under the leather flap and was now covered in mud. Evan grabbed a length of rope that he pulled from the pack, and then grabbed Toyota.

"What's going on?" the muddy Toyota asked, as Evan tied one end of the rope around the Didelphi boy's waist.

"Tie it on to something solid!" Evan barked.

"Tie what on to …" Toyota tried to say.

Toyota was in the air before he finished asking his question. Evan had launched him harder and higher than he did with Sydney. Toyota flew up toward the edge. As he reached the top, Sydney reappeared to wave at the group. He smacked hard into the girl and they both went tumbling backwards and out of view.

Up on the cliff, Toyota stood with the rope around his waist. "I think he wants me to tie this to something."

"There! That tree!" Sydney squealed through the whipping wind and rain, as she pointed to a large tree with massive roots coming up out of the ground.

Toyota quickly scampered over and began weaving in and out of the root system until the rope was snug. Sydney leaned back out over the edge with one foot holding onto the rope. "It's tied!"

Down below, Evan looked at *It* and Lucas and hollered out, "Okay, go for it," but before either one of them could grab a handful of hemp and climb up, they were mobbed by Ashmen grasping for the rope. Evan tried to push them back, but there was too many of him.

"Now what do we do?" *It* said.

"The only thing we can do," Evan said as he grabbed Lucas, lifted him up, and put him in his hand like he was a shotput. With another loud grunt, he thrusted Lucas into the air, who flapped his wings a few times to gain a few extra feet and reach the root system hanging over the edge of the muddy wall.

Evan began throwing the packs up to Lucas and Sydney who caught them and pulled them over the edge. All that was left was for Evan and *It* to get up. A few of the Ashmen managed to make it up the rope to the beginning of the root system, but everytime one was about to peek over the edge, Sydney's staff shot out, knocking them off the rope. A gleeful yip followed each strike.

The rushing water had finally reached them and came crashing down, washing most of the Ashmen further down into the valley. Evan's hulking body was withstanding the brunt of the first waves as he held *It* high out of the water. He put the boy on the rope and yelled at him to climb.

It reached up and climbed hand-over-hand until he made it to the roots. "Come on, use the rope!" he yelled back to Evan.

Evan began climbing, but the water was slamming against him, forcing him off to the side. He clenched his teeth and growled, with his muscles straining to not let go.

It got to the top and continued to yell, "Climb!"

Evan was making some headway, but the water was rising fast and pulling at him as though the current was alive and hungry.

It grabbed hold of the rope and yelled to the others to grab hold as well. They jumped into action and jerked as hard as they could, but Evan was nearly a thousand pounds without the added pressure of the water.

"Pull!" *It* shouted, but the rope wasn't moving at all.

"He's too heavy!" Lucas cried out.

The water was rising fast, but so was Evan. As long as he hung onto the rope, he would continue to rise up alongside of the cliff. *It* scooted along the side of the cliff until he saw that Evan was nearly at the roots. The Fallon began grabbing at the tangled mess branching out from the cliff face as he tried pulling himself up, but it was obvious to his friends that his strength was failing.

It climbed partially down the roots and grabbed hold of the Fallon's arm. The boy saw the look on Evan's face and knew that his Host Custodian, his friend, was going to give up and let go.

"Don't you do it! Don't you scrabb'n do it! Hang on!" *It* screamed as he pulled harder and harder. "Ahhhh!" He screamed as he strained. Then he felt his body begin to tingle. He was hit with an intense and sharp vibration throughout his whole being. Deep black lines veined out across the whites of his eyes as Evan and the rope began to move. The boy's face was red from the exertion.

Evan looked up and saw, for the first time, the black veins within the boy's eyes. A look of fear crossed the Fallon's face—was it the rising water, the boy's incredible new strength, or the demonic blackness in *It*'s eyes that gave the young Fallon his first real experience with fear?

With one last scream, *It* pulled as hard as he could, bringing Evan partially out of the water and into the roots, but in doing so he threw himself off balance and the large root he was standing on cracked and gave way, as the boy tumbled into the rushing water.

It looked back to see Evan clinging to the roots. Evan's eyes gave away his concern for the boy, as his human friend disappeared around the bend.

The turbulent water roared and rushed through the valley. Large bubbles broke the surface just as *It* appeared from the murky depths, gasping for air. He drifted helplessly as he did his best to swim towards the shore with the white churning water. Running out of strength himself, he reached the edge and grabbed onto some tree branches hanging low over the water. It took him a few agonizing moments, but he dragged himself up and onto the bank. He sat there breathing heavily when he saw something in the water near a fallen tree.

A young Ashman was clinging for his life. He couldn't have been much older than *It*. *It* got to his feet and stumbled over to the tree. He reached down to give a hand to the creature. The Ashman looked hesitatingly at the human boy.

"Come on, grab my hand or you'll die!" *It* hollered reassuringly to the Ashman boy.

After a few moments the creature reached out and took *It*'s hand. *It* pulled him to the shore and far up onto the bank. He smiled at the ashy creature while trying to catch his breath. This just may be the opportunity for a truce, and even a bond between their races.

"That was a close one," *It* said, still grinning. He turned his head and began looking around their surroundings, which is why he didn't see the young Ashman pull out a dagger that he wiped across his tongue.

When *It* looked back to the boy, the young Ashman plunged the dagger into his chest, and *It* fell back to the ground with blood running from his wound.

"Why?" *It* said with a bewildered look in his eyes. "Why?"

The creature jerked the knife out of *It* and raised it high above his head again to strike a final blow—*Thunk*—the Ashman boy flew backwards as a tire iron hit him in the head, knocking him unconscious.

Toyota and Sydney ran up to *It,* who was lying on his back staring at the sky. The pouring rain splashed down into the pool of blood bubbling up from the hole in his leather jerkin. He glanced over to his friends with his body trembling. "It's … It's my birthday today," he whispered, with his tears being washed away by the rain and a wiry smile disappearing from his lips.

As the human boy sank into darkness and the vision of his friends faded away, he heard Toyota cheerfully saying, "Happy Birthday."

A sporadic, yet constant tapping sound echoed in *It*'s ears. He wasn't so much annoyed by it as he was curious. Opening his eyes, he saw tree limbs high above him covered with leather tarps; holes and weak seams let the rain leak through. He leaned up to see Evan, Sydney, Lucas, and Toyota gathered around a small fire just under the edge of the tarp roof. Looking at his chest under his shirt, he saw that he was healed, but he had a vertical blackish scar near his sternum with some green pus around its edges.

"How long was I out?" he uttered, with his body shivering and weak.

"Oh, my Great Giver!" Sydney squealed as she bounded over to him and hugged him tightly.

"Ow!" *It* yelled and reached for his chest. Sydney pulled back when she realized she hurt him.

"Sorry," she squeaked.

Evan stomped over in an instant. "What in the scrabb'n world were you thinking?" he yelled. "You don't die for me! I die for you!" he pointed a thick finger at the boy. Evan's face glowed orange with anger.

The others moved over to be by *It*'s side. They glared up at Evan, both astonished and confused at his behavior.

Evan paused as he saw in the eyes of the others that he was way out of line. "Well ... dying is my job. Not yours," he huffed in embarrassment. "Besides, you had the others here scared half to death. Don't ever do that again," Evan said as he put his hand to the boy's head, clumsily checking for a fever.

Sydney slapped the big Fallon's hand. "Get out of there! That's my job. You don't see me stomping around like a big oaf and bellowing, do you?" Sydney scolded. She turned back to *It* and put her hand on his forehead. "Your fever broke."

"What fever?" the boy asked.

"You've been unconscious and unresponsive for three days," Lucas said, staring down at the boy with authentic concern.

"Three days?" *It* moaned.

"It shouldn't have taken that long—you became so sick. I think there was some kind of poison or something on the blade. You're going to need to be much more careful about who you try to save," Sydney chided him.

"Why did he do it? I was helping him. Why would he stab me?"

"Because that is his nature. You are going to have to learn that some things are just evil and there is no changing it," Evan grumbled.

"Yeah, no more trusting bad things to not stab you," Sydney squeaked.

Lucas stood upright, shaking his head with his feathers puffed and ruffled. "I am in agreement that your judgement in these matters needs be tempered with a healthy measure of prudent consideration."

"I got stabbed, and you guys are mad that I helped someone? Why am I the only one noticing this?"

"Hush, now. I think you're getting delirious," Sydney said, while placing her paw to his head.

"Well, hanging around nutters like you guys will make anyone delirious," he breathed out heavily and gave up trying to understand their brand of insanity. "So, what happen to the boy who stabbed me?"

The group shared tentative glances at one another. They couldn't have looked any guiltier.

"He .. took off." Sydney squeaked out slowly.

"Down the river." Evan added.

"I thought you threw ..." Toyota started to say to Evan when Sydney kicked him in the leg.

"We believe he is with his people," Lucas said.

"Good. I was afraid you would have hurt him ... and so you say it's been three whole days, huh?" *It* asked.

"Yeah, the big guy has been carrying you in my hammock, or at least when Sydney said it was okay to travel," Toyota said, waddling back to the fire to finish preparing a bowl of something that looked like it might be edible.

"And if I was big enough to stop him, we wouldn't have moved you at all in the last few days," Sydney squeaked angrily in Evan's direction.

Evan snorted. "Right, and if we stayed in one place those Ashmen that didn't die would have hunted us down and killed us in our sleep."

"He did the right thing," *It* said, while grasping Sydney's arm to calm his little friend down.

"Okay, enough is enough. Now it's time for me to do my job," Toyota said as he brought the bowl of something to the boy's chest and began spooning a black liquid into his mouth.

It couldn't say a word as Toyota began shoveling spoon after spoon of the spicy-tasting concoction into the boy's mouth. Of course, *It* didn't mind, as he was starving, and drank in as much of the soup as he could, though with much difficulty swallowing. "Wow, this stuff looks nasty, but it's really not that bad," *It* said, as he stopped Toyota's hand for a moment.

"It's all in the seasonings," Toyota said and then leaned in close. "But be careful, I added a little tarin root for a kick."

So, with the fire keeping them warm and their enemies being far away, the group felt that staying the night where they were was a grand idea. It might even give them time to dry out a few things.

They sat around the fire in silence. Occasionally *It* caught them looking at each other as though a lot was being said without a word being spoken. It wasn't long before Evan had to bring up the most obvious question burning in the back of his head. "So, what's up with the black lines in your eyes?"

"Actually, I think it's more relevant, or imperative, to ask how a one-hundred-and-ten-pound human boy was able to pull a half-ton Fallon out of the flood water," Lucas asked, tilting his head and raising his cheekbone as if to smile.

"Yeah, what gives with that?" Sydney squeaked excitedly.

"I have no idea," *It* offered weakly.

"Has it happened before?" Evan added with a snort of his trunk.

"A few times. The first was before the Host Custodian Ceremony."

"I think it's fascinating!" Sydney chittered.

"You think that's fascinating? Hand me your healing stone," *It* groaned as he reached his hand out.

Sydney dug her paw into her pouch, brought out the stone, and handed it to him. *It* held it out in front of them. "Rizon," he said with a wince, but nothing happened. "Wait a second. This happened last time. It may have to warm up, I don't know." He said the word over a few more times and nothing happened.

"You know, I don't know much about mysticism, but this doesn't feel very fascinating," Toyota grumbled, with a very disappointed look on his face.

"I don't get it. It worked before," *It* groaned.

"If I might interject, what were the particulars of the situation when this has occurred in the past?" Lucas asked.

"Well, there was the time when I was rushing to make it to the ceremony where Evan became my Host Custodian, and the time when I made this stone shoot up into the sky after I upset Sydney."

"And when you were trying to pull me out of the water," Evan included, with another shake of his gigantic head.

"Interesting. It appears evident that your mysticism is activated, or is utilized, through your emotions," Lucas surmised.

"I got an idea. Hold out the stone again, but this time don't use your brain to try and talk the stone into rising. Hope or wish for the stone to rise," Sydney suggested.

It held out the stone in front of him. He began to focus on the stone rising, but then realized he was thinking too hard. He closed his eyes for a moment and thought about the bright sky and the clouds and of his friends. He opened his eyes and began to open his mouth to say the word, but somehow, he knew he didn't have to say anything, so he thought the word "*Rizon.*" His eyes flashed with the black lines that instantly faded back to white as the stone shot up through the tarp above their heads, high into the sky, and out of sight.

In unison they all breathed, "Wow."

It motioned to the others. "Move back everyone." They all moved back, except Toyota.

"Why?" Toyota asked, but it was too late for him to get a reply, as the little stone fell out of the sky and slammed hard into his foot. He yelped, while jumping up and down holding his throbbing appendage.

"I told you to step back," *It* snickered, but winced with some pain to his chest.

Sydney bent over and picked up the stone. She clasped it in her hand and looked to him. In a half whisper born from shock, or maybe awe, she said, "You're a mystic."

"How can that be? I know nothing about magic," the boy questioned, as he was visibly a little concerned.

"As I understand it, mysticism chooses you. You don't choose it," Evan replied.

"So, what do I do now?"

"Well, you'll have to find out what kind a mystic you are, and then get trained. That means you'll have to find a diviner to perform a mystic identification enchantment, which is really scrabbed up since we just left Kandula a few days ago. He could've done it … and we will have to find someone to take you on as their student," Sydney chittered on in her factual tone.

"What if I don't do all that stuff? What if I can't find someone to help me?"

"If I may, based on mysticism history, you'll be labeled as a wild, or feral mystic among the mysticism community, and eventually be driven mad by the chaotic magics in your head," Lucas offered unreassuringly.

"What's a feral mystic?" *It* asked, as he was a little freaked out.

"Just what it sounds like. A mystic who is not focused and trained to corral their powers. They typically leave society either by their own choice, or not, since they can be a danger to those around them," Evan grunted, annoyed that there was yet another possible setback looming over their heads.

"Like the Feral Mystic of the Bloody Forest," Sydney squeaked with an eerie tone.

"Who of what?" *It* asked.

"It's nothing. Just a legend. A ghost story about a feral mystic who supposedly lives in a make-believe forest. As kids we were told not to venture far away from home or the Feral Mystic will come out of the Bloody Forest to get you—he's just a made-up story," Evan said dismissively.

"No! It's true. He exists. No one knows what he looks like. He roams around as a cloaked figure, more of a shadow than a real person. He is forever seeking something. Anyone who crosses his path is never seen or heard from again," Sydney tried to say in a spooky voice, but her squeaking made it sound more silly than scary.

"So, how long before I turn feral?" *It* asked jokingly.

"Actually, the becoming feral part is real." Evan replied.

"What? You're kidding, right?"

"Nope. When we reach the hooman kingdom you will need to seek out a diviner to discover what category your mystic powers will manifest in and begin training so you don't turn feral," Evan said with a touch of sincere concern to his voice.

"Agreed. I recommend we retire and get some much-needed respite. We can get an early start in the morning," Lucas offered with a respectful flourish to the group.

"Is anybody worried about my foot?" Toyota whined.

"I'll take care of it, you big baby," Sydney squeaked.

It's face was frozen, stunned by the knowledge that he may turn feral and become an outcast of society. Everyone else prepared for bed as is usual for the end of a normal day in the world of Fentiga.

TWENTY

CAN'T FOOL AN OLD SQUIRREL

Lord Stronghide's office was lit mostly by a blazing fire in the fireplace and a few sporadically placed candles. Like many Fallon dwellings, the room was humble and had just a large desk, two storage cabinets, and a few chairs. A large chest was stowed in the corner under a shelf. There were very few locks in the whole city, as nobody would try to steal from a Fallon, but there was a lock on Lord Stronghide's chest, and it was open.

Jagger, Kandula, and Stronghide stood around a table peering over a map. A loud, fast rapping on the door had them all looking up suddenly, as they weren't expecting visitors. Stronghide nodded to Jagger who lumbered to the door, while the Fallon Lord rolled up the map and casually walked to the chest where he locked it away.

Jagger opened the door and Edroy practically stormed in with Susanne just behind him. The hawk Ave, though looking peeved, still maintained his decorum by flourishing his arms and bowing.

"I implore you to forgive this intrusion." He maintained his bow until Lord Stronghide spoke.

"You are not at all an intrusion. Please speak your mind."

"It has been several days, and the young ones have not returned," Edroy said as he stood upright.

"And the celebration is tomorrow," Susanne added.

"Surely, by now you have received word as to their whereabouts,"

Edroy insisted.

Lord Stronghide shot a glance to Kandula, who nodded back to him, and then he looked back to Edroy and Susanne. "Now is when we make our apologies, but I hope you will understand the necessity when I tell you that they never left here for the village of Palham."

"What is this?" Edroy screeched with his feathers puffing up.

"Where are they, then?" Susanne asked very concerned, but calm.

"With the risk that there may be an information leak, we agreed ..." Stronghide gestured to Kandula and Jagger, "... that we should lead everyone into believing that the boy would be returned to the hooman kingdom via a caravan at the end of the rainy season. Instead, we felt it was a better strategy to send him with a small entourage via a route unknown to anyone."

"Again, please forgive my impropriety, and I wish no disrespect, but when were you going to share this information with us?" Edroy practically hissed, as he was much more upset than the Fallons had assumed he would be.

Kandula cleared his trunk and then spoke. "We had hoped you would be understanding of the desperate need for secrecy in order to keep them safe. You are here in concern of their safety, correct?" He stopped with a questioning look on his face, while crossing his arms over his chest and leaning in toward Edroy. The old Fallon knew well that the slightest hint of neglected attention to an issue would send an Ave politician scrambling to align himself with the socially correct position.

"Of course, their safety is our impetus and primary concern here and no other. It is just customary for all members of the Giverkind Collective to be forthright with information concerning issues affecting the other races," Edroy said with a frustrated flourish of his hands, as he fought to contain his anger.

"I have to agree with Edroy here. I certainly understand your motivations, but it would've been nice to have been informed before now of the details," Susanne added, with some reluctance in agreeing to anything remotely supportive of Edroy.

"Nice? Not only was it not nice, but it was a betrayal to our Giverkind union. The Regents Council will be inconsolable!" Edroy finally snapped at Stronghide.

Seeing the threatening mannerism of the Ave, Jagger stepped forward with his hand to the hilt of his sword. Lord Stronghide raised his hand to motion him back.

"What's done is done. You have our apologies. When we have word of their arrival in the hooman kingdom, you will be the first to know," Stronghide assured them.

"That is all well and good, but I cannot return to the Regents Council with no knowledge as to where our representative is, as well as the human boy. What route are they taking?" the Ave asserted, while he struggled to regain a politically correct bearing.

Kandula narrowed his eyes as he listened to Edroy's pronunciation of the word human, but he said nothing.

Stronghide stepped over to his desk, and Susanne crawled up onto the desk to be closer to his height. The Lord went over the plans, giving them a succinct summation of the route traveled by Evan's unit, including every detail. Though Prominence Susanne was more than satisfied with the strategy as it was completely explained, Edroy's irritation with the situation was obviously personal. He was physically shaken, as if this sequence of events had some undisclosed impact that he was not willing to share.

After they were through, Edroy quickly excused himself from the gathering and left without accepting an evening drink to salute the end of a Great Giver day.

"Did anyone else notice that he failed to fulfill a social propriety?" Kandula pointed out to the group.

"That bird is more nervous than a chicken in a den of wholven," Susanne chittered.

"It is odd," Stronghide added, with a knowing glance to Kandula.

"Odd, my furry tail. There is something seriously bothering him." She looked up at the Fallons who were not hiding their guilt as well as they thought they were. "So, who's going to tell me what's really going on here?" she said, noticing their reluctance to offer up anything. Her eyes squinted. "What are you gentleman up to?" Again, the Fallons just stood looking as guilty as could be. She held her paws down by her side as she spoke an incantation under her breath. Her hands began to glow with a purplish hue. "Don't make me angry, you wouldn't like me when I'm angry," she squeaked in her most menacing tone, which was still as cute as can be.

The three Fallons paused as they knew very well the destructive power of the tiny Seeuradi mystic. She stood staring at them with the tension growing. Just as she looked ready to release some terrible mystic force on them, she winked. "I had you going there, didn't I?"

Kandula snorted out louder than ever and chuckled uncontrollably. "I have so missed seeing you," he said between snorts.

Susanne gave in to a bout of chittering as well. "It's good to see you too, but seriously, what in all of Fentiga are you boys up to?"

Candles flickered around the walls of another sparsely furnished guest room in the Fallon central city of Utuska. Traveling trunks, sacks, and satchels were neatly stacked against the wall. The bed was covered with an ornate bright blue and red comforter blanket with gold trimmings. It did not look to be part of the room's standard decor.

A feverish scratching noise was the only sound heard, except for the occasional chirp of frustration. Seated at a large table was a nearly matured Finch Ave wearing a taupe cloak with a bronze brooch. With his quill squiggling back and forth, he hurriedly wrote on a piece of parchment.

Slam!—The door flew open and smacked hard against the wall. The young Ave leaped to his feet and leaned back against the table as Edroy rushed in, flailing his arms in the air and ranting in a gruff, yet restrained voice.

"They cannot do this! It is inappropriate!" he screeched while still trying not to be heard by anyone beyond his room. A satchel at his foot was kicked across the floor, scattering its contents everywhere. He stopped to see his trembling assistant trying hard to meld into his table. Edroy stalked over to him with long strides and turned his bad eye and scar toward the young Ave.

"That is not how it is done ... is it?" Edroy screeched.

The milky white coating of his bad eye bulged around in circles as the black pupil under it struggled to focus on the boy. The Ave assistant cringed at the sight and struggled to find the appropriate thing to say, but fear had him at a loss for words.

Edroy screeched a little louder. "Well, is it?"

The Young Ave, now visibly shaking with his feather raised high, looked back into the pale revolting eye. His beak cracked open slightly and a wisp of a chirp made its way out as he replied, "No?"

Edroy raised a claw and ran one talon down the Finch Ave's beak and hissed slowly, disturbingly, "No ... it's not. And you know why it is not, dear Roseem?"

"No," Roseem managed to whisper.

"Because." He raised the other talons of his claw and began tapping on the boy's beak as he spoke. "They lack decorum ... etiquette ... convention ... protocol." He leaned in even closer and whispered with his warm breath falling on the boy's face. "And without these things, you are nothing. They are nothing! That is why we are the dominant race of this world."

"Yes, my lord," the finch-boy replied

Edroy sniffed loudly near the boy's mouth and then cringed. "Shush. Leave me," Edroy said, noticeably calmer as he pushed the boy's face away.

Roseem scrambled to gather up his writing materials from the table and shuffled to the door with his arms full.

"And do something regarding your hygiene—it's disagreeable," Edroy said with a shake of his beak.

"Yes, my Lord," the boy called out as he closed the door behind him.

Edroy made several laps around the room while grumbling to himself and occasionally throwing his talons dramatically in the air and back to his sides. With an exaggerated huff, he opened one of the boxes on the floor and pulled out a Glamour Mirror that he hung delicately on the wall. After checking out his image for a moment, he picked up the satchel which he kicked earlier and riffled through it. Not finding what he wanted, he huffed again and searched through the items on the floor until he found a small beige bottle that he lifted in the air while he hissed, "Yes!"

He returned to the mirror and uncorked the bottle. He raised it to his beak and poured a small portion of its contents into his mouth. He swished it around violently. Moving close to the mirror he opened his beak and spit on the glass.

With his free claw, he tapped the tip of his talon against the mirror and drew symbols in the spittle. When he was done, he whispered, "Discours-etal."

The surface of the mirror began to vibrate and then rippled as if it were liquid. After a moment, the surface was smooth again. Edroy stood gazing at the mirror—waiting. Before long, the liquid shuddered and rippled as a raspy voice emanated from the reflective liquid.

"I've been waiting. I expected you to reach out to me before now," the raspy voice said.

"Yes, well, I have been preoccupied with the responsibilities of my post and the incompetence that assails me in this barbaric Fallon ghetto."

"I don't care about your obligations, or your current lodgings. It is your function to me that matters. Keep in mind you are not my only asset."

"Spare me your hollow threats. I am not intimidated by your shadowy demeanor and network of unscrupulous minions … but, for the sake of our continued and mutually beneficial affiliation, I have gathered some intelligence for you."

"It had better be good."

TWENTY-ONE

DEATH OF A FRIEND

The rains had not let up, and the group was still making less progress than they had hoped for. As they came across a road headed north, they stepped out onto it and paused. The river was not far in front of them. Evan reached into a pouch on his belt and pulled out a small box with a glass top. He shook it around and gazed down into it. A shiny black liquid was splashed all over the box inside, but slowly the droplets began to move. Like miniature living blobs of dark goo, they crept towards the bottom of the box and formed the shape of an arrow.

The big Fallon pointed up the road. "The direction box says we need to go that way, north."

"You know, on C-Earth, they had an ancient device like that called a compass," *It* offered with no hesitation. "Of course, now we just use GPS."

"Why wouldn't you call it what it does? A direction box gives you the direction you need to go in. I've never heard anyone ask what compass they needed to go in," Evan snarled.

"Well, you don't call a sword a pointy, stabby metal stick either. You call it a sword ..." *It* froze for a moment as Evan glared at him. "But then I guess I see your point ... no pun intended," he finished, and stepped away.

Evan lumbered to the side of the road toward the woods.

"Aren't we supposed to stay on the road? Remember the direction box?"

It asked.

"I know we need to make up some time, but there is no cover on the road," Evan grumbled as he peered off into the woods where there was plenty of thick foliage to conceal their movements.

"It's just so slow going in there," *It* whined again.

"Not to mention bemiring to our garments," Lucas added with an air of disgust.

Evan shook his head with his tusks sweeping wide and breathed in deeply as he resisted saying something that was sure to be insulting. He turned back to step off into the woods.

Lucas shuffled over to the big Fallon and said, "The man who risks nothing, risks all ... I was once told that ... We need to weigh those risks here. Off-road we are sure to meet with delays and a greatly reduced pace. On the road we will be fleet of foot and make up for lost time, but if we are not disciplined and vigilant, we risk confrontation." Lucas paused to look Evan in the eyes. "It is apparent that our decision be thoughtful, and not founded in our luck but rooted solidly in our abilities."

Evan's face tightened. If he chose to leave the road to sneak through the woods, he was acknowledging that he lacked the skill to travel the road safely. So, he sighed deeply, then tightened his hands into fist with a stern resolve. "The bird may be right. We will stick to the road, but everybody keeps on their toes."

"But Lucas doesn't have any toes," Sydney chittered.

Evan leaned down to her level and grumbled, "Then he can keep on his talons." After a moment of silence, Evan stood back up and began walking.

It put a hand on Sydney's shoulder. "Good thing I didn't remind him that you have paws."

"Yeah. I know. Right."

By now they had all learned to follow Evan's lead when it came to strategy. He was just too good at it to ignore him. So, they began the long walk down an equally long road. Lucky for them there was a break in the rain, which gave them the opportunity to dry off a little.

As they walked, Toyota stumbled around and waddled at a snail's pace.

"What are you doing?" Evan sneered at him.

"I'm trying to stay on my toes. It is a lot harder than you might think," Toyota replied.

Evan's eyes twitched, and he rubbed at the bridge of his trunk but said nothing as he shoved Toyota towards the group.

The time for drying was short-lived as it gave way to an unexpected downpour that fell harder than before. Evan had informed everyone that this worked in their benefit, as it was harder for anyone to see them from a distance. They made up for some lost time.

With *It*'s injury still on the mend and hurting, the choice to stay on the road was an even better idea. Evan thought it best to continue that way for as long as they could, or at least until they made it to Deadman's Bog.

During a break for a cold meal, Evan brought out the map and went over it. He had stopped to do this twice before. His young companions gave each other concerned looks. They were beginning to doubt that he knew where he was going.

"Is everything all right?" *It* asked.

"Sort of." He pointed to the map while everyone leaned in to see. "This is the road I believe we are on, but it has us heading westerly and shows no sign of turning back north. If anything, we seem to keep going northwest."

"What difference does it make, whether we go northwest or north?" Sydney squeaked.

"Well, if we go this way north, we should come out somewhere near the east end of Deadman's Bog." He indicated an area on the map. "But, if we go too far northwest, we end up on the west side of the bog in Kroncal territory where we will most certainly die," Evan said, with his own style of earnest, yet dark sarcasm.

"So, that's a big difference, right?" Toyota whispered to Sydney.

It leaned down and whispered to Toyota. "It all depends on how you feel about dying, I guess."

Toyota raised his hand.

"Yes," Evan said with a look of regret on his face for what was about to come from the opossum-monkey's mouth.

"Oh, I'm just raising my hand to vote that we go the way where we don't die."

Again, Evan grabbed his trunk in frustration.

"You could always have Sydney climb up one of the taller trees to get our bearings." Lucas added.

Evan shook his head. "The rain is too hard and it's too close to night.

She won't be able to see much of anything. We're better off traveling a little further down the road and then finding some cover to spend the night. In the morning, she can tell us where we are if the weather permits."

It looked at the trees shrouded by the rain and was surprised that Lucas would even make a suggestion with such obvious support against it. Of course, he shrugged it off, as he had learned not to be surprised by anything that happened in Fentiga.

They traveled for another two hours before they were forced to seek out shelter for the night. They had reached a bend in the road with a large field to one side. Lucas suggested they camp there, but Evan pointed out that they would be too exposed with the morning light, so he guided them into the edge of the woods alongside of the field, but far off the road. This way they would have a strategic vantage point of the road when they approached it in the morning, while still remaining out of sight.

Exhausted from the weather and the travel, the group got their lean-to shelters up as the last shimmer of light was sinking out of view. Sydney pulled together some kindling to start a fire with a mystic incantation and powder that she had been using since they left several days ago. With a flip of her paw, she spread the powder in the air while she chanted.

It watched on, almost mesmerized, following the powder with his eyes as it glowed with the purplish hue and was surrounded in a black mist. When the granules landed on the wet sticks—*Thwok*—every tiny particle of moisture evaporated instantaneously. Sydney explained to him that this was a special kind of mysticism that enchanted the powder so that it would dry whatever it touched.

It paid less attention to her words than he did to the enchanting aura created by the mystic magic itself. Each time he saw the glowing mist, it felt like it beckoned to him, drawing him into it as though they were one, or at least meant to be as one; but then the spell ended, and the kindling was dry. It ignited quicker than a desert-parched log—a quite handy spell to know in these conditions.

Evan stomped over and eyed Sydney for a second. "We don't know where we are or who is near, so I don't want to risk a fire. It's a cold camp tonight," the mammoth cautioned her.

"Can I at least dry our clothing and bedding?"

"Of course," he responded.

Lucas waved his hand and bowed slightly to Evan, which meant he was about to say something using more words than was necessary. "I am not one to offend, and I am always inclined to defer to your knowledge in such matters, but I'm sure our performance and endurance tomorrow would greatly benefit from a night's respite where we are both dry and warm ... surely we could risk a small fire."

"We surely are not going to risk a fire, and if anyone is dragging behind tomorrow because their butts weren't dry and warm tonight, they will find their butts having more issues than being warm and dry with my boot stuck in 'em," Evan growled.

Not wanting to have Evan's boot in their butts, the group voted against having a fire. Lucas' feathers ruffled and his eyes narrowed. It was obvious that he wasn't happy, but they would rather see Lucas unhappy than see Evan unhappy. So, to avoid any further fire related discussions, a watch schedule was set up with *It* going first, Sydney second, Toyota next, then Lucas and Evan taking up the last two slots.

The rain continued hard all night, but the group had found some high ground where they did not have to deal with any flooding. Sydney's drying powder and enchantments made all the difference when it came time for sleeping.

It was glad he had the first watch because his chest was still hurting from the stab wound, and he knew he wouldn't be able to fall asleep right away. Even though Sydney had healed the boy's injuries, she told him that it would hurt for a while, as the poison had done a great deal of damage by the time she had discovered it.

When it was Sydney's turn to relieve the boy, she gave him a sip of the nasty liquid Kandula had once given him for his nerves. She told him it should help him to sleep more soundly and reduce the pain. He was definitely looking forward to some sound sleep.

During her shift, Sydney practiced with her feather and smudge stick by chanting softly and bringing the spirit of the Dragon to watch over her friends and provide his blessings.

Though she couldn't conjure the full-formed misty dragon like the one Kandula created, she was able to produce a large blob of smoke with what looked like deformed wings. It drifted out from the smudge stick and was waved on by the feather. Effortlessly, it passed over her sleeping companions until it reached Toyota, when a cold sharp breeze blew it out from under the tarps, dispersing it into the rain.

Sydney's face crinkled with confusion, but she shook it off and didn't think anything of it. Besides, she realized it was time to wake him for his shift at watch anyway, so why worry about his spirit in that moment.

As one who never had trouble sleeping, Sydney was off in dreamland moments after her head hit the pack that she used for a pillow. Toyota stood under the tarp at the front with his Didelphi Fighting Staff in hand. He didn't mind that *It* now called his a tire iron. They were friends, and that was all that mattered.

He waited for several minutes, listening to the sounds of heavy breathing coming from the sleeping adventurers, and then turned to look them over with that unnerving toothy grin of his. Seeing everyone was deep asleep, Toyota put his poncho on and went out into the rain. When he was sure he was far enough away, he pulled out his tiny hearing horn. Placing it in front of his face, he called out, "Hello ... hello." Toyota listened, pressing it tight to his ear, but got frustrated when nothing happened. He called out a few more times and just as he was ready to give up, the horn vibrated, and he heard a voice.

"I'm here. Tell me what you know," the raspy voice came out from the horn.

Toyota went on to inform the person on the other end about the surprise start of their journey to the human kingdom. He mentioned the route they were taking and how they were approaching from a direction that no one would think to look for them.

He described the flooding in the valley and how the boy, *It*, might have mystic powers. He also detailed how the mysticism gave *It* the strength to pull Evan up out of the water and how it gave him power over a stone that he shot into the sky. He even told him how the boy stupidly tried to save a drowning Ashman and was stabbed in the chest for his troubles.

When he finished telling the stranger everything he knew, the voice on the other end just said, "Good," and then the horn went silent.

"Hello. Are you still there?" Toyota spoke into the horn but got no reply.

As he walked along, making his way back to camp, he thought he heard something and stopped. He sniffed the air, but the rain suppressed any odors. It didn't matter that he couldn't smell anything, he was sure there was something else out there. He began walking slower and quieter and paying attention to every sound and every sight. As he came around a tree, a tall form stepped out in front of him. He hissed unintentionally and went to swing his tire iron, but the form grabbed it before he could.

"Who were you talking to?" the angry voice of Lucas demanded.

"What? Nobody. I wasn't talking to nobody."

"I heard you talking to someone. Who was it?" Lucas demanded again, but with more intensity in his voice. There were no proprieties being observed here.

"Are you nutters? There is no one out here for me to talk to. I was talking to myself."

"No. It didn't sound like you were talking to yourself. It sounded like you were betraying our friend."

"What? I had to relieve myself—I talk to myself while I do it." Toyota shoved past Lucas. "There is no Giver law against someone peeing and talking to themselves that I know of."

Toyota waddled back into camp under the fierce gaze of Lucas; the feathers on the Blue Jay's head and neck were puffed up high and ruffled.

By morning, the rain had eased up to just a steady drizzle. Evan quietly woke everyone and had them pack their gear. Sydney used some more drying incantations and powder as they put away the wet supplies.

Once they were ready, the group trudged quietly in the direction of the field. They got right up to the edge of the woods when Evan's eyes nearly jumped out of his head. He stopped dead in his tracks and motioned to the others to stand still.

"What is it? Sydney whispered loudly as she climbed up Evan and stood on his shoulders. She almost fell over backwards with shock. In the field between them and the road was a unit of what appeared to be mantis-insect looking humanoids just slightly smaller than a Fallon.

Sydney climbed down Evan's back and hung off his pack near the bottom. *It* and Lucas leaned in.

"What is it?" *It* asked.

"Very, very bad things."

Lucas opened his arms wide. "What?"

"Our brave and wise leader had us camping right next to a bunch of Kroncal warriors—there is a good chance we are going to die today." Her factual tone once again under-emphasized the seriousness of the situation.

"What is she saying," Toyota hissed.

Evan quietly turned around and leaned over so everyone could hear him. "We will need to go back in the direction we came and circle around. The damp ground should make it so that we aren't heard."

"I'll protect the rear, you lead the way," Lucas whispered.

Silent as the dead, they all turned to head back—*Crack!*—The sound of a snapping branch rang out through the peaceful morning air. Evan turned back to see that Lucas had his clawed foot on a large dead branch. By the cringing look on the Ave's face, it was obvious that he was the one who accidentally made the noise.

Off in the field, a horn blared out in the Kroncal camp and the giant insect warriors could clearly see the tall Fallon just inside the wood line.

"Run!" Evan yelled.

They all took off running, with Evan calling out directions as to where to turn. The forest was making it difficult for them to navigate, but the Kroncal were having the same issue. Unfortunately, though, they were gaining ground.

Sydney was bounding around from the ground to the trees to Evan's back, pretty much all over the place so that she could keep an eye on the Kroncals as her group tried to escape. This time, *It* was the one moving the slowest because he was still a little weak from being stabbed.

Sydney realized that even if Evan picked the boy up and carried him, they wouldn't be able to get away. She needed to give them more time.

The group came across a small clearing and charged right out into it. While bounding from a tree to Evan's shoulder, Sydney called out to him. "You keep going and get *It* out of here. I can stay around here where they can't reach me. I'll distract them. I'll catch up later." She leaped off his shoulder, ricocheted off the ground, and up into the trees behind them. She was out of sight in an instant.

Evan had no time to argue. She was gone too quickly. The others were unaware of her intentions, so they had no say either.

⎯⎯⎯⎯⎯⎯⎯⎯⎯⎯

Sydney clung to some limbs just inside the tree line. She could see her friends still had not made it into the woods on the other side of the clearing. The Kroncals came into sight behind her. She just needed to stall for a little bit. By the look on her face, she wasn't sure how she was going to do it, but Sydney was not about to let her hooman buddy die. He would get the time he needed.

She had to think quickly as to where it was now best for her diversion: the treeline or the open grass. The trees gave her an escape route, but then the Kroncals may just ignore her and continue on after the boys, as they were in clear view of the creatures.

"No," she decided angrily. The open field gave her plenty of room to dodge, strike and stall them. "Yes, the field," she said, though not completely convinced.

It was the fastest she had ever run. She headed out into the field again and turned to face the way she came. Instead of grabbing her staff, she reached in a pouch and pulled out her feather, while the other hand pulled out a handful of some white powder. She began chanting as she ran, swinging her feather widely around her head. The drizzling rain started to swirl above her in a mini twister; another trick she leaned from Kandula.

She now saw the Kroncals clambering out into the clearing. They had pincer-like mouths and an exoskeleton instead of skin. Grasshopper-like legs propelled them forward with long barbed tails trailing behind.

Like the tail, the outside of their arms and legs were also barbed. They were born wearing armor designed for war and killing. She saw all this and remembered the horror stories behind their atrocities. She had heard how they ate their prisoners alive—yet she kept running at them.

Sydney's only thought was that her friend *It* was destined to end the isolation of the races and bring the humans back to the council. She knew he had to live and fulfill his destiny. Nothing else mattered. "For *It* and for victory!" she screamed, as she charged at the hideous creatures.

The Kroncals were also charging hard and fast and in just a few breaths they would be on top of the squirrel-girl in their path. The swirling air above her head frightened none of them as they had most likely seen worse, or at least they may have thought they did. Regardless, this was most certainly going to be the first time they had faced an angry Seeuradi mystic.

The first Kroncal warrior leapt into the air with a sickle swinging wide and high over his head, bringing it down at the oncoming furry squirrel-girl. As the blade sliced through the air, Sydney dodged to one side, causing the sickle to miss and dig deep into the ground.

Sydney bounded onto the blade's handle and scurried up the arm and then the shoulder of the giant insect. When she reached the top, she stepped on the Kroncal's head and launched herself into the swirling twister of air above.

Closing her eyes tight, she threw the white powder into the swirling air while screaming, "Transdential!" over and over in a loud chant. The powder was dispersed into the whirlwind, and it immediately began drying anything it contacted.

As she fell to the ground with her eyes still shut, the other Kroncals swarmed in on her, but as each one entered the twister, the powder blew into their eyes and dried up every hint of moisture. The creatures grabbed at their eyes and made hideous loud clicking noises instead of screams. They clashed into each other and even began to blindly swing their weapons into the air. One Kroncal was struck in the chest by another's sword and he fell hard, landing on top of Sydney.

She squealed in pain as two of the sharp barbs penetrated her leather armor on her side and back. Gray, gooey blood poured out of the Kroncal and over the little squirrel-girl. She gasped a few more times, and then nothing.

The boys sped through the forest with muscles aching and hearts pounding.

It called out to Evan, "What's the plan here?"

"We must find a place to stand and fight!" Evan replied, as he came to a stop and gestured to their left. "This outcropping of stones can be our sanctuary for now. Here we make our stand—remember your training! May the Great Giver be with us and may the Dragon breathe fire to give us strength and power of spirit!"

They rushed over to the stones and put their backs against them. "Be sure to meet their eyes and read their movements. The Kroncal are insects and all that matters to them is your death ... and keep in mind they will devour you as their trophy," Evan said through deep forced breaths.

"Where is Sydney?" *It* yelled as he looked around. "Is she hiding?"

Lucas looked around, but then Toyota said, "She turned back in the field. I thought it was odd."

"What!" *It* screamed. "We have to find her! We have to go back!"

Evan grabbed the hysterical boy. "No! We will stand and fight. You must run and hide. Do what you can to survive." The mighty Fallon pressed the map and direction box into the boy's hands. "You know where to go. Take this map and the direction box. It will show you the way. Leave! Now!" Evan barked.

It began backing away from Evan.

"Yes, go. Tell your people what happened here. Bring them back to the council."

It took a few more steps. "No! I will not leave Sydney to die!" he yelled, as he dropped the map and box and turned back the way they came. He took off running as fast as he could.

"No!" Evan trumpeted loudly. "Stop him!" he ordered the others as they took off after the boy.

Lucas was faster than Evan and Toyota, so he was the first to catch up to *It*. He called out to the boy. *It* turned his head back to gaze at the Blue Jay. The whites of the boy's eyes were filled with black veins that appeared to be pulsing, while tears poured out the sides. In that moment, *It* looked back in front of him and raced away as if Lucas were standing still.

It stopped at the edge of the field and saw the Kroncal warriors slashing with claws and swords at something that the boy couldn't see. His white hat flew off his head as he streaked off into the field screaming with a rage that came from deep within him.

The Kroncals heard the ear-piercing sound and turned in the direction of *It*, though their vision was fuzzy at best. The small human reached the first Kroncal and launched passed while striking him in the back of the head like he was trained to. The insect dropped to the ground. As *It* hit the grass, he rolled under the striking tail of another creature and drove his stiletto into the Kroncal's knee. As the beast went down, *It* cracked him with his tire iron.

Dodging and striking, screaming and crushing, the boy finished off the remaining Kroncal. They laid spread out in the field covered in gray goo.

Breathing like a mad man, *It* looked around for signs of his friend. He saw a reddish-brown, furry tail sticking out from under the body of a Kroncal. The small human grabbed the creature and tossed it aside like a sack of feathers.

Now the girl was in full view, her red fur saturated with rain and gray Kroncal blood. There was no hint of breath. Her bottom jaw gaped open with her tongue having fallen out to the side. A tiny rivulet of water ran down its length, cascading off the tip.

It dropped to his knees and wailed with every ounce of pain rising to the surface. The drizzling rain ran over his face, mingling with salty tears, as the boy wept like never before—and hopefully never again.

TWENTY-TWO

DRY SOCKS AND RENDER BEASTS

Evan, Lucas, and Toyota stepped out into the clearing. They could see *It* kneeling on the ground and, even with the distance between them, they heard him sobbing. Lucas reached down to pick up *It*'s hat and wipe the mud from the brim. As they reached the boy, they stopped just short of Sydney's body. Evan breathed in deeply with a glistening moisture forming in his eyes.

No one knew what to say, until Toyota bobbed his head back and forth and remarked, "Not bad, but I would have gone with a little more tongue. It would have made her look deader."

It raised his face to the monkey-opossum boy. "What?" he said with the black lines retreating from his eyes.

From the ground came a faint whisper. "Are they gone?" Sydney squeaked.

It knelt there motionless, unable to move as Sydney painfully rolled over and sat up. "Wow, those thorns of theirs hurt. I think it broke the skin a little," she said, as she turned to show *It* her side. "Does it look like it broke the skin? It sure feels like it did."

The human boy dropped back onto his butt and sat quietly in a puddle of water and gray, gooey blood. He just stared at the squirrel-girl as she twitched her tail around and wiped at her glasses in an attempt to get a better view of her injuries.

Lucas looked up to Evan. "It may be prudent for us to be somewhere else when the boy regains his senses," he whispered. With a slight bow, he placed the hat on *It*'s head and backed away.

Evan joined Lucas. "Yep. My bet is that she makes his eyes go black again," the Fallon grunted as he looked around at all the Kroncal carnage in the field.

Toyota stepped between the two and asked, "So, what are we talking about?"

Back on the run and breathing hard, the five companions ducked in and around trees as they moved quickly to give themselves distance from the field of dead Kroncals. They got back to the road and stopped to catch their breath. *It* hadn't said a word since they left the clearing, and he was pretty much following the others on autopilot.

On the road, Evan walked cautiously over to the boy and put his hand on his shoulder. "Are you okay? I know she put quite a scare into us," Evan said, while glaring at Sydney.

She just stuck her tongue out at him and turned to talk to Toyota.

Seeing that *It* wasn't responding, Evan gave him a little shake. "So, you going to be alright?"

"Bugs!" the boy finally said.

"What?"

"You never told me they were bugs!" *It* said, trying hard not to yell.

"Well, I also didn't tell you that the green stuff you drink in the mornings is tonk milk." Evan replied.

"What? What does that even mean?"

Evan straightened up and shrugged as he changed his tone from concern to that of instructional. "It means that I didn't tell you everything about everything. Some things are going to be left out and you'll have to learn them as you go."

"Telling me that a possible enemy that I may encounter looks like a giant insect ... is way different than telling me that something I'm drinking is a bodily excretion from another creature. Which, by the way, is disgusting ... but albeit yummy."

"What difference does it make what they look like?" Sydney added.

It held up a finger at Sydney. "Oh no, I'm not talking to you yet. You don't get to have anything to say in any conversation with me, especially not until you have apologized for that stunt you pulled."

"That stunt may have saved your life," she chittered back.

"I don't know, I seemed to have done fine."

"You only did fine because you went all feral mystic out there. Not to mention, they were blind," she huffed back.

"They were blind?" *It* asked, feeling a little less proud of himself.

Sydney nodded her head yes and glared at him over her glasses. "They had drying dust in their eyes."

Evan interrupted. "*It*, you can't be using your mystics anymore. It's too dangerous." The wrinkled brow of his head made it clear he was honestly concerned.

"How am I supposed to control that? You guys are the ones who told me it's somehow activated by my emotions. Are you asking me to not feel?" *It* said, raising his voice more than intended.

"That isn't such a bad idea. You could use a little less emotional reacting," the Fallon added, with a few nods and gesture of his trunk.

It tried to put his finger in Evan's face, but he only got as far as his chest. "Like your lack of emotions has done you a lot of favors. And I wouldn't have had to lose control of my emotions if somebody didn't have us sleeping right next to a bunch of ginormous cockroaches!"

"Like anyone else knew they were there? Besides, we should have been able to get away from them easily enough," Evan growled back.

It turned to Lucas with a snarl. "Yeah, Lucas, what was up with that? You walk around all day and I hardly hear you, then the one time we need everyone to be quiet, you sound like a herd of dancing Fallon."

"Look, gentlemen, tempers are running a little high at the moment. We are focusing on blame when we should be concerned with next steps," Lucas encouraged the others, while attempting to take the heat off himself.

"Yeah, big guy, what do we do now?" Sydney asked Evan.

"Based on the mountain over there and what I believe this road is, we need to head due north until we reach the bog."

No one else said a word as they followed Evan's lead and left the road, heading into the woods. As they trudged through the mud and vegetation, Sydney scampered up to *It*.

"So, this whole thing where you're not talking to me ... how long does it last?" Sydney playfully asked.

"I can't tell you that. I'm still not talking to you."

"So, does that mean another few minutes, or in an hour, maybe?"

Lucas leaned down toward Sydney. "My little experience with humans, or at least this human to be particular, tells me that we have a long walk ahead of us and I doubt he will be talking to you very soon."

While listening to Lucas and Sydney, something struck *It* as odd, but he couldn't put his finger on it. Something the Ave said sounded janky, but the boy shrugged it off and sped up to walk along side of Evan.

~

Night fell and they had to camp once again. *It* was busy holding his socks out in front of a fire just underneath the edge of the tarp canopy while Toyota was stirring a pot of nose tantalizing food hanging over the flames. Lucky for *It*, he brought a second pair of socks to wear while the first pair dried. He was also lucky that Lucas convinced Evan that another cold night would make this grumpy crowd much grumpier. So, the Fallon leader acquiesced early in the discussion of setting up a warm camp.

Sydney was busy checking on her supplies, as she wasted most of the drying powder that she used in her mini tornado enchantment.

"And can you tell him that we do have enough powder left to dry his socks," Sydney squeaked over her shoulder.

"Hey, *It*, Sydney said you can use some of the drying powder for your socks," Toyota called out while stirring the pot only a few feet from the boy.

"Oh, and let him know I need to check the wound on his chest again before bed," Sydney added.

"So, *It*, Sydney said that she will also need to check the wound on your chest. You know where the Ashman stabbed you," Toyota said, pointing the spoon at the boy like he was stabbing him with it.

It glared up at the Didelphi. "Yes, I know where he stabbed me ... you can tell her that we can wait until morning to check it out."

Toyota stood up and looked over *It*'s shoulder toward Sydney. "That's a no go on the checking out the chest wound for tonight. He said you can look at it in the morning."

"You tell him that I'm not going to be responsible if there is an infection that I don't know about, and he gets sick again!"

"Hey, *It*, so Sydney said she's not gonna be responsible if you get sick again."

"The infection ... you forgot to tell him about the infection," Sydney squeaked out loudly, though she, too, was only a few feet from *It*.

"Oh yeah, she said something about an infection," Toyota included.

"No, you twogg. Tell him that there could be an infection inside ..."

Evan leaped to his feet. "For crying out loud! Will you stop already! All day! All scrabb'n day the three of you have been doing this and you're driving me nutters!" Evan barked while glaring at the two stubborn kids as well as Toyota.

"Well, he started it," Sydney squeaked.

"Yeah, so? She still hasn't apologized or even admitted that she made a mistake," *It* sniped back.

"Just stop with it, or I'll stop it," Evan growled, with an orange hue to his face and his trunk jetting straight out in front of him—he was done with their maddening gibes.

"What are you going to do?" *It* sneered in defiance.

"Yeah, what are you going to do?" Sydney chittered.

~

The fire crackled and hissed as the occasional raindrop hit the flames. Evan sat alone on guard duty. It was peacefully quiet. He looked over to the others. *It* and Sydney were tied together facing each other on the ground. They were trying not to look at each other, but then *It* sneezed a few times uncontrollably.

"Can you stop that?" Sydney said, but not in an overly complaining voice. She made sure to not rile Evan.

"Your fur is tickling my nose," *It* replied while trying to stifle another sneeze.

"Sorry, I can't help it."

"Ah ha, you said sorry."

"Well, I didn't mean that kind of sorry ... you tricked me," she squeaked, but then softened. "I am sorry, though ... for upsetting you, that is."

"I guess I'm sorry for being a total twogg about the whole thing."

"And you were a twogg," she chittered back.

"I know," he said with a smile. He turned his head to the side and lifted it up. "Hey, Evan. We're not fighting anymore. We're talking now."

"Yeah, we're all good now. Can you untie us?" Sydney pleaded.

"Yep," Evan said, while stirring the fire with a stick, but he didn't move other than that, and the kids were getting nervous.

"So can you untie us now, please?" *It* called out again.

"I can, but I think it best to leave you that way all night—and during that time, I would like the two of you to consider the phrase 'what are you going to do about it' while you try to get some sleep."

"Seriously?" *It* moaned.

"Seriously," Evan snickered.

The morning came, but the rain didn't. For the first time in a while, they had a long break in the showers. Sydney was snugged up next to *It* with her head on his chest and his right arm around her shoulder. Toyota was under his other arm with his head also on the boy's chest. Sydney opened her eyes when she got a whiff of something very rancid. In front of her face was the opossum face of Toyota with his closed beady eyes and gnarly teeth.

"Ah, yuk!" She jumped away and woke up the other two.

"What the … why do I smell like wet dog?" *It* said, then noticed Toyota was still snuggled up to him. "What gives?"

Toyota pointed to Sydney. "She looked so comfortable sleeping on you, and I thought I would try—best sleep ever!" Toyota grinned.

It wiped at his clothes as if that would help rid him of the stench. "Well, don't do that again … either of you … aww … now I reek!"

Evan chuckled as he handed each of them a biscuit and dried meat for breakfast. "You all reek to me."

It looked around searching. "Where's Lucas?"

"He promised not to make any noise, so I let him scout ahead for us. Eat up and then pack up. I want to make some good time today while the rain has stopped."

It's brow furrowed and he looked questioningly at his boot. He pulled at the top and looked down into the boot.

"What's wrong?" Sydney asked.

"my sock is gone. Someone took my sock." *It* whined.

They both turned to look at Toyota.

"Don't look at me. I don't wear socks." Toyota said with a shrug.

"Let's go! We don't have time for this! Eat and pack!" Evan barked.

It reached into his pack and retrieved a clean sock. "This place is so weird."

They finished breakfast and packing in record time and headed north. The mud made it easy to track Lucas, but Evan was a little peeved that the Blue Jay went much further ahead than he was supposed to. At one point, Evan stopped and froze in place.

"What is it?' *It* asked.

"His tracks head west."

"Why would he go west?" Sydney said, looking at the Ave talon prints in the mud.

"I don't know. Something could have spooked him, or he lost his bearing. Let's follow the tracks for a ways," Evan grunted as he moved on.

They continued walking and came to another clearing up ahead.

"That's what I was afraid of," Evan whispered.

"What?" *It* whispered back.

"More tracks. They're not Lucas'."

"What are they?" Toyota said as he stepped his foot into one of the tracks on the ground. It was more than three times the size of his foot.

"Render beasts," Evan breathed.

Sydney stood still, sucking in air, too scared to speak.

"What the heck is a render beast?" *It* asked, as he noticed Sydney's reaction to the mention of the creature.

Evan sighed. "The Kroncal use them for hunting and battle. They ... they can render the flesh from a grown Fallon in minutes ..." He paused looking cautiously around. "They must have found their friends. The ones we left in that field yesterday. If we're lucky, they're not sure what they're looking for. Let's head back east, and fast."

"What about Lucas?" *It* whispered almost too loudly.

"He knows the route we're taking. If he's alive, he'll find us," Evan answered coldly and turned back the way they came.

"Wait a minute. He's our friend. We can't leave him," *It* protested and grabbed Evan's arm as if he could actually stop the giant Fallon.

"Look at those tracks. There are at least three of those creatures out there, which means there are at least ten Kroncal with them," he snapped at the boy.

"We still can't leave him."

"Yes, we can. He didn't follow the rules, and now he has to accept the consequences. Besides, his tracks look newer than theirs. He may have seen them and avoided them by turning back east further up."

"Why would he come this way if those tracks were already there?" Sydney said with a twitch of her nose. "It makes no sense."

"Because he is a birdbrain who has spent too much time at courtly ceremonies in fluffy clothes," Evan snarled.

Toyota's forehead wrinkled. "Fluffy clothes?"

"Never mind. We'll have to meet up with him later," Evan growled one last time before heading off.

They followed him back the way they came. All the while, *It* couldn't get the thought out of his head that Lucas may be in trouble. He hated leaving him behind, but he also realized that if they went to help the Ave, everyone else would be at risk as well. It just made no sense to any of them why Lucas would go off by himself. He must have had a very good reason.

With the knowledge that the render beasts were out there somewhere, the kids moved with haste and covered a great deal of ground. They traveled all day, and there was no sign of Lucas. By nightfall they had reached another well-traveled road. They decided to spend the night off the side of the road, but there was much debate as to whether or not they should light a fire.

The concern was that Lucas would not see them to the side of the road and he may keep walking past if he was traveling at night. Evan made the argument that if Lucas did pass them in the night, then they would surely catch up to him before they reached the human city of Squall. After a little more heated discussion and a few hurtful comments from Sydney about Evan's weight and girth, it was dictated that there would be no fire.

In the morning, they found some mountainous terrain and climbed to the highest point. From there they could see that to the north was a giant body of water. The humans named it the Tendril Sea even though it was far inland.

"If that is the Tendril Sea, then that road below we've been on must be this one here." Evan pointed to the map. "Bog Run Highway."

"Why Bog Run Highway?" Toyota asked while trying to stick his nose in the map.

"As I understand it, there was a time when the Kroncals didn't respect any boundaries and so merchants and travelers on the road would pretty much have to run fast from Deadman's Bog to Squall city."

"Okay. Should I just assume that Deadman's Bog is called that because some tragic event occurred there where thousands of men died some horrible death, and they continue to haunt it to this very day?" *It* sarcastically groaned, while brushing away some dried mud from his jacket with his hat.

"No, actually, it was named that by the early settlers of that area as a scare tactic to keep their children away from the bog. Evidently it worked," Evan surmised with a smile.

"By the Giver's beard! When did *It* get to be so morbid and negative," Sydney whispered loudly to Evan.

It's jaw dropped open. "What do you mean? I'm not being morbid and negative. It's just been my experience … since I've been here … that the average person ends up defending their life multiple times on a weekly basis, and for someone to stab someone else in the chest with a poisoned dagger seems to be commonplace—I'm not morbid and negative, this place is morbid and negative. I'm the happy guy, remember?"

"Whoa! Way to go in making us feel happy about our home and telling us how terrible it is … ya twogg," Sydney said with pursed lips and a scowling brow.

"I didn't mean that. You know I didn't," *It* pleaded.

Toyota nodded his head and plainly added, "People do die a lot here."

Evan too nodded. "Yeah, they do … and there's a lot of stabbing … and mauling."

It's face cringed with the overshared contributions to his point. "Okay, that's a bit much, but I think we're getting there." He turned back to Sydney. "I just feel that all of you expect me to accept everything here in Fentiga as the only reality that exists when I come from a world where we don't get chased every day by demonic people wielding poison daggers, or insects the size of a horse who devour their enemies alive."

"Well, it doesn't happen every day here," Sydney squeaked softly.

"I misspoke. I meant every other day," the boy said, smiling.

Sydney grinned her buck-toothy smile back at him.

"So, nobody kills nobody else in your world at all?" Toyota said with disbelief that such a place could be real.

"Nope, not at all." *It* said proudly.

"And no stabbing?" Toyota asked.

"None whatsoever," *It* continued with a smile.

Evan grunted, "Sounds like a boring place." He twisted back around and lumbered down in the direction of the road. "Let's go before the render beasts find us and rip us to pieces."

It thrust his hands out in a gesture to punctuate his sarcasm. "Yes ... of course ... as it is just another normal day in Fentiga." After a defeated huff, he fell in line behind Evan.

TWENTY-THREE

BEASTS OF A FEATHER

They made their way down the hill back to the road and started heading east. The weather had cleared up and, though the ground wasn't dry, it was also not nearly as slippery.

Occasionally riders, wagons, and even caravans would pass the group who kept to themselves and tried not to draw attention their way. Both Fallon and humans traveled past them, but the majority were human. *It* was relieved to see others of his kind and was tempted to talk to them, but Evan was cautious, thinking it best to wait until they met someone official to talk to.

It had asked Evan why he didn't approach any of the Fallons, but Evan was bothered by the question and only referred to them as not being members of a herd. His reaction to them was at best mild disgust.

To avoid unwanted attention, at times Toyota and Sydney would hide in their hammocks on Evan's back, as it was decided by the two of them early on that trying to conceal Evan would be as ridiculous an idea as putting a dress on a tonk. Actually, the two of them arguing over the age and weight of the tonk and the type of dress used had Evan so irritated that he made them ride in their hammocks.

Of course, a human boy wearing a white fedora hat and walking beside his Fallon bodyguard wasn't at all inconspicuous.

As they drew closer to Squall, the highway widened out and appeared to be very well traveled. The map made it clear that it wouldn't be long before they would start coming across small villages and farming communities. Toyota and Sydney made the long tedious journey much more enjoyable with their joking and singing, but *It* just couldn't shake the guilt and shame that they had not found Lucas yet—and nobody else seemed to care.

Along the way, Evan spent time trying to teach *It* about the many footprints in the mud that they were seeing. He hoped the boy would understand the importance of tracking as it pertains to survival. Sadly, the only track that *It* was interested in finding was that of an Ave, specifically Lucas—but, as the day wore on, it became more evident that their friend was lost.

Toward evening, they were walking along quietly when Evan stopped suddenly and stuck his trunk toward the sky while taking in several snorts of air. Sydney scrambled out of her hammock and up Evan's shoulder. She too began sniffing frantically.

"I smell it too," squeaked Sydney.

"It's upwind of us," Evan added.

It looked up and sighed, "More bad things?"

"Yes, and by the direction of the breeze, they are behind us," Evan grumbled.

"I wish I could smell things like that," Toyota moaned.

"Not these things, you don't. Everyone, get to the side!" Evan yelled.

Unfortunately for them, the section of road they were on had high, banked walls leading off into some raised open fields. This must have been a ravine at one time before the merchant traffic made it a road. Soaked by the rains, the muddy sides were too slippery to climb. Once again, Evan had to lift everyone up to the top which was only fifteen feet or so. When it came time for him to climb up, he had to stab his sword into the side of the muddy wall for leverage. He grimaced, as no warrior wants to abuse their weapon in such a manner.

He got over the top, and they all ducked low when they heard eerie howls further down the road from where they were. It was a soul-shuttering sound. Even Evan's trunk twisted, as anxious beads of sweat rolled down his leathery yellow face.

"Is that the render beast?" *It* asked.

"Can't be, we are already far inside the hooman kingdom. For the Kroncal to advance this far would be a declaration of war with the hoomans—

that is something they would not do," Evan whispered, unconvinced by his own shaky words.

"Yeah, and in the last couple months I have seen a lot of things that I would've said would never happen," *It* responded in a quick and condescending tone.

They waited and watched. After a moment, *It* noticed his hat on the road below. It must have flown off his head in the rush to get out of the ravine.

"My hat! It will give us away," *It* shouted, as he leapt off the edge of the bank and slid down to the mud below. When he hit the bottom, he lost his balance and tumbled into a mud puddle. He quickly scrambled over and grabbed his hat. Evan and the others shouted at him to hurry—the howls were getting louder.

It scurried back and made several failed attempts to scramble up the wall. On his last try, he slipped and rolled back down into the mud. He was laying with his back against the wall, completely covered in mud and muck with just a portion of his cheek showing through, when something came around the corner, running up the road—they were monstrous.

The creatures ran on all fours with strong meaty legs and large clawed paws. Their black hairless skin glistened with moisture. A row of small sharp quills ran from the front of their shoulders up their necks and met between their ears. Among the quills were forest green manes with dark streaks where the hair was matted down by the muck from the road.

Their heads were extended out unnaturally with the bottom jaws ending with two pointed tusks on each side of their drooling maws. Teeth the size of *It*'s fingers dripped with foaming saliva. Their muzzles were wide and rounded with huge flaring nostrils.

Two small antlers above and to the side of each eye poked slightly outward and then wrapped around the side of the head in line with their ears, causing the sharp tips to point away from the creature—even a sideswipe of their head could rip open a tonk's belly.

The beasts continued galloping down the road toward the group. *It*'s heart was beating fast as the hideous faces of the render beasts grew near.

Evan's voice whispered from above. "Calm … be very calm … breathe easily through your mouth and your nose. They may not see you through the mud."

"That's easy for you to say," *It* hissed back, but then got quiet. The beasts were now alongside of him on the road, and they stopped running. Their snouts began sniffing the air and the ground. One of them turned and looked in the direction of *It*, who clamped his eyes shut. He was covered in mud and muck which helped him blend almost completely into the side of the muddy ravine wall.

The biggest of the creatures left the road. It stalked slowly toward the human boy, placing each paw down with intense focus. The other two creatures followed the first. Its giant paws sank deep into the mud as it was not much smaller than a horse, but surely heavier. The lead render beast sniffed its way right up to where *It* was sitting with his back against the wall. As the creature got closer, the boy's entire being was screaming inside.

Fear welled up in *It*, and he was overwhelmed by the emotion. Gradually, he felt the painful familiar tingling, but he still did not move. The render beast crept right up to him with one of his tusks just inches from the boy's throat. *It* couldn't take the stress of not knowing what was happening. He heard the snorts and felt the hot breath on his exposed cheek. He forced his eyes open to find that he was gazing into the bright yellow eyes of the render beast. In that moment, the creature saw the black streaks filling the boy's eyes as they stared at each other.

The yellow eyes of the beast had the dark mist and purplish hue glowing within them. *It* was sure that he would be the only one to see it. It was the same mist he had seen on mystical items, or when spells were uttered. The creature maintained eye contact while it sniffed at the little human covered in mud. Then it moved in and gently began to nuzzle against *It*'s cheek.

Back down the road, a unit of Kroncal came around the corner riding giant cat-like steeds covered in plates of armor that looked like they were made from some form of reptile scales. At their current speed, they would be there in moments.

It looked deep into the eyes of the render beast and whispered, "Please, go."

He sucked in a deep breath when the creature's bottom jaw dropped open and then split in two. Razored teeth lined both halves of the jaw as viscous saliva dripped heavily onto the ground where each droplet bubbled as it hit the wet mud. The harsh corse tongue of the beast shot out and licked his cheek.

It was stunned with disbelief. Before he could regain his senses, the creature turned away. As it returned to the road, it kicked out its hind legs and tossed up more mud, striking the boy in the face, leaving him completely concealed by the mud.

The Kroncal rode up, making loud clicking and crackling noises. They didn't speak the same language as the others of this world, but *It* didn't need to know what they were saying to know they were furious. One small Kroncal remained completely silent and was hidden beneath a large cloak.

It risked opening one eye and saw the tall insect-like creatures arguing. One of them leaned to the side, then whipped his tail and leg over and off his cat-horse beast. With his massive grasshopper legs and feet, he left deep indents in the road as he stalked over to where the render beast had been sniffing at *It*.

On top of the hill Evan gripped his sword. He could see that both Sydney and Toyota were holding their weapons, ready to pounce, but they remained still as he motioned with his trunk softly like he was petting something on the ground, encouraging them to hold off.

The Kroncal in front of *It* scanned the area but didn't see anything. He was holding something in his hand—a sock, and not just any sock. It was one of *It*'s socks. The insect stomped back over to the lead render beast and clubbed it hard with his barbed arm while clicking loudly.

He held out the sock for the beasts to sniff. The render beast turned briefly to look at *It*, but its hideous face and fierce fangs weren't as scary now. The boy gazed into the face of the beasts and read the look of familiarity in the large yellow eyes. He knew he was safe—for now.

The hulking creature started off down the road, followed by the other two render beasts. All but the Kroncal on the ground jabbed their barbed feet into their riding beasts and took off after the render. The one Kroncal on the ground turned back to where *It* was lying still and concealed. He stood there for a moment curiously considering the wall of mud. He made one last click under his breath, which the boy assumed was a nasty curse word. The Kroncal leapt onto his steed and galloped away.

In a low, harsh whisper, Evan said, "Don't move … anyone. Stay still. Give them time to get further up the road."

They waited a little longer and when it was clear to move, Evan, Toyota, and Sydney slid down the edge of the small cliff wall. *It* stood up and

Sydney leaped on him with the biggest hug her little arms could muster. When she let go, Toyota, too, hugged him.

"Okay, okay. I'm fine. Enough with the hugging," *It* protested.

Evan looked hard at the boy. "I couldn't see much of anything. What just happened? Why didn't they tear you to pieces?"

"Well, first, thanks for waiting until they were going to tear me to pieces before doing something. Secondly, I don't know why they stopped, but one of them licked me."

"Whoa, how weird was that?" Sydney squeaked. "Was he tasting you? Maybe you didn't taste good to him and that is why he didn't eat you."

"Why was that?" Evan remarked, with a wrinkled brow.

"I don't know, but remember when I told you about the black mist and purple glow on mystical things that I see?"

"Yeah."

"I saw the same thing in their eyes. And I can tell that my eyes must have had the black streaks crossing them. There must be some connection that the beasts made between me and them. I think I even felt it … a little. Like we knew each other, but with a different kind of knowing."

"Or, maybe what Sydney said is true, and after it licked you it realized how nasty you tasted and decided not to eat you," Toyota said very seriously.

"I'm just glad they didn't eat you," Sydney added.

Evan grunted, "We'll need to figure it out later. Now we have to keep heading east without running into them again."

"How are we going to do that? They're going in the same direction we're going in," Sydney squeaked.

"My guess is that they won't be able to travel that way for long. The hooman city of Squall will certainly have soldiers stationed there as well as city guards. Unless the Kroncal are insane enough to ride straight out into the city, my guess is that they will have to veer off at some point and head back south."

"Yeah, you also thought it was a good idea to sleep right next to them the other night. And look how that turned out," *It* snickered with a smile.

"Very funny," Evan growled.

It stopped laughing and his face was grim. "There's something else I didn't tell you guys … They had one of my socks."

"What?" Evan growled.

"You gave them one of your socks? That's weird," Sydney squeaked.

"Yeah, I would've gone with a shirt or something. I like socks. They would keep my feet warm if I wore them," Toyota added.

"No, I didn't give them a sock. The Kroncal that got off the giant cat-thing had one of my socks and was having his render beasts sniff it. Why in the world would they do something gross like that?"

"You really have no clue, do you?" Evan asked as he began looking around. "You can train an animal to track by smell. All you have to do is give them a sniff of what they're hunting, and some creatures can track it that way."

"But how did they get my sock in the first place?" *It* said, confused.

"That's what really gets me," Evan said.

The four started down the road at a slower pace than before. *It* was still covered in mud from his hat to the inside of his boots, and it was going to be a very long uncomfortable walk.

TWENTY-FOUR

A BELLY FULL OF IT

An hour had passed since the encounter with the Kroncal and the render beasts when the lone silhouette of a large Fallon lumbered down the road. Evan appeared to be walking by himself, but as usual, Sydney and Toyota were kicking back in their hammocks while Evan carried *It* in his arms.

"When we get to the next stream, you're going to wash the mud and dirt out of your boots so I don't have to carry you anymore," Evan snorted with exaggerated irritation.

"What? I don't weigh anything to you," *It* snickered in response.

"That's not the point. It's the principle of the thing. Warriors don't carry other warriors in their arms because they have too much mud in their boots."

"Maybe we can start a trend," *It* continued with a snarky laugh.

Evan squinched an eye and cocked his head to one side in befuddlement.

"Let me guess. You don't know what the word trend means?" *It* asked, with less humor and more sympathy in his voice.

"No. I'm more for action and less for words—if you haven't noticed," the Fallon grumbled.

Before *It* could respond, Evan stopped walking and stared off toward the horizon. Far in the distance he saw smoke, and lots of it.

"What do you think that is?" the boy asked, with a nervous knowing to his voice.

"The same thing you're thinking it is," Evan responded with a sigh.

"The Kroncal?"

"That would be my guess. They may be burning a farm or village to see if you're hiding there."

"Put me down!" *It* yelled.

Evan dropped *It* to the ground and the boy took off running down the road toward the smoke.

"What are you doing?" Evan yelled, as he took off as well.

"I'm the one they're looking for! We have to help!"

Toyota peeked out from under the leather flap to see that Sydney was also partially out of her hammock and clinging on as Evan's running tussled the two passengers violently.

"What's happening?" Toyota managed to squeal out as he struggled to hang on.

"Something dangerous, I suppose," Sydney squeaked with an inappropriately eager smile.

Evan and *It* stopped suddenly when they came across a burning farmhouse. The large windows and doors made it clear it was a Fallon dwelling, though the design was obviously human, as smaller sized bricks and planks were used for the structure. Evan told the others to wait on the opposite side of the road by the edge of the forest. With squinted eyes and belligerent looks on their faces, they made it clear that they were not about to do that.

"If the Kroncal were looking for a hooman boy with a Fallon, a Seeuradi, and a Didelphi here, these people will not be happy to see you, or worse they will blame you," Evan tried to convince them.

"We can hide," Sydney said as she scurried up into her hammock with Toyota following.

"Open your cloak," *It* called out to Evan.

Evan opened his cloak and *It* grabbed onto his leather jerkin, swung his legs up, and wedged himself in.

"Close it up," the boy said, as he nuzzled in tight.

Evan wrapped the cloak up, but he looked very bulky; and the grimace on his face echoed his lack of faith in his hooman friend's plan.

"This isn't going to work," the Fallon complained, with uncharacteristic nervousness.

"Sure, it will. You look more like Floks now," a muffled voice from his chest chuckled. "Great Giver, you reek!" *It*'s tone changed dramatically.

"So now he's a believer in the Great Giver," Evan mumbled to himself as he made his way across the road with each step being awkward at best. He reached the farmhouse to find a family of Fallon outside near the barn. They were on guard at first until they saw that Evan was Fallon folk.

"What happened?" Evan asked.

"The Kroncal happened. They rode up on us without warning," a female Fallon snarled, while pressing a damp cloth to the head of a wounded Fallon male. "They said they were looking for a human. Barru was stabbed when he argued that we had no humans hidden here." She gestured toward the barn with her trunk. "My husband is in the barn over there with a hurt leg and head. He didn't even get a chance to tell them anything."

"Did they say who they were looking for? Or why?" Evan asked, but his words came across forced as he was unaccustomed to deception.

"No, they just kept insisting we might know something, or have seen something of this human." She gestured around. "Does this look like a human farm?"

Evan glanced around at the destroyed oversized farm tools and equipment and shook his head with some guilt. "Can we be of help?" he said honestly.

"We?" the lady looked at him oddly.

"I'm sorry. I meant we as the plural of I or me ... a fellow Fallon ... being of help that is." Evan's brow wrinkled as he knew he may have just blown his cover.

"Unless you're a healer or can help us get my nephew and my husband to the city."

"I think I can help," Evan said, as he reached around and fumbled with his backpack under the rain cloak where Sydney was in her hammock. "Just let me reach for a healing elixir that I have," he said, much louder than necessary.

From her hidden position, Sydney searched in her pouch for her bottle of shaman wound ointment. She was having trouble getting to it as Evan's hand kept knocking her around. Finally, she got frustrated enough that she bit down hard on one of his four giant fingers, causing Evan to jerk his hand out.

"Ow!" he hissed. "Sorry, I accidentally poked my finger on something irritatingly sharp." He reached back around and flicked Sydney hard with one of his good fingers.

"Ouch!" She squeaked

Evan forced a smile. "Sorry; poked myself again."

Sydney found the bottle and put it in Evan's hand. He handed the elixir to the woman and said, "Rub this in and around the wounds and it should heal if they're not too far gone. Be quick about it."

She raised her trunk with a grin. "Thank you so much. It is a wonderful thing to see Fallon folk helping each other like they used to."

"Fallon always help Fallon," Evan replied, as though it was a commonly known fact.

She laughed, shaking her head. "You're not from around here, are you?"

"No, actually I'm not."

"As much as your thoughtfulness is appreciated, the human kingdom of Aremac, and especially the city of Yolanrym and its provenances, are very much humanized. Even the Fallon folk act more like humans than their own kind."

Evan's trunk curled inward with curiosity. "How is that?"

"Just watch out for yourself and be cautious of everything, and you should be fine," she said without looking at him as she applied the ointment to Barru's bleeding shoulder. The skin around the gash pulled slowly together until only a scar remained. Releasing a burdened breath, the woman leaned back and looked to Evan as she said, "Humans are a selfish lot; and petty too."

A loud and frustrated huff came from under Evan's cloak, and the Fallon lady looked up to him as he pressed his hand against his bulging belly in an effort to stop *It* from squirming in protest.

"Are you alright?" she asked with squinted eyes, watching Evan's odd behavior closely.

"It's nothing. I ate something that doesn't agree with me." He got his belly under control. "Actually, could you tell me how far before we reach Squall?"

"Again, with the 'we' stuff," she said, with a squinted eye and her trunk sniffing the air with slight twisting motions. "You are a strange fellow." She pointed east and, without taking her eyes off him, said, "About another day and a half on foot."

Evan nodded his head. "Great. Then we ..." he laughed nervously. "I will be going and wish you good healing and health. The Great Giver bless you and yours." He turned to walk off.

Just as he twisted away, the beady eyes and snout of something retreated into his pack. The Fallon lady tilted her head and strained her eyes as she appeared to be unsure if she did or did not just see something.

TWENTY-FIVE

THE NAME BE VASILIK

Shortly before nightfall, they came across a small village with a public house and inn. From a distance, they could see that the structures had doorways big enough for Fallons, but the few people walking around town were far too small to be Fallons. Evan told the others to wait for him on the edge of town while he investigated. He made sure to lecture them on the necessity of staying out of sight and staying put, which was Evan-speak for "don't get into trouble." Though he lacked faith in their ability to follow instructions, he knew he had to make at least one pass through town without them to get the lay of the land, unimpeded by their antics.

He peered through the window of the first building he came to. Multiple makeshift shelving units and small tables were displaying everything from wooden plates with utensils to tools, tarps, and food items—a supply shack. To his surprise, he was greeted by a Fallon storekeeper instead of a human as he walked through the door. They hardly shared more than a few phrases to one another before she made sure to tell him about the Kroncal attack rumor going around town and how the town officials hired a local mystic to communicate the news to the Squall city guard several miles away. She was fairly confident that Squall riders would be arriving at any time.

"I don't even care that they're not Fallon kin, just as long as they get here and nip this Kroncal business at the root before it gets out of hand.

They may already be here, but I haven't had a chance to talk with anyone down at the Puddle since earlier today," she said, while unpacking a small crate.

Evan's hairless brow lifted. "Puddle?"

"It's down the road a short trot toward the center of town. You can get a snort and some more juicy news about them Kroncal down there because some of the folks that hang out in that place can't keep from run'n their gobs. You know, I also heard that them poor farmers did nothing to provoke them hateful Kroncal. I'll bet they even would've ate them if they could."

With his tusks dipping up and down, Evan nodded the whole time she spoke, as if this was the first he had heard of the attack. He knew, of course, the Kroncal had turned off the main road and headed south down a side path that he and the others had passed several miles before reaching the village they were now in. He was sure they were long gone.

When the shopkeeper slowed to catch her breath, he pretended to look over her wares before picking up a handful of sow-gum that he set down on the counter. She wrapped up the sweet treats in wax paper and traded them for the coin Evan held out to her. The Fallon warrior thanked her for the conversation and the sow-gum before leaving. As he walked out the door, he couldn't help but notice that she was looking at him with an inquisitive intent. Evan had the suspicion that he may be the topic of her next retelling of gossip at the Puddle, which was his next stop.

Evan was still in sight, walking into town toward the supply shack, when Sydney and Toyota had no trouble convincing *It* that they should sneak into town and be ready to help Evan should he get into trouble. Of course, *It* pointed out that Evan was one of the best warriors of Lord Stronghide's herd, but Sydney and Toyota assured the boy that it was a matter of honor that they provide backup. As *It* continuously struggled with what was and wasn't honorable in Fentiga, he deferred the decision to his comrades. Somehow, he wasn't surprised when Sydney and Toyota suggested they check the public house first, and maybe get something to eat while they were there.

Sydney and Toyota bounded off behind some huts and buildings in search of the public house. *It* was following behind, calling out to them to slow down, but they were too set on the mischief at hand to pay him any attention. This was an unusual situation for *It,* as he had always been the one to cause chaos for others and not the one dragged into mischief. When they reached the rear door of the public house, which was obviously built for a Fallon to pass through, Sydney and Toyota started through the door as *It* caught up to them. His face squinched in on itself as he saw the word PUTTLE crudely scratched into the door frame. The misspelling made it clear to him that the author of the sign was obviously not an intellectual giant. This did not give him hope as to whom or what they might find within.

A large burly Fallon with a filthy apron stopped them at the doorway before they got more than a few feet in. By the reek of ale permeating from his clothes, he was most likely the bartender, or town drunkard, or both.

"Wadda ya miscreants up to bak ere?" he asked with a sharp voice and spray of spittle.

"We're hungry," Toyota offered.

"They'll be no andouts ere for ya beg'r verms! Ya best be gone."

"We're not beggars," *It* said as he jingled his pouch. "We have money."

"An wher'd ya be get'n that kinda coin? Av ya been thiev'n off drunkards?"

"No, sir, we worked for it," the boy responded respectfully.

"Sir, ya be call'n me! Yor awfuly dirty fo be'n a gennelman."

"I could use a bath after we eat," *It* told him, while knocking at his dirty clothes with his hat.

"I'll no be hep'n ya there, but ya can clean up at the inn down er a piece," he nodded with his head and pointed with his trunk and tusk to the north of town.

"May we still eat first?" Sydney squeaked, while making the cutest face ever.

"Shor-thing. I ainn'a gonna be starv'n a face like'n that; specially one wit money to pay."

The kids looked at him with big eyes full of gratitude, and *It* started to walk towards the main room, hoping that the Fallon didn't change his mind and stop him. The bartender went on about his work, so they assumed he had no change of heart. When they got to the opening of the room, Sydney stopped in her tracks. She had seen cloaked humans on the road in the rain and could never get a good look, but here there were humans in full visibility.

"Oh, my Great Giver! There are hoomans here!" Her mouth dropped open for a moment. As *It* continued into the room, she grabbed his shoulder and pulled him back. "Here," she said as she snatched his white fedora out of his hands and slammed it on his head. "The hat will help us know it's you, but don't get separated, or we may never find you. I can't tell them apart."

It looked around the room, awestruck. It had just hit him that he had not seen another human face in what felt like forever. Sydney, who appeared authentically worried, had to shake the boy to get him to hear her rantings that he needed to stay near so they don't lose him.

It's brow dropped incredulously as he listened to Sydney's repeated request that he not get lost amongst all the indistinguishable faces. He shook his head, noticing there were only a few humans in the building, and they were all, obviously, of different human races. One had ebony skin with a handlebar mustache which curled in a loop at the ends, and he looked to be at least forty-five years old—and a hard forty-five at that. Standing at the end of the bar was a portly, pale-faced man who looked like a miniature Floks, but as a human. There were three other individuals who were obviously an elderly couple and their elderly friend. Two others toward the center of the room appeared to *It* as having Asian ancestry. At that distance, *It* could not be more specific. They had dark black hair and wore matching grey tunics. Most notably, they were all taller than *It*, and then some.

"Are you saying that you can't tell the difference between them and me?" *It* gestured widely.

"Don't they all look alike to you?" Sydney whispered to Toyota.

"Yes ... it's weird ... like they are all twins," Toyota hissed softly from the side of his mouth.

"And I've never seen so many before!" she added.

"Seven! There are only seven humans in this room. That's not a lot. And the reason you have never seen this many before is that you have never seen any before me," *It* griped, while trying to not draw attention to himself.

"So, I'm not allowed to be overwhelmed?" the little Seeuradi girl whined.

"I would say that overwhelmed is a little too dramatic," the boy replied, while shooting her a reprehensive look.

Toyota's mouth gaped and his eyes widened as a terrible thought hit him like a rampaging tonk. "What if they all have hats? What if they put them on?"

Sydney too was hit with this new desperation. They would surely lose track of their human friend if every human had a hat. She looked to *It* and his hat and then scoured the room with hectic glances. Her gaze settled on an overturned bottle poking out from a shelf above her head. The maker's mark pin stuck in the cork had a very unusual design to it.

Sydney scrambled up the to the shelf and grasped the bottle's neck with her paw. The maker's mark pin looked like a dead cat with a wagon wheel track over its midsection and a fancy feathered hat on its head. She grabbed the pin in her teeth and heaved back. The pin ripped its way out of the cork. Dull barbs on the pin shaft had held the pin in place. Following through with her backward tug on the pin, she flipped in the air, landing next to *It*. The entire action was over in a flash. Even if anyone had been looking, they wouldn't have been sure what they saw anyway.

"Here." Sydney called out as she slapped the pin hard against the side of *It*'s hat that was still on his head.

"Owwww!" *It* yelped. "Are you nutters! What are you doing?"

"Oh, don't be a big baby. This will help us know which hat is yours and which hooman is you."

The boy whipped the hat off his head and examined the pin sticking through to the inside with the little barbs holding it fast. As the point had not penetrated his skin, there was no blood. He flipped the hat and cringed as he saw the head of the pin. "Is that a cat?"

Sydney swiped the hat from the boy and, in one deft move, pushed it back on his head. The pin wasn't long enough to reach his scalp without the help of someone smacking it. "Keep it on when we are around hoomans."

The Floks-looking man at the bar turned and stumbled slightly as he tugged on his britches in preparation for a visit to the privy. As he walked up to the kids *It* stood staring up at the man.

Caught off guard, *It* grinned from ear to ear with his dented hat smashed on his head. "Hi! I'm a human too," he practically shouted with the excitement to have another human person standing in front of him.

The man steadied himself as best he could. "You don't say," he slurred, ending in a loud juicy belch. After a pause to get his bearings, he staggered to the back and out the door.

"Well, that was not very nice," Sydney whispered loudly in *It*'s ear. "Not nice at all."

Before the boy could respond, the two gentlemen with the black hair and dark tunics stopped talking to a Fallon barkeeper. One of them climbed up on top of a chair and began addressing the entire room.

"I am Constable Lin and this is Constable Chen of Squall city. As some of you may have heard, there has been a Kroncal assault just east of here. We have been dispatched as forerunners ahead of the unit of Squall city protectors. Until they arrive, we discourage all citizens from traveling west until order has been restored."

It was at this point Evan walked through the door and saw the kids standing on the other side of the room. His complexion switched from mustard yellow to angry orange, and he started to point and say something to the kids when he was distracted by Constable Lin.

"We have heard rumors that the Kroncal were looking for a human and Fallon traveling together. We wish to locate these individuals for questioning. If you have any information about them or the Kroncal invaders, please bring it to our attention. We will remain stationed here for the next few days."

Evan stopped pointing his finger and held back from saying anything to the kids, but he gave them a look suggesting that they not acknowledge each other. *It* nodded to Evan that he understood and herded the others to a table in the corner made for humans. They sat down.

Evan walked across the room, keeping some distance between him and the kids, and stopped at the bar, where he ordered a drink. He acted as though they weren't even there. Of course, that made him look suspicious, as everyone else took note of a Seeuradi, Didelphi, and human boy sitting together—Evan was the only one trying not to look.

The Fallon server came by to get drinks and food orders from the kids. At one point he laughed out loud and said the word "freat," very loudly. Evidently not many of the patrons drank nonalcoholic beverages in this pub, but he went to get their drinks and food. Occasionally Evan shot them dirty looks, and they would turn their faces away to avoid being the victims of his evil eye.

After their food arrived, the ebony-skinned human with the curly mustache limped over to the bar, using a cane as he walked. He stood next to Evan and asked the bartender to refill his tankard. While the bartender was busy getting the drink, the human continued looking forward but spoke out of the side of his mouth to Evan.

"I don't be know'n what be yor devious intentions for those snappers at the table, but I suggest ya stow them." He turned and stared a hole through Evan. Though the Fallon warrior knew he could crush the human with ease, there was something in the human's eyes and voice that suggested it was more than just a threat. Not to mention crushing a human was a sure way to draw negative attention to himself.

Evan swung his mammoth tusks slowly around and met the human's gaze full on. The aging man's eyes were drawn to the tattoo on Evan's right cheek. One of his bushy eyebrows jumped up high on his forehead with exaggerated curiosity. Evan could read on the man's face that he knew what the tattoo meant. It meant that the bearer of the tattoo was a Fallon warrior of the Stronghide herd and of high standing and skill—definitely not someone to trifle with.

The bartender delivered the tankard to the human who winked at Evan. "Remember our conversation, Fallon," he said to Evan before getting up stiffly. He lifted his glass in a mock salute to the mighty Fallon and then turned to limp the short distance to where the kids were seated. Without an invitation, he took a seat at their table.

The man had plopped himself down next to *It* with a huff as if the action was a laborious undertaking. "So, I no be the cheapest, but I be also no the most expensive. I accept coin, tools, livestock, and mystic devices as payment. Should ya be find'n yorself no happy with me services, ya forfeit yor deposit and any expenses. I be available to start today, but I reckon tomorrow would be better."

The kids just looked at each other not knowing what to say, and the human man sat there grinning until he took a long pull from his tankard of ale. After nothing was said for another moment, he set his cup down and drew his arm across his mustache, wiping away the foam.

"All right then, now that we be in agreement on the particulars, what services will ya snappers be need'n?"

Upon saying the word agreement, Toyota's ears perked up, and he leered seriously at the human. "Wait a minute, we have not made an arrangement with you. And you did not follow proper contractual etiquette," he hissed.

"Ha, me little Didelphi friend, we can always be count'n on yor like to make sure that the proprieties be followed."

Toyota grinned a very large toothy smile, knowing that he did the proper thing.

The human leaned down toward Toyota. "So, lad, what says ya be act'n as our arbiter for the arrangements so as to make sure we be follow'n proper procedures? I be sure ya have a nominal fee to charge for yor mediation of the negotiations."

"Of course, I would be happy to," Toyota said, smiling even more. He looked to *It* and Sydney. "So, what will be your opening request and price for …" He looked at the human man. "What is your name?"

"The name be Vasilik. Vasilik McCarthy, sir."

"So, guys, what will be your opening request and price for utilizing Mr. McCarthy's services?" Toyota said to his confused looking buddies.

"Just be call'n me Vasilik."

"Okay," Toyota responded, and glanced back at *It* and Sydney with anticipation of their answer.

"Actually, we don't need any help. Thank you very much," *It* said nervously and kicked at Toyota under the table. Unfortunately, he missed and kicked Sydney instead.

"Ow! Why'd you kick me?" Sydney squealed at *It*.

It looked at Evan and saw that he was still casting disapproving glances. Vasilik's left eyebrow raised high as he noticed the exchange of eye contact between Evan and the boy. He thought for a moment and then a grin crossed his face as he realized that he may have misread the situation previously.

"Tis a shame, I was be'n most certain I could av been of service to ya snappers, especially with the Kroncals look'n for ya and yor big friend at the bar."

"How did he know?" Sydney whispered too loudly to *It*.

Sydney leaned so far onto the table that her knees were well over the edge. "So, did you also know that we were on a quest to bring *It* to the human King?" Sydney gasped, with her ears pointed forward and her nose twitching with excitement under her glasses.

"An what kinda counsel would I be if'n I couldn't surmise yor purdickiment. I be already work'n out the details of yor passing unnoticed to the

Port of Squall and into Yolanrym proper to see King Mellis imself."

"We could use his help," Sydney excitedly squealed to *It*.

"Indeed, I be more than a sight helpful." Vasilik added, with a smile and a nod.

"What's your fee, then?" *It* asked.

"Hey, negotiating is my job. Cooking and negotiating contracts are what I do," Toyota complained.

"Fine," *It* said, motioning for Toyota to continue.

Toyota turned back to Vasilik. "And what is the fee for your services?" Toyota asked.

"Well then, I be not the one to break the purse of a snapper, so I could no take more than ten drach a day and expenses with the first three days paid in advance, so doncha even try to make me take any more than that."

Toyota looked to *It*, and the human boy just shrugged and said, "I've never used money before, so I have no idea."

"Wow, it seems he is worth so much more, but he is being kind, so it sounds like a very good deal," Sydney squeaked.

"Toyota, what do you think?" *It* asked.

"Yeah, I don't use money often either. All of my contracts are bartered, but it sounds good to me, and I really like the hair under his nose. I wish my whiskers curled around like that," Toyota responded.

It paused to think. "I guess we do need to have someone help us get there from here. So yes, let's do it," the boy piped up with a huge smile. It felt good to have something positive happen for a change.

"Okay, it looks like we have a deal. The two of you need to shake hands to make it binding, and you can spit in your hands to make it more official," Toyota instructed.

It looked at Toyota, not believing the part about spitting in his hand.

"I be no man to be shirk'n the legalities," Vasilik announced, as he raised his hand in front of his face and spit heavily into it and stuck it out toward *It*.

The boy's cheeks raised high on his face with a cringe of disgust like none he has ever felt before. He looked from Vasilik's now slimy, cracked and dirty hand to the aging man's face with a gaped tooth grin lifting his cheesy mustache.

Sydney held her head in her paws as she laid partially across the table shining a buck toothed smile at *It*. "Go on, it needs to be official."

Still cringing, the boy brought his hand up, spit in it, and reached it out toward Vasilik who greedily snatched the boy's hand into his and vigorously shook it.

As *It* was shaking Vasilik's hand, he noticed Evan watching them. The large Fallon's yellow face was the brightest orange he had ever seen. The boy could tell that he was upset about something and for the life of him he couldn't figure out what it could be, but he knew he would change the Fallon's attitude when he gave him the exciting news about hiring a guide. That was sure to cheer the big guy up.

"To begin, ya can be pay'n the thirty drach now, or to be make'n it easier, an even silver shek. Then we need be mak'n ar way to the inn an obtain'n lodge'n for a night."

Evan was fit to be tied as he watched *It* paying Vasilik money from his pouch. The giant Fallon shot a searing glare at Vasilik who had his back to him. Evan glanced around and saw that the constables were still in the room. He knew he could not be seen going near the kids and risk being identified as the provokers of the Kroncal. He glared back at Vasilik—not being able to crush people who annoy you is a huge inconvenience for a Fallon warrior.

When the three friends were done eating and drinking their fill, Vasilik led them toward the inn where they would get rooms for themselves and a bath for *It*. As they made their way down the muck-laden road, Sydney took a keen interest in Vasilik's bum leg.

"I can heal that, you know. I'm a healing mystic," she squeaked.

"No need there, snapper. That be a hurt that won't heal," Vasilik said with a chuckle.

She pulled out her smudging stick and tried to recite an incantation near Vasilik's leg, but he gave her a slight nudge with his boot that made her fall back on her tail.

"The best healer there ever be had done already tried everythin' a mystic could be doing for this twisted hunk." He smiled down at her as he slapped his leg. "But I do most appreciate yor offer." Sydney huffed her disapproval then got to her feet and followed as Vasilik led them into the inn.

TWENTY-SIX

JUST A HINT OF PROPHECY

When they first arrived inside the inn, Vasilik had the innkeeper give his current bill to *It* and he explained to the boy how they were expenses covered under the contract. As he was in a hurry to get a bath, *It* dug into his purse and paid for the charges.

They spent a night in beds; warm, clean, and happy. In the morning, everyone had an exceedingly enjoyable breakfast, which again Vasilik said was part of the expenses to be paid by *It*. Evan had stayed at the inn as well and kept his distance, but he never took his eyes off the group except for when they went to bed the night before. After breakfast, he followed them out of the inn and down the road. He lagged far behind until they were out of view of the village, at which point he sprinted to catch up to them.

When he did reach them, he charged towards Vasilik and stopped just short of him with his hand on the hilt of his sword. Vasilik, who had turned to face Evan, lifted up his cane and drew a sword from inside it. Before Evan could pull his sword, Vasilik's blade was at the Fallon's throat.

"Well now, we be wonder'n when ya was to be join'n us. I hope ya were no intend'n to draw that big meat cleaver of yorn. Cause that would be make'n me twitchy and I don'na think ya be want'n me a twitch'n."

Evan said nothing, breathing heavily and growling as he weighed the human in his mind. Judging by the swift and accurate placement of the sword, he knew this was an experienced swordsman—and the weathered lines of his face was that of a man who had seen the harder side of life. Though it was against his nature, Evan released his sword.

"T'was one smart move, Fallon," Vasilik said, as he deftly returned his sword into the cane scabbard.

"I don't know what you think you're doing, but you are done here. You don't have to go back, but you ain't going with us," Evan growled.

"As I be contracted and under the employ of this here young lad, I will be go'n where t'ever he instructs. Ya may choose to be join'n us, or no."

"He really can be of help, since none of us know anything about the human cities," *It* said, trying to calm the Fallon down.

"So, you run off with the first stranger that offers to help?"

"No. He was the only one who offered to help," Sydney chittered.

"That doesn't mean you can trust him. You just met him." Evan got louder and more frustrated as they talked.

"Yeah, well, the first time I met you, you tried to kill me. So how do you figure that into your philosophy?" *It* raised his voice.

"No … Ya didn'n. Tell me ya no did try an kill this wee one, did ya?" Vasilik carried on with forced concern.

Evan huffed and retreated a bit. "That was different."

It's eyes shot open wide. "How is that different?"

"It just is … and I didn't try to kill you," Evan said, with his tusks and eyes aimed toward the ground.

"Oh yeah, I'm sorry, you're right. You were only trying to kidnap me, which you did."

"Ya know laddie, I'm begin'n to question yor ability to select yor friends if'n they be apt to kidnap'n ya, or kill'n ya." Vasilik said to *It*, with melodramatic lines of concern across his forehead.

"Okay, this is going nowhere. I can see where having a guide couldn't hurt. I just want all of you to start considering your decisions before you make them." Evan turned to look at Vasilik. "And you … I am sworn to protect this hooman with my life."

"Be that the truth of it?" Vasilik asked, with a face full of doubt.

"Yes, he's my Host Custodian," *It* shared with mild enthusiasm.

Vasilik's eyes perked up with authentic interest. "Host Custodian ya be say'n."

"I'm sure you have no clue the depths of duty and honor of that position," Evan growled down at the man.

"To the contrary, me very large and seem'nly daft friend, I be understand'n it well. I be just at a loss as to the circumstances that be lead'n to such an extraordinary relationship." The expression on Vasilik face suggested he knew intimately the importance of a Host Custodian.

Evan sneered. "What you think doesn't matter beyond guiding us through to Yolanrym. So why don't you begin doing that."

"Then let's be on ar way," Vasilik said, as he began gleefully limping down the road and leaning heavily on his cane, dragging his left foot.

Toyota and Sydney started after Vasilik while *It* stood looking at Evan who was staring down at the boy's head.

"What's wrong now?" *It* asked.

"Is that a dead cat pinned to your hat?"

"It's there so you guys can tell me apart from other humans."

"But it's a dead cat." Evan stressed with immense incredulity.

It walked off after the others. What he grumbled went unheard.

As they traveled, Evan, *It*, Sydney, and Toyota saw things they had never seen before. They passed numerous people on the road, both human and Fallon, and some races they had no clue of. There were fewer wooden carts and wagons and many more vehicles from the Great Giver sites; most were rust-covered and only remnants of their past selves. Those few wooden carts they did see had axle and wheels from vehicles that *It* vaguely remembered from C-Earth's history.

Along the way, just before they got to Squall city, they came across various smaller villages and shanty towns where many Fallon lived. Evan was shocked to see so many of his kin living in poverty and on the outskirts of a large city. He stopped to ask some of the Fallons why the humans treated them this way, and they replied that the humans actually gave them a home, whereas the Fallon herd were the ones who treated them poorly.

He could not believe what they were saying was possible, and when he questioned them further, everyone had the same story. They, or their ancestors before them, were ostracized or banished from the Fallon herd because of something they did or something they didn't agree with. When one Fallon said he questioned the belief in the Great Giver, Evan understood why he was banished from the herd, as that was a heresy not tolerated, but the majority of the others have been unjustly treated.

It looked at Evan. "I once questioned you as to how no one in the herd committed crimes, but now I know and I can see that there were Fallon who made mistakes, or did wrong—this is what happens to them." *It* gestured to the squalor and indignant conditions surrounding him.

"And what of your world. A place where you are torn from your grandfather and forced to live with strangers who do not appreciate your courage and dedication to your friends, as well as your eagerness to accept people as they are. How could they take someone, who in our world is extraordinary, but in your world is treated with neglect or indifference?"

The boy sighed with a world of surfacing memories weighing down on him unexpectedly. "I guess no one is perfect."

"Except for the Seeuradi. We are probably the closest you're going to get to perfect. We appreciate life in all forms, and we're fun people," Sydney informed the others, as though repeating factual information.

"Yep, you squirrels are a far cry better than Fallons," Toyota said casually, and without noticing the grimace on Evan's face.

"What be this about ya lad an a different world that yor com'n from? I thought ya be human as well?" Vasilik asked with a raised eyebrow.

"I am human, I just accidentally ended up in Fentiga. I'm from a different world and it's a bit difficult to explain."

Vasilik's moustache raised high as a look of exaggerated shock crossed his face. "Can it be?" Vasilik whispered a little too dramatically, and much too loudly to himself for it to go unnoticed. "The child of prophecy?"

"What child of prophecy?" Sydney squeaked.

"There be a prophecy from many a year ago of a child from t'another world com'n here at a time when most needed an befriend'n the Giverkind. But that can't be, cause'n that child was to be av'n mystical powers."

"Oh, my Great Giver! He has mystical powers that we didn't know about," Sydney squealed as she pointed at *It*. She grabbed the boy by shoulders. "You're a prophecy child. Isn't that exciting?" Sydney squealed some more.

"It's just a bunch of tonk doppings," Evan mumbled as he looked menacingly at Vasilik.

"Ya do no need be so quick to be dismiss'n what ya do no understand. Of course, I would be think'n it a shovel full of tonk droppings too if'n I had no seen the prophecy me self," Vasilik added with more dramatic flair and using a deep eerie tone.

"Where exactly did you see this prophecy?" Evan hissed.

"T'was on a cave wall to the far east in the land of the Dead Echoes."

"What? Are you trying to say you've been to the Dead Echoes?" Evan said dismissively.

"Aye, that I did. So, I be know'n it be true."

"Bunk!" Evan barked.

It's forehead crinkled and his eyebrows raised up high. "What's the Dead Echoes?"

"Ooh, it's a place outside of the hooman and Giver kingdoms where no one ever goes because it's evil, and the land is dead," Sydney squeaked in a very serious tone.

"Not to mention that the only way to get to it is through Kroncal territory," Evan snorted.

Vasilik leaned down toward the kids and gave them a wink. "Tis all true, but there be another way if'n ya go by boat."

"By boat!" Evan barked. "Now I know you're lying. Only a fool would attempt to navigate through the rocks near the Dead Echoes shore. And how did you climb the cliffs if you did make it past the rocks and mer-people that feed there?"

"It be called courage and skill, me lad." Vasilik replied, with one brow raised high on his head and a tap of his cane against his chest.

"Bunk!" Evan barked again and turned to walk in the direction of Squall.

They still had another hour before they would arrive, so Vasilik continued to spin his tale about the prophecy child and the treacherous adventure that he had finding the cave.

TWENTY-SEVEN

O.M.G. IT'S A C.I.M.U.

Unlike the sturdily maintained walls towering over the perimeter of the Fallon central city of Utuska, the walls surrounding the land side of Squall were dilapidated at best, and the posted guards were more interested in the scantily-dressed female fruit vendors than the people passing through the gates unchallenged.

Just outside of the city gates, *It* and his protectors got mobbed by peddlers and merchants of all types and races. The boy was not at all impressed by the filth and squalor around him, but at least it reminded him of his own world and the cleanup they did to somewhat restore it. As he was walking along, he felt at home seeing so many objects from C-Earth. Scattered everywhere were lampshades from days gone past, clock faces with no hands, and even digital screens from old information processors, but his heart leapt into his throat and his eyes shot opened wide when he saw an item that looked even more familiar.

"A Cimu!" *It* yelled, as he ran over to a human vendor who had multiple handheld C.I.M.U. devices on a cart. "No way! I can't believe you have these!"

The vendor leaned over toward the boy. "Yes, I see you have good tastes, my friend."

Sydney was sitting on Evan's shoulder when they walked up with Vasilik to see what caught the boy's attention. Toyota must have wandered off, as he was nowhere in sight.

"And I have several of these wondrous serving trays and plates to choose from. Many sizes and colors. You can set your goblets and glasses on them and impress your friends. No finer coasters exist from here to Yolanrym," the vendor gushed, as he waved his hands over the many communication devices.

"Are you kidding me? These aren't …" *It* began to excitedly tell the vendor the truth about the items, but Vasilik quickly put his hand over the boy's mouth.

"Very attractive grub holders ya got there, but some of them be av'n scratches and by all means they no be completely match'n. But t'were the boy still interested, what would be yor price?" Vasilik said, while holding the boy to one side.

"I couldn't part with any one of them for less than a silver apiece," the vendor sighed, playing his role.

"Scoundrel! We'd pay half that an yor still robb'n us like babes in blankets," Vasilik bellowed, with one of his eyebrows arching high on his forehead.

"But I …" *It* tried to speak, but Vasilik tightened his grip on the boy's mouth.

"Surely they're worth more than half a silver each?" the vendor pleaded.

"And yet, we will be giv'n ya noth'n more than five drach a piece."

The vendor scowled, "How many were you looking to buy?"

"And how many of these would we be need'n, snapper?" Vasilik said, as he removed his hand from the boy's mouth.

"All," *It* replied.

"All?" the group said in unison, amazed that the boy even needed one cup, coaster, or dinner plate.

"*It*, we do not need all these plates. We don't even use plates most of the time," Evan protested.

It looked at Vasilik as he opened his mouth to make sure that the man wasn't going to place his filthy hands over his mouth again, and the boy did choose his words. "Trust me, Evan, we want as many of these as we can get."

"How many ya be av'n there?" Vasilik asked.

"Nine," said the vendor.

"Two silver it be. Ya need be giv'n the ninth as an incentive to be tak'n the lot off yor hands," Vasilik said to the man.

Though he didn't see any evidence of it, Vasilik knew the vendor was happy to get any price for worthless pieces of glass.

It gave the man his money and quickly shuffled off with his arms full of the small handheld communication devices. The boy found an area with a little more privacy, and he set his pack down and began cramming them in. After securing all but one of the devices, he lifted the remaining one in front of his face and studied it like it were a work of art, or a lost love. But then he did the oddest thing. He spoke to it. "Cimu, activate." After nothing happened, he placed it back in the pack and pulled out another one. He talked to four more of them with nothing happening and placed each one back in the pack. Evan began to worry about the boy's sanity, but on the sixth one, after *It* said, "Activate," the glass screen lit up.

"Yes!" *It* shouted excitedly and pumped his fist in the air.

"Wahoo!" Sydney squealed as she jumped up and down on Evan's shoulder. The big Fallon shrugged suddenly, and she dropped to the ground still cheering.

"What are you excited about?" Evan asked Sydney. "You don't even know what's going on."

"I know, but isn't it exciting?" she said to Evan, and then she bounded closer to *It*. "So, what is it?" she asked him, shaking with anticipation. "It looks like a mystic item."

"A Cimu," *It* whispered loudly.

"A see what?" Vasilik asked, gazing down at the device.

"Cimu—Comprehensive Interfacing Media Unit," *It* said, as if he was clearing up any misunderstanding.

By the looks on Vasilik's and Evan's faces, nothing had been cleared up. In fact, they were now more confused than ever.

"Oh, yeah, the seemoo. You've mentioned them before." Sydney saw the screen shining bright. "Wow. It's definitely a mystic ... doohickey. What was that incantation you used?"

"There's no incantation, it's not mysticism. It's just technology." The boy overflowed with elation. "And they're older models. So, it's older technology."

"I've never heard of technology mysticism," Evan grumbled, as he leaned in for a closer look.

"So, what do they be for, lad?" Vasilik said, hovering over him as well.

"We can use them to talk to one another when we're far away from each other. I just have to say the word 'activate' to make it work."

"Right, an incantation," Sydney insisted.

It glared at her for a moment, then shrugged. "I guess you could see it that way."

"So it is like a black bowl, or hearing horns?" Sydney asked, staring, amazed at the device.

"I don't know what those are, but if they make it so you can communicate with someone at a distance, then yeah." *It* picked another device out of the bag. "Cimu, activate," *It* said to the device, and it lit up. "Awesome, this one works too." He laughed and held them both up and said, "Cimu, deactivate." The devices went dark again.

"So, you're not going to eat off of them?" Evan asked, with Vasilik nodding and looking as if there were still a question about them being flatware.

"No, I'm not going to eat off of them." He shoved them back in his pack. "I'll work on syncing them up when we find a place with a little more privacy."

"Why would you want to sing to them?" Sydney squeaked, as she was now even more intrigued.

It looked down, shaking his head. "No, I'm not going to … no singing … there's no singing … never mind, let's keep moving."

⁓

They continued making their way towards the gate and, though *It* was excited about finding the C.I.M.U. devices, he was still bothered by the fact that they still had not found Lucas. He was also disturbed by the increasingly poor living conditions he saw as they got closer to the gate.

"Is it always like this?" *It* asked.

"Like what, laddie?" Vasilik replied.

"Like this. All the poor looking people and dirt and trash. The living conditions are horrible."

"Aye, it is no Yolanrym, but it be no different from any other port city in the kingdom. Actually, I be see'n worse."

"How can it be worse than this?" *It* gasped.

"Wait until we be get'n inside the city Gates," Vasilik said with a snicker.

They came within yards of the city's main entrance. Six guards stood near the gate, but only one was remotely interested in doing his job of checking out everybody entering the city. Vasilik stopped and raised his brow.

"That be an odd one there," he said out loud.

"What is it?" Evan asked.

Vasilik stopped for a minute to weigh the scene. "Tis' never so many watch'n at the gates. And they definitely don't be check'n each body for sure."

"What do you think is going on?" *It* asked.

"T'were I to be take'n a chance at a guess, I'd be say'n they were look'n for you and tusk face here." He gestured to Evan. "Yo're gonna be need'n to go in on yor own, Fallon."

"Not even by a demon's whip will I leave his side," Evan growled, as he pointed his trunk at *It*.

"If'n they be look'n for a Fallon and a human travel'n together ya may no get yor chance to be av'n any audience with the King."

Evan looked around to see that no other Fallons were associating with humans outside of basic business transactions. His face cringed as he appeared to be swearing under his breath. Then he said, "Fine. You all go in first and I'll take up the rear."

Evan dropped back as the others kept going.

"We need to also keep our eyes open for Toyota. He said he would meet us at the gate after finding the supplies we needed," *It* reminded the others.

As they walked up to the rotting posts of the city's main entrance, *It*'s face brightened up with a huge smile as he saw a familiar Blue Jay Ave sitting on the ground just off the road and leaning against the city wall. Both *It* and Sydney ran straight for him. Vasilik had trouble keeping up with his bum leg, but then, he also lacked the enthusiasm of the average teenager.

Lucas stood up when he saw *It* and Sydney coming and began to bow when he was nearly bowled over as they both crashed into him and hugged him like there was no tomorrow. He encased them in his feathered arms as he, too, was excited to see his friends alive.

"What happened to you? We thought you were dead," *It* practically yelled as he hugged him even tighter.

"Or worse," Sydney added, while latching on to the Ave's leg.

"My humblest apologies, I did not mean to distress you with my unintentional absence. I became disoriented," the Ave reported.

It caught his breath and shook his head in disbelief. "We thought the render beasts had gotten to you."

"I should say not. I was unaware that there were any render beasts in the kingdom."

Vasilik walked up and stood next to the trio as they talked.

Evan, who had been trailing behind, was now almost alongside of them but pretending not to be a part of their group. He busied himself by shopping at a vendor's cart selling scarves and bolts of material for making dresses.

"I did overhear some discussions regarding Kroncal attacks, but that must've transpired prior to my arrival. I didn't see or hear anything of them during my journey on the road, but my fear for you when I had been informed caused unmeasurable concern for your wellbeing and safe passage," Lucas said.

"How could you have missed them?" Sydney squeaked.

"Yeah, we followed your tracks and they led to many render beast tracks. Why did you go off in a different direction?" *It* asked.

"As our friend Evan has expressed on many occasions, I'm more suited for metropolitan environments. I had become disoriented and somewhat lost. By the time I located the road, I assumed you all preceded me, so I did not tarry, and journeyed fleet-footed here. Along the way, I persuaded a merchant to provide me space on his wagon amongst his merchandise for the last ten miles. Had I known I was ahead of you, I would not have continued," Lucas said, while a little distracted watching Evan pretend to shop. "Why is Evan perusing women's garments?" Lucas asked with a tilt of his head.

"Vasilik thought it best if Evan were to hang back since the city guards were looking for a Fallon and hooman traveling together," Sydney said, and then turned to Vasilik. "And this is our new friend, Vasilik. *It* hired him to help us get through to the King."

Lucas flourished his arms and began his long-winded introduction. "It's a pleasure to make your acquaintance, I am Lucas Alan Bourdillion Traherne, Second Assistant to the Established Regent Elect of the First Talon, Edroy Nalyd Kayne Grondol." He ended his introduction with an excessively deep bow which he held, waiting for an acknowledgement from Vasilik.

Vasilik gazed oddly at the bent over Ave boy. "I be no fancy dandy, so do no waste yor courtly flamboyants on me—I be Vasilik McCarthy, and pretty scrabb'n happy to meet ya," he said with an outstretched hand. Lucas stood up to his full height and was reluctant to shake hands with the unkempt human, but propriety dictated that he shake, which he did.

"So, I'm still bewildered as to how this all explains why Evan is fondling women's undergarments in a shanty market?" Lucas asked again.

"I think that is his way of being inconspicuous," *It* chuckled.

"I say, he is failing miserably if concealment is his objective," Lucas added with a chuckle as well.

"Yeah, but he would look cute in that lacey red scarf," Sydney squeaked with a giggle.

"And may I inquire as to where our friend Toyota may be?" Lucas asked, with a nearly undetectable snarl, as he resented having to use the word friend.

"He should be here by now with the supplies. He went shopping by himself. He wanted to show that he could be trusted to take on a task without help," *It* added.

Lucas shook his head as his feathers had ruffled on the back of his neck. "I'm sure he did wish to show he could be trusted."

"Well, snappers, we need be get'n gone while the get'n is good," Vasilik chortled as he wrangled everyone towards the gate. "Ya will be guests in me home this even'n. Switbo enjoys visitors."

"Who is Switbo?" Sydney asked, with a tweak of her nose to reposition her glasses.

"Aye, who she be indeed, but She Who Is To Be Obeyed … Switbo, me first wife."

"Your first wife?" asked *It,* with a questioning brow.

"First and only for more a year than I care to be remember'n—an angel; she be like none other. As did I, ya will be love'n her at first sight as she will you."

TWENTY-EIGHT

SHE WHO IS TO BE OBEYED

Nightfall was not far off as Evan's unit followed Vasilik through a very seedy part of town. Toyota was there as well. He met up with them just inside the city gate with two sacks bulging with food supplies.

Rotting trash, horse manure, and even dead verms were just a few of the nasty things lining the gutters of the streets. *It* covered his nose and shook his head, as this place made the shanty towns they passed on the road look like vacation villas. The many facial expressions of disgust made it clear how the group felt about their new surroundings.

"You weren't kidding when you said it was going to get worse once we got through the gates," *It* said.

"We av no got to the worse part yet. This here be me neighborhood," Vasilik boasted.

Evan stopped for a moment to wipe something off his foot. He wasn't sure what it was, but it smelled horrendous.

Vasilik nodded to the Fallon's crud covered foot. "Yeah, that be a bit of a muss you got there. I'd be no step'n in that t'were I you."

Toyota and Sydney sat perched atop Evan's pack as they were unwilling to let their feet touch the filth of the ground. They came to a slat wood structure with the boards stained black from years of grime buildup and with cracks in them wide enough that the slightest breeze would blow through freely. The door was of equal quality with the walls and large enough to fit a Fallon's bulk through with ease, but it looked to be precariously hinged on the frame. Of course, to the dread of the others, Vasilik stopped at the door.

"Ah, home be where the heart be, and me heart beats within," Vasilik mused as he opened the door and took a step in.

As his head passed through the doorway—*Twang*!—A dagger shot past his face and sunk solidly into the doorframe.

From inside, a woman's sharp, pointed voice called out after the dagger struck. "Yor two days late! What lie do you got for me this time?"

Vasilik threw open the door and pulled *It* in front of him as a shield. "T'was delayed on the account of the business I be av'n with me new friends here," he called back from his hiding spot behind the boy.

"Don't ya be bring'n gutter snipes in here again, or Webster will be the least of yor worries," said the tall, dark woman standing on the other side of the room, shaking a metal rod with a fluffy duster at one end of it. The way she shook the fluffy duster made it obvious that the cleaning implement was Webster. Her other hand was held suspiciously behind her back.

"No, me dear, these be business partners—pay'n business partners," he said, stressing the word 'paying' much more than it was necessary.

"Paying partners?" she repeated; a smile creeping to her lips.

"Yes ma'am. We've hired your husband to be our guide and use his connections to get us an audience with the King." *It* called out, and then paused as he saw that the duster rod in her hand had a slight purple glow with faint whiffs of black mist drifting around it.

The room was quiet and still as Switbo stood gawking at *It* with a world of questions on her face, but then she said. "Aye, of course this be what yor pay'n him for. Me husband there? ... and an audience with the king ... of Aremac? Our king? The one in Yolanrym?"

"Yes ma'am," *It* said, smiling.

"Huh ... good luck with that, wee snapper," she said sarcastically, but seeing how young he looked she used a softer voice. "Well, be get'n yorselves in out of the damp." She turned back around to place the dagger she was concealing behind her back onto the counter.

The weary bunch began to file into the house. Evan, who'd been hidden from view by the wall, thudded in as well. Switbo turned back when she heard the loud steps and saw Evan standing in her doorway. "The blazes and all that be cursed!" She gripped the rod of her duster tightly and whipped off the fuzzy cloth at the end to reveal that it was actually a weapon. *It* could now see the object clearly and noticed the rod she wielded had a familiar purple glow and dark mist emanating from it—it was a mystical item.

Switbo glared at Evan, and then back to Vasilik. "And yor be'n good with this?" she breathed to her husband as her empty hand reached slowly back toward the dagger on the counter.

"The Fallon be their muscle and protector, and one of me employers," Vasilik cautioned her. "Which be make'n im our friend and guest."

"This night will no be soon forgotten," she said as she motioned to Evan to come inside.

Evan stepped through the door. Switbo could now get a clear view of him and that he appeared to have three heads. Sydney and Toyota were peeking over his shoulders.

"So, Fallon, ya be have'n a wee bit of an infestation, I see," she said with a wiry smile.

"Oh, I'm not an infestation. I'm Sydney," the little Seeuradi girl squeaked, popping up and then leaping to the floor. "And that's Toyota. I can't truthfully say that he's not infested."

"Glory then! It be quite the menagerie ya be have'n here. Has this old swindler at least guided you to some food?" she said as she put some bread out on the table.

"No, he hasn't," Toyota said as he swung down off Evan's shoulder and landed near the table; and in a quick move he swiped up a piece of bread.

"Well, there be no much to eat here but we will be make'n do," she said reluctantly. The doorless cabinets above the counter confirmed that there was very little food to be found.

Evan sat down his pack, pulled out two sacks, and set them on the table. The sacks fell open and out fell a cornucopia of fruits, vegetables, and some salted meats. There were even several sugared dates.

"Not to worry, we've brought plenty," Evan said.

"And we can get more if you want," Sydney squeaked, with a huge smile on her face.

Switbo stood gazing at the food on the table and put her hand on Vasilik's shoulder as he stepped up to her. She leaned in and whispered, "Husband, ya have outdone yor self in yor mischief." She raised her eyes to Evan and her voice was warm and sincere. "Ya be welcome in our home."

After some quick introductions and one lengthy one from Lucas, Toyota finished chowing down his piece of bread and grabbed one of the food sacks. He swung it up to the counter and announced, "Just show me where your pots and pans are, and I'll get us supper in no time."

Switbo's eyes gleamed with the hint of a tear welling up. Vasilik leaned in and whispered in her ear, "And they be have'n coin," he said, with a peck on her cheek—yes, it was most definitely a tear in her eye.

"Okay then, if'n the two of ya don't mind manage'n the eats, our friend *It* here be in need of a diviner," Vasilik said out loud to Switbo.

"A mystic?" Switbo asked with a sneer on her face.

"Aye, evidently the boy be av'n a tad of the mysticism about him," Vasilik added.

"So, you'll be taking him to Sucram then?" she replied.

"And we shan't be long." Vasilik went to slap his wife on her backside, but her hand moved with lightning speed to block it.

"Wow! That was fast," Sydney gasped.

"Nope, t'was slow. Watch this," Vasilik went to slap Switbo on her bottom two more times, and each time she blocked it without even looking. "From years of work'n at the pub house, those reflexes be."

"That is just too awesome. Can I try?" Sydney asked, as she bounded over and behind Switbo. Without waiting for permission, Sydney swung her paw and tried to hit the human woman on her butt. Just like with Vasilik, Sydney was denied. She swung again and was blocked. Before long she was chittering and giggling as she attempted to play Switbo's buttocks like a drum, but with lightning speed Switbo moved her hands to deflect Sydney's paws. At one point, the woman even took a drink from her tankard and still didn't miss at blocking Sydney's strikes.

"Amazing. A human with Seeuradi speed," Toyota exclaimed with admiration.

"And though it does not appear to be so, my guess is that she is not in the spring of her years," Lucas respectfully commented to Evan in a hushed voice.

Vasilik watched his wife playing with the little Seeuradi girl, and for a moment there was an honest and sincere glimmer of some hidden truth in his eyes. He was smiling from the heart.

Evan leaned down towards Vasilik. "And this doesn't look odd to you?"

"No, lad, not one mite of a bit."

The boys joined in with the laughter and soon, the gaps in the boards on the wall not only let the breeze in, but they also let the mirthful and vibrant laughter seep out into the streets, where the joviality of sound was a stark contrast to the dismal sight of the squalor.

TWENTY-NINE

SOME MIRRORS ARE JUST NOT NICE

With Vasilik in the lead, *It*, Lucas, Sydney and Evan meandered down darkened streets and alleyways. Vasilik's eyes constantly darted around, as he stuck to the shadows. It began to look as if he, too, was avoiding being seen as much as the others. The reason for this became obvious when four large humans stepped out into the street as Vasilik approached a circle of buildings where multiple streets converged.

"There he is then, Mister Grifter himself, Vasilik," laughed one of the large humans with a long goatee beard and balding head.

"Aye, tis me gentlemen, but also tis a shame I av no the moment to be greet'n ya proper. I be sure ya be understand'n, Derger, me boy," Vasilik said.

"No, actually we do not understand, and neither will Brightskull. I'm sure, now, you would be willing to do business," said Derger.

"Nope, I'll still be need'n to pass," Vasilik replied.

"That's not one of your options. You owe Brightskull for the damages."

"An he be want'n payback fo da beat'n yo gav im," slurred a shaggy-headed cretin in the back with deformed lips that appeared to have been crushed on one side of his mouth.

"Shut it, Slurr!" Derger snapped.

"Tell him I'll no be pay'n for damages when he be the cause of it. And let him know I feel deeply sorrowful for the beat'n … tis sure he would av fared better had he no been full on into the bottle," Vasilik replied with a fake air of sympathy.

"Apparently you have misinterpreted the situation," the man said, pulling his sword out and resting in on his own shoulder. "It should not have come to this, but we all knew you would eventually end this way. It was just a matter of time."

"Aye, there be an end come'n, but no today caus'n tis no me ya be slow'n down." Vasilik turned his head back over his shoulder and called out, "Evan, lad!"

As Evan stepped out of the shadows, the men took a momentary step back in reaction to his size, but then broke out into laughter as his shape was more easily seen.

"You brought ya a farming oaf, eh? ... Or a dock tonk? He's a spineless tusker! Are we supposed to be afraid now?" Derger laughed.

There was only a sliver of moonlight shining through the cloudy sky, but it was enough to show the dark shade of orange spreading out over Evan's face.

It held his hand partially over his mouth and whispered to Lucas. "I know what a farmer is, but what are the other things he called him?"

"Not appropriate language, I can assure you. A dock tonk is a term which implies a strong, but insipid Fallon only useful to carry heavy burdens on the wharf. And the other word is an intolerant and vulgar insult to the whole Fallon race which would typically result in excessive violence when spoken in the presence of a Fallon warrior."

"Yep. And he spoke it in front of the wrong Fallon warrior," Sydney squeaked, as Evan stomped by them to stand next to Vasilik. "He shouldn't have used the 'T' word."

"Now, now. Ya should no av gone an used the 'T' word," Vasilik warned with a shake of his head and a snicker at Derger, as Evan stalked up to them. "Ya see, Evan here be a warrior of the Stronghide herd—an he be one of the finest of the lot."

Derger sneered. "That's a lie. There isn't a Fallon warrior within a thousand miles of here. Especially one of the Stronghides." He turned to look over his shoulder. "Kahlyn, what do you say?"

Standing behind Derger with a burst of dreadlocks covering his head and reaching down below his shoulders was a tall slender dark-skinned man. At any other time, and with the benefit of a razor, a bath, and some corrective dental care, he would be almost handsome. "Cannot say what's under the cloak, but I ain't never been afeared of a tusker, and I'm not going to start this night," the man hissed, as he stared at Evan. With one dreadlock hanging down his face, his eyes showed that there was no bluffing in his gaze.

The leather of Evan's sword hilt squealed under the pressure of his tightening grip when he heard the word "tusker" repeated. As he began to slide his sword out, Vasilik swung his cane up and let it come to rest on Evan's hand to stop him from drawing it.

Vasilik's left eyebrow shot up high on his forehead as he winked to Evan and said, "Even in defense, ya could be jailed for any kill'n done this night."

Evan bared his teeth, but let his blade drop back down into its sheath as he took a step forward and up to Derger.

Derger craned his head back, making eye contact with the menacing Fallon. He breathed in slowly and with much exaggeration, then let out a loud sigh as if he was being inconvenienced. As quick as a flash, he flipped his wrist while slinging out his sword in a leaping strike of his blade to the same spot on Evan's throat where Vasilik had threatened the Evan earlier that day—the sweet spot for killing a Fallon.

Twang!—The blade slammed hard into Evan's tusk as he twitched his head to block the telegraphed blow. Unfortunately for Derger, his leap sent him straight into Evan's meaty grasp. The Fallon grabbed him by his sword hand and his opposite shoulder. The human hovered in the air as Evan brought him in close with Derger's head between his tusks.

Evan growled deeper than any creature Derger ever heard as the Fallon roared, "Did you want to call me a tusker now?"

Before the man could answer, Evan twitched his head again, batting Derger's skull between his tusks until the would-be assassin's body went limp.

The shaggy-headed Slurr lunged forward toward Evan, but the Fallon warrior used Derger as a club to knock the man back. Kahlyn tried to take advantage of Evan's being turned slightly away and raised his sword to strike but was stopped dead by Evan's monstrous boot kicking the man in the chest and sending him sprawling several feet away.

Vasilik watched as Evan advanced. The sound of bodies being thrown violently through the air was accompanied by screams of extreme agony echoing in the dark. Unlike the others in the group who were cheering Evan on, Vasilik was doing more than mere spectating. He was examining the Fallon's every move—studying him. By the look on the old man's face, he admired the young warrior. Most Fallon fighters rely on brute force, but it was obvious that Evan was every bit the tactician—and this made him dangerous.

Vasilik knew the fight was over when he heard Evan say, "Did you call me the 'T' word?" one last time with the familiar thudding splash of a body hitting the mud.

The old man limped over to the Fallon who wasn't even breathing heavy and said, "That'll do, lad ... that'll do."

As *It* ran up with Sydney and Lucas, the boy held his arms out with his shoulder's shrugged. "Why didn't anyone tell me there was a 'T' word? I was surrounded by Fallons for months and nobody ever mentioned it."

"How are we supposed to know what words you know and which ones you don't? Do you even know what words you don't know?" Sydney squeaked.

"No. But that is besides the point. Are there any other words that could get me killed if I say them to the wrong people?"

Kneeling down into the mud, Vasilik began rummaging through the pockets of the unconscious men to retrieve four coin-pouches and anything else of value. "Aye, I wouldn't be call'n a Gold Tabard a piss-coat. That be mak'n them orney to deal with."

"Obviously I wouldn't say that. I meant any other common words and terms that I might say in conversation." *It* said.

"So, you were going to use the 'T' word in one of your conversations?" Evan growled.

"No. I didn't even know that the "T" word was a word until now. I mean I knew it was a word ... I mean ... never mind. Just drop it," *It* said, as Vasilik's activities caught his attention. "What are you doing?"

Evan also noticed and snarled, "You're robbing these men?"

"It's reimbursement for damages—a reparations of sorts," Vasilik said.

"But they didn't damage me," Evan hissed in disgust, as pilfering from a fallen enemy is not at all honorable.

"He's right. You shouldn't be doing that," Sydney squeaked with disapproval, though she has been known to swipe an apple or two at the occasional marketplace.

"Then we'll be calling it services rendered," Vasilik muttered, while grasping for any excuse that might justify his actions.

"Services? For what?" *It* added, with dwindling admiration reflected in his eyes.

"What services? Why, where else could they be receive'n such expert train'n in the art of self-defense?" Vasilik groaned, but changed his tune as he saw the looks on *It*'s and Sydney's faces that screamed of heartbreaking betrayal.

Vasilik jammed his cane into the mud. "Damned it all to blazes … I guess ya snappers be right." He tossed three pouches and the other items to the ground next to Slurr, who was now snoring loudly. "Are ya happy? Can we be get'n on with it?"

It and Sydney grinned up at the old man who just nudged them down the street and told them to "put a leg to it." As the kids took off with Lucas close behind, Evan and Vasilik brought up the rear. Vasilik couldn't help but feel the condescending stare and grimace emanating from the giant Fallon.

Vasilik glared up at Evan. "What be bite'n at yor south-end now?"

Evan's eyes tightened in. "There were four pouches—you dropped three."

Vasilik pursed his lips with his curled mustache dipping low on both sides as his voice took on a higher pitched sarcastic tone. "Saw that, ya did? Well, it be the thought that counts, lad."

They continued their trek to the Mystic Diviner's shop, but with an understandable lack of conversation between the two.

A small shop with mismatched shingles near an alleyway was lit by a lantern hanging from the building corner. The sign above the door showed two eyes looking at each other. Short, black, crooked lines streaked partially out into the whites of the eyes. The faded red background looked more like dried blood than paint. Silver dots resembling stars bespeckled the bloody background and frame. Painted on the window in crude dark letters were the words:

Mystic Designation And Sundries

A large figure stepped out from the alley, but still in the shadows. There was no doubt that it was Evan. Close behind him were Sydney, *It*, and

Lucas, and they stopped under the lantern, or at least most of the group was under the light; Evan couldn't fit. The sound of a familiar step, tap, and drag broke the silence as Vasilik pushed through the group.

"And why tis there no forward motion? Ya snappers got bricks in yor stockings." *Fwunk*—Vasilik came to a sudden stop when he attempted to push past Evan and the mammoth didn't budge. "Are ya gonna be get'n outta me way, or grow'n roots and sprout'n leaves?" Vasilik bellowed.

Evan let out a low grumble, or was it a growl? Either way, it wasn't friendly.

Vasilik glared up into Evan's unblinking eyes. "Someday, lad, I'm gonna learn ya a little someth'n about respect'n yor elders."

Evan continued to glare back at Vasilik as he moved to one side to let the human by.

The old cuss let out a slight snicker as he moved past the giant and to the door of the shop. "Tis where we need be, snappers." He peered in the window of the dark shop trying to make out if anyone was inside. "Me guess be the ole bugger be already t'sleep." He took his cane and rapped it against the glass. Nothing happened. He rapped louder. The glass rang out with each blow, threatening to shatter at any moment when, from inside, a candle flickered into view and a cloaked form headed towards the door.

As the door opened, a coarse and ancient sounding voice could be heard from within. "Oh, it's you."

"Tis most certainly," Vasilik answered back, with his curly mustache lifting with his grin.

The candle popped out of the door with a boney, clawed hand holding it. As the rest of the arm followed, the cloak turned out to not be a cloak, but a bunch of feathers instead. An old Ave leaned out in a sleeveless night shirt and trousers. Though his feathers were gray and tattered, it was obvious he was a once proud eagle. He glared hard at his night visitors and cringed. "Good Giver! What manner of company have you sunk to these days?"

He turned and motioned for them to follow him in. Around the room, shelves and display cases were filled with everything from potions to wands; from rune stones to enchanted parchments; and just about any and all other commonplace mystical accessories. There was even a stuffed, antlered rabbit that Sydney swore was always watching her.

Looming in the corner was a large object with a thick gray canvas draped over it. As *It* looked around, everything appeared to have a slight purple glow and dark mistiness to it. The shelves themselves appeared to billow the mystic smoke created by the enchanted items. While the youngsters marveled at all the strange gadgets and bobbles, Vasilik introduced his ragtag group to his oldest friend, Sucram.

Actually, the term friend was probably not the most accurate description of their mutual tolerance of each other, but it would do for now. Of course, the diviner didn't have to be a wise old bird to notice that Evan appeared to also have some distrust of Vasilik, but then again, who didn't feel that way?

For some reason, the guest that the old Ave found most interesting wasn't the person they were here about. His eagle eye fell upon Lucas, and he moved over to him for closer scrutinizing. "This is a sight I thought never to see." Sucram pulled at Lucas's clothing, prodded him with a claw, and finally lifted the boy's taloned hands up and inspected them. "A little recent wear and tear, but predominately a sophisticated lifestyle ... a politician I would say; and one under the tutelage of a prominent individual ... Regents Council, if I'm not wrong—correct?" He eyed the boy closely as he spoke.

"Yes, sir," Lucas answered, but for the first time since he has been with the group, the Blue Jay did not bow or offer any sort of respectful flamboyant presentation.

"Not happy at all to see me? I suppose you know of me, then?" the mystic asked.

"You are Sucram. You were once one of the great Ave mystics in service to the council. Respected, revered, and even feared," Lucas replied.

"The greatest of the Ave mystics," the old eagle said, with a raised and extended talon.

Lucas' beak couldn't sneer, but the look in his eyes could as he hissed, "Until you brought disgrace to our race and blasphemed the flock."

The cheeks on Sucram's face lifted though he could not smile. "To be so young and full of misplaced righteousness ... do you know the problem with the gift of divination?" Sucram asked Lucas, as he turned to walk away from the Blue Jay.

"You see too much?" Lucas said with a shrug.

"No ... I see the truth of things—as well as the deception, and that is the breaker of all vows. Be mindful. It is all too easy to fall from the flock, righteous Lucas." He strutted over to Vasilik, moving between the others crowded into his shop. "So, what brings you and your ..." He paused as he looked them over. "... horde to my shop after hours ... and uninvited?" Sucram ruffled his feathers as he stressed the uninvited part.

"We be in a bit o need of yor designation divination skills," Vasilik said with a gesture to *It*. "The boy can do things ... and his eyes ... well they be a scooch weird, I hear tell of it."

The old bird-man walked over to the human boy and, not so gently, grabbed his face. Gazing deep into *It*'s eyes, he said, "Weird eyes, huh?" He leaned in closer. "Tiny little black lines show up here at the edge of the eye?" He pointed one of his sharp talons at the white part of the boy's eye.

The tip was way too close for *It*'s comfort. "Yeah, how did you know?" *It*'s voice cracked from his nervousness.

"I wouldn't be good at my job if I didn't know these things." With an open hand against the young boy's face, he pushed *It* aside, as the feathered old Ave moved past him toward the large object in the corner. He knocked a few stools and containers out of the way to get to it.

"And we have here something that will shed light on what we don't know." He jerked the canvas down with little grace and a whole lot of dust. A second flourish of the old cloth sent another cloud of dust through the room. A brief moment of coughing and some waving away of the dust got interrupted as they all paused in awe of what they saw. A tall black slab held in place by a brass frame loomed over all except Evan—few things ever loomed over Evan.

Sydney let out a yip of excitement. "A black mirror of insight!" She scampered to Sucram. "Can I try it? Can I? Can I? Can I? Can I?" Her tail twitched with excitement and her glasses nearly bounced off her head.

"So, you know of this?" the old Ave asked her with a snicker.

"Of course! My Prominence used a black bowl to divine my mystic essence."

"The Black Bowl of Waters is a common practice of the rural mystic, but it sees much less than this mirror. May I presume you are training as a healer or prophet?" Sucram said, as he studied her with one and then the other of his eyes.

"More healer than prophet," she groaned, with some disappointment in her voice.

It giggled, but Evan laughed harder. "Yeah, her prophetic skills consist of flipping a coin and random guessing." the boy said and held up his hand. Evan, with a smirk of his own, high fived him from across the table.

Sydney dropped her head. "I'm trying."

Sucram put his hand on the girl's shoulder. "I'm sure you are." He guided her in front of the mirror as he described the process to the others. "As she peers into the mirror, her inner self and talent will be revealed to her, and her eyes will give us an indication of her power's strength as of this moment."

"Why as of this moment?" Vasilik questioned with a raised eyebrow.

Sucram tossed his head back and forth as he described time as being a variable in the development of all things, and that at any time something may be more or less than it once was. He placed his hand on Sydney's head. "What we see today may not be what we would see tomorrow."

Sydney was much less excited. "I could lose my powers?"

"Relax. Typically, we all grow stronger over time." Sucram smiled generously at her with his cheeks as his beak was rigid. "I'm sure what you and your friend see tonight will just be the beginning of your mystic journey." He took in a long breath and released it. "Now, relax and gaze into the mirror." The old mystic leaned in close. "Tell me what you see."

As Sydney peered into the darkness, she saw her reflection looking back at her. After a moment it waved at her, and she waved back with a huge grin. The reflection reached out from the mirror, grabbed her hand, and gave a bucktoothed-smile as it jerked Sydney into the mirror.

❦

The room she was in disappeared, as she was surrounded by darkness and felt herself falling into the stark black nothingness. Instead of fear, a warmth filled her body and soul. The blackness swirled around until a bright light broke through and she found herself in a field of brilliant yellow grass and a rainbow of colored flowers growing everywhere. To her left was a sick deer lying among the flowers, and as she walked past it, it jumped up full of life and scampered off. It was completely healed.

❦

Still standing in front of the black mirror in the Diviner's shop, Sydney was lost in a trance, but had been talking since she first stepped up to the mirror. "I can also see people. And they are getting up as I walk past." She continued to describe what she was seeing on the other side.

Sucram turned to the others. "These images tell us that she does indeed have the healer's gifts and an extensive one at that. Some healers are limited by species."

Suddenly, Sydney gasped. "The clouds are opening ... I see children ... oh ... one looks like me. I see our village. It has grown. My robes, they're not a Prominence's robes. They're not even Seeuradi." She paused and then gasped. "A king, or lord, or something ... a great king ... so big ... his kingdom ... his people follow him ... he relies on me." Tears began to roll down the little Seeuradi's face.

Sucram nodded knowingly. "The future. She sees what may come to be. With time, she will be a prophet as well as a healer—evidently an advisor to a king. She is very lucky to have more than one powerful talent. Quite unusual for her race."

Sydney gasped again, even louder, and shuddered as well. "No! Fire ... everywhere, fire!"

Sucram turned back to her. "Pull out from the flames, little one. Pull back. Don't touch them." He watched Sydney struggle to catch her breath, and then he calmed her down. "What do you see now?"

"Nothing," she squeaked. "It's empty, but full of light."

"Then return to us. Come back," the old Ave cooed in her ear. Sydney shuffled back from the mirror with the Diviner's help. He turned her to face the group. "See." He pointed to her eyes. Tiny, almost unnoticeable, black line segments stuck out from the outer edge in the whites of her eyes, but they didn't reach out much at all and they were very hard to see. "These little black marks indicate that she is strong with her talents, very strong." He pointed to his own eye and chanted a few times. "Look how the black reaches out more into the iris of my eye."

"And yor the most powerful mystic I be know'n," Vasilik boasted, with both eyebrows raised.

"There are those more powerful than me, for sure," Sucram chortled. "But not in this kingdom."

Sydney shook off the daze that she was in. "The fire. I have to go back home. My village was burning." She grabbed at Sucram's pant leg.

"No child. What you saw was only a possible future and one that may be centuries from now." He sat her down. "You have nothing to fear. These images are brought forward for you to learn of yourself. That is the purpose and the mysticism of the mirror. It brings forth the truth that is you. Even the vision of the king you will serve may only be a representation that you have something important in your future."

With his monstrously large hand, Evan cupped *It*'s entire back as he effortlessly pushed the boy toward the mirror. "I'd like to see you try and find some truth in this one," he snickered. "You'll be looking for water in the desert."

"Ok, boy. Your turn." Sucram guided *It* to the mirror. "Remember to relax, look deep into yourself, blah blah blah ... You know the routine."

"I'm a little hazy on the blah blah blah part, but I think I can do this and prove to Jumbo over there that he's wrong." *It* gestured with his head toward Evan, who responded with a snort from his trunk.

"It'll never happen," Evan grunted.

"We'll need to remove this," Sucram said, as he plucked the white hat off *It*'s head and set it down on the table.

It stood gazing into the black mirror. No reflection grabbed at his arm. In fact, he thought he should give up. It was obvious nothing was going to happen, but then his mind began to spin in circles as his thoughts leapt into the depths of the glossy blackness. Deeper he traveled. Images of animals and people drifted past him. Rocks, trees, the ocean, and the sky went by. Then planets and other unearthly sights passed around him.

In the room, *It* stood transfixed on the mirror. Sucram was at his side. "Tell me what you see. What fills your mind, your soul?" the old Ave said.

"I see animals and people."

Sucram nodded to Vasilik. "So, he also has skills pertaining to life ... maybe a healer as well he will be, or a mind reader," the old Ave said to Vasilik.

"Now I see boulders, the sea spray, and clouds."

"Ok ... maybe he will master material manipulation or the elements. Could be he will be a telekinetic or druid."

It began to wrinkle his brow and stutter as he talked. "There are shapes and forms ... I can't tell what they are."

"Ooo ... it looks like a conjurer is his destiny." The old mystic opened his beak in anticipation. "It has been a long time since I worked with one of those."

It began to sway, and his voice cracked. "It's all falling away … now I see everything."

Sucram put his claw on the boy's shoulder. "You mean nothing, my boy. It is nothing that you see. All whiteness."

"No. I see everything," ***It*** breathed, with his voice taking on strength.

"Maybe it's time to pull back. You're confused."

It began to chant in a deeper tone than ever before, "Light to dark, start to end! I see all." His voice was that of a grown man's, and it echoed eerily from his throat.

Sucram leaned in close. "Relax. Pull back, my son. Pull back now."

The boy's voice grew louder and deeper still. "Great and small is as everything and nothing!"

Evan took a step forward and grabbed his sword hilt, but he was frustrated as there was no one to fight. "What's happening to him?" he yelled out.

Without warning, ***It*** thrusted his hands out as he leaned into the mirror with its surface rippling like a pool of dark water.

Sucram pulled on the boy and yelled. "Enough! This is wrong! Something is wrong!" He tried harder to pull the human boy back out of the mirror, but nothing was happening as ***It*** continue to chant, "Light to dark! Start to end! Great and small! I see all!"

In the dark and damp cave where another black mirror was embedded in stalagmite stood the cloudy black form of the Empress. She gazed into the reflective dark surface as it seemed to be vibrating. "What is this?" she hissed to herself.

The mirrored surface exploded outward toward her but stayed intact with black viscous fingers stretching out at the demon shrouded in mist. As she floated backward in shock, the upper half of ***It***'s body was protruding out of the black, liquidy surface of the mirror.

"Light to dark! Start to finish! Great and small! I see all!" ***It*** chanted, with his eyes striped with long black veins. He reached out toward the Empress and gazed wickedly, manically, at her. He appeared older and somehow hard and rough—a grown man. "I see you! I see you!" his harsh voice called out, sending deep vibrations echoing through the cave and sending chills into small creatures cowering in the shadows.

"This can't be!" the cloudy form screeched with hatred.

"I see all. I see you!" *It* hissed in a dark, almost evil, voice and with an equally frightening smile. Under his right eye was half of a partially faded tattoo. The other half of the tattoo was covered by a scar from a fire long ago. Multiple other scars crossed his face with his skin being aged and worn.

"You can't have become this. You can't be ready this soon!" she hissed again, with a demonic visage just under the surface of her misty shroud. "And maybe you aren't," she said with her voice softening. A hint of smile crossed the clouded, demonic face. "Ooh my … you're caught between realities, aren't you? This is a divination of you; only a mirage of your strength and the future you … I see … yes, I now see you, child!"

Her misty form folded over multiple times as the tip of a dark red blade slid slowly from the folding mist. With a keen razored edge on one side and a row of sharply honed teeth lining the back of the curved blade, it continued to slip out from the mist with a hideous, clawed arm grasping at the handle. The flesh dangling off the claw arm appeared to have been badly burned with bits of skin barely clinging to the sinewy muscles as it wielded a hellish sickle.

From in the Diviner's store, panic prevailed as everyone called out in horror to *It*. Inside the mirror, they saw *It*'s torso and the misty demon empress. Sydney dashed under a table and cried out in unintelligible squeaks.

Evan had stepped up to the mirror and could see the scene unfolding on the other side. He reached out to put his hand through the mirror and grab *It*'s shoulder, but his giant hand crashed against the glassy surface as if he had punched into solid rock.

Sucram had one hand on *It*'s back, while he too had started chanting.

Evan glowered at the old Ave. "Hurry! Do Something!"

Sucram chanted louder as he began to tremble. Black lines dotted the edge of his eyes as he was reaching the maximum limits of his ability.

Evan turned back to the mirror and watched on helplessly as the sickle raised higher into the air and the black mist stalked closer to the boy. Evan could see that there was something just under the surface of the blackness; and for a moment it became almost tangible. A skull, or demonic visage with glowing purple eyes. The Empress snapped her gaze upward as she stopped in front of the human boy who hung there defenseless.

The demonic face smiled—but not at *It*. "I know you too." The creature leered at Evan—taunting him, making him watch as she readied to kill his human friend. Multiple snake-like tongues squirmed out and over her hideous up-turned lips.

"Urrrgh!" *Thwaack!* The boy and the old Ave mystic flew backwards as Evan swiped them both away from the mirror with a mighty strike that could have killed them both.

It was sprawled out on the floor face up. Evan, Lucas, and Vasilik gazed down at the boy whose eyes were filled with swirling blackness. The white was all but gone, and the hazel irises were replaced with a purple glow.

Sucram rolled over to check on the boy. He screeched and jumped back, scrambling across the floor after having seen *It*'s eyes.

Vasilik reached down to help Sucram to his feet. The old Ave whispered roughly, "Great Giver help us all!—he's a Molec!"

Vasilik steadied the old Ave. "No! That be not true!"

Evan, now kneeling down over *It* asked, "What's a Molec?"

Sucram trembled, and his voice was weak. "Their power is undefinable. They can have many talents, all talents, as they control the smallest pieces of life and all things."

Now, Vasilik's voice was shaky. "But … tis a good thing, or no?"

"No one can know. They are too rare and usually reclusive. And they definitely don't allow themselves to be tested or studied. I'm lucky to be alive. We all are." Everyone looked to *It*. The old diviner pulled on Vasilik's arm. "You know of a Molec who lived over a thousand years ago—he is of legend."

"Who?" Vasilik shook his head, as he couldn't think of anyone.

"Tro," the Ave whispered as he turned to *It*.

Evan straightened and took in a deep breath. "Tro … The End Bringer?" he whispered louder than intended.

The room was dead quiet as they all gazed at the deep black eyes of their lost friend who remained motionless on the floor. A long discomfort enveloped the room to join the eerie silence. When the long pause was over, Sydney, who had been quiet since she hid under the table, turned to the others, and said, "Is anyone else hungry? I'm starved … scary stuff makes me hungry."

Lucas dropped his head and shook it back and forth.

⁓

The diviner's shop was bright with candlelight. The group stood around *It*, who they had seated in a chair, still in a trance.

Lucas paced around. While walking back and forth, he asked Sucram, "Can you not cast a charm or something to bring him out of this? You are the Great Sucram!"

"So, now I am the Great Sucram?" he hissed back. After a pause, he shook his head. "No, I can't do any of that."

"Why not?"

"Because I can't." The old Ave let his head fall and his shoulders droop.

"You didn't even try!"

"It would have no effect." He saw the defiance in the young Ave's eyes. "Mystically speaking, it would be like your little squirrel friend trying to push over this brute." Sucram sighed as he glanced up at Evan. "No offense."

"Well, that's no problem," Sydney cheerfully squeaked, as she ran hard into Evans's leg thinking it would help *It*. Her feet skittered against the floor planks as they kept sliding out from under her. She twisted around and set her back against his gigantic thigh, but again her paws slid out from under her as before. She stopped to catch her breath from the exertion, and then in a flash she scrambled around and up the large Fallon until she was on his shoulders with her arms around his massive head. She tugged and pulled with all her might. Arching her back, she squeaked with ferocity, and she strained every muscle to pull on his head.

Lucas watched Sydney, as she now had her paws on both of Evan's ears and was jerking around widely as the huge Fallon groaned with annoyance. He felt nothing. Lucas turned back to Sucram. "I believe I understand your predicament."

Vasilik tilted his head to the side as his left eyebrow mischievously raised high on his forehead. He hovered over the boy. "I got me an idea, lads, but I ain't think'n yor gonna like it none too much, and tisn't at all mystical." He raised his hand up and out to the side with his palm flat as he stood next to the boy.

⁓

Deep in the darkness, *It* floated among the many celestial bodies of the universe. Off in the distance, he could see something slither out from behind a bright blue-ringed planet. Back and forth the form slithered as it got closer. The boy felt cold all over.

Closer and closer, the object weaved through the blackness and grew in size with each change of direction. The boy tried to flee, but he couldn't feel his legs or arms. The form began to take shape. A long tail—wings—scales—teeth! Terror filled the boy's soul as the ferocious beast was bearing down on him with jaws wide open.

Back in the diviner's shop, *It* screamed, "Dragon!" He would have hit the floor if Evan hadn't caught him after Vasilik slapped the boy so hard that he fell out of the chair. The word dragon shrilled out from the boy's mouth again as he screamed up at the ceiling. Candles flickered, as their flames leaped off from their wicks and hovered in the air for a brief moment. They flashed with a purple flame and then returned to their wicks, burning normally.

After several heavy breaths, *It* cleared his head and looked around. His face was burning with pain, as if hit by something very hard. Everything was fuzzy, but he saw a familiar reddish-brown streak that zipped across the room and to his side. His eyes slowly focused in. Sydney was so close her nose was touching his. All he could see were her happy, brown little eyes.

"Hi," he whispered, while trying to regain his voice.

"Welcome back … we're thinking of getting a bite to eat … You hungry?" Sydney squeaked.

"Famished, actually."

"Good, I'm beginning to get worried about Evan. He's been looking at you like you're a snack."

"What? I have not!" The big Fallon brushed the girl aside and lifted *It* into the air. He held the boy up with one hand and looked him over from top to bottom. "You okay?"

"I think so," *It* sighed. "But my face hurts. Did somebody hit me?"

Vasilik looked down at the floor and casually strolled over to stand next to Sucram.

Sucram nodded his head toward Vasilik and whispered, "Aren't you getting too old for these kinds of shenanigans?"

"Ya would be think'n so, but tis look'n like no," Vasilik shrugged.

Sucram sighed and strutted over to *It* as Evan set the boy down. He checked out his eyes that had turned back to normal. "I think someone under-explained the weird eyes situation." Sucram talked back over his shoulder to Vasilik. "I'm no longer the most powerful mystic in the kingdom."

"That's cool," Sydney squeaked.

"Yep, that's cool," the old Ave said with a shaky voice. "If it's cool to be capable of great and immense good or equally horrific and terrible evil."

"Well, the prophecy said that *It* will be great and good," Sydney said proudly.

"Which prophecy is this?" Sucram asked.

Evan pointed to *It*. "The hooman boy and his friends of many races will unite the land to face the darkness," he said.

"Wow, what an ambitious prophecy. And where did you learn of this prophecy?" Sucram asked, with more than a little sarcasm in his voice and an accusing glare at Vasilik.

"Vasilik tells us this," Evan snarled, with obvious skepticism.

Sucram turned to face Vasilik full on. "You don't say?"

Vasilik pretended to look away at something on the shelf.

"Seems odd that I have never divined this prophecy," Sucram said, staring at Vasilik.

"That's because it is on a cave wall in the Dead Echoes; Vasilik saw it there," Sydney chittered.

Sucram walked up to Vasilik and turned his head so one of his eyes was staring straight at him. He whispered harshly, "One of your old scams, I gather?"

"Aye, that it be. Sometime the ole ones be the best'ns," Vasilik whispered back.

Sucram leaned in even closer. "Just keep in mind that this boy isn't one of your usual marks … an inexperienced feral Molec … you have the worst luck … and I couldn't wish him on a more deserving human than you."

It got to his feet slowly and with much effort as everyone was heading for the door. The boy turned to Sucram who was walking away from his brief conversation with Vasilik. "Why can't I remember anything like Sydney did?" *It* said, rubbing his head and struggling to regain his thoughts of his experience with the mirror.

Sucram took in a deep breath that became a long sigh. "Because Sydney's current-self saw her vision. You viewed your visions as your future-self ... the person you are to become. When time catches up to you in that moment, it will all be clear to you. Until then, be happy in your ignorance."

"But I want to see them now. I want to know now," *It* whined in frustration and shrugged off Vasilik's hand as the man limped towards the others and attempted to move *It* toward the door as he went by.

"Then talk to your big friend, he saw more than any of us," Sucram said, and waved them off. "Now leave. I have a mess to clean."

It dropped his head and let Vasilik guide him out the door.

"Don'tcha worry no too much, snapper. When ya be far from here and in Yolanrym, tis will be but a dream," Vasilik assured the boy, as they disappeared out the door and into the night.

THIRTY

FUN IN FISHMONGER'S ALLEY

The door of Vasilik's dilapidated residence swung open as the aging man hobbled in, dragging his foot alongside of him. He motioned to Evan, who had *It* in his arms, to put the boy down on a cot in an adjoining room separated by a sheet that Vasilik held open.

"Lay the snapper here for the time be'n," Vasilik spoke, with more than a little concern in his voice.

Evan laid *It* down. He was awake, but obviously weak. Switbo turned to her husband. "Have ya got'n yor employer kilt already?"

"No, the boy be just a tad off his game. Sucram's divination mirror twas a touch too much for him."

"*It* is a powerful mystic!" Sydney cheerfully squeaked.

"Oh, be he now?" Switbo responded with a playful skepticism.

Vasilik walked behind his wife and leaned in as if to nuzzle her. "Actually, as Sucram be see'n it, the lad be probably the most powerful in the land," he whispered eagerly.

"For true? Ya not using yor lying voice," Switbo whispered back.

"Frighteningly true."

"Then, they actually are to be meeting the King?" Switbo said.

"Be look'n so."

"And what will be happen'n when they be find'n out that not only do ya be have'n no more contacts in the court, but ya be also banished from the king's sight?" Switbo chastised him, while keeping her voice down.

Both of Vasilk's eyes leapt open wide with counterfeit shock and offense. "Untrue, I still be know'n names, and it be King Ji Senior that be suggest'n I no return. Twasn't a decreed banishment. Which be mean'n it wearn't official."

"What part of 'on pain of death' sounds like a suggestion to ya?" she hissed.

Seeing as he would not be winning this argument, he kissed Switbo on the back of her head and gave up. "Well, I'll be cross'n that mire when I be come'n to it."

Switbo pulled away from him and gave him a swat with her towel. "Ya should be ask'n for a raise and a sizable advance. I can be use'n it to find me a new husband of higher quality after they be hang'n ya."

He smiled and tugged at his curled mustache. "Aye, twas for sure I married ya for a reason … always looking to the future, ya be."

At this time, the others noted the heavenly aroma filling the house.

"What have ya and the Didelphi got for us?" Vasilik remarked, as he breathed in heavily through his nose.

"A meal like none we et in some time," Switbo said with a broad smile.

Vasilik looked to the others and threw his hands open wide. "Okay, snappers, let's fill those bellies and make for the beds. We'll be av'n a time of it tomorrow, book'n passage and make'n ready for the jaunt at sea."

"What jaunt at sea?" Toyota asked, with a sudden shudder throughout his whole being.

"Ya was no think'n to walk around the inland sea, now was ya?"

"Um, yeah, actually," Toyota continued.

Evan snickered. "Didelphi don't swim."

"Good thing, caus'n we will be on a boat and no swim'n the distance … now, eat up."

The house echoed with the sound of Evan's snoring. Vasilik tip-toed around checking in on each of his guests/employers one last time before heading to bed.

"Do ya think ya be stepped into someth'n here that ya can't be wipe'n off yor boot with this lot?" Switbo whispered as Vasilik slipped into bed.

"Tsk, tis nothing. I'll be to Yolanrym and back before ya know it. Ya won't even be ave'n a chance to be wish'n me goodbye and I'll be back."

"I'm sure I won't, as I am to be go'n with."

"Ya aren't," Vasilik replied.

Switbo's eyes tightened, and a single nostril flared out. "Say ya aren't again and I'll be give'n ya the business end of me thump'n rod."

Having made the mistake once before of telling his wife what she couldn't do, Vasilik was not quick to repeat the incident. "I did no mean ya aren't in the sense that ya can't go, I meant that tis no necessary."

"I will not be made a widow by Yolanrym. Ya shouldn't be go'n, but see'n that ya are, I'm go'n with."

"I be a wise enough man to know not to fight ya on this."

"Wise? A wise man wouldn't be poke'n a sleep'n render beast as ya are."

"Or a chastising first wife." Vasilik wrapped his arms around Switbo and poked her in the belly with his finger.

She grabbed his hand and held on. "I'm glad ya be see'n things the right way in this."

"Always, me love," Vasilik said.

"So, I hear the boy be possibly the child of prophecy?" she said, with a knowing huff.

"That he might be," he snickered back.

"Been some years since I heard ya be use'n that one on a mark."

"I thought it be fit'n at the time."

"Be it the dream by the river one?"

"Nope, no with this lot ... the cave in the land of the Dead Echoes," he whispered, with a silly eerie voice.

"Oh, that be a favorite of mine," she giggled back.

"Yes, but the Fallon tis no buy'n it," Vasilik said, with a shake of his head.

"They never do," she whispered as she closed her eyes.

The next morning, Vasilik and *It* walked along the docks toward the port commission house where they would check departures for the next few days. Behind them was an eight-and-a-half-foot tall figure wearing a hooded cloak and following suspiciously close.

"Ya know lad, he ain't fool'n a soul," Vasilik hissed to *It* as they walked.

"Yeah, I know, but he is doing his job as a Host Custodian and a friend," *It* replied.

"That there be a head jarrer of a situation. To be hosted by them scrabb'n oafs be an honor at the least of it."

"You don't seem to like Fallon very much."

"And it be a day of darnation til I ever do."

"What's up with that?"

"What be up with it?" Vasilik slapped his bum leg with his cane. "Right there be what's up with that—a Fallon be to blame and I'd curse him to his death if I thought him no already dead."

"Did you kill him?" *It* said meekly.

"No, lad, for sure I be wish'n I had … be during the last Fallon-Kronc war it was when we human's sided with the overgrown trumpet blowers. A sad time it be for man and Giverkind."

"Is that why the humans pulled away from the world council?" *It* asked.

"No, boy, it be run'n much deeper than that. As I recall, there be a fallout with them other Giverkind over some secret concern'n the Great Giver, or some something or another. Sucram played his part in that. But, ya see, I was no always an independent agent as I be today. A member of the Gold Tabards, I once be."

"What's a Gold Tabard?"

Vasilik stopped, giving the boy a look that would scare a Kroncal out of its exoskeleton. "Shame on you snapper, for no even know'n at least that much about the kingdom of men."

"Sorry," *It* said, with a sagging brow.

"If I was to be a lesser man, I'd have a go at ya, lad, but as yor me employer, I'll be leave'n it to just a harsh word."

"As your employer, I am thankful for that."

"Just do no let it be happen'n again."

They stood staring at each other with an intense gaze, and then both burst out in laughter. "I knew I was to be like'n ya, lad. I knew all the way down to me bum foot, I did," Vasilik bellowed.

Evan hung back, not looking at all suspicious and growling under his breath as his dislike for Vasilik grew more as *It* grew closer to the man.

"Ya see, the Gold Tabard be elite soldiers for King Ji Mellis. The official name they be called be the King's Faith-Men. And the people be call'n them Gold Tabards because …"

"They wear gold tabards," *It* interrupted.

"Exactly, boy. That they do."

Vasilik looked up at the crudely crafted sign above an equally crudely crafted door. They had reached the commission house where the ship registries were logged. Vasilik held open the door for the boy as he walked past and made eye contact with Evan. Peering from under his hood, Evan sneered at the old man, who just sneered back with a crooked smile—and then he stuck his tongue out as he went in.

The Fallon warrior fidgeted outside, as he didn't like being separated from the boy—and he didn't like things that he didn't like. While he waited, a small frail human dressed in rags walked up and stood not far from Evan. After a few moments, five more humans in leather rain slickers walked up to the front of the building and met with the scrawny man. The little man immediately started reporting to the others.

"The boy with the white hat done went in here with that old swindler, Vasilik," said the small man.

One of the men leaned toward the man leading the group and said, "Kranf, don't let Vasilik's age fool you. That old lion has teeth and a few good fights left in him."

"Can I get me coin now?" the scrawny man asked shyly.

Kranf pulled a few coins from his pouch and dropped them on the ground. "Here, take it and go." As the little guy scraped up his money and skittered off down the wharf, Kranf turned to one of the men who had a long nasty scar on his chin and ordered, "Go get the others and meet us by Fishmonger's Alley." The man was off and running as Kranf continued. "They will walk back the way they came, and we'll take them there. Tell the others they can kill Vasilik, but we need to leave the boy alive for questioning."

"What if we have to kill them both?" asked one of the crew.

Kranf snarled with a menacing glare. "We don't. They want the boy alive—but they didn't say he couldn't be broken."

Vasilik and *It* walked out of the commission house, and the old man had a few pieces of paper clutched in his hand. They stepped into the lane and saw no sign of Evan.

"So, where be Chuckles gett'n off to?" Vasilik asked, happy to find Evan not there.

"Not sure, this is the first time in months that I haven't had him hovering over me. It's kinda freeing," *It* said.

"Well, there be no doubt that the tonk-headed fool be back soon. A Fallon's honor be everything, and be damned ya if ya come between them and their honor," Vasilik said, with a disdain born of experience.

"Should we wait?"

"He's know'n where home be, and he be a sizable lad, even if he no be quite twenty years."

"How did you know he wasn't twenty?"

Vasilik's eyes questioned the boy with a raised brow and smirk, lifting one end of his handle-bar mustache. "How can ya be no know'n it? Tis' be obvious."

With a curious tilt of his head, the boy was still not sure what to make of his wise, but quirky, guide. With as much time as *It* had spent with the Fallons, he still had trouble reading them, and yet Vasilik has some uncanny sixth sense about the race.

They began walking back the way they came. *It* looked around, expecting to see Evan shadowing their every move, but the big warrior was nowhere to be seen. However, he did notice two humans in rain slickers that had been keeping pace with them for some time. One of them was Kranf.

"So, have you noticed the two guys behind us?" *It* asked, a little nervous. "Are they following us?"

"Aye," Vasilik said without looking behind him.

"Yes, you have noticed them, or yes, you think they're following us?"

"Aye on both accounts."

"What do we do?"

"Do no be worry'n. Ya be hired the best guide and former Gold Tabard."

"Yeah, but they look a little younger and stronger ... no offense," *It* said, with his face cringing.

"A great mark ahead we be if'n they be think'n the same way as you. An' that'll be give'n us the advantage. Just keep walk'n and act'n all natural and the such. We just be need'n to get to the fishmongers' alley where we be change'n our heading."

They continued walking for a good distance, and the two men stayed right behind them. When *It* and Vasilik reached the alleyway, Vasilik pushed the boy in the direction of the alley and told him to run, as they both rushed off down the alley. The two men sprinted forward and continued to follow. When they came around the corner, they saw Vasilik and *It* mid-way down the alleyway, standing near some rubbish bins.

The men stalked towards them while the boy and old man held their ground, while wearing exaggerated smirks. Kranf gave them an evil, gapped-tooth smile and hissed, "You should've kept running."

Vasilik raised an eyebrow. "I be think'n the boy and me will be av'n no trouble with ya. And I be try'n to teach the snapper to be stand'n his ground when the wind be foul of temper."

"Well, you daft old man, not that we aren't enough to take you, but I think you'll find we aren't alone." He put his hand along the side of his mouth and hollered, "Show yourselves!"

A long uncomfortable silence had the men looking at each other.

Vasilik's yellow tooth grin showed from under his curly moustache. "By any chance be ya expect'n some company in yor nefarious endeavor here? And if so, be one of yor mates a tallish feller with a scar on his chin and miss'n an ear?"

"You're right about Pol having a scar, but he's not missing an ear," Kranf grumbled back.

Vasilik looked in one of the trash bins at a tall man with a scar across his chin and missing an ear, with blood covering the side of his face. Whether he was alive or dead was uncertain, but he wouldn't be causing anyone any trouble.

"Well, he be miss'n an ear now." Vasilik turned to *It*. "I do believe we be now know'n where the Fallon got off to."

Kranf and the other would-be assassin pulled swords from under their leather rain slickers when they heard loud stomps and splashes coming from behind them. When they turned, they found themselves face to chest with Evan who also had his sword in hand, and his blade was almost twice as long as theirs—sometimes, size does matter.

Kranf nodded to his partner, and they both pulled out a glass ball not much larger than their thumbs.

It could see a small portion of the glass ball as Kranf held it out to the side between his thumb and forefinger. It glowed ever so slightly with a purple hue and wisps of black mist floating around it.

Kranf and the other assassin slammed the glass globes on the ground. Even in the mud they shattered. A brief explosion of smoke billowed out, and for a moment the two men and Evan were enveloped in a white fog.

It and Vasilik heard some fast footsteps moving away from them, and a split second later they heard a familiar wet slicing sound, like that of a blade entering flesh.

"That can no be good for a body," Vasilik said, with that one eyebrow arching up high on his head.

The old scoundrel and the young boy cringed as they heard two loud thumping noises. After the thump, two men came flying out of the smoke and onto the ground not far from Vasilik and *It*. Before long, Evan appeared.

The giant Fallon sneered at the two unconscious bodies on the ground. "Yeah ... their friends tried that smoky camouflage mystic trick on me, too."

"By the looks of it, it be no work'n for them either," Vasilik laughed out loud.

"Not so much, no," Evan grunted with a wince, as he grabbed at his side.

"What did they want?" *It* asked.

"You," Evan answered with another wince.

Vasilik gave a quick look over at the men in the rubbish bins. "It appears, they no be go'n anywhere anytime soon, if they wake'n up at all," Vasilik said with a concerned look on his face, and then gave an accusatory glare at Evan.

"If it makes you feel any better, they were ordered to kill you," the Fallon grumbled back in response to Vasilik's ungrateful insinuation.

"As much as I be appreciat'n yor concern, I just be hope'n yor work here do no draw the city guard ... one of these men be a Gateman."

"Well, I wasn't trying to do you any favors. I'm just keeping the boy safe," Evan said.

"Yes, but if'n the city guard be in on this, then someone well connected be behind it." Vasilik hobbled over to where Kranf lay motionless on the ground. The old man knelt down to open the man's slicker jacket and found a pocket wallet. After he opened it and glanced in, he frowned and stood back up while cursing under his breath, "I be know'n he be look'n familiar. This one be a sergeant of the guard in Yolanrym. A good piece away from home he be." He motioned to Kranf and then to one of the men in a rubbish bin. "They must'a been here in case the other be need'n witnesses that no one would be question'n. An the word of a Yolanrym Blue Tabard carries a fine weight in a port town like'n this one."

Making sure *It* and Evan didn't see him, Vasilik slid Kranf's wallet under his cloak as he pulled out the slips of parchment that he got from the

Dock Commission House. He shook them at Evan and *It*. "I be think'n maybe we ought be check'n out these here ships and book'n passage before we get piked as criminals," Vasilik said, with a wink to the boy.

"Piked?" *It* said, not knowing what it meant, but assuming it wasn't good.

"He means that they will run us through with pikes for what we did here." Evan motioned to the unconscious thugs and winced again as he put a hand to his side.

"An I do no be know'n what ya mean by we, lad. It be you that done in these miscreants," Vasilik said, looking up to Evan. Evan just snarled back.

"I don't think I would like being piked very much," *It* said, and then noticed blood dripping onto Evan's boot from under the Fallon's cloak. "Is there something you're not telling us?" *It*'s voice cracked with concern, as he gestured to Evan's blood-soaked boot.

Evan winced again and then chuckled. "It's nothing Sydney won't be excited to see."

The three headed out of the alley and down the wharf toward the cargo piers.

THIRTY-ONE

THE MESSES FALLONS MAKE

In a dimly lit vacant storefront, Kranf and six other men stood before a man in a brilliant golden robe with a flash of green trim that glistened. The robed man pulled back his hood. It was Neevit. He began walking back and forth with an unreadable look on his face. No one said a word as they watched the man pace about the room.

"An old man and a young boy ... How much easier could I make it for you? That's all I asked of you. Bring me one boy and eliminate the old man. And yet you failed," Neevit grumbled, with many unintelligible curses that followed.

Pol, the tall man with a scar and now minus one ear, had a bandage around his head. He had been looking down at his feet and then built up the courage to say, "But we were jumped by a Fallon."

"One Fallon? A slow-moving dullard with no better purpose than to lift heavy things," Neevit said with a tilted head and sarcastic voice. He stepped up and grabbed Pol's head, turning it so that the bloody part of the bandaged covering Pol's missing ear was close to his lips. "Hello!" Neevit called into the bandaged ear hole. He paused for a moment and then thumped the bandage hard with his finger. "Is this thing working? Hello ... He was just one Fallon!"

Pol unintentionally pulled back from the pain, but he kept his head bowed down. "He wasn't like most Fallons. He moved fast, very fast, and he knew how to fight."

Neevit pulled a small pouch from his robe and began opening the pouch. "He moved very fast, and he knew how to fight?" Neevit repeated with a high-pitched, mimicking tone. "Well, I guess that's it then. If he moved fast and knew how to fight, there's nothing more that could be done … and nothing more to do here." He took a step forward toward Pol. As he did, Kranf took a slight step away from his bloody friend. "So, on to other things. Are you alone in the city?" Neevit's voice softened and became more sincere as he addressed Pol with mocking concern.

"I'm sorry," Pol said, looking completely lost.

"I'm just curious. Do you live alone in the city?" Neevit said, with some devious intent camouflaged in kindness.

"No, actually, I live with my wife and three tots on the tanner's block."

Neevit fumbled with the bag, then opened it and poured a little powder into his hand. He leaned in close to the frightened gateman. "A wife and tots … congratulations!"

"Thank you, your eminence." Pol relaxed and let out a sigh of relief.

"No, thank you. Thank you for being an utter and complete disappointment." Neevit held out the powder and with a short puff of breath, he blew it in the man's face. Pol jerked his head and coughed violently for a brief second and then stopped. He stared out in front of him at nothing particular at all. Neevit turned and walked away while replacing the pouch into his robe pocket.

Neevit stepped up to Kranf, staring a hole through him, while he called back over his shoulder. "Pol, leave this room and find the longest pier. Walk to the end of that pier and step over the edge. I want you to then swim as deep as you can go and don't stop … okay? Bye-bye." Neevit let out a malicious chuckle that he aimed into Kranf's face.

The hypnotized Pol spun around and walked out the door.

Neevit whispered in a gruff, restraining voice to Kranf. "So now, do you or your men have any more excuses you would like to share with me?" Neevit placed his hand on the pocket of his robe where he had his pouch of mystic powder.

"No, your eminence, we do not," Kranf stuttered, while bowing his head and shaking all over.

"And no mystery Fallon will be an issue for you?" Neevit added.

"Not even in the slightest …" Kranf began to answer, when the door slung open and two shabby, cloaked forms shuffled in.

Kranf's men all pulled their swords and set themselves ready to fight, with the intention to kill written across their faces.

The shorter of the two large strangers flipped down his hood. It was Derger. "Easy ladies ... No need in getting your knickers in a bunch," he said with every bit of disrespect intended.

The larger stranger behind Derger lowered his hood to show a head full of dreadlocks; it was Kahlyn.

Neevit's brow dropped, and one side of his mouth sneered. "What is this?" he hissed.

Kranf stepped quickly over to Derger and put his hand on his shoulder as though they were long time buddies. He looked back to Neevit with an eager smile. "These are the men I told you about last evening. They come from Yolanrym with high recommendations for their discretion in removing annoyances." He paused with a sinister smirk. "They hired on to help with the boy's guardians."

Derger glared at Kranf with a look that said he would break the man's hand if he didn't remove it from his shoulder. Kranf awkwardly lifted his hand and set it to his side.

Not immediately impressed, Neevit looked the new recruits up and down. "You have experience fighting Fallons?"

Derger and Kahlyn spent the last evening with a low-priced healer having their cuts and broken bones mystically repaired as the result of their last bout with Evan, but they chose not to inform Neevit of this. Instead, Derger gave a crooked smile to his buddy Kahlyn and then looked back to Neevit and said, "Experience fighting Fallons ... That we have."

Kranf grunted with a sadistic chortle. "I bet with them, there's lots of blood."

"Oh yeah, lots of blood and broken bits," Kahlyn offered, with the unsavory memory of his agony from hours ago still very fresh in his mind.

"Good, then. You can succeed where these dim-wits have failed," Neevit groaned, with a wave of his hand to Kranf and his men.

"But I want to be clear that Vasilik is ours to deal with," Derger insisted, stepping forward and shaking his open hand at Neevit.

"Be careful how you talk to the advisor to the king," Neevit warned Derger, with his voice dipping lower and his eyes penetrating the younger man.

Derger quickly pulled back and dropped his hands to his side. "I meant no disrespect, My Lord."

"Good." Neevit huffed and took in a deep breath. "But be careful of what you wish for. If Vasilik is a fraction of the man he was thirty years ago, he'll kill you without even trying—Trust me. I rode with the man during the Fallon-Kroncal war. His manners were deplorable even back then, but he was the only human I ever knew who could strike fear in those hideous Kroncal creatures."

"Well, he's old now," Kahlyn snickered.

Neevit's eyes narrowed toward the dreadlock-headed mercenary. "I'm old. Would you snicker at me?" He stalked up to Kahlyn who was much taller and turned his face up at the now trembling man. "I watched that man kill a render beast with a boot … Can you kill a render beast with a boot?" Neevit asked, with a sarcastic lilt in is voice.

"No, My Lord."

"I didn't think so." Neevit spun around and walked to a dilapidated counter where he picked up a small metallic cylinder tube. "Which is why I'm not trusting this last opportunity with the likes of you. Especially that git." Neevit pointed the tube at Kranf as he stressed the word git. He then walked over to Kranf and handed him the cylinder. "You will answer to Captain Vosvile. When you are well out to sea, use this to summon him—and don't mess this up."

"No, My Lord … I mean yes, My Lord, it will be as you request," Kranf stammered.

"Good." Neevit stopped and glanced around like he had heard something. After an uncomfortable moment, he shouted, "Go!" and pointed at the door.

Kranf and his men scampered off out the door while Derger and Kahlyn bowed slightly to Neevit and turned calmly to leave.

Before the door could close, Neevit called out one last time. "And if the boy makes it to the port of Yolanrym, there will be no place you can hide from me."

They were all well out the door and gone when from out of another room, a well-dressed Ave strutted in. It was Edroy in all his finery, and for him, this was being inconspicuous. As he walked around the room, he stuck a talon out and dragged it along, screeching through the dust on a table.

"I don't know which is worse, that you work with filth, or work in filth." He held up his finger with the dust on it. "Either way, it's repulsive."

"Well, I wouldn't have to do either if you had fulfilled your agreement. What happened with your connections to the Kroncal?"

"Regretfully, there was a bit of a rub in that."

"A rub, you call it? Am I to tell the Empress that we let the boy reach Yolanrym because of a rub?"

"Tell her what you wish, I didn't observe your men faring any better. Besides, I agreed to aid you in this endeavor, not do everything for you. I have even risked exposure by using your black mystics to bring me here. I must return before Stronghide, in his infinite ignorance, notices I'm no longer with them."

Neevit held his hands out in front of him. "With all that we have done for you and the flock, it would seem to me that we could receive a little more effort on your part, not to mention that this human boy has greatly upset your plans for a Fallon and Seeuradi war."

"Don't misunderstand me, the human and Ave relationship has been greatly appreciated and beneficial ... for both sides, I would say. As for the boy, he would have been deceased long before now had your Empress not intervened with her fickle and flippant obsessions."

"I don't pretend to know her intentions, and I don't recommend that you question them, or refer to them as fickle and flippant." Neevit hissed.

Edroy gave out a sigh, as he shook the ruffled feathers of his neck. "When we cease to question the powerful, the powerful cease being questioned." The elegant Ave walked to the door and opened it. "And that has been our downfall here," he said as he walked out the door.

"You don't even know the half of it," Neevit whispered, as he flipped up his hood and took his leave as well.

THIRTY-TWO

VASILIK IS SNEAKY. WHO KNEW?

After booking passage across the Tendril Sea, *It*, Vasilik, and Evan made their way through a local market picking up supplies which they would need for their short voyage and stay in Yolanrym. Prices in the king's city "be a personal violation to one's purse," as Vasilik put it.

"It be all about take'n advantage. The crown be take'n advantage of the people, the people be take'n advantage of each other, and that leaves us all to be scrabb'n fight'n for meat like we be buzzards," Vasilik lectured the boy as they walked. Neither of the two realizing that Evan has been lagging behind, slower than usual.

Vasilik put his arm around the boy's shoulder and said, "Take those black-hearts back there in the alley, they sought to be take'n advantage of an old man and a boy. Of course, they do no be know'n this old man and what would've come to them if the Fallon had no already be take'n fine care of them."

"They seem to know you," Evan grumbled, as more of an accusation than just his typical distrust of the old shyster.

Vasilik stopped in front of Evan. "What be ya mean'n in that, lad?"

Evan held his side and groaned, "At least they knew your name."

"They did, did they?"

"And in the alley one of the hoomans mentioned a Neevit, or something or other, but it could have just been him slurring, as his jaw was broken." Evan chuckled and then winced.

Vasilik face tightened as he stared intently up at the Fallon. "Now lad, I be need'n ya to be think'n clearly. Ya sure they be say'n the name Neevit?"

"I don't know if it's a name, but that's the word I heard." Evan winced again and looked to be dizzy as he swayed a little.

"Are you okay?" *It* asked and grabbed his friend's arm as if he could give any kind of support.

"I'll be fine, but the sooner we find Sydney the better," Evan said with effort.

"Maybe we can find a healer nearby?" *It* said, looking to Vasilik.

"No, I would no be do'n that. Them that be any good be expensive and them that be no good make matters worse. I say we be foot'n it to me abode now," Vasilik insisted with a very stern voice, as if he had other reasons to be heading back before gathering the rest of the supplies. The name Neevit brought about a strange change in his behavior.

They began moving quicker and were almost out of the marketplace as Vasilik caught a glimpse of a very shady character standing near a merchant's cart alongside of a smartly dressed customer. While limping as quickly as he could, Vasilik made his way over to the shady character. She was a shabbily dressed woman with very round features and at least half Vasilik's age. As he stepped alongside of her, he saw she was trying to lift a purse off of the customer who was distracted by the merchant. Vasilik grabbed the gal's hand with his cane, forcing her to drop the purse back in the customer's pocket. The pickpocket acted as if she accidentally bumped into the guy and made multiple, overly dramatic apologies.

"I'll be av'n words with ya, Loopa," Vasilik said to the woman as he pulled her away from her mark.

"Tis' ya insane?" Loopa scolded him while rubbing her hand and wiggling her fingers. "It be me livelihood yor smack'n with that stick."

"I be av'n a fatter chicken to pluck," Vasilik whispered harshly at her, as he leaned in closer to whisper awhile in her ear.

After Vasilik finished his whispering, he put something in Loopa's hand. She nodded her head and took off running, while Vasilik rejoined *It* and Evan as they continued toward home.

"What was that all about?" *It* asked.

"Information, laddie. Information," Vasilik said, as he gave more effort to moving his bum leg even faster than before.

Back at the McCarthy household, the small common area attached to the kitchen was dimly lit with just a few candles. The shades were drawn and the flimsy bolt on the door slid shut. A quiet hustle and bustle made the room look alive as everyone busied themselves packing. Sydney came out from behind the sheet of another room.

"How's he doing?" *It* asked.

"He'd be doing a lot better if he came here first before going to the market, but then it would've been less fun for me," Sydney squeaked, with her bucktoothed grin and twitching tail. "With all the blood he lost, it made it more of a challenge."

"Yor friend gets himself skewered like a pig, and tis fun for ya?" Switbo asked, disturbed by the squirrel-girl's careless remarks.

"That's how we know Evan's okay. It's when Sydney is upset that you really need to be worried," *It* called out with a loud snicker.

While the others joked and made light of Evan's pains, Switbo took a rolled-up piece of worn leather out of a nearby cabinet. She set it down gently on the table and wiped the dust off with one of her dish rags. After a moment, she lightly placed her hand on the roll and caressed it like it were a puppy. A smile crept across her face, as memories of times gone by were reflected in her eyes.

Switbo slapped the bundle on one side, and it quickly unrolled. Inside were shiny pieces of metal sticking out of pouches sewn into what now looked to be a leather belt or armor of some kind. In the center, two thinner straps of leather laid to one side. They, too, had small pieces of metal inserted into pockets. She held it up to show the others a harness.

Switbo was a woman in her late-fifties and feeling every bit of the rough road she'd traveled. Like the harness, some of her luster had faded, but it was still a beautiful piece of work, and every bit as deadly as ever. She pulled the harness over one shoulder and then the other. She brought the thicker portion around her waist like a belt and buckled it closed.

Thumbing one of the pieces of metal, she pulled it out and flipped it around with great speed and grace.

"Wow," Lucas gasped.

"Wow? Since when does a proper-speaking Ave say wow?" *It* teased Lucas.

"Contrary to popular belief, we Aves can use common vernacular when appropriate. We are, if nothing else, servants to communication," Lucas teased back.

"And arrogant gits," Vasilik whispered to himself.

Lucas looked up, as he wasn't sure what was just said. "Witty banter notwithstanding, that is one exceptional rig. May I examine one of your knives, please?" Lucas said greedily, as he turned back to Switbo.

"Don't be cutt'n yourself," Switbo replied, as she threw a knife, passing within inches of his head and sinking into the wall behind him.

With a slight twist of his head, Lucas gulped. The blade glistened next to his eye. He pulled it out of the wall and examined it. "This is forged from a Giver metal." After flipping it around a few times he threw it back, passing Switbo's head and into a cabinet. She pulled it out and put it back in the pouch on her harness with a smile of respect for the young Ave's skill.

"Are you sure that you're just a pub wench? I've never seen one throw a knife like that," Toyota said, eyeing Switbo curiously.

"Toyota! That was insulting!" *It* shouted.

"What?" Toyota asked with his hands held out.

Sydney whipped around to Toyota. "Great Giver! Don't you have any manners? They prefer to be called strumpets," she said, with her factual tone.

"No! That's not right either!" *It* barked louder than before.

"Actually, I be like'n strumpet better than wench," Switbo added, with a little nodding of her head while weighing the options.

"Okay, that didn't help in their education on proper etiquette," *It* said, while putting his face in his hands.

"No, but it be keep'n it entertain'n," Vasilik added with a chuckle.

With his cheeks raised in an Ave version of a smile, Lucas said, "I believe the correct term *It* was looking for is barmaid."

"Server ... She is a server. A public house server. Not a wench, not a strumpet, and not even a barmaid. A server!" *It* said, with his face still in his hands.

"No, barmaid be correct," Switbo said, turning to the frustrated boy.

"No way, really? So, none of you have heard of women's liberation and equality?" *It* pleaded.

"No, but it sounds really good ... Can we do that woman's libernation thing?" Sydney squeaked.

"Sure, why not? We should probably put *libernation* on our agenda for when we meet with the King," *It* groaned, defeated by the ignorant reality of this wonderful and frustrating world of Fentiga.

A knock at the door altered the mood drastically, as everyone produced a weapon and stood motionless in the silence. There was another knock. "Tis' Loopa," a harsh whisper came from the other side of the door.

"Ya alone?" Vasilik called out.

"By me-self, I be," the voice whispered back.

Vasilik went to open the door.

"How can you tell if she's telling the truth?" *It* asked, concerned and still holding his tire iron and stiletto at the ready.

"It be our code. If you are alone you say, 'by me-self, I be'. If'n someone's with ya, ya say any kind of other words." He unlatched the door. "Besides, this lock do no even keep the flies out if they be want'n to come in."

Loopa stumbled in, panting hard. Her hooded cloak had so many rips and tears in it that the rain had soaked her thoroughly.

"What have ya?" Vasilik asked and then handed her a tankard, which the freezing woman drank down before saying a word.

"There's be very little talk," she gasped.

Vasilik sighed and shook his head. "That be bad."

"Why is that bad?" Sydney asked.

"Yeah, it seems like we would want people not talking about us," *It* said, relieved.

"It be scrabb'n impossible to keep nare a crumb of a secret in Squall. And if'n someone be keep'n such a secret as kill'n this boy, then there be some heavy hands behind it. And Neevit be av'n a plenty enough heavy hand for the task."

"Who is Neevit?" Sydney squeaked, as she pressed her glasses tight against her face while looking Loopa over.

"He's an advisor to the human King and a mystic," Lucas said without thinking, then became very nervous with the feathers on his neck ruffling up. "My apologies."

"You don't have to ask for permission to speak every time, Lucas," *It* said, seeing that his Ave friend was skittish after speaking. He then turned to Vasilik. "Why would the king want me dead?"

Vasilik's eyes narrowed. "I be know'n King Ji Mellis since he was a wee snapper smaller than you. It be sure he's av'n no part of this."

"Then, why is this advisor of his after the boy?" Evan asked, as he pulled aside the sheet and stood in the doorless opening. It wasn't like he was going to get any sleep with all the noise this group makes.

"For sure it be a quandary of a thought. Which be mean'n that great caution be needed here," Vasilik said, with a sad drop of his head.

"Hoomans … Can't trust a one of them," Evan grunted. He turned his mighty head and tusks toward *It*, who stood staring holes through the Fallon. "Stare at me all you want. It doesn't make it any less true," Evan said, with a dismissive swing of his trunk at the boy.

Vasilik tapped Loopa on the shoulder with the back of his hand. "Be ya get'n them?"

She nodded her head vigorously, throwing water droplets to the ground. "Aye, and they t'were no easy to get holt of."

Vasilik extended his arm out towards *It*. "Lad, I'll be need'n yor purse."

It looked at Vasilik for a moment with many questions on his mind. Vasilik threw open his eyes wide and nodded his head down towards the boy's belt. The boy unhooked his money pouch and tossed it to Vasilik. The man took out some coins and put them in Loopa's hand. Loopa grinned with more gums than teeth and jammed the coins in a pocket under her cloak.

"And there be extra there to purchase yor tongue until we be far gone," Vasilik said with a very determined look into Loopa's eyes.

"On me honor. Let me tongue be cut out before it speaks of this," she promised, with more than a little sincerity in her voice.

She rustled through her jacket to produce several pieces of paper that she handed over to Vasilik.

"Good then, now go and be hide'n yorself away until we ship." Vasilik hustled her to the back of the dwelling where he pushed hard against what looked to be a shoddily built wardrobe. The rickety cabinet closet swung open to reveal a hidden door. Loopa slipped past him and out the door into the night, while the others looked curiously at the hidden doorway that they never even noticed before.

"How do you know we can trust her?" *It* asked.

Switbo chuckled. "Oh, we can be trust'n her all right … I killed her husband," Switbo said, still wiping oil on a throwing knife and then drying it off. Her tone was no different than if she had just acknowledged that she walked the lady's dog from time to time.

It, Sydney, and Lucas stood staring at Switbo with their mouths gaping open.

"T'was a very abusive man," Switbo commented, then slid the dagger back into the pocket of her harness and pulled out another to wipe down.

Evan looked over to *It*. "Yep, my trust in them is building every day," he grumbled, with a disappointed shake of his tusks.

"Ya be act'n as if ya no be like'n us, Fallon," Vasilik remarked, with a smirk on his face.

"I don't … now give the boy back his purse." Evan said, as he turned to gather his things.

It looked to his belt, realizing he didn't think to get the money pouch back from Vasilik.

"I be intended to do that very thing." Vasilik tossed the purse pouch across the table for the boy to catch.

"Right. I'm sure you did … because honor is just abounding in this place." Evan began packing his bag as he continued to grumble.

"So, are we going to hang around here until time to leave tomorrow?" *It* asked.

"Aye, but the time be now a scootch earlier," Vasilik said, as he placed the parchments on the table. "Today, before the sky and everyone to see, we be purchased our tickets on the cargo ship the Sun Skipper, leave'n tomorrow at midday. But we be actually go'n to board the Widow's Son in a few hours with these tickets Loopa be brought us … So ya best be get'n some rest before we shove off … and we'll be need'n watches tonight."

THIRTY-THREE

NOT A CREATURE STIRRED ... OK, MAYBE JUST ONE

Throughout the dark house, everything was still, but not at all quiet. Evan and Switbo seemed to be battling it out in a winner-take-all snoring contest, with neither one losing. Vasilik slept soundly amid the noise, but Sydney and *It* had pillows over their heads, as well as their cloaks and anything else they could find to block out the sound. Lucas was also stretched out and blissfully asleep as Toyota crept passed while wandering around the house checking on everyone during his watch.

Seeing that they were all asleep, Toyota snuck over to the door and unlatched it with great care. He took one last look into the house, then the little Didelphi eased out the door and closed it behind him. The door barely made a noise when it shut. Across the room Lucas' eyes sprung open wide. He got up to his feet and grabbed his cloak. Tiptoeing to the door was not easy with clawed feet, but he managed to not wake anyone as he, too, slipped out into the rainy night.

Splashing through the mud along the streets and down some alleys, Toyota moved with lightning speed. He came to a bakeshop near the market and stopped out front. In the shadows between the buildings a cloaked figure stood watching him. It was the same cloaked stranger from the woods in Utuska. He waved his hand as if patting something in the air, and Toyota turned around after feeling as though someone had just tapped him on the shoulder. He saw the stranger in the shadows and his heart sank.

Later, the door to the McCarthy home opened slowly. Beady little eyes peered into the room to make sure that the coast was clear. After a moment, Toyota skulked back in and set the latch on the door. Like before, he went around the rooms checking to make sure everyone was still asleep. When he got to a side room, he peeked in on Lucas. The Ave was sound asleep on a mat on the floor.

Toyota turned his head to the side curiously as he noticed Lucas' wet cloak and muddy claws. He shrugged his shoulders and waddled over to a chair by the table. He crawled up onto the chair and leaned back, letting out a depressing sigh. After a few moments of resting and having a few sips from a cup, he got up and waddled over to where Vasilik lay asleep next to his wife in an adjoining room. He leaned in towards Vasilik but stopped when he felt something poking him in his stomach. Looking down he saw a dagger at his belly and, the hilt was in the hand of the not-so-asleep Vasilik. Switbo continued to snore away.

"You said I should wake you at the end of my shift," Toyota whispered.

"And that ya did do, lad." Vasilik said, with his blade still in the Didelphi boy's stomach.

Toyota looked curiously at him. "Did you hear me come up to you?" Toyota asked, with an eager smile.

"Sadly, uh no. Twas yor stench."

"But I took a bath three days ago."

Vasilik put away his knife. "I no be doubt'n ya. That be an argument for you and yor body odor," Vasilik grunted, as he swung his feet off the bed and stood up in his baggy pajamas. "Wake the lot and be quiet about it."

As the boy waddled off, Vasilik turned back to his blissfully snoring wife. "And how long av ya been awake?" he whispered.

Her snoring came to a dead stop. "Since before the Ave and monkey-boy got back."

Vasilik grunted while putting on his pants. Switbo sat up and whispered up to him. "Ya gonna do someth'n about it?"

"Nope. I been around this lot long enough to be know'n that we be the worst of the bunch, but we need be keep'n our blades with us at all times on the boat … just to be safe."

She smiled. "It be always so reassur'n known'n I've married a man who set me status to that of the most despicable kind."

"And I be av'n no regrets neither."

Toyota went around the small house waking everyone up. As they did not get much sleep, he was not greeted with happy faces. Sydney even threw a boot at him, which made *It* even less happy since it was his boot.

With the house awake, packed, and ready, Vasilik took a moment to strategize. He glanced down at Toyota with a wiry smile that made the little Didelphi nervous.

"All right, lad. We be need'n yor special talent."

"Am I going to cook something?" Toyota asked excitedly.

"No, ya won't be cook'n. How be yor night vision? Well-practiced I would be imagine'n."

Toyota was confused, but responded, "Very good."

Vasilik motioned to Evan. "Come here Fallon," he said, but Evan didn't budge. "Be ya look'n for a 'please come here,' ya big git?"

Evan's knuckles cracked as he squeezed his fists tightly.

Switbo stepped between them. "Now, boys, let's be play'n nicely so we can live through this day," Switbo politely urged and then turned to Evan. "Sweetie, would ya please do as my idgit husband asks?"

Evan released his grip and moved where Vasilik asked him to stand.

Vasilik turned to Toyota. "See that there panel above Sweetie?" he asked as he watched Toyota nod his head yes. Evan, however, turned orange with his lips in a snarl. "Be get'n up there and go'n through that hatch. Ya will be find'n a slated vent. Get out onto the roof and be search'n up and down every alley and street ya can see, then report back."

Before Vasilik even finished talking, Toyota hopped onto the table and leaped up to grab Evan's tusk. From there it was a quick swing, which launched him onto Evan's head. When there, he popped open the panel, climbed through, and disappeared into the dark attic. After several minutes he reappeared, soaking wet.

"What did ya see, lad? Anything suspicious?" Vasilik questioned him the moment he was back in the house.

"Nope. All clear."

"Well then, let's be to it," Vasilik bellowed lowly, as he ushered everybody out of the house through the hidden door which Evan almost couldn't shimmy through. It didn't help matters that Sydney reminded the large Fallon that his bottom was the biggest she had ever seen—it wasn't the biggest, but she liked saying that, just to hear him growl.

THIRTY-FOUR

RUMORS ON THE HIGH SEAS

The sun hid behind dark clouds and, as always at this time of year, the Tendril Sea was choppy and cold. Hanging over the rail of the Widow's Son cargo vessel, *It* clung to the side as he lost the rest of his lunch and some of his dinner from the night before. Sydney laid stretched out on the rail a few feet away with the ocean spraying on her, while she watched the boy with a crinkled face and curious gaze.

"You hoomans can hold a lot of food in your stomachs. Not as much as a Fallon, but you had a lot in you. I don't see how you could hold so much and be so small," she squeaked.

Through bouts of retching he said, "I'm glad you can find something educational in my agony. I just wish you had something for seasickness." *It* got the last word out before he resumed his heaving over the side.

"But I do," she said with a big grin.

"What? Why didn't you say something? I'm suffering here."

"Well, I was talking to some of the other passengers, and I didn't even know you were sick. And by the time I got over here, you were well into it. You want me to give you something?"

"Yes! For the love of all … yes!"

Sydney leapt down to the deck and rustled through her pack. She pulled out what looked to be a seed, but when *It* got closer, he saw that familiar purplish glow and the hint of a dark mist. He eagerly swiped it from her and swallowed it down. In no time, his stomach stopped turning and it made him instantly feel better.

"I can't believe you would let me go through that before helping me with it."

"I can't believe you didn't ask earlier."

"What was so interesting about those other passengers that you couldn't be here for me to ask?"

She twitched her nose and reorganized the things in her pack as she talked. "Not much. They actually seemed more interested in what we had to say."

"Who's we?"

"Me and Toyota. We happened to be talking about the prophecy and some people asked about it, so we told them what we heard, and they found it interesting."

The boy's eyes widened as he grabbed her paw to get her attention. "Let me get this straight. You've been going around the ship telling everyone that I am a prophecy child?"

"No, of course not. That's silly. We did not go all around the ship. Many of the people came to us. I guess word spreads fast on a ship."

"You had better hope Evan doesn't find out, or you guys are foot paste."

"He won't stomp on us," Sydney chittered, as she went back to reorganizing her pack.

As she finished cinching up the pack's flap, Evan came out from around a platform full of crates covered in tarps. His face was orange, and his eyes grew tight with frustration as he searched intently for something. His gaze landed on *It* and Sydney.

"Sydney!" The giant Fallon bellowed, as he stormed in her direction.

"Correct me if I'm wrong, but that looks like the face of someone determined to stomp you into mush ... you may want to run," *It* said, snickering.

Sydney didn't wait for the raging Fallon to get there. With a terror-filled squeak, she bounded off with her pack, but the slick deck caused her claws to slide on the wood, increasing the fear as her little legs scrambled feverishly. With impending doom close behind her, she leapt on and over some tethered cargo—she was gone in a flash.

Evan reached *It* and was doing the best he could to control his anger. "Do you know what she did?" he growled.

"She told people about the cave prophecy," *It* replied, though Evan wasn't listening.

"She told people about the cave prophecy!"

"That's kind of what I just said."

"And now that ridiculous story has hoomans coming up to me and asking me if it's true. I could strangle that vagabond, Vasilik!"

It started giggling.

"Why are you laughing?"

"You said vagabond and Vasilik. They both start with 'V.' I don't know why, but it struck me as funny, coming from a Fallon's mouth."

"It's not funny!"

It huffed. "You act like anyone's going to believe her."

"They don't have to believe. It's the attention that it brings to you that concerns me. We are supposed to be traveling covertly," the giant Fallon grumbled, as he gripped at his trunk and paced up and back a few times.

"Alright, I'll go have a talk with Sydney and Toyota to make sure they stop spreading the rumor," *It* said, holding his hands out to calm Evan, but then the boy paused with his brow wrinkled while watching Evan pace. "So why aren't you seasick? You're not a seafaring guy."

"I asked Sydney for something as we were boarding. She may be a pain in my backside, but she is still our healer; it would have been irresponsible and stupid to not at least ask."

The boy sneered. "Yeah, irresponsible and stupid."

After a few days of stormy weather, the sun began to peek through the clouds, and the waters didn't seem so rough. Sydney's seeds kept everyone from getting sick, except for Vasilik and Switbo who didn't need them, as their previous experience of ship life left them unaffected by the voyage. If anything, they were at home and happy aboard a ship.

The young travelers managed to find ways of occupying their time, keeping the boredom at bay. Sydney practiced her healing mystics and utilized the time to create more of the purple healing goop that Kandula taught her to make. Toyota spent his free time annoying Evan and Lucas, while *It* spent time getting to know Vasilik and Switbo.

They taught him what he needed to know of the humans in this world of Fentiga and filled him with their stories of adventure. Of course, *It* gave them a questioning glare every time they tried to convince him of their previous careers as pirates. The boy never knew when they were joking or telling the truth. But it was obvious that the three of them were becoming like three peas in a pod, and the McCarthy's sincerely liked having the boy around.

It was also putting in some focused time getting the C.I.M.Us he bought in town working again. One afternoon, he had brought the devices on deck to tinker with them and he had asked the others to join him for a moment as he finished up. Sydney took a break from her studies, as Lucas and Evan were more than happy to do something that didn't involve Toyota pestering them. Vasilik and Switbo joined in, as they did pretty much whatever their employer asked. Of course, *It* almost never asked for anything, except for advice.

"What ya got there, snapper? We gonna eat?" Vasilik asked.

"No. These aren't for eating off of." He laid the devices next to each other. "I actually got all of them working and synced."

"That would be all and good if we had a clue what you are talking about," Evan said, as he looked over everyone's shoulder.

"Watch," the boy said, as he picked up one of the devices and leaned into it. "Cimu, activate." The device lit up upon receiving the order, and everyone "ooo'd" all at the same time.

"Okay, Sydney, your turn. Pick that one up," *It* instructed her, as he pointed to another device on the crate where he had placed them.

Sydney picked up the device and sniffed at it a few times before pulling back. "You want me to talk to it?" she asked *It*, with her eyes squinted through her glasses, looking the thing over.

"Yes. Just say, 'Cimu, activate'."

"Okay," she said, and then put the device in front of her face. "Seemoo, activate." The screen illuminated with a bright blue glow. Sydney giggled and chittered loudly.

"Now watch this," *It* said, giddy with excitement, as he held his device closer to his face. "Cimu, engage with Sydney Lapp."

Sydney's device began to make a repeating bleep noise. *It* leaned towards her and whispered, "Say, 'accept engagement from *It* Deepens.'"

"Accept engagement from *It* Deepens," she squeaked. Her device flashed, and *It*'s face appeared on the screen.

The boy waved into his device. "Hi Sydney!" he shouted and laughed.

Sydney turned to him and put her hand on his shoulder and gripped tightly. "Oh, my Great Giver, can you see me seeing you … I can see you

... You're waving at me," she squeaked endlessly.

"Okay, that is impressive," Evan murmured, while stroking his trunk and nodding.

"Impressive? That be downright bewilder'n!" Vasilik called out.

"What kind of mysticism be that?" Switbo asked, ogling over the face on Sydney's screen.

It held the device out and shook his head wildly. "It's not mystic, or magic. It's technology." He gestured back to Sydney's face, as he was overwhelmingly happy that something familiar was back in his life.

"Wow, Technology Mysticism. That is some cool stuff," Toyota breathed.

"That's nothing," *It* said, with a mischievous snicker. He hovered over the device again. "Cimu, activate hologram mode." His screen flashed again, and a 3-D image of Sydney's face popped up just above his display. He watched the miniature hologram of Sydney freak out when her head appeared next to her on *It*'s device.

"That is unreal!" Sydney screamed.

"Can I have one of these?" Toyota asked, as he pushed in close to get a better view of Sydney's device and got his face too close to hers.

On *It*'s device, the hologram face of Toyota appeared scrunched up next to Sydney's.

Sydney's hologram head barked at him. "Get away! Get your own!"

"I just want to see," the hologram head of Toyota yelled back.

It laughed hysterically as he watched the two hologram heads arguing, while his two little friends sitting next to him were doing the same.

"So, what do we use these for?" Toyota asked after Sydney pushed him away.

"To keep in touch with one another if we get separated," *It* replied.

"Why would we be separated?" Evan asked suspiciously, as his brow furrowed.

"I'm just saying, that as long as we are all within about a thousand miles or so of each other, we should be able to communicate. And if we had satellites in space, it wouldn't matter where we were on the planet," *It* commented nonchalantly. But when he looked around after a brief silence, he saw his friends staring at him. "What's going on?"

"I wouldn't like to be presumptuous of the collective thought, but I would hazard to guess that we are all wondering what a satellite in space means?" Lucas suggested.

"I'm also stuck on the word planet," Toyota included.

"Alright, wow, I guess we're talking about Astronomy 101," *It* gasped, while scratching his head.

Toyota dropped to a seated position with his arms crossed and a frustrated look on his face. "Okay, now I'm stuck on at least four words."

After explaining to everyone the general principle of the C.I.M.U. devices and how they communicate with each other through invisible signal waves, he left the group more dumbfounded than ever. Still, he passed out the devices and showed everyone how to operate them. That part didn't take long.

"The user-friendly aspect of the Cimu program makes it easy enough for a monkey to use … No offense Toyota," *It* said.

Toyota tilted his head. "Offense about what?"

"So, ultimately, we can talk to each other through these," *It* said, and then pointed to a small panel on the front of the C.I.M.U. "And as long as the sun occasionally shines on them here, the energy pack will stay charged. And when I mean occasionally, you could probably go underground for several months and use the devices daily without having to recharge. If it's turned off, the energy pack will hold its charge for years."

Toyota held his device up in the air and waddled around in circles, excited.

"You better be careful not to drop that thing," Evan scolded the Didelphi.

"Don't sweat it, Evan. These things are shatterproof and waterproof. They are even to some extent radiation and microwave proof," *It* added, but quickly realized he was only causing more confusion.

"Yeah, but are they Toyota-proof?" Sydney squeaked and laughed hysterically.

"Yep, they sure are. And you can use them as a flashlight," *It* added.

"A what light?" Switbo asked.

"Aim away from your face and say, 'Cimu, flashlight mode.'"

Toyota leaned in close to his C.I.M.U. device and said, "Seemoo, flashlight mode." A brilliant light flashed into Toyota's eyes, blinding him. The Didelphi boy screamed and threw the device across the deck, where it slammed into a freight crate and spun around a few times before coming to rest in a puddle.

"I told you to hold it away from your face," *It* scolded, as he walked over and picked up Toyota's device. He showed the unbroken screen to Evan. "See, it's even Toyota-proof."

THIRTY-FIVE

BETRAYAL REVEALED ... KINDA

A little more than two days away from reaching land, the group had been relaxing much more than ever before; this included sleeping late. *It* was snoozing away in his hammock below deck while the others were on deck, except for Vasilik. He was walking through one of the lower hallways when he saw a shabbily dressed deckhand lurking up the hall ahead and then turn the corner down another passageway.

At first Vasilik thought nothing of it as he continued limping along, but then he stopped and gave one of those expressions that said, *something sketchy was at hand*; and as a sketchy person, Vasilik had a nose for it. Quietly he eased up the passageway, but his bum leg and cane made it difficult to do with complete silence. Reaching the corner, he peeked around the wall and down the other hall. The shabbily dressed man stopped midway down the passage and called out to two other equally questionable people near the other end. "Kranf, over here."

"Scrabbit, Noggs, don't be screaming my name like that," Kranf whispered harshly, as he and Derger walked back towards Noggs, being careful to make as little noise as they could.

"Why not? People be call'n each other by their names all over the bleed'n ship. We would for sure be look'n suspicious if'n we didn't," the near toothless deck hand complained. His face was cracked and warn by the many years of sea spray, sun, and hard labor.

"Nevermind. Did you keep your eye on them?" Kranf scolded, with his nerves obviously frayed.

"I had me eyes on the big one, the squirrel, and the black-skinned woman. They be above on deck," Noggs whispered loudly.

Derger leaned closer. "And I saw the Didelphi talking to a cloaked man in the shadows down below. He seemed to be up to no good himself. I tried to listen in, but when I changed position to get closer, they done both disappeared, as if the shadows swallowed them whole."

"I don't care about a rat-headed monkey; what about Vasilik? Where is he?" Kranf groaned.

"I lost eye of the old cripple on deck ... and the kid ain't come out of his cabin neither," Derger said, with a motion of his head down the hall.

Noggs shuffled back and forth with nervous energy and his face strained with worry. "We run'n out of time. Be best to move soon, besides, the others are get'n a bit restless wait'n on your go ahead."

"Let them be restless. There's too much coin riding on this. We can't be scrabb'n it up," Kranf hissed, but relented when he took note of the sweaty brow and shaky eyes on Nogg's face. "Alright, get back up top. I'll be along when the job is done, and then the men can make their move."

Noggs skittered off through the passageway and disappeared as he bounded up some stairs at the other end.

Derger started to walk off, then turned back to Kranf. He looked as if he was going to say something, but then held his tongue and headed down the passageway where Vasilik was hiding around the corner.

Vasilik was waiting around the corner. The old swindler gave his mustache a twirl, then reached down to slide out the sword hidden in his cane. It didn't move more than two inches before Vasilik felt something poking him in his back, and a voice came out from behind him.

"I know what you be think'n, but you'd be best leav'n that hideaway in its sheath," a raspy voice whispered over his shoulder.

Vasilik slid the blade back down into the cane and held his hands out. He turned to see Kahlyn holding a rusty, jagged dagger at his gut, as Derger came up behind him.

"What you got here, Kahlyn?" Derger asked, with a knowing grin.

"You have been slip'n to let an old codger be sneak'n up on you," Kahlyn snickered back.

"It didn't do him no good to hear us, now did it?" he said, scratching at his goatee.

"Ya lads have noth'n to be worry'n with me. I'm just under the boy's employ and av me no pony in this race," Vasilik said in an all too convincing tone.

"We'll see which way the wind blows your sail," Kahlyn whispered in Vasilik's ear, while twisting the dagger. He then looked to Derger. "Do what you have to. I got this one."

"Since that tonk-brained Kranf is not following the plan anymore and is heading down there to kill the boy, I'm going to secure a place for us to lock this one up until we hit port. Keep him quiet until I get back. And don't get tied up with that Fallon without me," Derger said, and then walked off deeper into the ship.

Kahlyn nodded his head at Vasilik. "If'n you be only in it for coin, then we may have a use for you."

Vasilik smiled with his left eyebrow raised up high. "Of course, where the coin be, I be. Although, I be av'n a question of ya."

"What?"

"Do ya have a seemoo activate?" Vasilik said, with a muffled pinging noise sounding from under his cloak.

"A what?" Kahlyn asked nervously, looking around as he was sure he heard something.

Vasilik acted as though he didn't hear anything and continued talking. "Or maybe ya av a seemoo request engagement with Switbo?" he said louder, with yet another muffled pinging noise after it.

Again, Kahlyn looked around for the noise. "What you gabb'n on about, old man? You're not mak'n any sense."

"Well, I be figure'n since we be down below in this passageway near the aft of the ship, we should be get'n to know each other. Because I sure be hate'n for you to stick me with that blade of yorn," Vasilik spoke out loud and towards his cloak.

"Are you daft? I know where we are, and I ain't here to get to know you," Kahlyn yelled, getting more frustrated with Vasilik's lunacy. "I think the many years have yor head off plum."

"That they have. When ya be get'n to be my age, day be sometimes night, and left be sometimes right. I can no even tell when I be com'n and go'n."

"If that be true, you can forget work'n with us," Kahlyn said.

"Us? Who be us? Ya talk'n about Kranf, the boss?"

"Scrab, no. Kranf ain't no boss. He's about as daft as you. I'm talk'n about Cap'n Vosvile."

Vasilik's face lost all its playful guise, and his voice was strained as he grumbled, "The Cap'n of the Red Lion?"

"One and the same he is, but he won't be tak'n you on with all them loose pebbles in your nogg'n. When the signal goes up and he comes roar'n in, you will be lucky if you are only sent adrift."

"So, who be give'n that signal?" Vasilik asked.

Kahlyn's eyes narrowed suspiciously. "You know, I think we best be quiet until Derger gets back."

"I be feel'n quite certain that ya will be quiet'n up for some time," Vasilik hissed.

"What do you mean by that?"

Thunk! —"This," Switbo's voice could be heard just as Kahlyn dropped to the ground. She was standing there holding a belaying pin from the ships rail in one hand and her C.I.M.U. device in the other. She shook the device at Vasilik. "I'm think'n I be go'n to like this thang."

"The boy!" Vasilik shouted as he turned to run down the hall. Switbo followed, but he stopped her. "Go get the beast. No tell'n how many of these scalawags there be."

"Aye." Switbo turned around and headed back the way she came and stepped down hard on Kahlyn as she went by.

Kranf crept down the passageway, making sure not to make a sound. He drew a dagger from under his coat. It was every bit as rusty as the one Kahlyn had, but this one was longer and nothing short of sinister, with small metal teeth along the edge on one side of the blade.

The assassin set his eyes on the door just down from a stairwell. He eased up to it and placed his ear against the aged wooden surface. There was no sound other than that made by the ship creaking as it rolled back and forth. With his empty hand he pressed lightly on the door until it started to move. It squeaked as it opened, but then again, the whole ship creaked and squeaked constantly.

Creeping into the room, Kranf's eyes quickly fell upon a hammock with bulging blankets and a white Fedora hat at one end. A smile wormed across his face as he practically slithered right up to *It*. The smile widened into a gaping grin, half filled with rotting teeth, as he brought the dagger above his head and then slammed it down into the blanket.

The rusty metal sliced straight through the bedding and stuck out the canvas bottom of the hammock. Kranf's eyes opened wide as he jerked the blade out and threw the blankets to the floor. There was nothing there. He turned and rushed out the door and into the hall. He stopped to see *It* standing on the stairway buckling his pants, as he had just returned from relieving himself over the deck rail. They locked eyes, and *It* saw the dagger in the man's hand.

Vasilik popped out around the corner at the opposite end of the hall. He was winded and trying to catch his breath. Kranf looked back to Vasilik and smiled, then he turned back towards the boy.

"Run, lad! Run!" Vasilik hollered out, as he hobbled down the hallway.

It's eyes shot open, and he bounded back up the stairs as if he were imbued with Seeuradi abilities. Kranf chased after him with no chance of Vasilik catching up before he could kill the boy. *It* had one more set of stairs to climb up to reach the deck. Kranf threw the dagger, and it passed just in front of *It*, causing the boy to stop as the corroded metal blade sunk into one of the ship's support beams.

It continued out onto the deck and Kranf grabbed his dagger as he ran past, following the boy out into the wind. *It* reached the rail of the ship and grabbed one of the belay pins.

"Not very smart of you boy. You really gonna bring a stick to a knife fight?" Kranf said, his maniacal laugher added an extra level of fear to the boy's dilemma, until something made *It* smile.

"That depends. Are you really going to bring a knife to a Fallon fight?" the boy laughed, with every bit of snarkiness intended.

Evan stepped out from behind a stack of crates. His narrowing eyes and his crackling knuckles were a sure sign that there was about to be a whole lot of pain on deck today.

The wind was whipping hard and loud. Kranf's thin hair lashed around his face, adding to his crazed appearance. He continued grinning. "I guess you got me boy, but can your Fallon get to me before I run you through?" He winked at *It*. "I don't think so." He lunged full on at the boy.

It stood his ground. Evan charged, but it was obvious that Kranf was right when he said he would get to *It* first. The Fallon could only hope that the first strike at *It* missed. Kranf was only a few feet from *It* when the familiar reddish-brown flash appeared. Even before Sydney's staff took out Kranf's knee, a shiny little throwing dagger zipped from out of nowhere and sliced across the assassin's hand, making him drop the dagger. Both Kranf and the dagger hit the deck in front of *It*, who took his belaying pin, gave it a flip in the air, and then wacked Kranf on the head with it.

Evan got there with his face glowing a bright orange and his breath coming in deep loud grunts. His fists were trembling with anger, as he looked down onto the moaning and helpless Kranf. The Fallon was consumed with frustration, as he was all wound up and ready to crush someone—but now there was nothing to crush.

It knelt down by his would-be killer. "I guess I didn't need the Fallon," he said with a cheesy grin. He looked up to Evan with concern in seeing his friend so tense and orange in the face. "You really need to loosen up, man!"

Kranf, too, began laughing, but his laughter was disturbing and twisted. "You think this is it, you little twogg?" He continued laughing until it turned into a cough, forcing him to stop. With his sleeve, he wiped the spittle that had formed in the corners of his lips and then put two fingers in his mouth. A loud piercing whistle came from between his fingers, as he put everything into a single breath. At midship, Noggs stepped out from behind some other passengers. He saw Kranf and gave him a nod. Reaching into his coat, Noggs pulled out what looked to be two glass spheres. He threw them up at the main mast and they shattered against it, spraying flames onto the sail.

If the smaller commotion didn't draw a big enough crowd, the fiery blast definitely did. A flurry of crew, including the captain, appeared on deck in moments to fight the fire. A warning bell rang out as one sailor banged at it furiously. Men shouted above the roar of the flames while the cold wind spread the fire through the sails as if it were a blazing creature, crawling and leaping from sail to sail.

"Cut the lines! Man the buckets! Step lively, scrabbit, or I'll be the fire burn'n your backside with the lash!" Captain Danner called out to the men, who scrambled around in what seemed like a chaotic display, but in reality, they were containing the fire and keeping it from spreading to the rest of the ship with each man and woman performing their role.

Kranf glared up to *It*. "Now what? You can't make it to Yolanrym without a sail."

"There be more sail down below. This be just a delay," Switbo huffed.

"Yes, but our daggers made short work of them as well. There are always your blankets." He laughed in defiance of the murderous stare the woman gave him.

Toyota came from down below, scurrying quickly between the frantic crew. He stopped next to *It*. "What did I miss?"

Vasilik's eyes flew open with an unexpected rage, as he remembered that one of Kranf's men had heard Toyota conspiring with a shadowy figure below decks. Vasilik took two swift strides, followed with a solid kick, which knocked the Didelphi several feet to the rail. "Not me boot, that be for sure!"

"What are you doing!" *It* yelled at Vasilik, as he threw himself over Toyota to protect him from Vasilik's next blow.

The aging man's voice was harsh and sharp as he yelled again. "Tell him, lad! Tell him how ya be tell'n that cloaked stranger where we be! The man *It* be concern'n about!"

"Stranger? What stranger?" *It* called out to Vasilik over the roar of flames and screaming of men. The boy looked at Toyota. "What is he talking about?"

Vasilik stopped advancing on Toyota when Evan grabbed his arm, but he was still seething with anger. "The only souls to be know'n we be on this ship be stand'n here right now. He told them where we be." Vasilik thrusted his cane at Toyota who shrunk even deeper into *It*'s body.

"What about that friend of yours who got us the tickets? She knew we were on the ship. Maybe she told," *It* yelled back at Vasilik.

"Loopa would have died before tell'n. She hid herself so they could no be tortur'n her for information. And that be the truth of that," Vasilik replied.

"Yeah, but she is no better than ..." Evan started to say.

"Us," Vasilik snapped, stepping over to Switbo after Evan let him go. "She be no better than us be what ya mean'n to say?" Vasilik snarled.

"Actually, yes. I trust Toyota far more than I do the likes of you," Evan growled.

Vasilik gestured back to *It*. "I'm tell'n ya that the one who betrayed this boy be on this ship."

Lucas stepped forward with a slight bow. "I witnessed Toyota take his leave last night during his shift as guard."

Everyone froze. All eyes were on Toyota. *It* looked down at the frightened opossum face of the Didelphi boy in his arms. "Did you leave last night? Did you tell the cloaked stranger where we were going?"

Toyota dropped his head and looked down at the deck. His body heaved with a heavy sigh. "I told him."

It's eyes filled with water, and his lips trembled. For several months he had shared more adventures and more emotions with these people than he had in all of his lifetime on C-Earth.

"I had to. I have a contract with him. It's an inherited contract from my father. I had to fulfill it. I had to," Toyota pleaded, with tears welling up in his beady eyes.

It let go of Toyota, letting him fall to the deck. The human boy pulled away while staring off into the flames above and then whispered, "We trusted you. I trusted …"

In the distraction, Kranf reached into his coat and pulled out the cylinder he had been given by Neevit. He held it up towards the sky.

"Stop him!" Vasilik screamed.

Sydney swung her staff, knocking the cylinder out of Kranf's hand. It rolled across the deck and stopped next to Lucas' foot. The Ave picked it up. Kranf made an attempt to scramble away, but Evan stepped on his leg and held him in place, while the man screamed in tremendous pain.

"It be some form of signal to be call'n the Red Lion," Vasilik said, relieved that the cylinder had not been activated.

"What's the Red Lion?" Sydney asked.

"It be a ship, and run by a ruthless pirate," Switbo added, with her voice cracking.

It, who was already emotionally distraught, turned and then yelled at the entire group. "Pirates? You got pirates? Really? C'mon, you guys are killing me, here! I guess I shouldn't be shocked. If you're going to have giant bugs with render beasts and a feral mystic trying to kill me, why not pirates too! While you're at it, do you have any space aliens or dinosaurs you haven't told me about?"

Sydney took a step toward Evan as they watched *It* catching his breath. "Is he going to be ok?" she squeaked.

"I can no speak about an aleean or dinasewer, but aye, the pirates that be come'n be a lot ya no want to meet," Vasilik said, with an unsettling expression on his face, including his one raised eyebrow.

"Of course not, why should there be anything on the face of this planet that isn't trying to hurt me. I guess that's too much to ask," ***It*** ranted, with a double dose of angry sarcasm.

"It be noth'n to worry about. We be have'n the signal. They will no be find'n us before we reach Yolanrym, even without the mainsail," Vasilik encouraged, with sincere relief in his voice.

It turned back to Toyota. "But there's still you. I can't believe you. I was your friend. Not because we had a contract, and not because it was a responsibility. It was because I was your friend and I cared about you, and I thought you cared about me!"

"I do care about you. I still care about you!" Toyota cried out.

"You tried to have me killed. You gave one of my socks to the Kroncal so they could hunt me down and kill me. Friends don't do that to each other ... On other planets that is."

"I didn't do that," Toyota said, with a twist of his head and an honestly confused look.

It pointed at him. "You just said you did! You said you told the cloaked stranger where we were."

"Yeah, but he has nothing to do with that or with Kroncals. He's just a bit ... strange," Toyota said with a shrug.

Tiny black lines stretched out a short distance into the whites of ***It***'s eyes while he struggled to not strangle Toyota. "He tried to kill me when we fought the Ashmen."

Toyota shook his head with knowing confidence. "Nope. I'm sure he didn't."

"I saw him try to kill me."

"Trust me, if he wanted you dead you would not be here right now," Toyota said, with Sydney's typical matter-of-fact attitude.

"Who is he, Toyota? Tell us!" Evan barked, as he finally got over the initial shock that he was wrong about Vasilik and Toyota.

Toyota mumbled, and the only words they heard over the chaos on deck were "feral" and "mystic".

"You're kidding me. A feral mystic is after ***It***?" Sydney chittered, getting mad herself—and getting a Seeuradi mad was not an easy task.

"Sort of," Toyota said, sheepishly.

Evan leaned down. With his tusks near Toyota's face and tension in his lips, he grumbled, "How is it just sort of?"

"I didn't say he is a feral mystic … I said he is The Feral Mystic."

With slack faces, all eyes turned to Toyota.

"You mean the crazy mystic from the Bloody Forest that they tell scary stories about? The powerful mystic that Evan said is only a fairytale? A myth?" *It* questioned him while successfully fighting off his own anger, although the black lines were faintly still there in his eyes, and the familiar tingle was beginning to course through his body.

"Yeah, that one," Toyota said nonchalantly.

It turned to Evan. "I bet you're really not happy about your Host Custodian title, now, are you?"

"Yeah, not so much. But we still have a problem. If Toyota didn't tell the hoomans where we were going, who did?" Evan grunted.

It stood pondering for a moment. The tingle in his body shifted to his head. He began processing memories and information from every aspect of his life. Even the boring facts that his friend, Izak, constantly droned on about back on C-Earth stuck out in his mind. Millions of images and thoughts careened through his brain, twisting around and folding in on themselves, until they came to a screeching halt and one word stood out in full clarity. "Human," *It* said in a low voice.

"Yes, you are a hooman," Sydney replied, a little concerned for *It*, as he was acting weird.

"That's my point. You all say hooman, like some dumb owl … No offense," *It* said.

"None taken," Evan huffed.

"I take offense," Sydney squeaked.

"But you," *It* pointed to Lucas. "Last night I thought you were nervous from speaking out of turn, but I heard you say human." *It* reached even deeper into his thoughts and, as if talking to himself, he said, "You pronounced human correctly. How did you know to do that? When we camped out next to the Kroncals, you stepped on the twig that alerted them … You disappeared among their render beast tracks … and when they rode by us, someone smaller than them was on a horse wearing a cloak. That's how you got to Squall before us." He looked over to Lucas. "Why? Why would you do this?"

There was a long pause, as they all turned to Lucas. A single tear beaded up and rolled down across the blue feathers of his cheek as he answered,

"For the flock." His voice cracked, and his arms moved with reluctance as he raised the signal device above his head.

It could see the purple glow and a black mist surrounding the cylinder in Lucas's claw.

The Blue Jay Ave mumbled the word "Firlon." Sparks burst out the cylinder's top end. Red, blue, green and every other color under the sun exploded into the sky as a leathery toad-like creature with a spiked tail and bat wings crawled out of the tube. It briefly glanced around with glowing yellow eyes and then leapt into the air, following the sparks into the sky before turning southeast. It flew with great speed until disappearing into the clouds.

Normally, Evan would be pounding the life out of the Ave boy for such treachery, but everyone continued to stand still; frozen again in a deathly quiet, staring at Lucas with disbelief. The tear from his cheek fell, crashing on one of the weathered and worn wooden planks of the deck, as the signal tube dropped from his clawed hand. No words were spoken—there was nothing to say.

The black streaks stretched out further across the whites of *It*'s eyes, and his body tingled with overwhelming mystic energy. His hands trembled as he stared at Lucas, but he did nothing. If he let out the feral mystic power in him now, it would consume him and everything around him. He would lose all his friends—all that he has come to love.

The Ave looked as if he wanted *It* to destroy him; to take his life and in turn ease his suffering, but when he saw that *It*'s devotion kept him from lashing out, Lucas turned and walked away with slow dreadful steps—what he had done could not be undone, or ever forgotten.

"Ha, so this whole time, you didn't know you had two spies among your group of needle quilters?" Kranf cackled, with a forced laugh.

Evan leaned over and gave a light flip of his backhand to Kranf's cheek and knocked the assassin out cold.

Sydney looked to Switbo and in a loud whisper said, "Needle quilters?"

"It be mean'n shiftless old women, dear," Switbo responded with a motherly tone that had no deception to it.

Sydney chittered something in Seeuradi at Kranf that sounded like it was too nasty to say in common tongue.

Again, there was a long moment of silence among the group, until Toyota cleared his throat and said, "So, am I not in trouble since I'm not the bad guy anymore?"

"You want me to throw him overboard?" Evan asked *It* with a guttural growl, while looking at Toyota.

It stood there thinking.

Toyota's eyes sprung open wide. "No! You can't do that. *It*, don't let him do it," Toyota begged with tears welling up in his eyes—a Didelphi's worse nightmare is drowning.

Switbo leaned in to Vasilik. "He's not go'n to let the Fallon do it, is he?"

"It no be in the boy to be do'n such a thing. He be just sweat'n the little scamp … I reckon," Vasilik whispered, with a lift of his eyebrow and a tilt of his head that indicated he had no confidence in his own words.

It continued to not move for a few moments longer. "Do whatever you want." He turned to the hatchway leading below. "There's a feral mystic I'm going to have words with."

"I'm going with," Evan said, throwing his shoulders back.

It spun around with the black lines pulsing in his eyes. "I don't need your help!" he hissed in a deep raspy voice that sent chills through everyone.

Evan shrunk back for the first time in his life and watched *It* walk off.

Sydney's eyes were glistening, and her voice was shaky. "Are we breaking up?"

"No dear, they be take'n a brief breather. They be boys being boys," Switbo said, with uncertainty in her words. She looked to her husband who just threw his arms out and shrugged his shoulders.

Evan turned around to face Toyota. The little Didelphi screamed, "Ahhhhh! Don't let him throw me over," as he scuttled over to hide behind Switbo. Evan started to bend over, and Switbo moved her hand inside her coat and grasped a throwing knife. Evan dismissed her bravado gesture with a snort and shake of his head. He bent the rest of the way down and grabbed the unconscious Kranf by the collar and lifted him off the ground.

With a rare softness in his eyes and a kinder voice, he looked down at the trembling Toyota. "Why don't you go get started on lunch. *It*'s going to be hungry when he gets back," the Fallon warrior said, just louder than a whisper, as he walked off with Kranf's feet dragging the ground.

Sydney huffed and straightened her little cloak while pushing her gaudy teal glasses high onto her little nose. Clutching her staff in her hand, she started marching towards the hatch to down below.

"And where be it ya go'n, lassy?" Vasilik called out.

"I'm going to help *It*. He's my friend," she squeaked angrily.

"Twas clear he be not need'n any help," Switbo cautioned.

"He told Evan he didn't need help. I'm sure he wasn't including me in that. Besides, I have to be there to heal him when The Feral Mystic beats him up."

"I do no trust where to be put'n my coin on that fight. Sucram says the boy be a Molec, and the lad looks to be in a fierce arse-kicking mood," Vasilik muttered to himself more than to anyone particular.

"I hope not, I need the healing practice," she squeaked back at him, as she bounded off through the hatch.

Vasilik looked to his wife. "I ain't be get'n paid enough for this."

"Well, this be definitely the most excit'n con you run in a great many year," Switbo said in a long drawn out breath.

"That it be. That it be," Vasilik said with a sigh.

They paused, staring off at the empty hatchway. Switbo closed her eyes and gave a little shake of her head in agitation. "You can be let'n go of me leg, now," she said, as she looked down at Toyota. "And if'n you don't want to be get'n thrown into the sea, you best get to mak'n that grub."

Toyota waddled off rapidly as a large piece of burning sail flopped through the air and landed in front of Switbo and Vasilik. She laid her head on her adoring husband's shoulder, as they watched the inferno and its continued chaos unfold on deck with pleasant content looks on their faces, as if, somehow, they felt refreshingly at home.

THIRTY-SIX

WHICH FERAL MYSTIC?

The passageway down below was completely dark except for the glow from *It*'s C.I.M.U. He walked with a determination and some innate knowledge of where he was going, as if being guided from something deep within him. He came to a door leading into a large cargo compartment. As he opened the door, his nose was accosted by the reek of mildew and rot. He continued into the cargo hold filled with crates and barrels and made his way to the center of the room where there were less crates, but more oddly shaped freight.

When he reached the middle, he stopped and stood still, searching the darkness. Nothing was there, yet he felt that he was not alone. "I want to talk to you," *It* called out, still fueled by anger and sadness. He waited a moment, listening, but heard nothing but the sounds of verms scurrying around. "You must have misunderstood me. I wasn't asking. I want to see you and I want to see you now!"

"And who are you to make demands of me?" a harsh voice called out from the darkness.

"I'm the one who just lost a trusted friend because of you. I'm the one you've been following for months … cowering in the darkness."

"Cowering? That's a strong accusation, don't you think?"

"Call it what you will. You are either going to come out and face me now and kill me now or stay the scrab away from me and my friends." *It* continued to look around.

"Who said that I wanted to kill you?"

"You tried to before … with the Ashmen."

"You are an ignorant boy. I wasn't trying to kill you. I was trying to save you … which I did."

It's face contorted. "Why? Or better yet, why didn't you just approach me. Talk to me."

The voice in the darkness lost its harsh tone and became more casual. "That's not my thing. I don't do social etiquette."

It huffed with frustration, as he much preferred seeing who he was talking to. "What do you want from me?"

"Information, data."

The boy's brow perked up. "Data? How do you know that word?"

"Like you, I come from another world … over thirty years ago."

It's face lit up, and for a moment he forgot this was a possible enemy he was dealing with. "Are there others like us?"

"Only one that I know of," the voice called back.

"Who is it? Can I speak to them?"

From the blackness came an eerie chuckle. The kind that makes the skin crawl and the heart race. "Oh … I wouldn't rush that encounter."

Unhappy with all the shady theatrics and deceit, *It* called out, "So what do we do now?"

"I've learned some of what I need to know from you, but there is much more that interests me."

"So, ask."

"Not now."

"Why not now?" *It* cried out. He felt the tingling coursing through his body, and his eyes pulsed. As he strained to see through the darkness, he began to make out images. Directly in front of him was a cloaked figure.

"Because, you have more important things to worry about."

"Like what?" *It* asked with a slight delay in his words, as he willed himself to see more. The blackness began to fade away, and he could see that the Feral Mystic was only ten feet away from him, though the man's voice came from all angles of the room.

"The Red Lion for one, and a demon witch for another," the Feral Mystic said, then waved his hand and the room was black again. *It* could see nothing beyond the light from his communication device.

"What demon witch?" *It* yelled out into the darkness.

"Tell the Didelphi his contract is fulfilled," the voice called out, and then there was nothing.

The boy took two steps toward the darkness and called out again. "What demon witch?"

It waited a few long moments, but he knew he would hear no reply, and a feeling in his gut made it clear that he was now alone in the compartment. Being more confused than when he first got there, the boy turned and headed back out the door. Closing the door behind him, he began walking through another compartment. He stopped to sniff the air and then winced. "Whoa, is that you Sydney?"

"And how did you know I was here? Your nose must be getting more sensitive," Sydney squeaked at him, as she came out from under some tarp-covered cargo.

"Nope. You just haven't bathed in a couple days, and you're damp."

"What are you saying?" she asked, with a deep, piercing stare and her glasses resting dangerously close to the edge of her nose. She was trying oh-so-hard to be intimidating. Of course, something that cute would be hard pressed to intimidate a fluff-bug.

The black lines in *It*'s eyes vanished, and a weak smile cracked across his lips. "Nothing. Let's go eat."

Though Toyota made a lunch large enough for a small army, nobody seemed very hungry, except for Sydney, that is. She was never upset enough to not be able to eat. Back on deck, *It*, Evan, and the McCarthy's silently watched the sailors darning large pieces of sail to get the ship moving back on course and make up time.

"So, what do we do now?" *It* asked the quiet lot.

"The way I see it, that signal may have just been a misdirection to make us focus on something that isn't there," Evan replied, with false encouragement.

It gazed out to the back of the ship. A trail of glowing black and purple mist led from the middle of the ship up into the sky and disappeared to the southeast. "It wasn't a misdirection. I can see the trail in the sky."

"And the Red Lion will be sure to be follow'n it," Vasilik said with certainty, as he used his cane to push around a biscuit he had dropped on the deck.

"We'll have to bring the Captain in on this and find out what defenses he will have to repel the attack," Evan added.

"Yor no go'n repel the Red Lion. If'n we be her target, this ship and all who be on her be scrabbed," Vasilik grumbled, tapping at the biscuit until it broke under his cane.

"How will they do it?" *It* asked.

Evan shrugged, as he was unfamiliar with battle at sea.

"She'll be catch'n up to us before the sails be mended, lay in her hooks, and board us," Switbo said, staring off into the distance.

"Then we'll make our stand when they come aboard and take them out as they do," Evan said, pushing his chest out.

"And that be last'n all of a few moments as they swarm us and burn the ship to its keel," Vasilik snickered with some unknown irony.

"They would kill all these innocent people?" Sydney squeaked between mouthfuls of some stringy meat with beans.

"Aye, to be get'n to the lad, they would," Vasilik said, pointing his cane at *It*.

It paused and watched some passengers on deck offer to help the sailors with the sails. A few human children played on deck while their parents discussed the delay and possible new arrival times for reaching Yolanrym, none of them realizing that this may be the last evening they share together.

Toyota came out from the hatch with a pot in hand. He waddled over to the rail and emptied the contents into the water. Briefly he made eye contact with *It*, but he dropped his head in shame and self-loathing, dragging the pot behind him through the hatch and down below.

It started shaking his head no, and he slapped a column of crates with his hand. "No. These people are not going to die for me!"

"Sorry, me boy. Ya ain't gonna be hav'n much to say in the matter when the Lion be get'n here," Vasilik said.

"Is that what you think? All of you?" *It* looked at his companions and they each had a defeated look in their eyes and dread on their faces, even Evan. "Well, you're wrong. Because we're going to attack first. We are going to board the Red Lion," *It* declared to now-shocked faces.

"Are ya mad?" Vasilik said, looking at the boy's eyes for signs of a mental break or black streaks.

In hearing the boy, Evan did something he rarely ever did; he smiled broadly and with pride. "When they set the first hooks," he gasped, as he understood *It*'s intentions.

"That's what I'm thinking. When we cross over on to the Lion, we have Captain Danner and his men cut the lines from here," *It* said with eager, albeit naïve, excitement.

"But where be the part where we don't die?" Switbo questioned the boy with a wink.

"I haven't thought that part through yet. I kinda hoped Evan would figure that out," *It* replied, with an expression of trust on his face.

"That be a mighty important element of yor plan to be poorly formulated," Vasilik added.

"That's why we brainstorm this out," *It* said.

"What kind of storm?" Sydney mumbled, with beans falling out of her mouth.

In no time at all, *It* had gotten his emotional second wind and brought the group together to strategize their attack on the Red Lion. It wasn't much more of a plan than he had already described, so Evan had to take it from there and fill in the details. Everything was going to rely on them keeping the crew of the Red Lion occupied while the Widow's Son made its escape. As much as he hated their only option, the Fallon figured that if *It* was the pirate's main target, then the Red Lion wouldn't pursue the others after the boy was aboard their ship. Or at least this was their hope.

They informed the captain of the situation and found him to be less than happy with the predicament they had caused. But he was quick to buy in on their plan, as it involved fewer risks of casualties from his vessel and included an escape with both ship and cargo.

They spent their time preparing for much of the evening and into the night which helped to occupy their minds, as it didn't look like anyone was going to sleep much, if any. The moon peeked through the clouds that had opened up in the sky. Standing alone at the aft of the ship was a tall form leaning on the rail and watching the water. It was Lucas. He had stayed hidden during the day but came up top to breathe.

From the shadows, another form walked slowly up behind him and paused just feet from the Ave. Lucas' head tilted slightly, indicating that he knew someone was behind him, but he made no move of defense, or of any other kind. If this was his time to die, he welcomed it. After a few tense moments, the shadowy form stepped over to Lucas and leaned on the rail alongside of him.

"I could say it's a nice night, but we both know it's not," *It* said, while looking at the water below. His voice was dry and pointed and lacking even the slightest of the once-familiar affection.

"Did you come to inquire as to the impetus of my betrayal? If you did, I have already offered my response earlier and no additional intercourse will change the situation," Lucas said, never once turning to look at *It*.

"No. I know why you did it. I don't understand it, and I don't know why you didn't come to me before, but I am clear on the why. You did it for the flock. Of course, I don't understand why the flock would need me dead."

"Neither do I," Lucas breathed out heavily.

"If I ask you for the details of who made this request of you, would you tell me?"

"No."

"I thought as much. And Evan seems to think that the flock will deny knowing anything of it, which means they will deny you."

Lucas turned to *It* with a look of honest confusion and frustration on his face. "Why did you not have the Fallon kill me? That's how it was supposed to go."

It turned and peered deep into the Ave's face. "Friends don't kill friends." The boy turned to walk away and then stopped. He glanced back over his shoulder and said, "When the Lion comes, the captain here will need you to help him and the crew to cut the lines and break for safety … You owe me this much." *It* walked away, leaving Lucas to the torment of his own guilt. The Ave stared out at the waves as they crashed into and over each other, devouring themselves from the inside out.

Daybreak came fast, and all hands were frantically making ready. The other passengers were made aware of the situation and those brave enough, and strong enough, were recruited to help with the escape plan. Most of them thanked *It* and his friends for their sacrifice, while a few others blamed the boy for putting them in the situation to begin with. There were also those who told *It* that they believed in him as the prophecy child. Of course, each time it was mentioned, Vasilik would have to look away as to not laugh or give away his guilt—and Evan's reaction needed no explanation.

As they had not eaten the night before, everyone's appetite was not only back, but they were all eating breakfast like it was their last meal. Toyota couldn't be happier that, though he wasn't forgiven, he wasn't forsaken like Lucas, and now he was useful again.

After filling his stomach, *It* excused himself early, as he said he had something to take care of. He made his way back down to the cargo hold and entered the same way he did the day before. Somehow it managed to smell even worse than yesterday.

Back in his spot amongst the crates and barrels, he called out, "I'm assuming you're there." There was no reply. "I thought you should know that when the Red Lion comes to board us, we will be taking the offensive and boarding them first." *It* waited to see if this was going to be a one-way conversation. The silence confirmed that it was. "Well, anyway, if you want this ship to make it to Yolanrym, you would do yourself a favor by helping the crew with the hooks and any boarders coming from the Lion."

"I don't need this ship to get to shore," the harsh voice called back from the shadows, breaking the silence, and causing several verms to scurry off for safety.

"So, you are there ... I believe you ... You saved me once when you didn't have to. There are children on this ship that need saving," *It* called out.

"Isn't that what you're doing with your suicide; saving the children?" the Feral Mystic said, with a dismissive air to his voice.

"Yes. It's the right thing to do."

"So, my efforts to save you before were for nothing?"

It bobbed his head back and forth with a crinkled brow. "That's one way to look at it."

"It is the way I look at it. Why are you doing this?" For whatever reason, the mystic stranger expressed actual concern in his questioning.

It laughed as he took a second to consider the real reason why, then he smiled. "A friend once told me, 'we do what we have to for our herd and for honor' ... and right now that seems to be a good enough excuse for me."

"Spoken like a true Fallon ... Are you done?" asked the Feral Mystic.

"I suppose." *It* turned to walk away and stopped. "Oh, and if you should decide to help and fight, Vasilik suggests we aim to wound and not kill. He said that it will be our best chance at mercy once we are on the Lion."

"There is no mercy on the Lion," the mystic hissed.

The cargo hold fell silent. *It* walked down the aisle, out the door, and closed it behind him. He had an odd look of contentment on his face, and for a boy with just hours left to live, the look seemed out of place.

The long wait was all that was ahead for *It* and his eclectic band of mis-adventurers, but it was much shorter than expected. Off on the horizon, a speck had appeared. The captain's men were working feverishly to have the mainsail ready to unfurl when given the signal, and at this point, they were cutting it close. Evan's plan was to have burned pieces of sail hanging from the rigging and smoking pots of burning tar to give the illusion that the ship was disabled and on fire.

The crew of the Red Lion would be sure to fall for the ruse long enough for *It* and his friends to put their portion of the plan into action. Sections of the rail had been partially cut through so as to have many of the hooks fail when the rails break away. A few bowmen from the crew of the Widow's Son would help to repel boarders while *It* and the rest made their way to the Red Lion; at that time the Widow's Son would have their newly-sewn sails raised and have focused all attention on cutting any remaining hook lines.

"The captain says they will be upon us before noon," Evan told the group.

"No, that won't do. I have planned a talon fish stew with potatoes and sweet onions for lunch. I don't suppose we can ask them to wait." Toyota said, with sincere disappointment.

They all glared down at the Didelphi with chastising looks. Vasilik leaned in towards Toyota and said, "It be a bit soon for ya to be chat'n with them others, so you might want to be give'n it a day or two."

"Or a year," Evan grumbled.

"Has anyone seen Lucas?" *It* asked.

They all looked at *It* as if he were insane.

"Why would we be want'n to be see'n him?" hissed Switbo.

"I asked him to help the captain with boarders," *It* replied.

"You asked him to help repel the people he signaled to come kill us?" Evan snarled.

"They could use every hand and blade available. Like you said, he most likely has no life to return to in the flock. Whatever his reasons for doing what he did, I know he authentically cared for us. He will do this one last thing to honor the friendship we had."

"How do you know he would do that?" Evan asked.

"Wouldn't you?" *It* asked.

"I know I'm not supposed to talk, but I assume I'm coming with you guys ... right?" Toyota said, with a pleading voice and with that same unnerving sinister grin.

"You should probably stay over here and help out. You too, Sydney. There is no need in you giving up your life," *It* said, while tousling the fur on his little Seeuradi friend's head.

Vasilik gave a heart-wrenching look to his wife at hearing the boy's words. He took in a deep breath while putting his hand on Sydney's shoulder. "Well, it probably be a good idea for some of us to be stay'n back and help'n the others here. Me wife and me will be sure the lass makes it to home alright."

Evan sneered and growled at the older man's cowardice, but *It* just let out a nervous laugh. "It's okay. You and Switbo have done more than you signed on for." The boy unhooked his coin purse from his belt and tossed it to Vasilik. "I won't be needing this after today. You've been good friends to us." *It* rushed over and threw his arms around Vasilik. "I'm going to miss you ... or at least for the short while I'm still alive," the boy's voice cracked, as he fought to hold back the tears, while still laughing.

Vasilik's eyes glossed over, and he, too, struggled to maintain control. "Aye, it be a pleasure do'n business with you too, lad. Now go hug the woman, she be live'n for that kind of nonsense." Vasilik pushed *It* into Switbo who wrapped her arms around the boy.

"There, now. You don't go talk'n like that. It will be fine." Switbo took the boy's hat off and pressed her cheek against his head. "You just be let'n those black eyes of yorn go wild when you get over there and give them what for."

"I will," *It* said, and wiped his sleeve across his face.

Sydney broke into tears and leapt on the boy, hugging him as tight as her little arms would let her, which made Toyota break down crying and launch himself on the boy as well.

"For the Great Giver's sake, let the boy die with some dignity," Evan barked at Sydney and Toyota with his own huge eyes looking glossier than normal. "You got me wishing the Red Lion would be here already."

Switbo leaned into her husband and put her arm around his waist. She pressed her lips gently against his ear with what looked to be the sweetest of sentiments. "I be hate'n you with a powerful hate, and from the hottest blazes for put'n me through this with that beautiful boy. You can be start'n yor search for yor second wife before we even be gett'n off this ship." She stood back upright with a sad smile.

Vasilik's eyebrow raised up high, and his mouth dropped open. "And what be I do'n wrong now?"

THIRTY-SEVEN

THE RED LION

The Red Lion was equal in size to that of the cargo vessel, the Widow's Son, but instead of having boxes and barrels of freight on the deck, there were several large ballistae with grappling hooks at the ready and armed crewmen with unsavory dispositions. The ship was painted a rusty, weathered red with equally weathered yellow stripes down the side to match the yellow rails. At the front, a faded, red lion's head with the mane flowing down to the water's edge was poised with its mouth open in mid-roar and a skeleton hanging from its teeth.

Around the main mast, crossbows and boarding pikes were secured into storage racks for quick access. Every crewman had a cutlass or axe as they made ready for the assault. A tall lanky sailor in a burgundy leather vest and bandana on his head stood on the forecastle at the front of the ship peering through a small telescope. He closed the scope and turned on his heels.

"Yo there, tell the cap'n we'll be overrunning them within the hour," he called out to a squat crewman who had years of wear on his face.

"Aye, Halman, sir!" the crewman replied.

The man stumbled as he made his way across the deck to the aft of the ship and into a door. Halman began barking orders, preparing the ship for battle. Buckets of water were prepared for dowsing the ship prior to engagement and then refilled in preparation for firebombs of oil-filled bottles with strips of cloth jammed in the openings. They would be lit on fire before throwing.

The sailor who ran off to inform the captain of the situation came stumbling back across the deck. He panted loudly, as he was unaccustomed to running at all. "Mr. Halman, sir!"

"What have you?"

"The cap'n expects ya to handle it an earn yor keep for once, sir ... His words, no mine," he shouted, and then took in a gulp of air, as he feared some reprisal.

"Then we won't be disappoint'n him," Halman shouted back. He looked through his telescope again and saw the smoke floating up from the Widow's Son. "It be appeare'n the king's man be done his part." He turned back to the crew. "She's float'n adrift ... twill' be easy pick'ns today!"

On the Widow's Son, it was the quiet before the storm, as nervous men watched and waited, while the Red Lion drew closer and approached from the port side, just as they had hoped. Sailors waved rags in the air to a show that they thought the Red Lion was there to help, which was a detail Switbo added to the overall plan.

Evan had to hide behind the tarped freight, as his bulk would be easily seen. The others mingled in amongst the crew and waved eagerly to their supposed saviors. They saw some of the men from the Red Lion waving back and laughing. So far, the strategy seemed to be working.

As the Lion glided in closer through the choppy water, Halman gave the signal to change course and close the gap between the ships. The two vessels were alongside each other when the ballistae of the Red Lion fired their hooks, which soared over to the Widow's Son. The men on the Red Lion scrambled over and grabbed the ropes and began pulling.

Vasilik stood amidship with Switbo and began yelling. "Wait for it!"

Many of the hooks latched onto the loosened rails and fell to the water below, but the other hooks held fast, and the ships were drawn even closer together. When the first few men from the Red Lion swarmed over by swinging on ropes and climbing the hook lines, Vasilik yelled again. "Now, be damned ya! Now!"

Arrows flew from the Widow's Son and took out the first couple men. But then things turned for the worse. Several of the sailors on the Widow's Son pulled swords and began fighting with other men on their own ship.

"Traitors!" Captain Danner yelled.

Evan burst out from behind the crates to see more men flying over from the pirate ship, and the bowmen of his ship were busy fighting their own crew. Evan's face flashed orange and his knuckles cracked. He came across the first traitor and slapped him with the back of his hand, resulting in the sound of bones breaking. Vasilik and Switbo took out two more traitors as Sydney whacked one in the head with a staff, allowing the crew to subdue him. They had quelled the mutiny, but now there were too many Red Lions on the Widow's Son. Evan's plan had been felled by a more sinister plot.

There was all-out chaos as the Fallon's strategy continued to unravel, but then an aft hatch of the Widow's Son flew open, and a hooded figure leaped out on deck and began running along the port side of the ship. It was the Feral Mystic. Whipping his cloak over his shoulder, he revealed two pistols in holsters strapped to his waist. He drew out both weapons and began firing. Shot after shot was hitting its mark and taking out Red Lions in the shoulder and in the legs. As *It* had requested, the mystic was not making any intentional kill shots. For a moment, things were back on schedule.

"Let's go!" *It* yelled to Evan, as he clubbed a boarding pirate and took his cutlass.

"Wait!" Evan yelled, but it was too late. *It* was already swinging across.

As the boy landed, his hat fell off and rolled away. He thought he saw someone grab it, but he was too busy defending himself from the crewmen who charged him as he stood up.

Seeing his human friend already on the Lion, Evan leapt over the rail and grabbed the rope of an incoming pirate and crushed him in the process. The Fallon was now on his way over to help *It*.

The crew cut two of the hooks free from the pirate ship and the third was shot loose by the Feral Mystic. Sydney saw that the ships were free and, disobeying *It*, she darted to the rail. Leaping high into the air, she grabbed a rope to swing across. On the way over, she saw Toyota alongside of her swinging … and waving to her … and she smiled.

It and Evan were back-to-back with a few unconscious sailors at their feet when Toyota and Sydney hit the deck and bounded over to them. The four were doing well in fighting off the pirate crew, when Vasilik and

Switbo landed on the deck next to them. Switbo was graceful and nimble in her tumble as she leapt to her feet. Vasilik, on the other hand, hit the deck like a discarded sack of potatoes and groaned as he tried to stand up.

"I be always hate'n that part," he yelled to his wife.

"Yes, but now be come'n the fun part." She pulled out her battle rod and said, "Extensium" and the rod mystically extended from both ends into a six-foot metal staff. She howled with pleasure as she began parrying cutlasses away and cracking heads.

"God, I be love'n that woman," Vasilik said to the crewman in front of him as he smacked the pirate's hand with his cane and dislodged his axe. Vasilik caught the axe before it hit the ground and used it to conk the sailor in the head. "I'll be need'n that, thank you very much."

It saw his friends fighting for their lives. His face tensed at the sight, as they shouldn't even be on the Lion; that wasn't part of the plan. Fear and anger welled up inside him and his eyes grew dark, as the black streaks made their appearance in his eyes. He began moving quicker than Sydney and hitting as hard as Evan, but even in his growing fevered state he made sure to just wound.

The ragtag group were doing better than could have been imagined, but it wasn't long before the sheer numbers were going to overwhelm them. A huge sailor with a burned face and wiry beard charged at *It* when he wasn't looking. Just as he was a few steps from slamming into the boy, a loud screech drew everyone's attention skyward.

Lucas had leapt from the crow's nest of the Widow's Son and was gliding swiftly toward the Red Lion. He pulled in his wings slightly and began to spin in the air, as daggers flew out from the feathery blur and into the knee and arm of the big man charging at *It*. The pirate dropped hard to the deck. Lucas landed next to his former friend with daggers in hand.

"Thanks for the help, but I think now you're gonna wish you brought a sword," *It* said to Lucas, with more than a little distrust in his eyes.

"I have one," Lucas said, as he threw his two daggers into an oncoming pirate; and as the man went down, the Ave snatched away his cutlass. "See."

"Convenient," *It* said, and parried the next strike from another of the Lion's crew.

―

Back on the Widow's Son, the Feral Mystic holstered his weapons as there were no more targets to shoot. He raised his arms high in the air and made short circles with his hands. The air and smoke above his head twisted and swirled with each arm creating its own funneled shaped tempest. With one quick motion, he brought them down hard in separate directions. One palm stretched out towards the sails that had now been unfurled by the crew of the Widow's Son and the other palm faced the sails of the Red Lion. In a voice louder than all the chaos around him, he yelled, "Aeorn!"

The maelstroms from each hand struck out toward their intended marks. When struck by the gale force winds, both ships lurched forward and away from each other, with tremendous creaking and groaning from the sail masts and the ships' wooden hull. Everyone on both decks were thrown off balance with a few crew members from the Red Lion's decks being cast overboard. With a flip of the Feral Mystic's wrist pointing at the Red Lion, the ship began a steep bank, turning completely away until it was facing in the opposite direction. Despite only half the sails being set, the pirate ship was set on a speedy course away from the Widow's Son.

Halman stood on the forecastle of the Red Lion, watching the Widow's Son making its escape. "Nice try, but we can be follow'n ya to the ends of the sea!" he yelled and pulled out a small crystal that he looked through at the sky. He saw the glowing mystic trail leading from the Widow's Son. He then lifted his telescope in time to see the Feral Mystic bring his closed fist to the front of his hood and then thrust his hand out like he blew a kiss.

Halman quickly raised the crystal back up to his face and gazed through it upward. He watched as the misty trail started to fade and disappear, as if being erased along its length. "No! no! no! Scrab ya!" Halman cursed, as he watched the last of the mystic glow vanish right up to the Red Lion.

Halman whipped around to see that his men were not getting the upper hand as quickly as they should. He reached into his pocket and pulled out a whistle. He blew one long shrill with two smaller ones after it. His men backed off of *It* and the others, but after another three whistles, the pirates formed a line. They stood in two ranks, one in front of the other. The front rank had all grabbed little crates and barrels to act as make-shift shields, while the second rank held boarding pikes out like spears. They moved in slow.

"Okay, this does not look good," Sydney squeaked, as she scrambled up Evan to perch on his shoulder.

"Aye, be steady, lads, with them teeth pickers. They be a mite pointy," Vasilik said to the advancing line of the Lion crew.

The door to the captain's quarters slung open, slamming hard against a pirate, knocking him out completely. The noise drew everyone's attention. An old man in a faded red leather jacket stepped out onto the deck. It was Captain Vosvile. His ebony skin was wrinkled from time and the harsh elements. For the most part he was thin, but he had an obvious beer belly that stuck out and over his belt. *It* noticed a familiar look to his face, as the old pirate had a curly grey mustache exactly like Vasilik's, but much, much longer. The old captain also had an equally grey wiry beard with blotches where there were scars instead of whiskers.

"Where's me cocked bonnet?" The captain yelled back toward the hatchway. "Scrabbed and be hang ya, girl! Where be me bonnet?"

"Here me Cap'n, sir," said a tiny Didelphi girl, rushing out with a large faded black captain's hat with three corners and a bulge in the middle for his head. Several tattered feathers extended out from a tarnished brass hat band. It had seen many years of battles and use.

"Contract, or no. I should be rid of ya if'n ya leave me head bare another time," he barked, as he snatched the hat from the Didelphi's hands.

The captain set his hat on his head and turned towards *It* and the others. He walked with direct and measured steps, with his right hand resting on his sword hilt and the other hand stroking his long mustache whiskers. He began to walk past Evan as he reached him first, but Evan turned to point his sword at him. With two quick reflexes of his right hand, the captain drew his sword and cut Evan's hand, making him drop his blade, and then slapped the sword skidding across the deck near to the edge. His movements were beyond fast.

The captain slid his sword back into its sheath. "Don't be testing me again, youngon," he said to Evan, without raising his voice. Seeing Sydney on Evan's shoulder, the captain turned his head to one side with a questionable look on his face. "An that be one odd look'n parrot yer got there ... an ugly to boot."

"Hey! That wasn't nice!" Sydney squeaked.

"Shut it," Evan whispered to the dejected girl.

"Well, it wasn't nice," she complained.

The captain continued walking and came across a pirate with a white Fedora on his head. "Be that yor bonnet?" he asked the pirate.

"No, sir. Cap'n, sir," he responded nervously.

"An whose might it be then?"

"The boy's, Cap'n, sir."

"An what be me orders concern'n other person's bonnets?"

"Don't touch them, Cap'n, sir."

"Aye, don't be touch'n them. An what did ya do?"

"I touched it, sir," the pirate said while cringing.

"Uh huh."

The captain snatched the white Fedora off the pirate's head. "Go flog yourself, until the boy is happy," the captain ordered. The pirate ran off to the other side of the ship and began flogging himself with a knotted rope he found on the deck.

The potbellied old pirate faced the crew and addressed them with a loud bellowing voice. "What be me number one rule?"

In unison the whole crew called back, "Don't touch another's bonnet, Cap'n, Sir."

"Then why do ya keep do'n it?" the captain yelled, with more frustration than the situation seemed to warrant.

The crew looked at him blankly; everyone afraid to say anything.

"Scrabbit all," he mumbled to himself and turned back around. He walked over to *It* while briefly examining the hat. He paused and looked confusingly at the dead cat pin overlapping the black band. He huffed disapprovingly and placed the hat on the boy's head. "Me apologies about yor bonnet, youngon."

"Thank you? Sir?" *It* said and cringed, as he saw the pirate on the other side of the ship flogging himself. As the captain started to walk away *It* stopped him. "Pardon me, sir," *It* said submissively.

"Aye," the captain responded.

"I'm quite happy having my hat back. He can stop doing that now," *It* said, pointing his finger in the direction of the pirate swinging the knotted rope against his back.

"Halman?" the captain called out.

"Aye, sir, Cap'n," Halman called back from the forecastle.

"The boy be happy," the captain commented with the same enthusiasm as stating that the weather was mild. He resumed his leisurely walk.

Halman put his hand to the side of his mouth as he yelled out to the man flogging himself. "The boy be happy!" With that, the man stopped flogging himself and dropped to his knees.

The captain finally reached Vasilik and leaned in to look at his mustache. "I see yor still imitate'n me," he said with a gregarious laugh, as he grabbed Vasilik and hugged him tightly, followed by a kiss on his cheek. "I be miss'n ya, son. How be yor muther?"

Vasilik hugged him back. "I be miss'n ya too … and mums been be'n dead near thirteen year."

"Tis a shame. Lovely woman twas she."

It, Evan, and Lucas stood with their jaws open wide with shock. Sydney looked sad as she leaned down to Evan's ear and whispered, "That's too bad about Vasilik's mom."

Vosvile pulled back away from Vasilik and turned to Switbo. "An you, lass! Many a nights I still be av'n impure thoughts of ya, Margaret, me girl." He pulled Switbo into him and gave her a quick kiss on her lips, like that of a friend or distant relation who wished they were more than just friends.

"And I still be dream'n about you, Vossy me love," she said, as she threw her arms around his neck. "It be too many year." She hugged him tightly and with all sincerity.

"Aye, it be," he replied, pushing her back to take a better look at her. "An them years be a mighty good friend to ya. Now be tell'n me how yer done got'n into this mess."

Switbo put her arm around her husband, leaned her head towards him and said to the captain. "I'll be giv'n you one guess."

The captain gave out a loud forced laugh. "Ya be up to yor scoundrel ways again, have ya, Vasilik me boy?"

"Only in some sense of the word," Vasilik replied, much more relaxed.

"Well then, let's be dispatch'n with this lot and be catch'n up over some wine and bread," the captain said in a very cheery voice, as he gestured that *It* and his friends were the ones to be dispatched.

Again, *It*, Evan, and Lucas had their jaws still open wide. This time even Sydney and Toyota looked very concerned.

"Aye, that would be right and good, but there be a rub in that I be need'n that we no be dispatch'n this lot of snappers," Vasilik said, with a voice of uncertainty in his request.

"A rub it be indeed. I be lose'n a sizable purse, no to mention bring'n the king's advisor and his dark witch down on me if'n we don't be dispatch'n em," Vosvile said with a wink.

"What witch?" *It* blurted out, with no thought to proprieties.

"The one that be need'n ya dead. An' one evil witch she be. How could such a wee bite as yorself be putt'n a needle in her craw? It be a dumfound'n one for sure," Vosvile replied.

It turned to Evan. "The Feral Mystic mentioned a witch. This may be the one he was talking about." *It* and Evan both sidestepped over to Switbo and Vasilik. "We need to find out who she is and where she is. But most of all, why she is after me," *It* whispered.

"We can be get'n that information from Neevit, but he won't be give'n it freely," Vasilik replied.

"Excuse me," the captain tried to interrupt.

"That's if he be know'n who she be and where she be at … and who be the puppet master of the two," Switbo added.

"Or are they partners?" Lucas interjected, but the group just gave him a scornful look and he withdrew.

"He is right. We don't know if they're partners, or if one is subordinate," *It* said intently, as his mind was working in high gear.

"Excuse me. Hello. I be still in charge here," the captain interrupted again.

"Sorry, dear." Switbo put her hand on the captain's shoulder. She looked to the rest of the group. "We need to no be rude to our host."

"Much appreciated," the captain said to Switbo. "I be sure ye have yor own agenda to jaw on, but me be think'n it not as immediate of an importance then me hav'n to kill the lot of ya today. So can we be focus'n on that issue for the time being?" He turned to the forecastle. "Halman!"

"Aye, Captain, sir!" Halman called back.

"Where be the scrabbn' Widow's Son and why be she not our vessel to command?" Vosvile called out, as he looked out to the sea.

"She had a powerful mystic with her, and he set our sails wayward."

The captain growled and tugged on his gray mustache. "It ain't look'n good for ya, boy. I was count'n on that cargo as well," he said to *It*.

Vasilik reached under his coat and brought out the pouch of coin that *It* gave him and he held it out to the captain. "There be this for the lad's life and for the other snappers. I'll be sign'n on to the Red Lion to pay the rest."

Captain Vosvile, like the others, gawked at Vasilik as if he must be ill in his head. Switbo was not only amazed, but she had a tear of pride in one eye.

"That purse wouldn't pay me galley sums. And an old gimp be only a liability on me decks. Keep yor coin," he said, tired of the discussion. "Let's eat and be enjoy'n each other's company. On the morrow, we be chum'n the waters with them young ones as per the contract."

THIRTY-EIGHT

GETTING AWAY ... HAT AND ALL

The captain's quarters were brightly lit by the many candles throughout the room. At the table, the captain entertained the prisoners with a feast prepared by his personal cook with the aid of Toyota. Roast hen, seasoned potatoes, fresh bread, and fruits galore stretched across the table and filled their bellies.

Prior to being served, Vasilik and Vosvile cleared up some questions the others had regarding their relationship. Vasilik told them that his mother, Araia, and the captain had been romantic acquaintances around the time Vasilik was born. The captain added that Araia and he both had other acquaintances, but he had a special place for her in his heart, so he eventually accepted that Vasilik had some likelihood of being his son. When Vasilik was old enough, at the age of twelve, he joined Vosvile's crew.

Both men had differing opinions as to the details of how Vasilik left the sailor's life to serve the king, but they did agree that for many years there was some resentment, until Vasilik returned with a wife and a bum leg after the war.

Evan leaned over the table while Vosvile was preoccupied with a servant, and he pointed his trunk accusingly at Vasilik. "You could have shared this information about you and your papa when we were planning for the attack."

"And it would av been do'n no bit of good but to cause you to be distrust'n me to no end," Vasilik replied.

"Oh, yeah? And now I have so much more trust in you," Evan groaned, with his eyes turned up to the ceiling.

There was an uncomfortable lull in conversation.

Sydney noticed plaques along the bulkhead with swords attached and names printed on each. She climbed up on a shelf underneath them, pressed her glasses high on her nose, and crinkled her face as she struggled to discern their purpose. "Were these the captains of the Red Lion before you?"

Vosvile paused his conversation with the servant to respond. "No lass, those be the arms of the cap'ns who done got in me way or wouldn't be given in to surrender'n proper."

He finished talking to the servant and sent him away. With a sneaky smile, he shuffled over to a chest on the other side of the cabin. "Of course, those be just the cap'ns of note." He opened the chest to show many swords, daggers, and dirks. "These be belong'n to them that I heard nary a word of fame about."

"Oh ... that's nice," Sydney said, uncertain if she should be impressed.

"So, Captain, could you tell us about the witch?" *It* asked, not being at all as casual as he thought he was.

"Why would ya be want'n to jaw on that dark subject?" he asked, walking back to the table. "If'n yor dead t'marrow, what good be it to ya t'day?"

"To be die'n without unanswered questions be a mighty comfort to the condemned," Vasilik pointed out. "Ya can be give'n that much to the lad."

"That it be, I reckon." The captain wiped his mouth after a deep drink of wine. "Well, boy, I'll be tell'n ya what I know, but it ain't even a tankard full." He placed his hands on the table and leaned in for all to hear. "So, t'was thirty year or more that they say the demon witch came to be. She was a powerful mystic and a powerful horror to lay eyes on. They say she be born to the land of the Dead Echoes."

"Who is they?" Evan asked, suspicious of the story.

"What? They? They be they. Them what first told the story ... now be let'n me finish," Vosvile grumbled.

"The Dead Echoes, isn't that where the cave prophecy is located?" Sydney squeaked excitedly.

"What? Cave what?" The captain sat up, annoyed that he was interrupted during a knee thumper of a good story.

"Prophecy. Vasilik told us of the cave prophecy where there is a drawing on the wall of me and my friends saving the world from an evil force," *It* said, as if presenting some factual data.

Vosvile glared at Vasilik with a chastising look and whispered harshly, "Not that old one? Shame be on ya for it."

"Let them be av'n this one?" Vasilik said with a pleading look, to not be exposed the night before the little ones were to die.

"What is it?" *It* asked.

"Tis nothing. I just be feel'n ya too young to be know'n of such things as the prophecy." The captain shot Vasilik and Switbo another chastising look. "Where be I in me own tale?"

"A dark witch born to the Dead Echoes," Evan said, as if bored to tears.

"Aye, she be born to that evil land to the west and with a heap'n lust for power. She's be made a pact with the Kroncal and even be connected with a demon dragon or the like," he said with a deep, eerie voice, as he saw Sydney and *It* hanging on every word.

"And what about the prophecy?" Sydney squeaked, with a great big innocent grin on her face while her tail twitched away.

"Aye, as I be remember'n it, there be somebody of prophecy scratched on a cave wall," he said like more of a question than a statement, as he glanced to Vasilik.

"Child!" Vasilik interrupted.

"Ah, yes. It be a child. And this evil darkness that he must be destroy'n with his cadre of cavaliers … or some matter, or other of such …"

"Ooo. We're a cadre of cavaliers," Sydney said, giving *It* a friendly punch to the shoulder.

"Aye, but the darkness be only banished and no destroyed," Vasilik corrected the captain.

"No, I be remember'n you spinn'n it as she be'n destroyed," the captain argued back with a hiss.

"Banished," Vasilik disagreed.

"And how be it different if'n when it be banished it be gone any-o-way?" Vosvile pointed to the kids. "Besides, on the marrow they aren't to be care'n whether t'were banished or destroyed … I'm tell'n it me own way." He took a breath and continued. "And I be recall'n there be a quest and some mystical item that elped them to be save'n the world of Fentiga.

The end ... now off to bed with the lot of ya. I av many a thing to do t'morrow, and most of you av dying to do."

As they stood, Sydney gave the captain a quick hug on his side and thanked him for his story. *It* also thanked him for his hospitality. Both the boy and girl were sure they wouldn't be dying tomorrow at the hands of someone who fed and entertained them like that.

The captain ushered them out onto the deck where guards stood waiting to take them to a supply hold for the night. As they got closer to the hold, Sydney was still chittering away after listening to the captain's story.

"You know, I don't think he is actually going to kill us tomorrow," she squeaked factually.

"No, he be goin'n to kill ya snappers for sure," Vasilik said with certainty.

"Well, he won't like doing it," Sydney protested.

Vasilik smiled weakly. "Ya got me there, wee lass. He won't be like'n it one smidge."

"But he'll be do'n it all the same. He be haven to, or Neevit would give the king cause to be hunt'n the Lion down ... nope, he can't just be lett'n ya go," Switbo added, with a crack in her voice.

As they were led into the supply hold, Toyota and Lucas were already there waiting.

"Which be why we be need'n to escape before morn," Vasilik added, as he walked in and laid back on a sack of grain.

"We are on a ship in the middle of the inland sea. We can't escape," Evan grumbled and paced around in atypical behavior.

"Yet we be av'n to," Vasilik responded. "Besides, he be want'n us to. It be the only way he be save'n face with his men and no be in over his head with Neevit."

"How can you be sure?" *It* asked, apprehensive of the response.

"For one, he left me with me cane," Vasilik said, holding the cane above his chest.

"And two, he be locked us in here and not the brig ... and three, there be only one guard outside the door," Switbo added.

"How can you be certain there is only one guard?" Lucas risked a question.

Evan sneered at the Ave boy but answered all the same. "The other one walked off after they closed the door," he said from the side of his mouth.

It looked at Evan, still confused, and Evan continued, "He shuffled his feet while he walked. I heard him go off."

"So now we be wait'n until two bells and take'n our leave then," Vasilik said lazily.

"You still didn't tell us how we will be getting off the boat," Evan grumbled some more.

"Cause, I ain't be figured that part out yet." Vasilik said, and rolled over to nap.

"You lot best get some sleep. It go'n to be a long hard day tomorrow, or a very short one, depend'n on how things be go'n tonight," Switbo said sweetly, with the intent on easing their minds—but it didn't work.

Evan stayed awake to take the first watch as everyone kicked back. *It* was propped up against Evan's side, Sydney was leaning on *It*, and Toyota was at the boy's feet. An unspoken restriction forced Lucas to huddle in an opposite corner by himself. Vasilik and Switbo were the only ones who looked to be asleep—it's not like their heads were on the block, so they had nothing at risk.

"You don't trust them one bit do you … Vasilik and Switbo, that is?" *It* whispered to Evan.

"They're hoomans. What's to trust?" Evan grumbled with a smirk.

It jabbed the Fallon in the side, but it felt like less than a mosquito bite to the mighty mammoth. "So, you don't trust me?"

"I trust you least of all," Evan said, with another smirk.

"Hey," the boy protested.

"If you don't trust them, why are you listening to them?" Sydney asked.

"Because they seem to at least have a plan. I have nothing. I've never been so helpless." Evan breathed in deep.

For the first time, it dawned on *It* that for a proud Fallon like Evan, being helpless may be worse than death, and that the reason he wasn't protesting the oncoming execution is because it would be a relief to his suffering.

It sighed. "If we don't escape, I'm glad to be with you guys in the end … You're my herd and …" Sydney joined in with *It* as they said in unison, "We do what we have to for our herd and for honor."

Evan's eye twitched, and his face tightened. It took all his will and focus, but the Fallon let no emotions show through.

Sydney reached over *It* and put her paw on Evan's hand. "I like our herd. We are weird and unpredictable," Sydney chittered.

"And we got the most butt-kickingest Fallon as a leader, so I don't think they will be able to kill us tomorrow. Evan will take care of us," Toyota said, as if it was a plain and simple truth; he seemed to be forgetting that just yesterday, Evan was offering to throw the Didelphi overboard for betraying *It*.

Again, with the full strength of his inner being, the Fallon was stoic.

Across from them, Vasilik and Switbo laid facing away from the young ones, which was good since they weren't nearly as strong as Evan and the tears streamed down their faces.

After a few hours, Evan stood up and nudged Vasilik with his foot.

"I be awake, Fallon," Vasilik whispered.

"If we're going to do something, now's the time." Evan whispered.

"That be true," Vasilik replied, as he got slowly to his feet with a few grunts and groans.

They woke everyone up, as the battle from earlier in the day had worn them all out and made it possible to sleep. With whispered hushes, they huddled together to go over the plan.

"So, how is this going to work?" Evan asked.

"We get the wee lass to be call'n out with a belly ache and when the guard be open'n the door, the Fallon will be give'n him a scant tap to dreamland," Vasilik said, while hammering his fist into his hand.

"Then what?" *It* asked.

"Then we be get'n a longboat, lower it down and off we go," Vasilik added.

Evan looked at him with his face growing orange and his jaw tightening. "That's your plan? Sydney acts sick to draw a guard and then we escape in a boat?"

"And a right fair plan it be," Vasilik sneered.

"No, it's not. Everyone knows the sick prisoner ploy! The guard would have to be a complete dimwitted twogg to fall for that. And then there is the problem of reaching shore?" Evan complained.

"One step at a time, lad," Vasilik said, and turned to Sydney. "Ok now, lass, get to belly ach'n, and we will be reeling in a whopper of a dimwitted twogg."

Sydney started moaning and fake crying, but nothing happened.

"Louder!" Switbo whispered, as she pinched the little Seeuradi.

"Ow!" Sydney yelped and then continued crying out loud.

The door started jiggling as someone worked at the lock. When it swung open, the guard leaned in. "Shut it or I'll be ..."

Before the pirate finished his sentence. Evan reached out from the side where he had been standing and brought his hand down on the guard's head. The human's knees buckled, as he crumpled to the deck

Vasilik looked sideways at the guard and then glanced up to Evan. "Be ya no understand'n what a scant tap be, lad?"

"That was my scant tap," Evan growled.

Switbo turned to Sydney. "Can you be heal'n him a touch? We shouldn't be make'n Vossy any more vexed."

After Sydney provided some makeshift first aid for the guard, they made their way above deck. As they came through the hatch, Vasilik was surprised by a pirate at the hatchway and began to strike out at him, but Evan grabbed the old scoundrel's arm. On closer examination, the crew member was out cold and propped up against a wall. After a few more encounters with comatose sailors, they quickly came to the conclusion that the entire ship was passed out drunk.

They reached the first longboat and Vasilik lifted the tarp covering it to look inside. "It won't be this one," Vasilik said with a loud whisper and then moved on.

"What's wrong with this one?" Evan demanded, but was left standing there as everyone followed Vasilik.

They checked out two more longboats and Vasilik rejected them both. Evan was livid but held his tongue. They came to another long boat and after looking inside, Vasilik pulled his head out and announced, "Here she be."

"What difference is there between this one and the last three?" Evan hissed.

"This one be provisioned," Vasilik announced, as he whipped the tarp back to reveal their backpacks, weapons, sacks of food and barrels of fresh water. Vasilik pointed to one small keg in the back of the boat. "Of course, that one there be belong'n to me and the missus. The captain sure do be know'n how to bid ya farwell, he does."

"Bless his old black heart," Switbo said, as she placed one of the launch hooks through a ring attached to the boat. After the rigging was ready to go, Evan had everyone climb in, except for Toyota, whose fear of water had him latched to Evan's leg. The Fallon could have easily ripped the Didelphi from his leg, but he knew it would hurt him, so he had a better idea. "Sydney, toss me something with tarin root."

"Raw or fermented?" she called back.

"Definitely fermented," Evan replied.

She retrieved a small vial from her pack and tossed it to him. Evan tilted it back into Toyota's mouth, and after a few moments, the little Didelphi was so relaxed that Evan poured him into the longboat.

As Evan was tending to Toyota, Vasilik unexpectedly climbed back out of the boat. "I be almost forget'n," he whispered as he started to sneak off.

"Where are you going?" Evan hissed and looked at Switbo. "Where is he going?"

"I'm sure I don't be know'n," she whispered back, and then her eyes shot open wide and her mouth slowly opened. "Oh no ... but be for sure he won't be do'n that."

"Doing what?" *It* whispered, as he looked out over the deck in fear of being caught.

They all waited in the darkness for what felt like a lifetime, when they heard the familiar step and drag of Vasilik's footsteps. The man moved quickly to climb back into the boat, a little winded. With a harsh whisper at Evan, he said, "Be shove'n off already."

Now that they were all finally aboard and ready, Evan pulled on the rigging lines with one hand and pushed the boat out over the edge with the other hand. What usually took several sailors to do, Evan did with only a few grunts. Once he lowered them to the water, he swung out and climbed down the rope.

Normally, multiple sailors would sit on opposite sides of the boat to row. That wasn't the case here. Evan took a seat in the middle of the boat and began rowing with an oar on each side and set the boat on a course away from the Red Lion.

"What was so scrabb'n important that you had to go back?" Evan grunted, as he rowed quickly, while also being conscious to avoid splashing.

"I figured we be owe'n a little payback for our troubles," he snickered, as he held up Captain Vosvile's three-pointed hat.

The oars stopped in mid-row, and the boat glided silently, as all eyes were on Vasilik.

"Twas fear'n that be what you be up to," Switbo said, with a sad shake of her head.

Evan turned to *It* with his face partially visible in the half moonlight. "Please let me kill him—just a little bit."

"Sorry, big guy. He's my employee, and I'm sure Human Resources would not approve."

Everyone was either too shocked, or too angry, at Vasilik to question the boy about yet another unintelligible human term.

Vasilik set the Captain's hat down and began the work of rigging up the sail. He either pretended to not care, or actually didn't care, that everyone disapproved of his little stunt—*It*, for one, knew how a harmless stunt could go tragically wrong, as the memory of his chute ride into the Bin was forever etched in his mind.

THIRTY-NINE

A LONG, SHORT BOAT RIDE

The next morning was cloudy with a steady rise and fall of waves rocking the boat in near rhythmical fashion. Everyone was asleep except for Switbo, who was piloting the boat with one hand on the sail line and the other on the rudder. The cold breeze was stinging, but at least the rain took a break for a while.

Lucas woke up before the rest. The wind ruffled his blue feathers as it blew across his face, and he pulled his cloak in tighter before taking a good look around.

"Yeah, you still be alive boy, but not on any account of mine," Switbo called out to him, more frigid then the biting wind.

Lucas just glanced around, not sure how to reply, or even if he should.

"Ya can also be sure that me and me old man have made many a bad mistakes in our lives, and we still be here. It be the mov'n on part that be difficult. This lot of snappers ain't likely to be forgive'n ya soon … if'n at all. And if we don't all be drowned to our deaths, then you'll be know'n where ya stand with them when we trod land next. Just don't be hold'n to any hope. Hope … She be a heartbreaker and a villainous life stealer. Like the mermaid to a man's soul, her song will be lull'n ya long enough for her to be dig'n her teeth into yor throat."

"Very vivid and poignant imagery," Lucas' voice cracked, as he risked speaking.

"That it be." She paused for a moment and looked to the sky. "Dawn be break'n," she said and then pointed to the bottom of the boat. "Ya see that cane of me husband's?"

"Yes."

"Pick'er up."

Lucas stretched out a feathered arm, wrapping his claws around the cane and lifting it as if to hand it to her.

She nodded toward Evan. "Now, smack up that big one awake."

"I beg your pardon?" Lucas said, to what struck him as the most insane request he had ever heard.

Her eyes narrowed. "It be like this; I be the kind you never see com'n, whereas he comes at ya head on and mak'n a fierce noise. Now who should ya be fear'n most?" she said, with her voice taking on a darker tone.

Lucas thought for a few moments and then saw a gleam of something in her eye that disturbed him to his core. He raised the cane up and dropped it hard on Evan, who popped up instantly with his sword drawn. He cleared his head and looked straight at Lucas with death in the shaking of his eyes.

Lucas sheepishly pointed at Switbo. "I was complying with the lady's orders."

"Yeah, but who are you more afraid of," Evan growled.

The bird-boy looked at Switbo and Evan who were both giving him an evil stare. "With gentle and earnest respect to you both, I find you as equally terrifying as you are imposing, and I leave it as such." He tossed the cane down, which hit Toyota and woke him up. The monkey-opossum stood up all sleepy-eyed, and while rubbing his face, he began walking along the seat bench until he walked completely off the edge of the boat and splashed into the freezing water.

The shrieks that followed woke the rest of the group. *It* had his tire iron in his hand, which he unwittingly swung at Vasilik, but was blocked by Evan. Vasilik had a dagger in hand, and Sydney held a wooden spoon in a very threatening manner. *It* looked over to her and her spoon with a huge question reading on his face.

Sydney shrugged. "What? It was all I had."

The shrieks from outside the boat continued even after Evan scooped Toyota out of the water and held him inches above the seat. The Fallon held up the soaking-wet Didelphi, who still hadn't figured out that he was no longer drowning. His legs and arms were frantically flailing while he continued trying to swim.

After Sydney began drying Toyota with a blanket, the group paused to notice Switbo sailing the boat. *It* called out to her from the front seat. "How do you know if we're going in the right direction?"

"With this." She reached down by her foot to pick up a little box and tossed it to the boy. When he opened the box, he found that it had a glass top inside and a similar arrow to that of Evan's direction box. There was even the glowing black and purple mist surrounding the needle.

By the look on the boy's face, he still didn't understand how Switbo knew if land was in the direction they were sailing. She pointed at the box and said, "It be mystical. I done found it in the supplies that Vossy be leav'n for us. I asked it which way it be to Yolanrym and it be giv'n the heading."

"How long before we reach land?" *It* asked her.

"I be not knowing that."

"Hand it to me," Sydney said.

It tossed the box to her. She took out her feather and passed it around and over the box as she chanted and then stopped.

"So?" *It* said with a shrug.

"I tried the divination chant Kandula taught me, but I'm still learning it. So, we are either going to be there in two days, two weeks, two months, or two years," Sydney said with confidence.

"Well, let's be pray'n for the first one then," Vasilik yawned.

"So, we're going to spend the next two days in this boat?" Toyota whined.

"It looks to be that way," Evan said, as he began rummaging through the sack and rationing out bread and fruit for their breakfast.

There was a brief break in conversation, as everyone was hungry, and the meager feast was consumed with great speed. Toyota was the first to clear his throat and interrupt the silence as he turned to *It* and said, "I was wondering … is our contract still valid, since it turned out I'm not your enemy and he is?" Toyota pointed with his foot at Lucas, who had taken up a place in the back near Switbo.

"No. You voided that contract," *It* said, without looking at the Didelphi.

"Does that mean we have to make a new contract?" Toyota offered with a wishful intent in his eyes.

It slapped his hand to his forehead. "You betrayed my trust! As a matter of fact, nearly a third of the people in this boat has betrayed my trust at one point or another … unless of course any of you have some confessions to make."

"Well, actually, I did report on your activities to Lord Stronghide," Evan said, while bobbing his head with a slight shoulder shrug.

"What?" the boy cried out.

"And I did have to report back to our Prominence the things that I learned about you," Sydney said, as she nibbled on some more bread.

It looked at Vasilik and Switbo to see if the betrayal was complete. They both glanced at each other and then back to him, shaking their heads.

"No, we be good," Vasilik said.

"Be no confessions here," Switbo added.

"I can't believe that the people I can trust the most are the ones I met only a few days ago," *It* ranted.

"The herd appears to be having its culling," Lucas said, just above a whisper.

"No. You don't get to talk yet. Maybe soon, but right now, you don't get to talk," *It* yelled, as he pointed some sort of guava fruit at Lucas.

"What do you mean soon? You can't seriously be considering … You're not letting him back in the herd," Evan hollered at *It,* as he stood up and towered over the group.

"Why not?" *It* responded.

"The fact that he nearly got us killed is why not," Evan leaned over toward the boy with his tusks on either side of his head.

"You tried to kill me the first time I met you."

Evan straightened. "Are you ever going to let that go? That's not even the same thing." He sat back down.

Now *It* stood up. "Let go that you were going to kill me? And how is it not the same thing?"

"I wasn't trying to kill you. I was trying to kidnap you. It's different."

"No, that isn't different. Kidnapping somebody is still a bad thing."

"I've said sorry. We talked about this already." Evan crossed his arms in frustration.

"First off, saying sorry doesn't fix it. Second off, you never said sorry."

"I was meaning to. It was implied," Evan grumbled back.

It threw his hands up. "Okay, you know what? We are going to reboot to the default settings of this herd ... right here ... right now!"

"What of a what?" Vasilik asked Sydney.

The girl just shrugged and said, "That's his language from the other place. It all sounds like gibberish."

It made a rolling motion with his hands. "It's a start over! We are starting our friendships over! Here, Toyota shake my hand!" *It* yelled, as he stuck his hand out to Toyota.

Toyota recoiled in fear of *It*'s behavior and was reluctant to shake, but he reached over and shook *It*'s hand, when he noticed the boy's eyes had a twinge of black threatening to stretch out from the sides—this was not the place for a feral mysticism outbreak.

After shaking Toyota's hand, *It* said, "We now have a contract to be friends again ... but with a clause stating that if you do something stupid like that ever again, you will never be my friend ... and ... and I will probably cut holes in all your underwear or something heinous like that."

"That works for me," Toyota said, and then looked to Sydney and whispered, "I already found a loophole in the contract. I don't wear underwear."

Sydney cringed.

It turned on Evan while he was still on a roll. "You, Evan ... You are one of my best friends! I'm going to trust you and you're going to trust me! And you're going to start telling people you're my friend when they ask you if you're my friend!"

Evan sat nodding his head reluctantly. "Okay."

The boy snapped his head in Sydney's direction, and she squeaked unintentionally. She was afraid of what the boy was going to say next. *It* looked as though he were going to launch into a tirade, but he paused to think and then said, "You, Sydney. I love you just the way you are. Never change. Never!"

Now it was the McCarthy's turn to hear what was on the boy's mind. "Vasilik and Switbo, you guys are the best! You've always been there for me ... even though always covers a very short amount of time, but I trust you with everything." He looked at the group as a whole. "Now we are a functioning herd again and I don't want to hear anymore infighting, or I swear my eyes will go black and this boat will be a very unhappy place to be!"

"But it's already an unhappy place to be," Toyota whined, clinging to Evan's leg.

"Tell me about it," Evan said, looking down at Toyota.

"What about him?" Vasilik called out, as he pointed his cane at Lucas.

It glared at the Ave. "I'm still so scrabbing mad at you for doing this to us, that I don't know what to say to you … I don't want to talk to you for a while, but I'm sure I will eventually."

"Considering the circumstances, awhile is an improvement over never," Sydney squeaked to Lucas as she went back to eating.

Lucas nodded his head, knowing that no words would be proper at this time.

For the next day and a half, Switbo taught *It*, Sydney, and Toyota what she knew about sailing, and that was quite a bit. She even let the kids take turns guiding the boat on its course and maintaining its heading according to the mystic compass.

Coming on the evening of the second day, Vasilik and Switbo were awakened as they felt themselves being roughly thrown back and forth. A storm had snuck up behind them. Sydney and Toyota, who had been piloting the boat, hadn't been paying any attention to the sky.

"Get over luvs!" Switbo yelled, as she took a seat by the rudder, while pushing Toyota and Sydney aside.

Vasilik took hold of the sail as the wind began blowing them in the wrong direction.

Switbo hollered out, "Take her down. The gale will be throw'n us off course … Fallon, take hold of those oars and be gett'n us point'n the right way!"

Vasilik grabbed the direction box from Toyota and tossed it to *It*. "Keep hold of that lad, and be make'n sure that Evan be stay'n true to the course."

"We're already going off course!" *It* cried out.

"Just be get'n us to land, lad! Get to land!"

Vasilik began pulling the gear out and repacking everything away into the leather pouches. The day before, he taught everyone how to use oils and waxes from the supplies to help waterproof their packs and make them usable for flotation. Now was the time to have them ready. Of course, Toyota was barely useful, as he spent his time curled up on the bottom of the boat, shrieking and hissing.

Evan fought the waves as best he could. Within moments, a downpour of rain fell upon them. Lightning streaked across the sky, and the thunder was so loud that they felt each rumble down to their bones.

"I see it. I see it," the boy started yelling, looking away from the direction box and out across the sea.

"What do you see, snapper?" Vasilik called out.

"Land. I see land—that way, Evan." *It* pointed into the darkness.

"What be you say'n, boy. There be nothing out there," Vasilik yelled back to *It,* as he could not see what the boy was pointing at in the black night.

It turned back to Vasilik. The man saw the boy's eyes were streaked with black as he kept pointing off in the distance. "Trust me. It's there," *It* shouted, with no rebuttal from Vasilik.

Evan put his back into it, and they fought their way inland. As they got closer, lightning streaked across the sky. For a moment, the night sky was as bright as midday. Switbo's face cringed and Vasilik's eyebrow leapt high on his head as the flash of light revealed large swells of white foam coming at them and jagged rocks just below the foam—they found land.

"You be steer'n us into the rocks!" Vasilik yelled at Evan. "Be turn'n the boat! Turn the scrabbin boat!"

Evan tried to change direction and thought he had spun them to face away from danger, but the current and waves continued to push them toward the rocks. Unfortunately, their boat was turned sideways.

"Blast ya scrabbin Fallon. Ya be killed us all!" Vasilik yelled as he made sure everyone was clinging to a pack. "When we hit, do no be try'n to stay in the boat! Ya be get'n hurt worse that way! And don't be fight'n the current. It be only tire'n ya out! Ride it into shore and try to stay together!"

"And be keep'n hold of each other! Link arms! Keep eyes on one another," Switbo shouted, as she gave up the rudder and grabbed a pack for herself.

The boat rose up high on the waves and dropped down several times. Before long, they had taken on so much water that they were nearly full. One last wave brought the craft high into the sky and then it came crashing down onto the rocks below. Splinters of wood shot off in different directions. Sydney was the first to be launched into the water, with

Toyota and Switbo following behind her. One more rough wave came in right behind the first and finished the job as they were all washed away.

It popped up out of the water and was tossed around helplessly by the churning water. He saw Sydney hit a rock and then disappear under the waves. *It* struggled to get to her, but a giant hand dragged him screaming toward shore.

Evan threw the boy on shore. *It* collapsed with each attempt to stand. Vasilik pulled a shrieking Toyota onto land with Evan's help. The Fallon and old human looked back to see Lucas pulling a partially unconscious Switbo toward shore. Evan snatched her up and got her to land. *It* began screaming Sydney's name, but there was no sign of her.

It's eyes met Lucas' gaze. The Ave must have known what the boy expected of him, as he turned back into the waves and dove under the foaming water. They wouldn't be in this situation if it wasn't for Lucas so, for *It*, the Ave boy's life was far away from a priority compared to that of Sydney's.

It called out for Sydney again and there was nothing but foam and spray coming out from the shore's edge. Lucas broke the surface empty-handed and dove back down. Vasilik and Evan spread out knee deep in the water, prepared to dive in if they caught a glimpse of her.

Again, Lucas broke the surface, and he looked to be struggling with something. Evan waded out as far as he could and when he was close to Lucas, Lucas shoved the motionless body of Sydney into Evan's hands. Evan tossed Sydney to Vasilik, who quickly hobbled with her back onto the beach. When Evan turned back, Lucas was gone.

Seconds passed as the mammoth warrior was torn between what he should do versus what he wanted to do. He turned, as if to go back to shore, but instead, he dove out and down where he last saw Lucas. He caught a glimpse of some feathers tumbling under the waves and he swam for them. He cradled the Ave boy under a wing and brought him to shore where they found *It* kneeling over a limp and lifeless Sydney—this time, she wasn't pretending.

"No! Do something!" He pleaded with Vasilik who could only offer more tears of sorrow to add to the boy's. *It* looked at the girl's mouth and remembered that in the old days of earth they had to breathe into the mouth of a drowned person. For a moment, all time stopped, and *It* had memory flashes of recorded vids and articles whirling in his brain and stopping long enough for the information to be revitalized in his mind.

He remembered having glanced at the information during some class he had attended at the education center on C-Earth, but it was never retained or consciously noted. Now it all seemed so clear and even overwhelming. The boy knew CPR. He tilted Sydney's head back and placed his mouth over her mouth and nose and blew. The Seeuradi girl's chest rose and fell with his breath.

Vasilik's face cringed as he watched the boy with disapproval. "What be ya doing, Lad? I no be think'n this be the time for that," Vasilik called out.

It started to press on her chest as the forgotten information was now a solid part of his knowledge, but nothing was happening. He raised his hands above his head and screamed one last time. His eyes flashed black, and his hands were glowing with a dark lightning shooting between the finger tips. He brought his hand down and touched Sydney's chest. She lurched as the lightning shot from the boy's hands and into her body.

Water sprayed from her mouth as she screamed in pain. "What are you doing! Are you completely nutters? That hurt!"

It swept her up in his arms and cried into her neck.

Sydney's eyes darted back and forth from *It* to Vasilik and Evan a few times. "Okay, am I the only one thinking this is weird?" Sydney squeaked weakly as she coughed.

It's tears turned to laughter. After he let Sydney go, he walked over to Lucas and stood for a long moment, watching the Blue Jay as he lay in the sand trying to catch his breath. "Thanks," *It* finally said, after a long debate with his conscience.

"It was my responsibility ... my obligation." Lucas tried to get up and bow, but he didn't have it in him.

"Yes, it was, but thank you all the same. This doesn't fix everything, but it is a start," the boy said with a nod and walked away to help gather the gear.

They found shelter in a nearby alcove in a cliff and rested from their ordeal. With driftwood and Sydney's drying spell, they had a roaring fire to warm their cold bones.

Slivers of light broke through the clouds and began the warming of the day. Though they were all happy to see the morning, it came much too fast for those still recovering from the rough shore landing the night before. Sydney's head was still aching, causing her left eye to wince, but with a groggy wave of her mystic feather and a half-mumbled chant, the pain was gone. If only she had taken the time before they set out to learn a revitalization spell from her Prominence Susanne or a chant from her new teacher Kandula.

The weary, but grateful, hodgepodge of Evan's unit gathered what gear they had left and hiked up a cliff trail to the ridge of a small mountain. When they crested the top, they looked down and caught a glimpse of a massive walled city a day's walk away. The walls and buildings with their aged white stones were a direct contrast to the multicolored forest surrounding what was most certainly Yolanrym.

Tall and majestic were the mountains with their own broken patterns of gray rock, purple and red leaved forest, and white snow caps reaching up to the blue cloudy sky—but even with the beauty of the human kingdom below and the promise of living with his own kind, *It* still wondered how he could stay there when Utuska had become his new memory of home and the Fallons his people.

"Well, I told you I would get you to the hooman land," Evan said, swelling with self-pride.

"You didn't lie there … You are going in with me, aren't you?" *It* asked, knowing the answer.

"Of course, he will. He has to. He's leading this herd," Sydney squeaked.

Evan grinned widely and walked out in front, leading the motley group down the path.

"Did he just smile?" *It* gasped.

"Don't be question'n it, lad. Ya snappers may never be see'n him do it again." Vasilik laughed as he put his arm around the boy's shoulder and followed Evan down through the tall grass. Off in the distance, the old scoundrel's voice could be heard as it trailed off, "And, for a price, I'll be let'n ya use me contacts in the city—yeah, stick with me, snappers. Stick with me."

Switbo lagged behind, mumbling to herself. "That's if'n the guards don't be kill'n us on sight at the gates." She shook her head and stepped faster to catch up to the others. "If'n one be damned, then damned be we all!"

The group stopped to turn and look at Switbo. She smirked and said nothing.

Sydney climbed up Evan's arm so her face was nose to nose with Switbo. She twitched her nose, causing her glasses to shift and then cracked a toothy grin. "I don't always understand you, but you are so my kind of hooman."

Switbo smiled.

EPILOGUE

A WARM WELCOME AHEAD ... UNLIKELY!

Inside a large palace chamber, many long, golden-hued drapes flowed from the vaulted ceiling to the floor. Soft rays of light shining through the drape openings made the room glow with dust drifting through the air like tiny snowflakes of pure gold. The few pieces of furniture throughout the room were exquisitely crafted and only affordable by royalty. A long, drawn-out sigh emanated from an elegantly crafted chair near a massive redwood desk. Sitting among the inlaid gold leaf spiral designs of the high-backed seat was a slender man of not quite thirty-five years. A thin band of silver with a single amber gem in its middle encircled his forehead just above his wrinkled brow. It held his straight black hair tightly in place. Only a few renegade strands stretched out over his pale cheeks.

The regal man was engrossed in his work, as he scanned over the many parchments and scrolls scattered over his desk, which had the same inlaid gold leaf designs as the chair. He pulled at the short black hairs of the thin-cut beard framing his face. After a few more sighs, he reached for a large, plumed quill and scratched his signature across the bottom of one of the documents ... *King Ji Mellis.*

From the opposite side of the room, a great metal-plated double door opened and a young court attendant strolled midway across the marbled floor, stopped just before the family crest of a shield and dragon embedded in the marble, and bowed deeply with practiced reverence.

"Your highness?"

Annoyed, King Mellis shook his head. "What now?"

"High Counselor Neevit Prewt, and Commander Etsumi Sha-Ron of the Gold Tabards to see you, my king."

Before King Mellis could respond, Neevit strode through the doorway with the commander right on his heels. They passed the boy and stopped when they reached the desk. The years of opulent living had the advisor breathing heavily while the Commander who stood a head taller and fully donned in armor gave no sign of fatigue. Creases in her yellowed, ivory skin betrayed her many years of experience, and her silky short-cropped ebony hair bore more than a few traces of gray. Though well into her fifties, her endless brown eyes could still break a man's heart, or fill it with terror, depending on what side of her sword he stood.

Mellis leaned back into his chair. "By all means, enter and approach. It's not like you need to adhere to royal protocol just because I'm your King."

In the background, the court's attendant fought to hide his smirk as he backed away to the double doors, making sure to close them quietly as he exited.

"Sorry, my King. It is a force of habit left over from your father's preference," Sha-Ron said, with a slight bow of her head. She then leaned over and set a handful of parchments onto the desk, adding to the numerous others that stretched across its surface. "We have received many more reports throughout the city regarding the pirate attack on a merchant vessel and the mysterious heroes who sacrificed themselves for the safety of the crew and passengers." She paused for a moment. "They say the heroes were led by a Fallon warrior and a child. A child said to be of some prophecy."

King Mellis waved his arms over the table. "As it has been recorded in almost every one of these initial reports ... tell me something I do not know."

"Some say the boy was headed here. To Yolanrym. He seeks an audience with you, my King," Sha-Ron added.

"Me? Why is this?" The king stared down at the papers for a moment in silence and then looked up to Neevit. "And what have you discovered of this prophecy?"

"Nothing more than before, your highness. I used extensive divination spells and have scoured the ancient tomes. I found no mention of such a prophecy," Neevit responded with a bowed head. "The only reference at all to be found is that of an old sailor's tale; a rumor born of drink and superstition."

"So, then there is some substance to it," the King grumbled.

"An unreliable substance," Neevit tried to insist.

"I, too, have heard the tale in my younger years, my King. Some nonsense of a great evil being defeated by a boy and his mates. A relatively trite and uncreative bunch of drivel, in my opinion. Stories of prophecies are inked by the unintelligent and consumed by the ignorant," Sha-Ron ended with a pompous huff.

"Yes, but my father often remarked that the moment you discount the fantastic, the fantastic will make a discount of you." The King looked up to Neevit. "You remember the stories that you and father used to go on about? There was the one I loved most of all where a Gold Tabard slew a render beast with nothing but a boot … A boot for the Giver's sake! No, if that story can be true, as it was told to me by a King of Yolanrym, then by the Dragon's Breath, we should keep our minds open to what we don't know until it becomes known."

Neevit's eyes narrowed with concern—or was it fear? If the Empress knew the boy was still alive, and on his way to see the King, her displeasure would be deadly. "Yes, your highness, but what would you have us do?"

"Be proactive. If this boy is destined to find me, then let us be the first to find him. I will question him myself."

"Is that truly wise if we do not know his intent? What if he perceives you to be the evil that he seeks to destroy?" Neevit pleaded.

"That thought occurred to me," Mellis replied.

"No boy will make it past me and sixty Gold Tabards to do harm to my King," Sha-Ron said, with her chest pushed out and a hand on her sword.

"Don't forget, he has a warrior Fallon and a mysterious mystic with wands that shoots fire," Neevit said.

"How did you know that?" Sha-Ron questioned, with her eyes squinting at the aged advisor.

"Uh, what?" Neevit stuttered.

"I've been overseeing the investigation into this while you were sequestered in the city records library. When would you have heard the details that I only recently was aware of?" Sha-Ron inquired, with earnest confusion.

"Well, you see ... I have been researching and divining on the subject ... also, there is the city administration that is one of my responsibilities ... and one of the city guards had informed me of such happenings as reported by supposed passengers from the merchant ship," Neevit replied.

Both the King and Sha-Ron listened with bewildered looks until Neevit finished his nervous and sputtered response.

Neevit continued. "And it was then that it occurred to me that this boy could be a disturbance to the city if even just a story such as that gets out of hand."

King Mellis leaned back in his chair. "You have a point. The one thing in all this, that is surely true, is the belief in the hearts of the people of some darkness not far on our horizon. The threat of war between the Fallon and Seeuradi have everyone concerned about our position when the violence begins. We can't allow such imaginations to rise to the point of panic at a time like this." Mellis paused as he gazed out over the reports on his desk. "As I said before, let's be sure to find this boy quickly."

This was the opportunity Neevit was looking for to engage his men in a legal capacity to search openly for the boy and dispatch of him lawfully. "At once, your highness. I shall meet with the city guards and send word to the village elders to apprehend the boy at all costs," Neevit said, while turning to leave.

"Hold now! Don't turn this into a dead or alive man hunt. Until we hear to the contrary, this boy is still reported to be a hero. And at worst, he may just be the unfortunate victim of a wild and rampant rumor," the King chastised Neevit.

"Yes, your highness," Neevit replied with a bow, and then headed across the floor and out the door.

King Mellis turned back to Sha-Ron. "I want you and your Tabards to find the boy first, should he show."

"I understand, my King, but I'm confident the city guard will be efficient in apprehending him if he tries to enter the city," Sha-Ron said.

"I have no doubt that they will, but in recent months, I have found that many of those who were to come before me had mysteriously vanished or were killed by the city guards in the service of their duties. I would actually like this suspect to live long enough to stand before me."

"Then that is what will be, my King. I shall have my men make their presence known in the streets to ensure that justice is upheld. Also, as long as the boy and his men do not resist, he will not give the city guards any reason to overreact."

"Yes. I have hope that he does come peacefully. Sadly, peaceful can sometimes be an ambiguous word." The King's lips lifted in an uneasy smile.

The End ... Of Book One.

ALL ABOUT ME
BEING ALL ABOUT YOU
BEING SOMEWHAT ABOUT ME

Wow! You made it to the end of Book One. Good on you. As I know it's common for some writers to dwell in self-deprecating behavior at this point, I will instead just say … thank you!

Without your support, I would still be dreaming of weird worlds instead of writing about them. I greatly appreciate you and your time.

If you enjoyed Book One of *The Boy Called It* (*TBCI*), please leave your review wherever you purchased your copy. I know you readers don't need us writers nearly as much as we need you—your reviews matter. Keep up the good work … wink wink.

And keep an eye out for Book Two:

The Boy Called It: The Prophesy's Child? … Huh?

It is due to release early in 2024.

For more about the *TBCI* series, check me out at:

Facebook.com/WallaceEdsonBooks

SHOUT-OUT

I'm always being asked who I read since the stories I write aren't like what I read. I decided to answer that question here by giving a shout-out to some of the authors I enjoy. As I am dyslexic, most all my book intake is through audio narrations. My preference tends to be for Fantasy, but you will find the Fantasy subsets to vary. LitRPG is my current fascination.

Look up these authors and give them a try. You won't be disappointed:

Benjamin Kerei • Brady Frost • Drew Hayes • E.A. Winters
Eric Ugland • James Hunter • Jez Cajiao • JF Brink • Matt Dinniman
Ryan Rimmel • Seth Ring • Tomi Adeyemi • Tracy Deonn
William Shakespeare

THE AUTHOR

Authors spend their days weaving lies. Therefore, they are an incredulous source at best when it comes to their own bio, or any other so-called fact pertaining to reality. They even try to trick you by writing their bios in third person so you think it is someone else bragging about them. Who has ever fallen for that?

It is for this reason I suggest that you create an image of Wallace E. Edson that makes you happy and meets all your expectations. He, who may or may not be me, will in turn assure you that your image of him is correct and without contestation (refer to the statement of authors as lie weavers in the above paragraph).

If you happen to be someone with an incurable sense of curiosity or FOMO, try perusing any of his online options:

- **WallaceEdsonBooks@gmail.com** to join his newsletter
- **Facebook.com/wallaceeedson** Facebook Author Page
- **@WallaceEdsonBooks** to see him embarrassing himself on **TikTok**
- **Patreon.com/wallaceeedson** for the VIP treatment
- I'd say check him out on Twitter … but, com'on … Twitter? Really?

Made in United States
Troutdale, OR
10/14/2023